OXFORD WORLD'S CLASSICS

GRETTIR'S SAGA

GRETTIR'S SAGA is the most famous of the outlaw sagas and one of Iceland's great epics. The saga spans two centuries of the Viking Age and begins with the migration of Grettir's Norwegian ancestors to Iceland in the years following Iceland's discovery in the ninth century. The core of the saga recounts Grettir's childhood and long years of outlawry before turning to a story of revenge among viking warriors in Constantinople. A troubled soul, Grettir displays loyalty and nobility, along with a highly developed sense of humour, to become the most beloved of Iceland's outcast heroes. He fights men, berserker warriors, and otherworldly creatures, and his contest with the walking corpse Glam is one of the most memorable episodes in saga literature.

Iceland's Viking Age sagas are one of the world's great literatures, telling of heroes, warriors, outlaws, feuds, honour, valour, and passion. They blend fiction and history with unusual realism, reflecting Iceland's medieval society, and bring alive the world of the far north a thousand years ago.

JESSE BYOCK is Professor of Old Norse and Medieval Scandinavian Studies in the Scandinavian Section at the University of California, Los Angeles, and Professor at UCLA's Cotsen Institute of Archaeology. He is the director of the Mosfell Archaeological Project in Iceland. Professor Byock has written widely on the Viking Age and Icelandic society and is the author of *Viking Age Iceland*, *Medieval Iceland*, and *Feud in the Icelandic Saga*. His previous translations include *The Prose Edda*, *The Saga of the Volsungs*, *The Saga of King Hrolf Kraki*, and *Sagas and Myths of the Northmen*.

RUSSELL POOLE is Professor of English at the University of Western Ontario, Canada. He is the author of *Viking Poems on War and Peace* and *Old English Wisdom Poetry*.

DAVIDE ZORI is a Ph.D. candidate in Viking archaeology at the Cotsen Institute of Archaeology, UCLA, and the field director of the Mosfell Archaeological Project.

OXFORD WORLD'S CLASSICS

For over 100 years Oxford World's Classics have brought readers closer to the world's great literature. Now with over 700 titles—from the 4,000-year-old myths of Mesopotamia to the twentieth century's greatest novels—the series makes available lesser-known as well as celebrated writing.

The pocket-sized hardbacks of the early years contained introductions by Virginia Woolf, T. S. Eliot, Graham Greene, and other literary figures which enriched the experience of reading. Today the series is recognized for its fine scholarship and reliability in texts that span world literature, drama and poetry, religion, philosophy, and politics. Each edition includes perceptive commentary and essential background information to meet the changing needs of readers.

OXFORD WORLD'S CLASSICS

Grettir's Saga

Translated with Notes by
JESSE BYOCK

With an Introduction by
DAVIDE ZORI and JESSE BYOCK

Skaldic Verses by
RUSSELL POOLE

OXFORD
UNIVERSITY PRESS

OXFORD

UNIVERSITY PRESS

Great Clarendon Street, Oxford OX2 6DP

Oxford University Press is a department of the University of Oxford.
It furthers the University's objective of excellence in research, scholarship,
and education by publishing worldwide in

Oxford New York

Auckland Cape Town Dar es Salaam Hong Kong Karachi
Kuala Lumpur Madrid Melbourne Mexico City Nairobi
New Delhi Shanghai Taipei Toronto

With offices in

Argentina Austria Brazil Chile Czech Republic France Greece
Guatemala Hungary Italy Japan Poland Portugal Singapore
South Korea Switzerland Thailand Turkey Ukraine Vietnam

Oxford is a registered trade mark of Oxford University Press
in the UK and in certain other countries

Published in the United States
by Oxford University Press Inc., New York

© Jesse Byock 2009

The moral rights of the author have been asserted
Database right Oxford University Press (maker)

First published as an Oxford World's Classics paperback 2009

British Library Cataloguing in Publication Data

Data available

Library of Congress Cataloging-in-Publication Data

Data available

Typeset by Cepha Imaging Private Ltd., Bangalore, India
Printed in Great Britain by
Clays Ltd., St Ives plc

ISBN 978-0-19-280152-4

7

CONTENTS

ILLUSTRATIONS AND MAPS

INTRODUCTION

Grettir's Saga is a sweeping tale of the Viking Age written by an unknown Icelandic author at the start of the fourteenth century. Drawing on earlier oral and written sources, the saga recounts the life of Grettir the Strong, an outlaw who survives for decades while his enemies hunt him. *Grettir's Saga* is psychological, passionate, and criminal. It is a drama about a man who values his independence above all else. Resourceful but often his own worst enemy, Grettir is Iceland's most famous and beloved outcast hero. Marked more by the attribute of extreme strength than cunning, Grettir has the capacity to harm his fellow men as well as serve them.

Forced to live on the margins of society but still bound by its rules, Grettir is a poet, killer, and thief who preys on farmsteads yet helps the weak. A loner who attracts trouble, he fights people from all ranks of life: outlaws, hired hands, farmers, warriors, and chieftains. Grettir roams through Iceland and Norway ridding isolated farmsteads of berserkers, bears, monsters, and the walking dead. The saga refrains from making clear judgements about his character, and the resultant ambiguity has stirred centuries-long debate, leaving it to each reader to evaluate Grettir's culpability and the justice of his exclusion from society.

Saga and Social Framework

Iceland's sagas are episodic and follow a historical time-line set within the framework of the Viking Age from *c.* AD 800 to 1100. Iceland was a remote island, and ancestral sagas, drawn from the lives of free farmers and small-scale chieftains, became a dominant focus of cultural expression. For centuries, saga-telling, whether orally narrated or read aloud from manuscripts, conveyed Icelandic social memory about not-so-distant ancestors who shared with the saga audience a similar lifestyle on the very same farms. For Icelanders, the sagas reinforced awareness of their roots in Norway and defined their place within the world.

Grettir's Saga divides into three narrative parts: a core central section preceded by his ancestry and followed by the vengeance taken for his death. The first part begins in Norway in the mid-800s, introducing Grettir's great-grandfather, the warrior Onund Tree-Foot (Peg-Leg). Immediately, the saga plunges into viking conflicts and voyages west from Norway to the Celtic lands of the British Isles. Returning to Norway, Onund opposes the unifying king, Harald Finehair (*c*.865–930). The saga depicts Harald as a tyrant, usurping the rights of freemen and outlawing independent-minded opponents such as Onund. This Icelandic view of Harald is repeated throughout the sagas, and reinforces the concept that Iceland was a refuge for strong individualists resisting the growth of monarchy in Norway. Iceland's greatest outlaw saga starts with an aristocratic ancestral outlaw three generations before Grettir.

Following Onund Tree-Foot's battles, the saga recounts the transforming event in the family's and Iceland's history: the migration from Norway to newly discovered and previously uninhabited Iceland. Beginning around the year 870, the 'land-taking' continued for sixty or so years, until all the good land was occupied. The settlers or 'land-takers' (*landnámsmenn*, a term which includes women) emigrated principally from mainland Scandinavia, especially Norway, and from the viking encampments in the British Isles, particularly the Norwegian outposts in the Hebrides and Ireland. The land-takers navigated 600 miles (1000 km) west into the North Atlantic with their families, livestock, farm implements, and followers in tow. *Grettir's Saga* gives us an idea of how new homesteads were parcelled out in Iceland without having to fight an indigenous population for the land—a significant factor that is unusual in European expansion. During the years of Iceland's settlement, 10,000 to 20,000 people came in search of new farmsteads. Iceland was a place where even hardened warriors, such as Onund Tree-Foot, could bring their families and settle peacefully.

Grettir's Saga offers a twist to the familiar story of heroic opposition to King Harald. In contrast with other principal settlers who bask in the prosperity of their new lands, an air of tragedy marks the fortunes of Grettir's ancestors. In order to honourably settle his scores with Harald, Onund stays behind too long in Norway. He arrives in Iceland later than other prominent land-takers, and consequently he has to accept a less desirable parcel. His new property is marginal, and Onund mourns the loss of his rich Norwegian grainfields. He composes poetic laments about replacing his previous good fortune with the icy slopes of Kaldbak (Cold Back Mountain), the chilly name of his new farm. Having explained the reduced circumstances of the formerly prosperous family, the saga author finishes the first part of the saga by describing the fortunes of Tree-Foot's descendants in Iceland, Grettir's grandfather and father.

The second and major part of the saga recounts the life of Grettir, the longest-surviving Icelandic outlaw. This part begins with Grettir's boyhood pranks and continues until his three-year stay on the fortress-like island of Drangey. Grettir develops into the strongest man in Iceland. He is courageous, intelligent, and renowned but also imprudent, undisciplined, indolent, hot-tempered, arrogant, abusive, and tragic. He steals from farmers, even the small ones, and they in turn repeatedly attack him. Few can stand up to him, as Grettir is almost a giant, able to fight huge man-eating trolls and revenants from the grave. As Grettir ages he becomes more likeable. The result is a confounding character whose stand against the privileges of social rank and the ability to form loyal friendships have made him an icon of personal independence. Almost without exception, everyone in Iceland knows about Grettir. Only a few other saga characters can make such a claim today or over the centuries.

The saga's third part focuses on vengeance-seeking for Grettir. It tells of the journey to the Byzantine empire undertaken by Grettir's half-brother, Thorstein the Galleon (so named because he walked with the rhythmic motion of a *drómundr*, a galleon-like sailing-ship). This part takes place at the end of the Viking Age in the eleventh century, when the Norse regions become part of the larger Christian world. Men and women now travel from Iceland all the way south to Mediterranean lands. In Constantinople Thorstein takes service with the Varangians, the emperor's bodyguard composed mainly of Norsemen. In contrast to Grettir, Thorstein is a man of good luck who, when he gets into difficulties, is rescued by a Greek noblewoman named Spes. This concluding section of the saga becomes a humorous tale of cuckolding and convoluted deceit, followed by acts of Christian contrition, redemption, and charity.

The Althing, Blood Feud, and Survival

The settlement period formally ended around the year 930, when the first generations of Icelanders formed a rudimentary government.

They established a national assembly, the Althing (*thing*, Old Norse for assembly), which had legislative and judicial functions, but not executive powers. At the Althing chieftains vied for power, arbitrated conflicts, settled marriage terms, and made laws. The Althing met for two weeks each summer at Thingvellir (Assembly Plains), and was attended by chieftains from all over the country and by their free farmer followers called thingmen. There were no police or armed forces to keep the peace. This function was left to the private action of chieftains and farmers.

The Althing is frequently mentioned in *Grettir's Saga*, as are the regional springtime assemblies. For example, a scene set at the Hegraness Thing in Skagafjord gives one of the best descriptions in the sagas of how people amused themselves at such assemblies. The springtime things could last a week or more, and met each year in May after the spring thaw when rivers became fordable. These regional things were held before the annual trek to the Althing, a journey which could take several weeks each way.

Medieval Iceland was what anthropologists call a chiefdom-level society, and the sagas offer a good view of the power dynamics in Iceland and in Norway. *Grettir's Saga* displays competitive contests common among individuals vying for the respect of a chieftain. Two examples are Grettir's conflict with the braggart Bjorn at Thorkel's hall in Norway, and Grettir's trouble in Iceland with the overbearing foster-brothers at the chieftain Thorgil's farmstead. In the Old Norse world, controlling violence was a primary function of a chieftain, and these two incidents offer a picture of the ideal leader who can maintain peace among a retinue of violent men. Grettir runs afoul of the values of such men, and no chieftain openly champions his cause.

Feud is at the core of saga-telling, providing the literature with a cohesive sense of discord, and *Grettir's Saga* is a tale of conflict with blood feuds running throughout. Starting with Onund Tree-Foot, the author links episodes from the family's feuds into narrative feud chains, recounting long-running, violent quarrels. Basic incitements of feud such as insults, acts of violence, and calls for vengeance are reciprocal, providing characters with ready motivation for responses. Violent or insulting reactions lead to new episodes. Exchanges, such as the long conflict involving Grettir's family, the people from Thoroddsstead (Thorodd's Farm), and the people from

Mel, fit logically into the saga's chronological framework and draw additional individuals and groups into feud.

Competition among neighbours for the island's limited resources frequently stirs animosities in the saga. Viking Age Icelanders practised a form of sedentary pastoralism. They were not nomadic herders but lived on fixed farmsteads raising sheep and cattle. The Icelanders' staple diet was based on dairy products. Milk, cheese, and curd production was supplemented by fishing and hunting wildfowl as well as gathering birds' eggs. Grass for livestock fodder was the main summer crop, a form of agriculture which left time for men to attend assemblies and to set out on vengeance-taking raids. The cultivation of grain was rare.

Survival in Iceland's marginal environment often depended on a high degree of cooperation. The autumn sheep round-up and manning the small coastal fishing vessels especially required group work. There was need for competitive readiness to seize opportunistic moments such as cutting up or flensing beached whales before carcasses rotted. On two occasions, members of Grettir's family battle with neighbouring farmers over whales washed ashore during times of famine. Using their long flensing knives as weapons, men kill each other from right on top of the whale, and violent feud erupts. Among Iceland's written sources, *Grettir's Saga* offers some of the most detailed information about the importance of beached whales. Sometimes live or dying whales beached themselves, but mostly they were already dead when they reached land. Bloated and raised to the surface by the gases of decay in their stomachs and bowels, these dead creatures were such huge treasures of meat and fat that men were prepared to fight over whale carcasses washed ashore following storms. The author's interest in whales is matched by an array of information about the material culture and subsistence strategies. We learn what people ate, how they fished, the tools they employed, the clothes they wore, and the layout of their houses.

Family Sagas and Outlaw Sagas

The four greatest 'family sagas' are *Egil's Saga*, *Grettir's Saga*, *Laxdaela Saga*, and *Njal's Saga*. *Grettir's Saga*, which was written after the others, probably between 1310 and 1320 (no one can be absolutely sure), incorporates more supernatural elements than the other major sagas. The family sagas, a group of anonymous Icelandic prose stories, are so named because they recount stories about the people and regions of early Iceland. Unlike many medieval stories from other European lands written in Latin, the sagas are told in Old Norse/Icelandic, the everyday language of the medieval Icelander brought by the first Scandinavian settlers.

As a literature, the family sagas are set in the functioning world of early Iceland, replete with folkloristic beliefs. The texts explore personal issues while stressing economic and social relationships fundamental to the lives of common people. Providing invaluable information about daily life, the family sagas are a window into a lost culture, describing the operation of normative codes and cultural ethics. Acts of heroism and villainy are set in the context of isolated cattle-raising and sheep-herding communities. Lovers' quarrels, feasts, and conflicts among neighbours over hayfields, insults, and the rights to driftage, especially whales and wood, take place in everyday settings. Most of the main characters of the family sagas lived just before and after Iceland's peaceful conversion to Christianity in the year 1000. From the saga's clear time-line, we estimate that Grettir died in 1031. His birth-date in 996 is less secure. Placing a lifespan such as Grettir's within a chronology calculated by generations and events is classic saga technique—creative storytelling set within a historical context.

Grettir's Saga is an outlaw saga. This very small subgroup of the family sagas also includes *The Saga of Gisli* and *The Saga of Hord*. Outlaw sagas tend towards biography, exploring the psychology of the underdog hero. *Grettir's Saga* provides considerable insight into its hero's mental state. When his father treats him with animosity, Grettir answers by cruelly harming his father's animals. Grettir retains the love of his brothers and the devotion of his mother, and he returns both. Two of his Icelandic brothers die violently as part of his troubles, and his Norwegian half-brother abandons a secure life in order to avenge him. It is worth noting that Grettir is not unique in facing paternal issues. Almost like a Greek tragedy, the saga details a pattern of discord between fathers and sons existing for generations in Grettir's family.

Outlawed, Grettir lives as a liminal character on the boundaries of human society. The combination of extraordinary strength and a desire to excel constantly pushes him to test his own limits. Repeatedly,

Grettir publicly competes against himself in feats of strength where he raises large stones, and local folklore throughout Iceland associates him with boulders, calling them Grettir's lifts—almost all are beyond human capacity to move. Some of his most foolhardy actions can be interpreted in the light of his uncontrollable need to prove that he can get away with more than others. During his stay on Drangey Island he risks his and his brother's life by attending the local Hegraness assembly on the mainland, even though many of his enemies are present.

A Character on the Move

Grettir is constantly on the move, journeying widely in Iceland and Norway. Repeatedly he yields to the temptation to undertake new feats of courage and strength, actions which rarely help him to escape from the growing tragedy of his outlawry. Saga characters frequently plan aggressive measures as a means of advancing their ends. Grettir is not of this sort. He harbours grudges for years, but his attacks are rarely part of a plan which takes the future into consideration. He consistently reaps little value from the way he injures people or responds to insult. His exaggerated sense of personal honour is closely linked to his predisposition to violence, and in most situations of conflict he ignores early Iceland's conflict-resolution mechanisms.

By disregarding the options of arbitration and payment of compensation, Grettir leaves himself no way out of feud. For instance, Grettir ignores a mediated settlement offered by Thorkel, his host, and places personal honour above accepting compensation or respecting the wishes of his host: 'Thorkel said: "It is my wish, Grettir, that you do not avenge yourself on Bjorn. To make sure of that, I offer to pay as compensation the full worth of a man, if you will be reconciled with him"' (Ch. 21). Grettir refuses this honourable option of customary law. Bjorn is well born, with powerful Norwegian kinsmen. They in turn will seek vengeance, leading to further killings and Grettir's banishment from Norway.

In many ways, *Grettir's Saga* is a tale of conceit and its costs. In early youth Grettir manifests his arrogance through unwillingness to work on his father's farm, and this trait repeatedly gets him into trouble in a society requiring hard work from all its members. Grettir makes it clear that he considers normal tasks beneath him, and instead devotes himself to accomplishing great deeds. He refuses to take orders, and individuals outside his immediate family find it impossible to control him. Chieftains keep their distance. The powerful chieftain Vermund the Slender from the West Fjords refuses to admit Grettir into his household, stating: 'You are not easily disposed to becoming a follower of other men' (Ch. 52). For his part, Grettir delights in tricking and mocking chieftains. He frequently disguises himself, and once even gives false directions to his most embittered enemy, the chieftain Thorir of Gard, sending Thorir and his men into an impassable swamp where their horses get bogged down.

Although Grettir spends a large part of his life trying to counter the legal case against him, he never attacks this chieftain, Thorir of Gard, who brought the case. Likewise, he spares the life of the son of the powerful chieftain Snorri Godi. As a strategy for securing the good-will and indebtedness of his neighbours, Grettir supports his friends and engages in gift-giving. In a series of episodes, Grettir favours the followers of the chieftain Bjorn the Champion of Hitardal and robs only the thingmen of Bjorn's rival chieftain. Concerning his nearest neighbours in Skagafjord, those who live right across the water from his lair on the island of Drangey, the saga tells us: 'He always had good relations with those who lived nearest to him and never held back from them whatever he acquired' (Ch. 72).

Poetry, Quips, and Women

The sagas are famed for their poetry, memorable quips, and understatements. *Grettir's Saga* is foremost among them in this respect, and few equal the understatement of Atli, Grettir's unfortunate brother. Surprised by his enemy while he is standing in the doorway to his longhouse, Atli looks down at the spear just thrust through his belly and deadpans: 'Broad spears are now in fashion' (Ch. 45), thus assuring himself a thousand years of fame.

When Grettir leaves the family farm, he asks his father Asmund for a weapon, the mark of a man. His father answers: 'You have not been obedient, and I have no idea how you would use weapons if put to the test, so I will give you none' (Ch. 17). To this refusal Grettir replies laconically: 'Nothing given, nothing owed' (Ch. 17). The saga itself quips in the next line, underscoring the lack of affection which surrounds Grettir even as a boy: 'Following this, father and son parted with little love. Many wished him farewell, but few a safe return.'

Quips define Grettir's defiant nature. In Norway, an outlawed berserker named Snaekoll confronts Grettir and his host, an ageing farmer. When Snaekoll says: 'You would truly become scared of dealing with me, should I become angered,' Grettir replies: 'Only what is tested is known' (Ch. 40). Later, back in Iceland, Grettir runs into a string of bad luck in the West Fjords. Once when sleeping, he is surprised by local farmers, who tie him up. Helpless and pathetic, he is questioned by a commanding woman, Thorbjorg the Stout, the daughter of the chieftain Olaf the Peacock and the wife of the chieftain Vermund. She asks: 'What drove you to this, Grettir, that you trouble my thingmen?' Grettir's reply captures an endearing side of him that gradually becomes more noticeable as he ages: 'Some things just happen. And I have to be somewhere' (Ch. 52).

The saga contains over seventy verses. Most are attributed to Grettir, his masterful poetry complementing his other skills. In Iceland poetry was both an art and a game. Poets called skalds created images in the form of word-puzzles employing metres, kennings (poetic circumlocutions), intermittent internal rhyme, assonance, and alliteration. Audiences responded by unravelling poetic diction and commenting on the imagery. Good poets often gave more than one choice of meaning, and skill in the play was a sign of intellect and learning. Grettir excelled at this game, and the saga presents his poetry with a personal stamp. His poems possess a sardonic, riddling, and ironic quality, reflective of his character.

Uncommonly for saga heroes, Grettir's verses are often sexually explicit. The poetry helps to uncover Grettir's personal side, including his penchant for women. He beds the wife of a ship's captain, a widow, a servant-girl, and giant-like supernatural women. Few readers miss the humour in the verse addressed to the servant-girl at Reykir after she alludes to the size of his penis. After he caught hold of this imprudent woman at Reykir, the saga says: 'The maid servant screamed at the top of her lungs, but by the time they parted, she no longer taunted Grettir' (Ch. 76). Grettir's relationship is calmer with the daughter of Hallmund, the unusually large, gentle-minded woman whom he consoles in a cave in the wild interior of Iceland. He also has an easy relationship with the daughters of the half-troll Thorir. Sometimes the relationships are damaging to Grettir. This is

the case on the crossing from Iceland to Norway, when he offends the
sailors by dallying with the young wife of Bard, the ship's captain.
Interestingly, we do not hear much of Bard's view.

That the captain of the *knorr* (a Norse trading ship) had a young
wife on-board indicates that women sailed the high seas on trading
vessels, not just as travellers but as companions to their men. Here
again saga description informs our understanding of medieval
Scandinavia, and *Grettir's Saga* gives considerable information about
women. In addition to travellers, it portrays a range of women's roles,
including guardians of family honour, political leaders, wives, lovers,
mistresses of houses, independent widows, nuns, serving-maids, and
witches.

Grettir's laziness on-board the *knorr* offers insight into how the
medieval audience regarded Grettir's behaviour. The saga tells that
the sailors 'got no work out of him and became angrier than before.
They said Grettir would be made to pay, both for his verses and for
breaking the rules. "You think it better", they said, "to stroke the belly
of Bard's wife than to fulfil your duties on-board. Such conduct is
intolerable."' Finally roused, Grettir stands up and replies in verse:

> All right, I'm up, despite
> the sea and its constant pitching.
> I know she won't be pleased
> if Grettir lies down on the job.
> She's a fine woman, fair of
> complexion—yes, she'll take
> a dim view of things if others
> must slave on my behalf.
>   (Ch. 17)

Jumping down into the hold, Grettir starts bailing out the water.
The sailors marvel at his enormous strength and change their opinion
of him.

Even today, modern Icelanders readily attribute clever statements
to Grettir, and many know his poetry by heart. Part of the appeal is
that the verses conceal intentions with double meanings. When
addressing berserkers in Norway, Grettir inserts a conditional phrase
that initially sounds friendly but subtly expresses his true intention: 'If,
however, we are still such good friends when you leave, as I think most
likely, then I would like to join your group' (Ch. 19). The berserkers do
not seem to notice. Skilled at repartee, Grettir utters proverbs and

speaks through aphorisms. When his uncle Jokul offers him senten-tious advice, Grettir notes that Jokul might best look to his own interest: 'Danger is at your own door when it has entered your neighbour's' (Ch. 34).

Bad Luck and Sorcery

Characters in the saga, including Grettir's half-brother Thorstein the Galleon and his uncle Jokul, refer to Grettir as a man of ill luck, an *ógæfumaðr* (an unlucky man). Repeatedly, the saga returns to the concept of luck, an important notion in the Old Norse world that differs from our modern concept. Called *gæfa* in Old Norse, a term connected with the verb *gefa* (to give) and related to the noun *gipt* (gift), luck in the sagas is quantitative. Close to fate, luck could be inherited from ancestors, granted, spent, given, taken away, or lost. Both vocabulary and usage in the sagas indicate that luck is a gift from nature, a kind of natural endowment.

Grettir's ill luck surfaces when he appeals for a judgement from St Olaf, the holy king of Norway. Grettir had accidentally set fire to a house in Norway, killing twelve innocent men, including two sons of the Icelander Thorir from Gard, an old friend of King Olaf. To stay in Norway, Grettir must have Olaf's protection. Olaf is the epitome of the saintly and righteous Christian evaluator, and rejection by him is equivalent to rejection by Christian society. The burning of Thorir's sons weighs on Olaf's judgement.

In an exchange that highlights the difference between luck and prowess, Grettir asks to join the king's retinue, saying to the king: 'You have many men with you who will not be thought more warrior-like than I' (Ch. 39). The king replies: 'I can see that there are few men like you, on account of your strength and courage. But more than this, you are so much a man of ill luck that you cannot be with us. Go now in peace and stay wherever you wish throughout the winter. But when the summer comes, go back to Iceland, because it is there that your bones are fated to lie.' Before parting, Olaf adds: 'If ever there was a man who was cursed, then he must be you.' As if to prove the king's foresight, when Grettir returns to Iceland he finds himself outlawed, his father dead, and his brother Atli killed.

Luck is not always against Grettir. Material objects, such as swords or rings, have their own luck, and possession of such objects, with their inherent quantity of good or bad luck, affects a person's fate. Grettir possesses weapons with good luck, including Jokul's-Gift, the sword given to him by his mother. Most important is the good sax or short-sword called Kar's-Gift, which he takes from the mound-dweller Kar the Old. This famous viking lay guarding his treasure in his underground burial chamber until Grettir broke into the mound and robbed him. The sax is not a weapon that fights by itself but an implement suitable only for a hero capable of wielding it. With his cunning, Grettir is the right person, and he employs the sax with success in several encounters.

Supernatural influences, especially sorcery, also affect Grettir's luck and fate. In general, his dealings with supernatural creatures worsen his luck. While fighting the revenant Glam, the clouds suddenly part and the two look at each other in the moonlight. In one of the most famous passages from the sagas, Glam casts his evil eyes on Grettir and curses him in an almost analytic tone. The result leaves Grettir afraid for the rest of his life of being alone in the dark: 'Most of what you do will now turn against you, bringing ill luck (*ógæfa*) and no joy (*hamingjuleysi*). You will be made an outlaw, forced always to live in the wilds and to live alone. And further I lay this curse upon you: these eyes will always be within your sight, and you will find it difficult to be alone. This will drag you to your death' (Ch. 35).

The concept of *hamingjuleysi* in the above passage is close in meaning to *ógæfa*, but the term carries the understanding of lacking the joy of personal success. After his cursed encounter with Glam, Grettir's only hope for relief is reincorporation into the society which has rejected him. Grettir tries. He travels throughout Iceland appealing to chieftains for assistance, but, the saga tells us, 'always something got in the way' (Ch. 52).

Sorcery also plagues Grettir, especially the conjuring of the old witch Thurid, whom Grettir's opponent Thorbjorn Hook enlists to disable Grettir. The saga connects Thurid with pagan practices: 'People dismissed her as feeble, but, when she was young and people were still pagan, she had been skilled in magic and sorcery. Now it seemed as if she had forgotten everything, but even though the country had become Christian many sparks of heathenism remained' (Ch. 78). Thurid curses Grettir's good luck (*heill*) and seeks to seal his fate by removing all his *gæfa* (luck) and *gipt* (naturally endowed gifts). The saga presents sorcery and magic in Christian terms, and Thurid is sinister.

Sorcerers use their powers to control people and things, and Thurid's spells redirect winds and currents. Grettir's enemies find themselves vilified because they rely on sorcery. The issue becomes a legal one, and people take sides in deciding which is more dangerous, the sorcery of his opponents or Grettir's criminal acts.

Creatures and Land-Cleansing

Grettir's outlawry frequently places him in contact with threats whose origins reach far back into Scandinavian folklore. He fights a variety of humans and creatures including berserkers, revenants, trolls, and cave-bears. These encounters, while overtly successful, contribute to his bad luck. The saga uses the specific term 'land-cleansing' (*land-hreinsun*) to describe Grettir's ridding the countryside of dangers. Grettir's liminal status also places him on the border of human imagination, but he is not superhuman. He is an exceptional man with giant strength, courage, special weapons, and the diverse skills needed to defeat a variety of creatures and enemies.

Grettir's physical prowess does not exceed the limits of credibility. The saga tells us: 'Grettir once said that he thought he was secure in a fight against most men, even if three came against him at once. Nor would he give way without trying, even if he had to face four men. But he would fight with more than that only if he was forced to defend himself' (Ch. 31). Grettir is not concerned with fantastic beings such as flying fiery dragons. His opponents are threats drawn from the anxieties and belief systems of Iceland's rural society and understood by its medieval church. They arise from pre-Christian traditions but are presented in the Christian context of the period when the saga was written.

Several times in Norway Grettir fights berserkers, warriors who roam the countryside as brigands preying on isolated farmsteads. Berserkers are an old phenomenon, and Grettir's ancestor Onund Tree-Foot also fights them. The English word 'berserk' is derived from the Old Norse *berserkr*, a compound of *serkr* (shirt) and *berr* or *beri* (referring probably to the animal 'bear', but also possibly meaning 'bare' as in without protection). Berserkers were especially feared because in battle they threw themselves into a rage and possibly a trance called *berserksgangr* (going berserk). Berserkers, drawing this frenzy down upon themselves, became terrifying fighters and almost invulnerable. They threw off their armour, howled like dogs, foamed at the mouth, and bit their shields before plunging into the ranks of their enemies. *Ynglinga Saga* (*The Saga of the Ynglings*), an Old Icelandic text attributed to the thirteenth-century Icelandic chieftain Snorri Sturluson, describes berserkers as warriors devoted to the war–god Odin, possibly part of an Odinic cult: 'His [Odin's] men went to battle without armour and acted like mad dogs or wolves. They bit into their shields and were as strong as bears or bulls. They killed people, but neither fire nor iron harmed them. This madness is called berserker-fury.'[1]

The cultic origin of the berserk practice seems to have come from an old North Germanic shamanistic tradition in which warriors put on bear-skins and in a trance-like state became bears. *The Saga of King Hrolf Kraki* offers some of the best examples of bear warriors in the sagas. Pictorial evidence has been found on artefacts pre-dating the Viking period, such as a seventh-century bronze helmet decoration from Torslunda, Sweden, showing a weapon-bearing man in an animal skin and a one-eyed, dancing god-like figure, perhaps Odin. Centuries later in Iceland, around the time *Grettir's Saga* was written, the Icelandic Grey Goose Law (*Grágás*) specifically outlaws *berserksgangr*. This entry suggests that the practice of going berserk was still a concern in the twelfth century when the oral laws were written down.

Grettir's Saga also speaks of 'wolfskins' (*úlfheðnar*). These were ferocious warriors who wore wolfskins and exhibited supernatural, wolf-like qualities. *Heimskringla* reports that King Harald Fairhair had a small group of wolfskins. *Grettir's Saga* notes that these warriors were also berserkers. At a crucial moment in the great sea-battle of Haursfjord, 'King Harald ordered his berserkers to advance. They were called the wolfskins and no iron could bite them. When they burst forward, nothing could withstand their assault' (Ch. 2). After King Harald and his descendants took control of Norway, berserkers lost their importance as royal troops. Hard to control, they were outlawed in Norway and pushed to the fringes of society. They became pirates and bandits, and it is in this role that Grettir encounters them in this saga.

---

[1] For an English translation of *Ynglinga Saga* see Snorri Sturluson, *Heimskringla: History of the Kings of Norway*, 3rd edn., tr. Lee M. Hollander (Austin, Tex.: University of Texas Press and American Scandinavian Foundation, 1999), 6–50.

He also challenges revenants, which in Old Icelandic tradition are physically strong, corporeal walking dead. Unlike in many other cultures, revenants of the sagas are not shades of former individuals or ghost-like apparitions, but large, dangerous, animated corpses, who return to terrorize their former local communities. They often bring harm to former friends, family, enemies, and employers. Frequently they re-enter and try to take possession of the farmhouses where they previously lived. Burying people properly, so they cannot return, was of crucial importance.

The Icelandic walking dead are probably an old cultural feature in Scandinavian folk tradition. They are connected with the fear and power of darkness and reflect the possibility of continued material life of the individual after death.

Christianity did not uproot this belief, and revenants in Iceland were recognized and exorcized by the church. Icelandic practices, as known from medieval writings, were frequently different from church practices on the mainland. Christian teachings treat soulless bodies as animated by the devil or demons, whereas Icelandic ghosts (*draugar*) come back to life by their own volition and not by external possession. Icelandic sources portray a nuanced and extensive picture of what might once have been beliefs concerning the living dead and life after death in northern Europe before Christian theology took hold.

Sometimes revenants can be reasonable. For example, *Laxdaela Saga* features a crew of drowned sailors who return from the dead to occupy the house of one of the sailors' wives. In saga style based on social and legal processes, the living occupants of the house prepare a legal case against the dead intruders. When the revenants lose their case, they obey the jurisdiction of the living and leave the mortal world. This is an example of the mix of folkloristic content and Icelandic legal structure. The law sets the rules, whether for the living or the dead.

Grettir fights the walking dead as an exceptional human, not as a sorcerer or a magician. In his first fight with a revenant he relies on the heirloom sword, Jokul's-Gift. The saga tells us that Grettir 'cut off the head and placed the head against Kar's buttocks' (Ch. 18). In the Glam episode, Grettir uses the sax and repeats his technique of placing the revenant's head alongside the buttocks, perhaps a reflection of ritual actions associated with permanently killing revenants.

Glam is the best-known ghost in the sagas. His meeting with Grettirs' occurs in the middle of *Grettir's Saga*, and marks a turning-point in the story. Grettir tastes fear for the first time and acquires his tragic weakness: his inability to be alone because of his fear of the dark. While alive, Glam was a large, surly man who shunned company and neglected Christian traditions. These character traits foreshadow his post-mortem existence, intensifying his antisocial qualities. Shortly after Glam is killed by a previous revenant, his body begins to move of its own volition, and it shies away from the priest who wants to bury it in the churchyard. Glam begins to haunt the valley and 'ride the roof' at Thorhallsstead. He beats his heels against the sides of the roof and starts killing people on the farmstead, until the farm is in a shambles. When Glam's haunting is at its worst, Grettir arrives and confronts the revenant in the middle of the night.

Grettir also fights trolls, monstrous beings who live in the wilds and at night break into the world of men, seeking human flesh to eat. Grettir is unable to stay away from danger and seeks opportunities to challenge such creatures. After hearing of a series of Christmas Eve killings over two previous years, Grettir journeys to the farm of Sandhaugar in the north of Iceland. Disguised as a mysterious stranger, he arrives at the very darkest moment of the winter. There he finds two trolls. The local farmers and the Christian priest have been unable to mount any opposition to the incursions of these monsters, and Grettir, an outsider, takes on the task of facing them.

Not all of Grettir's encounters with trolls are negative. The shadowy, giant-like character Hallmund, almost a troll himself, leads Grettir to his lonely daughter. Hallmund also shows Grettir the way to an enchanted green valley hidden in the middle of Geitland Glacier, a kind of Icelandic Shangri-la where Grettir spends a winter. There is something magical in the allusions to the hours Grettir wiles away with the daughters of Thorir, the half-troll (*blendingr*, a blending of troll and human) who rules over this lost valley. From our perspective we can see that Grettir's sexual relationships in the wild are inappropriate for his society. Such liaisons underscore his position as an outsider, a person beyond the law.

Although Iceland had no indigenous bears or any predatory animals beyond arctic foxes, in Norway Grettir encounters a powerful cave-bear attacking the farm of his host. Worship of the cave-bear is an ancient phenomenon in Scandinavia, and partial memory of this practice continued well after the conversion to Christianity. Although the bear episode in *Grettir's Saga* is not connected with cultic worship, the story is somewhat strange for an Icelandic hero. Probably the episode incorporates aspects of older tales accredited to Grettir during the telling of his travels. The bear episode is what folklorists would recognize as a nature–culture encounter. Grettir, a hero with the strength of a bear, seeks out the animal in its own environment. When Grettir returns to human society, he brings with him the animal's paw as a token of his victory, and the story connects Grettir to a tradition of bear warriors.

There are numerous Scandinavian stories of contacts between humans and cave-bears in addition to the memory of berserker 'bear' warriors. Bears, which live private lives deep in caves, are in many ways human-like. They can walk on two legs and have human-like eyes, giving the appearance of intelligence and memory. Bears are masters of the forest in the way that humans are masters of the cultivated fields. At times bears hunt in the pastures and tilled fields of humans, whereas humans hunt in the forest. The two compete for space and food.

In the sagas some people are named Bjorn, a name which means bear. Sometimes people are transformed into bears, and sometimes humans engage in sexual activities with them. Grettir's fight with the cave-bear in Norway comes about through a competition with a man named Bjorn, who claims he can kill a cave-bear troubling their host's farm. Bjorn is a cowardly braggart who humiliates others to gain the admiration of younger warriors, and in the end, it is Grettir who fights the bear. In what is perhaps the remnant of an older bear-warrior story, Grettir also takes Bjorn's life and retakes his fur cloak, the one which Bjorn had tossed into the cave-bear's den.

Grettir's Saga *and Other Medieval Tales*

Scholars have long noticed that Grettir's slayings of trolls at the farm of Sandhaugar in the valley of Bardardal and his killing of the walking corpse Glam show affinities with the episodes in the Old English epic poem *Beowulf* where the hero kills Grendel and Grendel's mother. Both prose saga and Old English poem draw on ancient northern European traditions about champions who free the countryside from aggressive otherworldly creatures harming society.

The two champions, Grettir and Beowulf, are land-cleansers, but ultimately they have very different roles in their society. Grettir is an outlaw, whereas Beowulf becomes a prominent king.

In Bardardal Grettir fights a female and then a male troll in actions analogous to Beowulf's contests with Grendel then with Grendel's mother. In saga and poem, the hero waits alone indoors during the night to confront a man-eating monster seeking men to kill and drag back to devour in a watery cave. In both instances the monster is fatally wounded by losing an arm and flees back to its lair. The hero pursues, dives under water, and enters the cave, where he confronts and kills a second monster of the opposite sex. In Grettir's case the first monster is female, the second male. In Beowulf's case, it is the other way round. The saga makes no mention of a parental relationship between the trolls, but that does not mean that such a relationship was absent in other tellings. Unlike Grettir's fight with the trolls, analogies between Grettir's contest with the revenant Glam and Beowulf's monster-slayings are less clear. Glam is not a member of a man-eating male–female pair associated with water. Glam is a walking dead man who kills people but does not eat them. The similarity between the Glam and Grendel episodes is principally that the monster ravages the world of men and that Grettir and Beowulf wait inside the hall at night to fight the intruder in single combat.

With Icelandic saga and the Old English poem separated by perhaps 500 years, it is difficult to postulate a direct connection as some scholars have done. The *Beowulf* story, although preserved in an Anglo-Saxon version, is originally a Scandinavian tale, and the similarities between *Grettir's Saga* and *Beowulf* most likely derive from a common heritage of oral storytelling. Grettir and Beowulf are cultural heroes with bear-like characteristics, including strength sufficient to compete with monsters. The stories of these heroes integrate elements from myth, folklore, and history.

Some episodes in *Grettir's Saga* are probably influenced by the *Romance of Tristan and Isolde*. This borrowing from the French romance occurs in the third and final part of the saga, when the tale turns to the exploits of Thorstein the Galleon. Thorstein journeys from Norway to the Greek Byzantine Empire, and in Constantinople he becomes involved in amorous adventures with Spes, a married noblewoman. Romantic love suddenly becomes a central theme in the saga. Known as 'The Story of Spes' (*Spesar páttur*), this exotic section of the saga includes motifs similar to the romance, such as the unfaithful wife's dubious oath. These episodes are almost certainly late additions to the Grettir story, probably added by the fourteenth-century author or a later scribe. Nevertheless, they are well integrated into the narrative, serving to contrast Thorstein's and Grettir's luck.

From other sources we know that the *Romance of Tristan and Isolde* was translated into Old Norse by command of the king of Norway in the early thirteenth century. King Hakon (later called Hakon the Old) was interested in becoming a powerful European monarch. Wanting to educate his retainers in courtly European culture, the king commissioned a monk, Brother Robert, to translate the saga from French into Old Norse. Brother Robert's translation seems to have been reasonably well known in medieval Iceland, and is preserved in Icelandic sources. One can imagine an Icelandic saga author incorporating this imported material into the more traditional elements of the Grettir story in order to make the saga more entertaining and modern. The integration is an example of how sagas adapted to changing tastes without altering the core nature of an eleventh-century story.

Grettir's Saga is one of Iceland's greatest tales. Within a chronological frame spanning two centuries, the saga is both fictional and historical. Combining a wide range of elements into an effective whole, it details social relationships, acts of feuding, and the circumstances of life in the medieval North Atlantic. It also tells a Viking Age story on a personal level. Grettir is a troubled soul with a noble side, whose struggle with the revenant Glam is one of the most famous passages in the sagas. His perseverance, wit, and independence have gained him an assured place in Icelandic history and world literature.

Davide Zori and Jesse Byock

NOTE ON THE TEXT AND TRANSLATION

THE goal of this volume is to provide a readable translation that accurately captures the nuances and style of the original. To assist the reader in navigating unfamiliar aspects of the saga, the translation contains chapter titles, maps, and illustrations. The endmatter contains notes, an appendix on Grettir's years of outlawry, and genealogies. An asterisk in the text indicates the presence of a note at the back of the book, where they are listed by page number. A Glossary of two parts serves as an index, providing the reader with a tool for locating characters (both human and supernatural), groups, animals, objects, and places in the story.

Manuscripts and Editions

Grettir's Saga remained highly popular in Iceland from medieval times down to the modern period. There are many extant manuscripts, but most are late paper copies of earlier vellum or skin books. Beginning in early modern times and continuing to the end of the nineteenth century, copying older vellums on to the pages of inexpensive blank paper books became a passion among Icelanders.

The major extant vellum manuscripts are from the late medieval period. Three of the four principal ones, AM 551a 4to, AM 556a 4to, and AM 152 fol., are housed in the Árni Magnússon Manuscript Institute in Reykjavík, Iceland. The fourth, DG (Delagardie) 10 fol., is found in Uppsala, Sweden. Although the skin manuscripts of *Grettir's Saga* fall into two groups, all four trace back to a single lost manuscript, and all offer the same version of the saga without great differences. Many other sagas have contrasting variants preserved in different manuscripts.

The medieval manuscripts of *Grettir's Saga* have been transcribed into modern scholarly editions, and the translation in this book is based on two editions of the saga. Each of these, *Grettis saga Ásmundarsonar*, edited by Guðni Jónsson, *Íslenzk fornrit*, vol. 7 (Reykjavík, 1946), and *Grettis saga*, edited by Örnólfur Thorsson (Reykjavík: Mál og menning, 1994), assembles a complete text of the saga after comparing the major vellum manuscripts. When there were differences between the two editions, I followed the more recent 1994 edition.

Verses

Russell Poole translated the poetry in this book. He based his translation of the verses on the *Íslenzk fornrit* (1946) edition and also consulted the Mál og menning (1994) edition. The verses in this translation loosely contain two-stress or three-stress lines, suggesting the metrical characteristics of the original without being strictly bound to them. Intermittent internal rhymes, assonances, and alliterations give a general, although diluted, impression of the compulsory internal rhyme and alliteration characteristic of much medieval Icelandic poetry. In a few instances the kennings (poetic circumlocutions) are closely imitated. More often the meanings of the kennings emerge through word choice.

Spelling

Names and terms in the translation are anglicized, and Old Icelandic case endings omitted. The closest English equivalents replace non-English letters such as þ, ð, æ, and ö, but when a name is familiar to English speakers in another form, I use that. For example, the Hebrides are called by their English name rather than by the Norse term the 'Southern Isles' (*Suðreyjar*). When the action is set in Iceland, the translation employs Icelandic place-names or names close to the Icelandic original, since the reader can still find many of these sites on a modern map.

Place-names offer considerable information, and where possible, English translations are given in parentheses. In many instances, landscape descriptions replace Icelandic names, for example, 'Geitland Glacier' instead of *Geitlandsjökull*. Many farmsteads in Iceland use a person's name followed by *staðir*, and these names are anglicized by using the word 'stead'. When the saga takes place in Norway, Norwegian spelling often replaces the Icelandic unless there is a good English alternative to both.

Acknowledgements

Translating *Grettir's Saga* was a pleasure, particularly because of the quality of the assistance I received. My outstanding doctoral student in Viking Age archaeology, Davide Zori, was a valuable partner in writing the Introduction. My friend Kristján Jóhann Jónsson and I had much fun reading over the translation and debating the nuances. Russell Poole, Davide Zori, Gayle Byock, David Lasson, Brooks Walker, and Collin Connors all contributed significant comments and suggestions. Guðmundur Ólafur Ingvarsson made the extensive series of maps, and I enjoyed working with a cartographer of such great skill and knowledge. The same can be said for the time I spent working with the architects Grétar Markússon and Stefán Örn Stefánsson. They turned their interest in historical architecture to the project and Grétar drew from the saga descriptions an Icelandic turf-walled longhouse and a Norwegian timber storage building. Robert Guillemette used his many talents on the graphics and design. Judith Luna, my editor at Oxford University Press, is a thorough professional and the book owes much to her. I also wish to thank the Arcadia Fund, the Alcoa Foundation, the Institute for Viking and North Atlantic Studies, the John Simon Guggenheim Foundation, the UCLA Center for Medieval and Renaissance Studies, and the Gelsinger Memorial Fund for their generous support.

SELECT BIBLIOGRAPHY

Studies

Amory, Frederic, 'The Medieval Icelandic Outlaw: Life-style, Saga, and Legend', in Gísli Pálsson (ed.), *From Sagas to Society* (Enfield Lock: Hisarlik Press, 1992), 189–203.

Arent, A. Margaret, 'The Heroic Pattern: Old Germanic Helmets, *Beowulf*, and *Grettis saga*', in Edgar C. Polomé (ed.), *Old Norse Literature and Society: A Symposium* (Austin and London: University of Texas Press, 1969).

Beard, D. J., 'The Berserker in Icelandic Literature', in Robin Thelwall (ed.), *Approaches to Oral Literature* (Belfast: New University of Ulster, 1978), 99–114.

Berger, Alan, 'Bad Weather and Whales: Old Icelandic Literary Ecotypes', *Arkiv för nordisk middelalder*, 92 (1969), 92–7.

Blaney, Benjamin, 'The Berserk Suitor: The Literary Application of a Stereotyped Theme', *Scandinavian Studies*, 54.4 (1982), 279–94.

Bruce-Mitford, R. L. S., 'Fresh Observations on the Torslunda Plates', *Frümittelalterliche Studien*, 2 (1968), 233–6.

Ciklamini, Marlene, 'The Literary Mold of the *hólmgöngumaðr*', *Scandinavian Studies*, 37.2 (1965), 117–38.

—— 'Grettir and Ketill Hængr, the Giant-Killers', *Arv*, 22 (1966), 136–55.

Caciola, Nancy, 'Wraiths, Revenants and Ritual in Medieval Culture', *Past and Present*, 152 (Aug. 1996), 3–45.

Chadwick, N. K., 'Norse Ghosts (A Study in *Draugr* and *Haugbúi*)', *Folklore*, 57.2 (1946), 50–65.

—— 'Norse Ghosts II (Continued)', *Folklore*, 57.3 (1946), 106–27.

Cook, Robert, 'The Reader in *Grettis saga*', *Saga-Book*, 21 (1985), 133–54.

Damico, Helen, 'Dystopic Conditions of the Mind: Toward a Study of Landscape in *Grettis saga*'. *Geardagum* VII. *Essays in Old English Language and Literature* (1986), 1–15.

de Looze, Laurence, 'The Outlaw Poet, the Poetic Outlaw: Self-Consciousness in *Grettis saga Ásmundarsonar*', *Arkiv för nordisk filologi*, 106 (1991), 85–103.

Fjalldal, Magnús, *The Long Arm of Coincidence: The Frustrated Connection Between 'Beowulf' and 'Grettis saga'* (Toronto: University of Toronto Press, 1998).

Glendinning, Robert J., '*Grettis Saga* and European Literature in the Late Middle Ages', *Mosaic*, 4.2 (1970), 49–61.

Hastrup, Kirsten, 'Tracing Tradition—an Anthropological Perspective on *Grettis saga Ásmundarsonar*', in John Lindow *et al.* (eds.), *Structure and Meaning in Old Norse Literature*, The Viking Collection 3 (Odense: Odense University Press, 1986), 281–313.

Hawes, Janice, 'The Monstrosity of Heroism—Grettir Asmundarson as an Outsider', *Scandinavian Studies*, 80.1 (2008), 19–50.

Heslop, Kate, 'Grettisfærsla: The Handing on of Grettir', *Saga-Book*, 30 (2006), 65–94.

Hume, Kathryn, 'From Saga to Romance: The Uses of Monsters in Old Norse Literature', *Studies in Philology*, 77 (1980), 1–25.

—— 'The Thematic Design of *Grettis saga*', *Journal of English and Germanic Philology*, 73 (1974), 469–86.

Liberman, Anatoly, 'Beowulf—Grettir', in Bela Brogyani and Thomas Krömmelbein (eds.), *Germanic Dialects, Amsterdam Studies in the Theory and History of Linguistic Science*, 38 (Amsterdam: John Benjamins, 1986), 353–401.

Motz, Lotte, 'Withdrawal and Return: A Ritual Pattern in *Grettis saga*', *Arkiv för nordisk filologi*, 88 (1973), 91–110.

Orchard, Andy, *Pride and Prodigies: Studies in the Monsters of the Beowulf Manuscript* (Toronto: University of Toronto Press, 2003).

Ólason, Vésteinn, 'Arrogance and Misfortune—Grettir', tr. Andrew Wawn, in *Dialogues with the Viking Age* (Reykjavík: Heimskringla, 1998), 186–90.

Poole, Russell, 'Lof en eigi háð? The Riddle of *Grettis saga* Verse 14', *Saga-Book*, 27 (2003), 25–47.

—— 'Myth, Psychology, and Society in *Grettis saga*', *Alvíssmál*, 11 (2004), 3–16.

Richardson, Peter, 'Vera varð ek nokkur: The Reader, the Women and the Berserks in *Grettir's saga*', *Arkiv för nordisk filologi*, 113 (1998), 65–75.

The Saga of King Hrolf Kraki, tr. Jesse L. Byock (London and New York: Penguin Books, 1998).

Turville-Petre, G., 'Outlawry', in Jakob Benediktsson (ed.), *Sjötíu Ritgerðir*, 2 (1977), 767–78.

Turville-Petre, Joan, '*Beowulf* and *Grettis saga*: An Excursion', *Saga-Book*, 19 (1977), 347–57.

Whitaker, Ian, 'Some Anthropological Perspectives on *Grettla*: A Response to Motz', *Arkiv för nordisk filologi*, 92 (1977), 145–54.

Sagas and Society

Boberg, Inger M., *Motif-Index of Early Icelandic Literature*, Bibliotheca Arnamagnæana, 27 (Copenhagen: Munksgaard, 1966).

Byock, Jesse L., *Feud in the Icelandic Saga* (Berkeley: University of California Press, 1993).

—— *Viking Age Iceland* (London: Penguin Books, 2001).

Dubois, Thomas A., *Nordic Religions in the Viking Age* (Philadelphia: University of Pennsylvania Press, 1999).

Foote, Peter G., and David M. Wilson, *The Viking Achievement: A Survey of the Society and Culture of Early Medieval Scandinavia* (New York: Praeger Publishers, 1970).

Karlsson, Gunnar, *Iceland's 1100 Years: the History of a Marginal Society* (Reykjavík: Mál og Menning, 2001).

Kristjánsson, Jónas, *Eddas and Sagas* (Reykjavík: Hið íslenska bókmenntafélag, 2007).

Laws of Early Iceland: Grágás I: The Codex Regius of Grágás, with Material from Other Manuscripts, ed. Andrew Dennis, Peter Foote, and Richard Perkins (Winnipeg: University of Manitoba Press, 1980).

Thorlaksson [Þorláksson], Helgi, 'Historical Background: Iceland 870–1400', in Rory McTurk (ed.), *Old Norse-Icelandic Literature and Culture* (Oxford: Blackwell Publishing, 2005).

Vikings: The North Atlantic Saga, ed. William Fitzhugh and Elisabeth Ward (Washington, DC: Smithsonian Institution Press, 2000).

Reference Works

Cleasby, Richard, and Gudbrand Vigfusson, *An Icelandic–English Dictionary*, 2nd edn. with a Supplement by Sir William A. Craigie (Oxford: Clarendon Press, 1975).

Haywood, John, *The Penguin Historical Atlas of the Vikings* (London and New York: Penguin Books, 1995).

Medieval Scandinavia: An Encyclopedia, ed. Philip Pulsiano *et al.* (New York: Garland Publishing, Inc., 1993).

Orchard, Andy, *Cassell's Dictionary of Norse Myth and Legend* (London: Cassell, 2002).

Further Reading in Oxford World's Classics

The Anglo-Saxon World, tr. Kevin Crossley-Holland.

Beowulf, tr. Kevin Crossley-Holland, ed. Heather O'Donoghue.

GRETTIR'S SAGA

CONTENTS

Contents

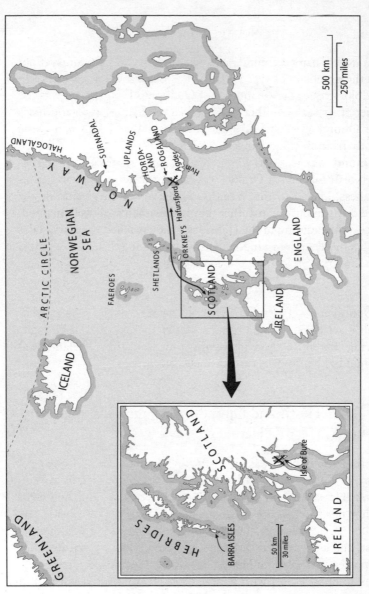

Map 1. The Viking World of Grettir's Ancestor Onund Tree-Foot. Onund and his companions raid in Scotland, the Hebrides, the Shetlands, Ireland, England, and Norway. In the Hebrides they fight sea-battles at the Barra Isles and the Isle of Bute. Returning home to Norway, they take part in the great sea-battle of Hafursfjord against King Harald Finehair.

1. The Norwegian Viking Onund

A MAN was named Onund.* He was the son of Ofeig Clumsy-Foot and the grandson of Ivar Horse-Prick. Onund was the brother of Gudbjorg. She was the mother of Gudbrand Hump, who was the father of Asta, the mother of King Olaf the Saint. On his mother's side Onund was an Uplander, but his father's kinsmen came mostly from Rogaland and Hordaland.

Onund was a great viking who raided in the West* across the North Sea. With Onund was Balki, the son of Blaeing from Sotaness, and Orm the Wealthy. Hallvard was the name of the third companion, and together they had five ships, all well manned. Once, while raiding in the Hebrides,* they reached the Barra Isles and chanced upon a king named Kjarval. He too had five ships, and Onund and his companions attacked him. The battle was fierce. Onund's men fought bravely, and many fell on both sides. The fight ended when the king escaped with only one of his ships.

Onund and his men, having acquired both ships and a store of wealth, settled in for the coming winter there in the Barra Isles. During the next three summers they raided in Ireland and Scotland. Then they returned home to Norway.

2. Thorir and Onund Battle Against King Harald of Norway

AT that time there was no peace in Norway. Harald Shaggy-Haired,* the son of Halfdan the Black, was fighting his way to power. He started out as a king from the Uplands, but then went farther north where he fought many battles and was always the victor. Turning south, Harald fought his way down along the coast, and as he passed through each region, he brought it under his power. By the time Harald drew near Hordaland, men made plans to oppose him with a large force. Kjotvi the Wealthy and Thorir Long-Chin were the leaders of the Hordalanders, and the men of Rogaland followed their king Sulki.

At the time Geirmund Helskin* was in the West across the sea. Although he was a chieftain among the Hordalanders, he took no part in the battle. That same autumn Onund and his companions returned home from raiding in the West. When Thorir Long-Chin and King Kjotvi learned of Onund's return, they sent messengers, promising both honour and wealth if Onund and his men joined them. Now Onund and his companions chose to side with Thorir and Kjotvi. They were eager for an opportunity to distinguish themselves and asked to be placed where the fighting would be thickest.

The meeting between King Harald and his opponents took place in Rogaland in Hafursfjord.* Each side assembled a large force, and the battle was one of the most important ever fought in Norway. Many sagas recount the event, because, as is to be expected, the sagas record the most important happenings. Men came to the battle from all regions of the country. There were also groups from other lands and large contingents of vikings.

Onund placed his ship alongside Thorir Long-Chin's in the centre of the fleet.* King Harald attacked Thorir Long-Chin's ship first, because Thorir, a famous berserker,* was known to be fearless. Both sides fought furiously, and finally King Harald ordered his berserkers to advance. They were called 'the wolfskins', and no iron could bite them. When they burst forward, nothing could withstand their assault. Thorir fought valiantly, but he was killed on-board. His ship was cleared from stem to stern of all defenders, and the lines tying it to the other craft were cut. It drifted slowly back among the other ships.

Now the king's men attacked Onund's ship. Onund placed himself in the prow and fought with great courage. One of the king's men said: 'That man stands firm in the prow. Let's remind him that he is in some danger.'

Onund was just then striking at a man, and as he stood with one foot up on the gunwale, an opponent aimed a blow at him. In warding it off, he bent his knee forward, and at that instant one of the king's forecastle men* struck Onund's leg. The blow landed below the knee, cutting off the lower leg. Onund was immediately out of the fight, and now the majority of his men fell.

Onund was carried onto a ship. The owner, a man named Thrand, was the son of Bjorn and the brother of Eyvind the Easterner. Thrand faced King Harald's attack and his ship lay alongside Onund's.

The allies' fleet now began to break up. In the rout that followed, Thrand and the other vikings sought to escape as best they could. They set sail west across the sea. Onund remained aboard Thrand's ship, together with Balki and Hallvard the Stormy. Onund's wound was healed, but for the rest of his life he walked with a wooden leg. For this reason, he was called Onund Tree-Foot as long as he lived.

3. Outlaws from Norway

By then, many men of excellent family were abroad in the West. They had fled their ancestral lands in Norway because King Harald outlawed all those who had fought against him and seized their property.

When Onund's stump was healed, he went with Thrand and eight others to meet with Geirmund Helskin. At that time Geirmund was the most famous viking in the West, and the men asked Geirmund whether he was ready to try to regain his lost power in Hordaland. They offered him their support. They all thought they must make a claim for their lands, and Onund* was a rich man from a great family. Geirmund replied that Harald's power had become too entrenched. He thought there was little hope of finding either honour or success through war, because Harald had already defeated an army drawn from the entire population. He said that he had no desire to become the slave of a king, having to ask for what he had previously owned in his own right. He would rather consider some other plan, because at the time he was well past the years of his youth. Onund and his companions returned to the Hebrides, where many of their companions had gathered.

There was a man named Ofeig; he was called Grettir.* Ofeig was the son of Einar, who was the son of Olvir the Child-Sparer.

His brother was Oleif the Broad, the father of Thormod Skapti. Steinolf was another son of Olvir the Child-Sparer. He was the father of Una, who was married to Thorbjorn the Salmoner. The third son of Olvir the Child-Sparer was named Steinmod. He was the father of Konal, who was the father of Alfdis from the Barra Isles. Konal's son was named Steinmod. He was the father of Halldora, who married Eilif, the son of Ketil the One-Handed. Ofeig Grettir was married to Asny. She was the daughter of Vestar, who was the son of Haeng. Ofeig Grettir's sons were named Asmund the Beardless and Asbjorn, and his daughters were Aldis, Aesa, and Asvor.

Ofeig had fled west across the sea because of King Harald's hostility. His kinsman Thormod Skapti was with him. They brought along with them their households and relatives. In the West, Ofeig and his men raided widely.

Thrand and Onund Tree-Foot now decided to sail west to Ireland to meet with Eyvind the Easterner.* Eyvind, Thrand's brother, had taken over the coastal defence of Ireland.

Eyvind's mother was Hlif, the great-granddaughter of King Frodi. Hlif was the daughter of Hrolf, who was the son of Ingjald, who was the son of King Frodi. Thrand's mother was Helga, the daughter of Ondott Crow.* The father of both men was Bjorn. Bjorn was the son of Hrolf from Ar, and was originally from Gautland. Bjorn fled after killing Sigfast, an in-law of King Solvi, having burned him to death in his house.

Bjorn escaped to Norway, where he spent the summer and then settled in for the winter with Grim the Hersir,* the son of Kolbjorn Shame-Bringer. Grim wanted to murder Bjorn for his valuables, so Bjorn left and went to Ondott Crow, who lived at Hvinisfjord in Agder. Ondott welcomed Bjorn warmly, and Bjorn stayed there during the winters. In the summers he went raiding, and continued to do so until Hlif, his wife, died. After Hlif's death, Ondott married his daughter Helga to Bjorn, who then gave up his war voyages.

Bjorn's son Eyvind then took over command of his father Bjorn's warships, and by this time Eyvind had become a great chieftain in the West. Eyvind married Rafarta, the daughter of

Kjarval, king of the Irish. Their sons were Helgi the Lean and Snaebjorn.*

When Thrand and Onund returned to the Hebrides they encountered Ofeig Grettir and Thormod Skapti. Strong friendships were forged among them because it seemed they had come back from the dead, after being in Norway where the troubles were the worst.

Onund fell into a brooding silence. When Thrand became aware of Onund's mood, he asked what was bothering him. Onund answered with this verse:

> 1. The day we faced the music
>   of sword blades clanging on shields
>   destroyed my life's joy:
>   hardships grip us too soon.
>   The axe hexed me with a maiming
>   stroke. Who now would pick me
>   as a man of consequence?
>   That's the cause of my despair.*

Thrand replied that Onund, wherever he went, would be regarded as a vigorous man. 'The best choice for you would be to settle down and marry. I offer my support and would lend my voice if I knew where you wanted to look for a wife.'

Onund replied that Thrand was a generous friend. He said that the best matches were now lost to him, at least those that were truly desirable. Thrand answered: 'Ofeig has a daughter named Aesa. We might look in that direction, if you find the idea agreeable.' Onund consented.

Next they raised the matter with Ofeig, who said he recognized that the suitor came from a prominent family and was rich in movable goods and wealth. 'But,' said Ofeig, 'I consider his lands [in Norway] of little value. Onund also seems to me to be less than fully capable in his walking. Further, my daughter is still only a child.'

Thrand responded that Onund was more vigorous than many men who still had both their legs. With Thrand's support, Onund and Ofeig eventually struck a bargain. Ofeig agreed to give his daughter's dowry in movable goods when she left home, because neither party placed much value on the lands still in Norway. Not long afterwards Thrand married Thormod Skapti's daughter. Both young women were bound by agreement to wait three winters. Onund and Thrand spent their summers raiding, returning each winter to the Barra Isles.

4. Onund and the Vikings

VIGBJOD and Vestmar were the names of two vikings from the Hebrides. They raided with eight ships in the waters around Ireland, remaining on-board both winter and summer. They caused much damage until Eyvind the Easterner took over defence of the coast. Then they withdrew and returned to the Hebrides. From there they raided, sailing deep into the fjords of western Scotland.

Thrand and Onund set out to find these vikings, and learned that Vigbjod and Vestmar had sailed to an island called Bute. Onund arrived with seven ships. The vikings saw the ships approaching, but when they realized the size of the force, they felt secure in their strength to handle the danger. Arming themselves, the vikings put to sea to meet the attackers.

Onund ordered his men to manoeuvre their ships into a narrow but deep sound, lying between two cliffs. There they could be attacked only from one direction and not by more than five ships at a time. Onund, who was a clever man, placed five of his ships at the entrance to the channel. Arranged in this way, they could choose to withdraw slowly, because open water lay behind them. A small island lay on one side. Onund placed one of his ships under its cliff. He had his men collect a large supply of heavy stones. They piled these on the cliff above, in places where they could not be seen from the ships below.

The vikings, thinking their opponents had fallen into a trap, threw themselves into the attack. Vigbjod called out, asking who had allowed themselves to be so penned in. Thrand answered that he was the brother of Eyvind the Easterner, 'and I am here with my companion Onund Tree-Foot'.

The vikings laughed and chanted:

> 2.   The trolls* take
>   each inch of Tree-Foot!
>   The trolls sink
>   the whole boatload!*

Then they added: 'It is difficult for us to see why men who cannot look after themselves go into battle.' Onund replied that the matter would remain unclear until put to the test.

The two sides manoeuvred their ships alongside each other, and a savage battle began. Each side fought bravely, but when the battle became fiercest Onund ordered his men to fall back towards the cliff. Once the vikings realized that Onund was retreating, they assumed that he was preparing to flee and made straight for his ship. In their effort to reach him, the vikings came under the cliff. Now Onund's men, who had been placed up on the cliff, moved out to the edge. The stones they hurled down onto the vikings were so large that the men below could not possibly shield themselves. Many vikings were killed outright; others were wounded so badly that they were unable to use their weapons.

Now the vikings wanted to escape, but they were unable to. By then their ships were in the narrowest part of the channel and, in the strong current, they could not be steered. Onund's men boldly assaulted Vigbjod's ships, but Thrand's men made little headway against Vestmar. As the defenders thinned out on Vigbjod's ship, Onund, along with some of his men, began to board it. When Vigbjod realized what was happening, he urged his men to stand firm. Then he turned to attack Onund, and the other men moved away. Onund was himself a forceful man, and he told his men that the time had come to determine how a meeting between Vigbjod and himself would go. Onund's companions now shoved a log under his knee, enabling him to stand steady.

Vigbjod advanced towards the stern of Onund's ship, and when the viking reached Onund he struck at him with his sword. The blow sliced off a piece of Onund's shield. Then the blade continued downward, sinking into the log supporting Onund's stump. There it stuck fast, and Vigbjod was forced to bend forward as he

pulled on the sword, trying to free it. At that moment Onund
struck at Vigbjod's shoulder, cutting off his arm. The viking was
so badly wounded that he had to drop out of the fight.

When Vestmar realized that his companion had fallen, he leapt
onto the ship which lay farthest from the fighting. He escaped and
took with him those of his men able to reach that ship. Then
Onund's men stripped the dead. Vigbjod was on the brink of
death. Onund went up to him and said this verse:

> 3.   See how your wounds are bleeding!
>   But I don't flinch, my friend.
>   I'm a one-legged chieftain, yes,
>   but I carry no wounds from you.
>   Many would-be warriors*
>   mouth off but fail to think.
>   Your type sadly lacks practice
>   in fighting it out to the end.

Onund and Thrand seized a large store of war spoils before
returning in the autumn to the Barra Isles.

5. Land in Iceland

THAT following summer, the two companions readied their ships
to sail west to Ireland. At the same time, Balki and Hallvard
decided to end their stay in the West. They had heard that good
land was available for the taking in Iceland,* and decided to
sail there. Balki claimed land in Hrutafjord (Rams' Fjord) and
lived at the two farms called Balkasteads, both named after him.
Hallvard claimed for himself Sugandafjord and took possession of
Skalavik* (Long House Bay) as far as Stigi (Ladder). He settled
there.

Thrand and Onund arrived in Ireland and went to meet
Eyvind the Easterner, who greeted his brother Thrand warmly.
When Eyvind realized that Onund was among the new arrivals,
he was infuriated and wanted to strike him. Thrand intervened,
asking his brother to stop. He said there was no sense in Norsemen

fighting among themselves, particularly when a man had given no offence. Eyvind said that Onund had earlier caused damage when he attacked King Kjarval [Eyvind's father-in-law], and now would have to pay for his actions. The brothers fell into a long argument over the issue, until Thrand said he would share the same fate as Onund. Only then did Eyvind let himself be appeased.

Thrand and Onund stayed in Ireland long into the summer. They accompanied Eyvind on his war voyages, and Eyvind came to respect Onund's courage and boldness. In the autumn Thrand and Onund returned to the Hebrides. Eyvind had promised Thrand his entire share in the expected inheritance from Bjorn, their father, if Bjorn died before Thrand. Onund and Thrand remained in the Hebrides until they both got married, and even for some years after that.

6. Thrand Sails for Iceland

NEXT the news came that Bjorn, Thrand's father, had died. When Grim the Hersir heard of the death, he went to meet with Ondott Crow to lay claim to Bjorn's property. Ondott said that Thrand, as Bjorn's son, was the rightful heir. Grim retorted that Thrand was abroad in the West.* Further, Bjorn was a Gautlander by origin, and it was the king's right to inherit the property of all foreigners. Ondott declared his intention to hold the wealth in safe-keeping for Thrand,* his grandson. With this, Grim now left, having been unable to establish claim to the property.

Thrand now learned of his father's death and, accompanied by Onund Tree-Foot, he immediately set out from the Hebrides for Norway. At the same time, Ofeig Grettir and Thormod Skapti sailed for Iceland, taking their households with them. They landed at Eyrar (Sand Banks) in the south of the island, where they stayed for the first winter with Thorbjorn the Salmoner. Later the two laid claim to the region called Gnupverja-Hrepp (Hill-Men's Commune). Ofeig took the western part, which lay between the Thver (Tributary) River and the Kalf (Calf) River, and built his farm at Ofeigsstead near Steinsholt (Stony Hill). Thormod claimed the eastern section of the district and built a farm at Skaftaholt* (Skafti's Wood). Thormod's daughters were Thorvor, the mother of Thorodd the Godi* from Hjalli (Mountain Ledge), and Thorve, who was the mother of Thorstein the Godi, the father of Bjarni the Wise.

Now there is more to tell about Thrand and Onund. In sailing back to Norway from the West, they encountered so favourable a wind that no news of their voyage preceded their landing at Ondott Crow's. Ondott, greeting Thrand well, told him about Grim the Hersir's attempt to claim Bjorn's property. 'It seems to me more proper, kinsman,' said Ondott, 'that you, rather than the king's slaves, inherit from your father. Luck is with you that no one yet knows about your voyage here, because I suspect that if Grim finds the opportunity, he will direct his animosity against one of us. It is my wish that you take the wealth into your keeping and sail abroad with it.'

Thrand replied that he would do so. He gathered together all the possessions and, as quickly as he could, prepared to leave Norway.

Before setting sail, Thrand asked Onund Tree-Foot whether he was not of a mind to try his luck in Iceland. Onund replied that, before such an undertaking, he first wanted to meet with his kinsmen and friends there in the south of the land. Thrand said: 'Then we will now have to go our separate ways. I would like you to keep an eye on my kinsmen, because, if I succeed in getting away, they will be targets for vengeance. For my part, I intend to sail out to Iceland and hope that you will do the same.' Onund promised that he would, and the two separated with deep affection.

When Thrand sailed out to Iceland, he was received well by Ofeig and Thormod Skapti. He settled at Thrandarholt (Thrand's Wood), to the west of the Thjors (Bull's) River.*

7. Onund and Asmund Sail for Iceland

ONUND went south to Rogaland, where he met many of his kinsmen and friends. He stayed secretly with a man named Kolbein. Onund learned that King Harald had confiscated his lands and that his property had been placed under the management of a man named Harek, one of the king's stewards. Onund went there in the night and seized control; Harek was led out and executed. Onund took all the possessions that they could find and then burned the farmhouse. He spent the rest of the winter in various places.

That autumn Grim the Hersir, having failed to acquire Bjorn's property for the king, killed Ondott Crow. Immediately, the very same night, Signy, Ondott's wife, loaded all their possessions onto a ship. Together with her sons Asmund and Asgrim, she returned to her father Sighvat. Soon afterwards Signy sent her sons to Hedin, her foster-father,* who lived in Soknadal.* But the boys became dissatisfied after only a short time and returned to their mother. Now they set out again, arriving at Yuletide* at Hvin, the farm where Ingjald Tryggvi lived. Ingjald, urged by his wife Gyda, took the boys in, and they stayed there over the winter.

In the spring Onund travelled to the northern part of Agder.* He had learned of Ondott's death and how he had been killed. When Onund located Signy, he asked her what assistance she and her sons would like to receive from him. Signy said that they longed to take vengeance on Grim the Hersir for Ondott's killing. The sons of Ondott were sent for. They met with Onund Tree-Foot, and all parties agreed to join forces. A watch was now kept on Grim's movements.

That summer there was much ale brewing at Grim's, because Grim had invited Jarl* Audun to a feast. When Onund and the sons of Ondott got wind of these plans, they made their way to Grim's farm. They arrived unexpectedly and set fire to the houses, burning Grim the Hersir to death inside along with nearly thirty of his men. The attackers seized many valuable possessions. Onund then withdrew into the forest, while the brothers, who were in the boat of Ingjald their foster-father, rowed out along the shore and then hid themselves a short distance from the farm.

When Jarl Audun arrived for the feast, as had been agreed, he realized that his friends were lost. He gathered some men and stayed there several nights, but he was unable to learn anything concerning the whereabouts of Onund or the others. Together with two of his men, the jarl slept in a loft.

Onund followed closely all that happened at the farm and then sent for the brothers. When they met, he asked them whether they wanted to keep watch outside or to attack the jarl. They chose to attack the jarl and, using a timber beam, they battered the door of the loft until it gave way. Asmund grabbed hold of the two men who were with the jarl, and threw them down with such force that they were almost killed. At the same time, Asgrim rushed the jarl and ordered him to pay compensation for their father, because the jarl had been a party to Hersir Grim's plans to kill Ondott. The jarl said that he was not carrying money with him, and asked that the payment be postponed. In reply, Asmund placed the point of his spear against the jarl's chest, telling him to pay on the spot. The jarl took off a necklace, which Asgrim accepted, together with three gold arm-rings and a costly velvet cloak. Then Asgrim gave the jarl a name, calling him Audun Nanny-Goat.

When the farmers and men of the district became aware that an attack was under way, they assembled, intending to come to the jarl's assistance. Because Onund had a large force, it turned into a hard fight and many prominent farmers as well as retainers of the jarl were killed. The brothers now rejoined Onund and reported the outcome of their dealings with the jarl. Onund said that they had chosen badly in not killing the jarl. 'Such an act would have counted as suitable vengeance-taking against King Harald, and we would have gained some return for what we have lost to him.' They answered that the jarl had suffered even more disgrace.

Now they made good their escape and went up into Surnadal. Eirik the Ale-Lover lived there. He was a landed-man.* He received the group well and gave them all lodgings for the winter.

At Yuletide they exchanged drinking-feasts with a man named Hallstein. He was called Horse. Eirik's turn came first, and he treated his guests with generosity, showing them honour. Next it was Hallstein's turn, but a quarrel broke out and Hallstein struck Eirik with a drinking-horn. Eirik was unable to avenge this dishonour, and returned home leaving matters as they stood. This exchange rankled with the sons of Ondott, and a little later Asgrim went to Hallstein's farm and, on entering, gave Hallstein a severe wound. The men who were inside jumped to their feet and attacked Asgrim, but he defended himself well and slipped through their hands in the dark. The men were sure they had killed him.

Word about this event came to Onund and Asmund and, thinking that Asgrim was dead, there seemed little they could do. Eirik now advised them that they should go to Iceland. He said that matters would turn out badly for them if they were still in Norway when the king found time to give his attention to such matters. They followed Eirik's advice and made preparations to sail to Iceland. Each one had his own ship.

Hallstein, in bed with his wounds, died before Onund and Asmund set sail. Kolbein, who was mentioned earlier, decided to sail with Onund.

8. A Stormy Voyage

WHEN they were ready, Onund and Asmund put to sea. They sailed alongside each other. Onund recited this verse:

> 4.　Folk saw us two in our prime
> 　　fearless and strong in the clamour
> 　　as spears went screaming past us,
> 　　Hallvard Stormy and I.
> 　　Now, one-legged, it's my lot
> 　　to clamber aboard my mount*
> 　　and set my course for Iceland.
> 　　This poet's stars are sinking.

It was a rough crossing. Strong winds from the south continually drove them northwards, off course. They sighted Iceland and, when finally able to take their bearings, realized they were already north of Langaness (Long Headland). The ships were sailing so closc to each other that the men were able to talk between them. Asmund said that they should sail to Eyjafjord (Island Fjord), and they all agreed. They tacked* along the coast until a storm came out of the south-east. When Onund tried to face the wind, the boom broke. They lowered the sail but were then driven out to sea. Asmund reached Hris (Brushwood) Island,* and waited in its shelter until a wind took him into Eyjafjord.

Helgi the Lean gave all of Kraeklingshlid (Shell Slope) to Asmund, and he settled there at South Gler River. A few winters later his brother Asgrim came out to Iceland and lived at North Gler River. Asgrim was the father of Ellida-Grim, who was the father of Asgrim.*

9. Onund Settles in Iceland

NEXT there is something to be told about Onund Tree-Foot. For several days he was driven by the storm, but then the wind shifted. Now it came from the north, blowing in off the sea, and so they sailed towards land. Those aboard who had previously made the trip realized that they had been driven beyond the west-ern part of Skagi. They now sailed into Strandafloi (Bay of Strands) and approached the South Strands. Then six men came rowing towards them in a ten-oared boat. The men called out to the larger ocean-going vessel and asked who was in charge. Onund named himself and enquired where they were from. They identified themselves as housemen* of Thorvald from Drangar.

Onund asked if all the land in the Strands had been claimed. They replied that small parcels of unclaimed land remained in the Inner Strands, but nothing was available farther to the north. Onund asked his shipmates if they wanted to look farther to the west or if they should claim the land that they just learned about. They chose to look at that land first, then sailed southwards into the bay. Putting in at a small inlet off Arness (River Headland), they lowered the ship's boat and rowed to land. At that time a rich man named Eirik Snare lived there. He had taken the land between

Ingolf's Fjord and the place called Ofaera (Inaccessible) in Veidileysa (Scarce Hunting).

When Eirik learned that Onund had landed, he offered to let him take from his claim whatever parcel he wished. He added, however, that there remained very little unsettled land. Onund said that, before deciding, he wanted first to see what was available. So they headed southwards across the fjords. When they reached Ofaera, Eirik said: 'This is the place to begin looking. The land is unclaimed from here all the way to where Bjorn has settled.'

A large mountain on that side of the fjord was covered with snow. Onund looked at the mountain and said this verse:

> 5. While the ship careens ahead,
>   life goes adrift for a man
>   whose spears were always honed;
>   my power, my estates have foundered.
>   My lands and my many kinsfolk
>   I fled, and now a new blow:
>   what use the bargain, if I quit
>   my fields to buy Cold Back?*

Eirik replied: 'Many have lost so much in Norway that they cannot be compensated. As far as I know, all land in the main regions has now been claimed. For this reason I cannot easily advise you to leave and look elsewhere, but I will keep to my word and you may take from my claim what suits you.'

Onund said he would accept this offer, and claimed the land beginning at Ofaera and extending all the way to Kaldbak (Cold Back) Cliffs,* including the three inlets Byrgisvik, Kolbeinsvik, and Kaldbaksvik. Afterward, Eirik gave him all of Veidileysa, as well as Reykjarfjord (Smokey or Steamy Fjord) and all of Reykjaness (Steamy Headland) on that side.* But the rights to driftage were not defined, because at that time wood and other driftage* was so plentiful that everybody was able to take whatever was needed.

Onund built a farm at Kaldbak, and had many people in service. When his wealth began to grow, he built another farm in Reykjarfjord.

Kolbein settled in at Kolbeinsvik, and Onund remained quietly at home for the next few winters.

10. Onund Assists Aud the Deep-Minded

ONUND was so brave that few able-bodied men could stand against him. He was also a man whose name was recognized all through the land because of his ancestry.

Next a quarrel broke out between Ofeig Grettir and Thorbjorn the Jarl's Champion. The dispute ended when Thorbjorn killed Ofeig at Grettisgeil (Narrow Passage) at Haeli. In the aftermath of the killing, the sons of Ofeig set about assembling a large following to prosecute their case. They sent for Onund Tree-Foot, and in the spring he rode south.* On the way he stayed at Hvamm (Grassy Hollow) as the guest of Aud the Deep-Minded.* She greeted Onund with much affection, because he had been with her in the West over the seas.

By then Olaf Feilan, her grandson, was an active, grown man. Aud herself had reached a great age, and she confided to Onund that she wanted to find a wife for her kinsman Olaf. She had in mind that he ask for the hand of Alfdis of the Barra Isles, who was a cousin of Aesa, Onund's wife. Onund thought the proposal promising, and Olaf now rode south with him.

When Onund met his friends and brothers-in-law they invited him home with them. The legal case was discussed. The prosecution was to be presented at the Kjalarness Thing,* because at that time the Althing had not yet been established. In the end the case was placed in arbitration. A very large fine was awarded for the killing, and Thorbjorn the Jarl's Champion was made an outlaw. Thorbjorn's son was Solmund, who was the father of Singed Kari.* These kinsmen, father and son, remained abroad for a long time afterwards.

Thrand invited Onund, together with Olaf, to come home with him, and Thormod Skapti likewise invited them. The visitors then presented Olaf's marriage proposal. It was an easy pleading, because people were well aware of how outstanding a woman

Aud was. After the marriage agreement was completed, Onund and Olaf rode home. Aud thanked Onund for the assistance he had given to Olaf. In the autumn, Olaf Feilan married Alfdis of the Barra Isles. Then Aud the Deep-Minded died, as told in *Laxdaela Saga*.

11. Peace Dies with the Older Generation

ONUND and Aesa had two sons. The older one was named Thorgeir, and the younger Ofeig Grettir. A little later Aesa died, and Onund then married a woman named Thordis. Thordis was the daughter of Thorgrim from Gnup (Peak) in Midfjord (Middle Fjord), a kinsman of Midfjord-Skeggi.* With Thordis, Onund had a son named Thorgrim. From early on Thorgrim grew big and strong. As well as being a wise man, he was a very skilful farmer.

Onund lived at Kaldbak until his old age. He died of illness and was buried in Tree-Foot's Mound. He was the bravest and the most agile one-legged man ever in Iceland.

Thorgrim was the acknowledged leader of Onund's sons, even though there were others who were older. When he was only twenty-five years old his hair turned grey, and for this reason he was called Grey-Streak. Thordis, his mother, later married a man named Audun Shaft, who lived to the north in Vididal (Willow Valley). Their son was Asgeir, who lived at Asgeir's River. Thorgrim Grey-Streak and his brothers together owned a great deal of property, which they held in common without any divisions.

Eirik Snare, as noted earlier, lived in Arness. His wife was Olof, the daughter of Ingolf from Ingolfsfjord, and their son was named Flosi. Eirik was a capable man who had many kinsmen.

Three brothers, Ingolf, Ofeig, and Eyvind, had earlier come out to Iceland. They took the three fjords that afterwards were known by the men's names, and they lived there. Olaf was the son of Eyvind. He lived first in Eyvindarfjord and afterwards at Drangar. He was an aggressive man.

There were no serious disagreements among people in the region as long as the older generation lived. But after Eirik Snare died, it seemed to his son Flosi that the people of Kaldbak had no legal claim to the properties that Eirik had given to Onund. A serious dispute arose from this contention, with Thorgrim and his brothers holding fast to their claim of ownership. Now it was no longer possible for the men of the regions to hold games* together.

Thorgeir oversaw the brothers' farm in Reykjarfjord, which was owned by Thorgrim and his brothers. Thorgeir often rowed out fishing, because at that time the fjords were full of fish.

Back in Vik, Flosi and his men now made plans. There was a man named Thorfinn; he was a hired hand* on Flosi's farm at Arness. Flosi sent the man to Reykjarfjord to take Thorgeir's head. Thorfinn hid in the boathouse, and that same morning Thorgeir made ready to row out to sea. With him were two men, one named Hamund, and the other Brand. Thorgeir walked first, carrying on his back a large leather flask filled with drink. It was very dark outside, and as Thorgeir made his way down past the boathouse Thorfinn rushed at him. He struck with his axe between Thorgeir's shoulders. The axe sank in, making a squishy sound. Thorfinn let the axe fall loose from his grip, because he was sure that, as the saying goes, 'there was no need to bind the wound', and he wanted to save himself by getting away as quickly as possible.

About Thorfinn there is this to be told. He ran north to Arness, arriving just before full light. He reported Thorgeir's killing, saying that he would require Flosi's protection. He then declared that the only option for the people at Arness was to offer a settlement, 'and that would be best, given our situation and the seriousness of what has occurred'. Flosi said they ought first to have some news, as 'I see you are thoroughly scared after this great deed'.

There is this to tell about Thorgeir. He turned with the blow, so that the axe struck the drinking-flask, and he received no wound. They didn't try to track the man because it was so dark. Instead, they rowed down the fjord and out to Kaldbak, where they reported what had happened. The people at Kaldbak made great fun of the event, and started calling Thorgeir 'Flask-Back', so that the name stuck from then on. This verse was said:

6. In better days men renowned
   for their gifts and glory bathed
   swords gleaming like fish
   in wounds cut deep as trenches.
   But that creep, who's lost the respect
   of one and all, a pure
   coward, dips both cheeks
   of his axe in a skinful of whey.*

12. A Beached Whale

AT that time a famine descended on Iceland. It was so devastating that its like has never again been experienced, and few fish were caught and no whales or other driftage washed ashore. This situation continued for several years.

One autumn, seafaring Norwegian merchants in an ocean-going ship were driven ashore in Vik. The ship broke up and Flosi took four or five of the men into his house, including Stein, their captain. The rest of the crew found lodgings throughout the Vik region. The merchants tried to repair their ship. They used pieces from the wreck, but that proved to be difficult. The result was a ship with scarcely a stem or stern, yet broad in the middle.

In the spring a powerful storm blew in from the north. It continued for nearly a whole week, and after the storm men went out to check their driftage.

There was a man named Thorstein. He lived at Reykjaness and found a whale where it had washed ashore on the farthest tip of the headland, at a place called Rifsker (Rib-bone Rocks). It was a big finback whale. Thorstein immediately sent one of his men to Vik to tell Flosi, and another man to the people at the next farm.

There was a man named Einar who lived at Gjogur (Cleft). He was a tenant of the Kaldbak people. It was his job to look after the

Kaldbak driftage on that side of the fjord. When Einar learned that a whale had washed ashore, he immediately took his boat and rowed across the fjord to Byrgisvik. From there he sent a man to Kaldbak.

When Thorgrim* heard the news, he and his brothers set out as quickly as they could. Together, they were twelve in a ten-oared boat. The sons of Kolbein, Ivar and Leif, went with them and took along four of their men. All the farmers, those that could, set off for the whale.

Now there is this to tell about Flosi. He sent word to his kinsmen, up north in Ingolfsfjord and in Ofeigsfjord, and also sent for Olaf, the son of Eyvind, who was then living at Drangar. Flosi arrived first, along with the men from Vik. Immediately they began to cut up the whale. The pieces that were sliced off were dragged up onto the land. There were nearly twenty people at the beginning, but their number quickly increased.

At that point the men of Kaldbak arrived, in four ships. Thorgrim formally laid claim to the whale, forbidding the men of Vik the right to cut, divide, or take away any pieces of the whale. Flosi responded by demanding that Thorgrim prove that Flosi's father, Eirik, had formally and with the proper wording granted Onund Tree-Foot rights to the driftage. Otherwise, Flosi said, he would defend his rights by force. Thorgrim realized that he had too few men, and decided not to attack.

Then a ship was sighted out on the fjord coming in from the south. The men were hard at their oars and the ship advanced swiftly. It was Svan from Hol (Hill) in Bjarnarfjord, together with

---

Map 2. The Strands. Fleeing Norway, Onund and his companion Asmund sail 'out to Iceland' in two ships. After sighting the Langaness headland, the ships separate in a gale. Asmund takes shelter at Hrisey Island in Eyjafjord and claims land there. Onund, driven northwards by the storm, finally comes ashore in the Strands (named for its wide beaches), where he claims Kaldbak (Cold Back Mountain). In the next generation, during a famine, a dead whale washes ashore at Rifsker. Rival leaders claim the meat and a fight starts. Men up and down the coast become involved and the map traces the sailing routes to the battle. After the battles, Onund's son Thorgrim (Grettir's grandfather) moves the family south from the Strands. They settle at the farm of Bjarg (Sea Cliff) in Midfjord (Middle Fjord), where Grettir is raised.

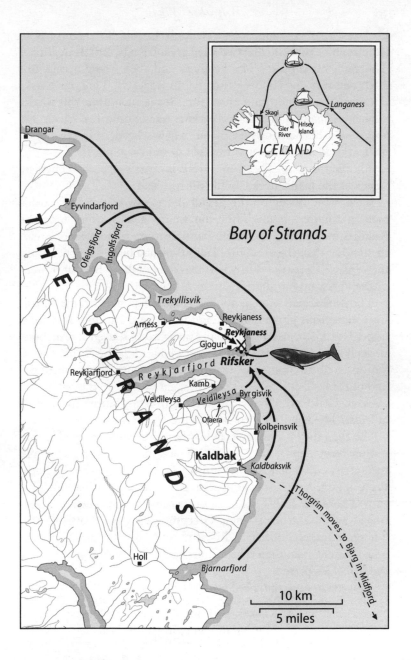

Bay of Strands

Drangar

Eyvindarfjord

T H E

S T R A N D S

Trekyllisvik

Arness

Reykjaness

Reykjaness

Gjogur

Rifsker

Reykjarfjord

R e y k j a r f j o r d

Kamb

Veidileysa

Veidileysa

Byrgisvik

Ofaera

Kolbeinsvik

Kaldbak

Kaldbaksvik

Thorgrim moves to Bjarg in Midfjord

Holl

Bjarnarfjord

10 km

5 miles

Langaness

Skagi

Gler River

Hrisey Island

ICELAND

his housemen. As soon as Svan landed, he told Thorgrim not to let himself be robbed. The two were great friends, and Svan offered Thorgrim his support. The brothers said they would accept this offer, and now the Kaldbak men boldly attacked. Thorgeir Flask-Back led the assault, and went for Flosi's men atop the whale. Thorfinn, the one mentioned earlier, was cutting the whale. He had placed himself forward at the whale's head, and stood with his feet in foot-holes which he had cut out for himself.

Thorgeir said to Thorfinn: 'Here is your axe back.' Then he struck at the man's neck, slicing off his head.

Flosi, who was up on the gravel shore, saw this and urged his men to counter-attack. They fought for a long time, with the Kaldbak men getting the upper hand. Few men had weapons with them other than the axes and blades they had been using to cut up the whale. Then the Vik men abandoned the whale and were pushed back up the shore.

The Norwegian merchants had their weapons with them, and were dangerous opponents. Stein the Captain cut off a foot from under Ivar Kolbeinsson, but Leif, Ivar's brother, used a whalebone to send one of Stein's companions to Hel.* By then they were fighting with anything they could lay their hands on, and men fell on both sides.

Next, Olaf from Drangar arrived with many ships* in support of Flosi. The Kaldbak men now found themselves outnumbered, but by then they had loaded their ships. Svan now ordered everyone on-board, but as they made their way out to the ships the Vik men attacked. When Svan reached the water he hacked at Stein the Captain, wounding him seriously. Then he leapt onto his ship. Thorgrim dealt Flosi a serious wound and succeeded in getting away. Olaf struck at Ofeig Grettir, and it was a death-wound. Thorgeir gathered Ofeig in his arms and got on-board the ship. The Kaldbak men then rowed into the fjord, heading south. Now the two sides parted.

This verse was composed about the encounter:

> 7.   At Rifsker, so I hear,
>   crude weapons came in handy,

> when a bunch of unarmed men
> struck out with chunks of whale.
> Back, with brute force and zest,
> the enemy hurled the meat.
> Since when was this a battle?
> I call it childish pranks.*

A truce was arranged between the two sides, and the case was referred to the Althing. Thorodd the Godi, Midfjord-Skeggi, and many men from the south of Iceland supported the Kaldbak men. Flosi was outlawed, along with a number of the men who had been with him. Flosi, who insisted on paying all the fines himself, now fell deeply in debt. When Flosi in turn brought a counter-suit, Thorgrim and his brothers were unable to show that they had paid a lawful sum in return for the land and the driftage rights.

Thorkel Moon was the law-speaker* at this time, and he was asked to make a ruling. He said it seemed to him that an agreement had been legally made if some form of payment had been given, even if the payment was not of full worth. 'Because', he noted, 'Steinun the Old had made such an agreement with my grandfather Ingolf,* so that Steinun received from Ingolf the whole of Rosmhvalaness (Walrus' Headland). In return, she gave a cloak of many colours. This agreement has never been disputed, even though much more was at stake than in the current case. Here, then, I give my opinion,' he said. 'The disputed lands should be divided, with each of the parties receiving an equal share of the driftage. And from now on, it should be accepted as law that each property-owner shall have full rights to all driftage on his land.'

This was done. The land was divided so that Thorgrim and his brothers gave up Reykjarfjord and all land farther out from it on that side of the fjord. In return, they received full ownership of Kamb. Ofeig's killing was compensated by a large payment. Thorfinn was found unworthy of payment, whereas Thorgeir was compensated for the attempt on his life. With this settlement, the parties were reconciled. Flosi made preparations for a trip to

Norway with Stein the captain. He sold his lands in Vik to Geirmund
the Unstable, who lived there from then on.

The ship the merchants had rebuilt was unusually wide and was
called 'the wooden tub'. Trekyllisvik (Tub Bay) is named after it.
Flosi sailed on it but was driven back ashore in Oxarfjord (Axe
Fjord). The *Saga of Bodmod, Grimolf, and Gerpi** describes the
events that followed.

13. Grettir's Parents

AFTERWARDS Thorgrim and his brothers divided their property.
Thorgrim took all the movable goods and Thorgeir got the land.
Thorgrim moved south to Midfjord where, counselled by Skeggi,
he bought land at Bjarg (Sea Cliff). Thorgrim was married to
Thordis, the daughter of Asmund from under Asmundargnupi
(Asmund's Peak). He was the settler who had first claimed the
Thingeyrar District.

Thorgrim and Thordis had a son named Asmund. He was a
big man, strong and intelligent, with a fine head of hair. He
went grey early, and for this reason he was called Grey-Streak or
Grey-Locks.* Thorgrim became a dedicated farmer, who kept
all his men hard at work. Because Asmund did not want to work,
there was little affection between father and son. Things
continued in this way until Asmund reached manhood. Then
he asked his father for some marketable goods so that he could
travel abroad. Thorgrim replied that there was little for him to
have, but nevertheless gave him a few goods of small value. Asmund
then travelled abroad and quickly acquired wealth. He sailed to
different lands, becoming a prominent and rich merchant. He was
a popular and reliable man, with many kinsmen in Norway who
were well born.

One autumn Asmund went east to the Oslo region in Norway,
and stayed with a well-born man named Thorstein, an Uplander
by family. Thorstein had a sister named Rannveig, who was
thought to be a fine match. Asmund asked for her hand and, with

the counsel of her kinsman Thorstein, the offer was accepted. Asmund settled there for a time and was well respected.

Asmund and Rannveig had a son who was called Thorstein. He was the handsomest of men, strong and with a fine voice. A tall man, he moved rather slowly and was nicknamed Dromund (the Galleon).

When Thorstein was still a small child his mother Rannveig took sick and died. After this, Asmund no longer found joy in Norway. Thorstein was then looked after by his mother's kinsmen. They managed his property, while Asmund once again returned to seafaring and became a famous man.

Asmund landed his ship at Hunavatn in Iceland. At that time Thorkel the Scratcher was the foremost leader among the people of Vatnsdal (Lake Valley). When he learned of Asmund's arrival, he rode to the ship and invited Asmund to come to his home. Thorkel lived at Mar's Stead in Vatnsdal, and Asmund went there to stay. Thorkel was the son of Thorgrim, the chieftain from Karn's River. He was a man of surpassing wisdom. These events took place after the arrival in Iceland of Bishop Frederick and Thorvald Kodransson, who were living at Laekjamot (Stream's Meeting). They were the first to preach Christianity in the northern part of the country. Thorkel, along with many other men, accepted to be prime-signed.* There are many stories about Frederick and Thorvald's exchanges with the men in the north, but these are not part of this saga.

Thorkel was raising a woman named Asdis in his home. She was the daughter of Bard, who was the son of Jokul, the son of Ingimund the Old. Ingimund was the son of Thorstein, the son of Ketil Raum. Asdis's mother was Aldis, the daughter of Ofeig Grettir, who was mentioned earlier. She had not yet been promised in marriage, but was thought a fine choice both on account of her kinship and her property.

Asmund, now tired of seafaring, wanted to settle down in Iceland. He made a proposal, asking for Asdis's hand. Thorkel was already familiar with Asmund and realized that he was a rich man, well able to manage his affairs. So this is how Asmund won Asdis. From then on Asmund became Thorkel's trusted friend. He developed into a prosperous farmer, who knew the law and was ambitious. Shortly afterwards, Thorgrim Grey-Streak from Bjarg died. Asmund inherited the property.

14. A Troubled Childhood

ASMUND set up his farm at Bjarg. It was a large and impressive household. He kept many men around him and was a popular man. His children with Asdis are these:* Atli was the oldest. He was an honest man, unassuming and gentle, and he was well liked by everyone. They had a second son, who was called Grettir. He was exceptionally troublesome as a youth. He said little and was difficult in both what he said and what he did. His father Asmund gave him little affection, but his mother adored him. Grettir Asmundarson was a handsome youth, with a broad, squarish face. He was red-haired and had freckles. He developed slowly as a child. Thordis was the name of Asmund's daughter, the one who later married Glum, the son of Ospak Kjallakson from Skridinsenni. Rannveig was the name of the second daughter. She married Gamli, the son of Thorhall the Vinlander. They lived at Melar in Hrutafjord. Their son was Grim. The son of Glum and Thordis was Ospak, who disputed with Odd Ofeigsson, as related in *The Saga of the Confederates*.*

Grettir lived at Bjarg until he was ten years old. Then he began to take on strength, and Asmund asked him to do a little work. Grettir replied that he was not sure it suited him, but he asked what he should do.

Asmund replied: 'You will look after my geese.'

Grettir answered, saying: 'An unimportant little job.'

Asmund replied: 'Do this well, and things will go better between us.'

So Grettir began to look after the geese. There were fifty of them, even more counting the young ones. It was not long before he found them difficult to herd, and the goslings were especially annoying. This began to irritate him, especially because he had little control over his temper. Not long after, some vagrants found the goslings lying about dead, while the geese had their wings broken. This event took place in the autumn. Asmund was thoroughly displeased, and asked Grettir whether he had killed the birds. The boy grinned and answered:

> 8. When winter comes, I attend
>   to wringing the goslings' necks.
>   If an older bird crops up,
>   victory still goes to me.

'And you will no longer need to concern yourself with them,' said Asmund.

'He is a friend, who spares others from problems,' said Grettir.

'I will find you some other work,' said Asmund.

'He learns more, who tries more,' said Grettir. 'What is it that I should do now?'

Asmund replied: 'You will rub my back at the fire, in the way I have always had it done.'

'That would be hot work for the hand,' said Grettir. 'But it's a weakling's job.'

Matters now continued in the same way for a time, with Grettir holding this job. As summer turned to autumn, Asmund craved more heat and urged Grettir to rub his back strongly.

At that time it was the custom on the farms to build large long-houses, and in the evenings people sat on both sides of the central long fire.* Tables would be set up for eating, and afterwards, people slept alongside the fires. During the day it was here that the women worked the wool. One evening, when it was time for Grettir to rub Asmund's back, the old man said to him: 'You weakling, stop being so lazy.'

'It's rash to incite the stubborn,' said Grettir.

Asmund said: 'There's no stamina in you.'

Grettir saw some wool-combs lying on the bench. He took a comb, and with it he scraped down along Asmund's back. Asmund jumped up and was furious. He set about trying to hit Grettir with his cane, but the boy ducked under the blows. At that moment the mistress of the house came in and asked what was going on. Grettir answered with this poem:

> 9. Your purse-proud lord and master
>   takes it into his cruel mind

> to burn my hands: I feel it
> keenly, treasured lady.
> I set my grasp on him grimly
> with untrimmed nails, and see,
> owner of linen finery,
> how carrion-birds home in!*

Grettir's mother was disappointed by his conduct, and remarked that he would not be the type of man to avoid trouble. The relationship between father and son did not improve.

A while later Asmund spoke to Grettir, telling him that he was to look after the horses. Grettir said that he thought that was a better job than giving back-rubs.

'But you will do', said Asmund, 'exactly as I tell you. I have a fawn-coloured mare that I call Kengala.* She is so wise about wind and water that if she resists going out to pasture, it never fails but a storm is on the way. When this happens let the horses stay inside the stable, but when the winter comes keep them up north along the ridge. It seems to me that you will need to carry out this task better than the two that I previously gave you.'

Grettir replied: 'That is cold and manly work. But I do not like trusting the mare. I know of no one who has done so before.'

Grettir now set himself to herding the horses, and so matters continued until Yule was past. Then the weather turned very cold. There was snow and grazing was difficult. Grettir had few good clothes and was not yet a hardened man. Often he was very cold, and in every storm Kengala chose to graze in the most exposed places. No matter how early she left in the morning, Kengala would not return home before the sun had set. Grettir began to think he ought to do something to repay Kengala for forcing him to stay outdoors.

Early one morning Grettir came to the stable and opened the door. Kengala stood in front of the hay-trough. Even though all the horses had been given fodder, she took it all for herself. Now Grettir got up on her back. He had a sharp knife in his hand and with it made cuts across Kengala's shoulders and then down her back on both sides of her spine. The horse reacted violently. She was well fed, strong, and mean. Kengala reared up, smashing her hooves against the wall, and Grettir fell off. When he got to his feet he tried once again to get onto her back. The two struggled violently, but in the end he flayed the hide off her back all the way down to the flanks. Following this, he drove the horses out to pasture. Kengala had no interest in grazing and only nipped at her back. Just past midday she turned around and ran home to the stable.

Grettir locked up the stable and went home. Asmund asked where the horses were, and Grettir said they were locked up in the stable as usual. Asmund said that they could expect a storm if the horses did not want to stay out in such weather.

Grettir said: 'Many lack wisdom, even those from whom you expect more.'

The night passed without a storm. In the morning Grettir drove the horses out, but Kengala could not tolerate being outside in the pasture. Asmund found it strange that the weather remained unchanged.

The third morning, Asmund went out to look at the horses. He approached Kengala and said: 'Considering that this has been such a good winter, the horses do not appear to have done as well as they might have, but your back, Kengala, will nevertheless be firm.'

'The expected happens,' said Grettir, 'and also the unexpected.'

Asmund stroked the horse's back, and its hide came off in his hand. He found it unbelievable that this had happened, and said Grettir had caused it. Grettir grinned, but said nothing.

The farmer walked back to the house, so angry he could barely speak. He entered the main fire-hall only to hear his wife say: 'By now my young kinsman should have proved himself by minding the horses. Asmund spoke this verse:

> 10. That fine mare of mine,
> Kengala, flayed by Grettir!
> What a mean trick he played on me!
> Proud mothers do blather on.
> The fact is, for ages now

that smart young lad of yours
has been brushing off my orders.
Please heed my poetic words.*

Asdis answered, 'I don't know which I find more unpleasant: your constantly finding jobs for him or the way that he always carries them out.'

'I will put an end to that,' said Asmund, 'but he will be treated the worse for it.'

'And neither of us shall hold the other responsible,' added Grettir. And so matters continued in this way for a time. Asmund had Kengala killed.

Grettir played many other childish pranks, but they are not mentioned in this saga.

He now grew very large, but people had scarcely any idea of his strength because he was so clumsy. He continually composed poems and short verses which were thought insulting. He did not hang about in the hall by the fire, and for the most part he said little.

15. The Ball Game

At that time there were many young men coming of age in Midfjord. Skald-Torfa lived at Torfustead. She had a son named Bersi, who was a very handsome man and a good poet. The brothers Kormak and Thorgils lived at Mel. A man called Odd grew up with them. He was their dependant, and was called Odd the Orphan-Skald. Audun was the name of a man who grew up at Audunarstead in Vididal. He was honest and good-natured, and the strongest man in the Northern Quarter among those of his age. Kalf Asgeirsson and his brother Thorvald lived at Asgeir's River. Grettir's brother Atli developed into an imposing young man. A peaceful sort, he was well liked by everyone.

These young men would get together to play ball at Midfjord Lake. People from Midfjord and from Vididal would also come, as did many from Vesturhop (Tidal Inlet) and Vatnsness, as well as from Hrutafjord. The ones who had to travel a distance would stay locally. Those who were of equal strength were arranged to play against each other, and the games provided much enjoyment, particularly in the autumn.

When Grettir was fourteen years old, his brother Atli invited him to take part in the games. Partners were chosen, and Grettir was set to play against Audun, who has been mentioned earlier. He was the older of the two by a few winters. Audun hit the ball so high over Grettir's head that he could not reach it. It landed far out on the ice. This angered Grettir, who assumed that Audun wanted to make a fool of him. Still, Grettir walked out and found the ball. When he came back, he went right up to Audun and hit him on the forehead with the ball so hard that the skin broke. Audun then swung at Grettir with the stick he was holding, but Grettir ducked under the blow and was not hurt. Next they grabbed each other, each trying to throw the other to the ground. Now people noticed that Grettir was stronger than anyone had realized, because Audun was powerful. The two stood struggling with each other for a long time, but the fight ended with Grettir falling. Audun then shoved his knee into Grettir's stomach and gave him a good beating. Atli and Bersi ran up, along with many others, and the two were separated.

Grettir said that he did not need to be held like a wild dog. 'Only a slave immediately takes vengeance, but a coward, never.'

People chose not to let this fight cause problems, because the brothers Kalf and Thorvald wanted the two to be reconciled. Besides, Audun and Grettir were distantly related. The game went on as before with no more quarrelling.

16. A First Killing, Lesser Outlawry

THORKEL THE SCRATCHER now began to grow old. He held the Vatnsdal chieftaincy, and was an important leader. He was an old and trusted friend of Asmund Grey-Streak and, as befitted their close relationship, Thorkel's practice each spring was to ride to Bjarg for a visit. He did so once again in the spring following the events just related.

Asmund and Asdis greeted Thorkel with open arms. He stayed with them for three days, and the brothers-in-law discussed many things between them. Thorkel asked Asmund what he had to say about the nature of his sons, and whether they would be capable men. Asmund replied that he believed that Atli would be a fine farmer, careful and prosperous.

Thorkel answered: 'A useful man, one like yourself. And what do you have to say about Grettir?'

Asmund replied: 'About him, it could be said that he will become a powerful man but an uncontrollable one. With me he has been stubborn and difficult.'

Thorkel answered: 'That is not promising, kinsman.' Then he asked: 'And how shall we arrange our trip to the Althing this coming summer?'

Asmund answered: 'Travelling has now become difficult for me, and I would like to stay at home.'

'Would you like Atli to go for you?' said Thorkel.

'I don't believe I can afford to lose him,' said Asmund, 'on account of the work and the provisions we have to get in. But Grettir will not work. I think he has enough cleverness. Under your watchful eye, he could carry out my legal responsibilities.'

Thorkel said: 'It's your decision, kinsman.'

Thorkel prepared to ride home when he was ready, and Asmund saw him off with fine gifts.

A while later Thorkel left for the Althing. He rode with sixty men; all those who were members of his chieftaincy rode with him. He came to Bjarg, where Grettir joined him. They rode south over Tvidaegra (Two–Day) Heath. Because there were few

---

Map 3. Grettir's Home Region in Northern Iceland. Grettir's family farm at Bjarg in Midfjord is surrounded by kinsmen, friends, and enemies. Grettir's kinsman Audun, whom he fights at a ball game, lives at Audunarstead in neigh bouring Vididal. Grettir's sister lives at Melar in Hrutafjord. Her farm is close to Thoroddsstead, the home of Thorbjorn Oxen-Might, an enemy of Grettir's family. The map inset traces Grettir's trip to the Althing at the age of fourteen winters. In Chapter 35 Grettir rides from Bjarg to Thorhallsstead in Forsaeludal, where he fights Glam.

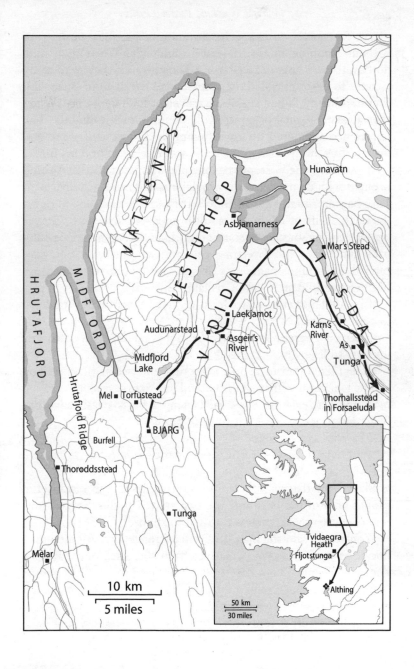

HRUTAFJORD

MIDFJORD

HRUTAFJORD RIDGE

VATNSNESS

VESTURHOP

VIDIDAL

VATNSDAL

Hunavatn

Asbjarnarness

Mar's Stead

Laekjamot

Karn's River

As

Audunarstead

Asgeir's River

Tunga

Midfjord Lake

Mel ■ Torfustead

Thorhallsstead in Forsaeludal

■ BJARG

Burfell

■ Thoroddsstead

■ Tunga

Melar

10 km

5 miles

Tvidaegra Heath

Fljotstunga

50 km

30 miles

Althing

places for horses to graze in the mountains, they pushed on without stopping in the deserted highlands. When they rode down into the Fljotstunga (River's Tongue) area, they were ready to rest. So they unbridled their horses and left them to graze with their saddles on. They lay down and slept for a long time. When they awoke, the men began to look around for their mounts. The horses had wandered off in different directions, and some had been rolling on the ground. Grettir was the last to find his horse.

It was then the custom that people who went to the Althing brought with them their own provisions, and most travelled with food-bags tied to their saddles. Grettir's saddle had slipped down under the belly of his horse, and the food-bag was gone. Grettir started looking, but could not find it. Then he saw a man dashing back and forth, and Grettir asked him who he was. The man replied. He said his name was Skeggi, and that he was a member of the household at As in Vatnsdal in the north.

'I am in Thorkel's party,' he said, 'but I was careless and have lost my food-bag.'

Grettir answered: 'It never rains but it pours. I have also lost my bag, so let's look together.'

Skeggi liked that idea, and for a time the two of them walked about, looking together. All of a sudden Skeggi dashed across a field. He reached down and picked up a bag. Grettir saw him bend down, and asked what he had found.

'My bag,' said Skeggi.

'Who says so,' said Grettir, 'and let me see it. Many things are not what they seem.'

Skeggi said that no man would take away what was his. Grettir caught hold of the bag, and the two started pulling it back and forth between them, each wanting it for himself.

'You seem', said the man, 'to have a strange idea. All men may not be as wealthy as your relatives from Vatnsdal, but that does not mean people do not dare to defend their property from you.'

Grettir said that a man's rank was not the issue, but that each person has a right to what is his.

Skeggi said: 'If Audun were only closer, he would wring your neck like he did at the ball game.'

'So much the better,' said Grettir, 'but you are not going to wring my neck, however this turns out.'

Skeggi then reached for his axe and struck at Grettir. But when Grettir saw what was coming, he grabbed the axe with his left hand, just above Skeggi's grip. Grettir then quickly yanked it free and swung the same axe down into Skeggi's head. It sank right into the brain, and the man fell down dead.

Grettir took the food–bag and threw it over his saddle. Then he rode after the others. Thorkel had ridden off, because he had no idea what was happening. People from the group now began to notice that Skeggi was missing. When Grettir caught up with them, they asked him if he knew anything about Skeggi.

Grettir replied with this verse:

> 11. A singular troll creature
> known for its cutting jibes
> swooped down just now on Skeggi.
> It was thirsting after blood.
> Its hard mouth stretched in a grin
> as it touched his skull; its bite
> cleanly split his forehead.
> I was witness to this myself.

Thorkel's followers reacted quickly, saying that no troll would have taken the man in full daylight.

Thorkel thought quietly for a while. Finally he said: 'Something else has taken place here, and Grettir probably killed him. So what did happen?' Grettir then gave a full account of the dealings between them.

Thorkel said: 'Matters have taken a turn for the worse. Skeggi was part of my following and a man of good family. I will take responsibility in this way: I will pay whatever compensation will be judged, but as for the question of outlawry, there is little that I can do. You now have two choices, Grettir. Either you can continue on to the Althing and see how matters turn out, or you can turn around now and return home.'

Grettir chose to continue to the Althing. The case was prosecuted by the dead man's heirs. Thorkel supported Grettir.

He offered to make a formal agreement by handshake* for the compensation, and paid it on the spot. But Grettir could not avoid being outlawed, and was to leave the country for three years.*

When the Althing broke up, the chieftains rode off in a group. They stopped under Sledaass (Sledge Ridge) before going their different ways. It was then that Grettir lifted the stone which lay there in the grass and which now is called Grettir's-Lift.* Many people went to look at the stone, thinking it a great feat that such a young man was able to lift so big a boulder.

Grettir rode home to Bjarg, and he told his father what had happened. Asmund said little, only that Grettir would be a troublesome man.

17. Grettir Sails for Norway

A MAN was named Haflidi. He lived in Reydarfell (Reddish Mountain), alongside the Hvit River (White River). He was a seafaring man and owned a trading ship, which was beached on the Hvit River. On the ship with him was a man named Bard, who had a beautiful young wife.

Asmund sent a message to Haflidi, requesting that he take Grettir aboard and help him. Haflidi said that he had heard that Grettir was difficult to control. However, on account of their friendship he agreed to take Grettir on-board. Then Grettir set about preparing for the journey abroad. Aside from a little home-spun cloth and some provisions for the ocean crossing, Asmund chose not to give Grettir any saleable goods.

Grettir asked his father to give him a weapon. Asmund replied: 'You have not been obedient, and I have no idea how you would use weapons if put to the test, so I will give you none.'

Grettir replied: 'Nothing given, nothing owed.'

Following this, father and son parted with little love. Many wished him farewell, but few a safe return.

His mother accompanied him for a way, and before they parted she said the following: 'You were sent from home, kinsman, without the honour that I would have wished for a man as well born as you. It seems to me that you most lack good weapons, and my heart tells me that you will need them.'

Then she took from under her cloak an inlaid sword. It was a fine weapon. She said: 'Jokul, my grandfather, owned this sword, as did others of the Vatnsdal men, and it brought them victory. Now I want to give this sword to you. Use it well.'

Grettir thanked her affectionately for the gift. He said that to him this was better than if he had received items of greater value. Following this, he went on his way and Asdis sent him off with her good wishes.

Grettir rode south over the heath without stopping, until he arrived at the ship. Haflidi greeted him well and asked about his goods.

Grettir spoke this verse:

> 12. As a seafaring man, sail set
> for a following wind, let me
> tell you that some rich people
> equipped me poorly for this trip.
> A strong woman bettered my lot
> when she made this sword her gift:
> once more the saying's borne out
> that 'the mother is best for the child'.*

Haflidi said it was clear that she was the one who thought most of him.

They made ready and set out to sea. A good wind came up and, when they had passed the shallows, they set sail. Grettir made a place for himself beneath where the ship's rowboat was stored, and would not move from there. He would neither bail water nor work the sail. He refused all of the work which, on a ship, he should have shared equally with the other men. He likewise refused to pay others to do his work.

They sailed south around the Reykjaness headland, and then continued southwards along the coast. Just as the shoreline dropped from view, they were met by the driving winds of a storm. The ship was leaky and was scarcely strong enough for the driving wind. The crew was soaked through, while Grettir rained scornful verses down on them. The men detested this.

Then one day, as a strong, cold wind blew, the crewmen called to Grettir, asking his help 'because our fingers are freezing'. Grettir looked up and said:

> 13.   What a blessing if the shivering
>   idiots get cramp in their fingers!

The men got no work out of him, and became angrier than before. They said he would be made to pay, both for his verses and for breaking the rules.

'You think it better', they said, 'to stroke the belly of Captain Bard's wife than to fulfil duties on-board. Such conduct is intolerable.'

The weather continued to worsen, and the crew was forced to bail both day and night. They began to threaten Grettir.

When Haflidi heard this, he went to where Grettir lay and said: 'I do not like this exchange between you and the merchant crew. You refuse what is required of you and then taunt them. They are threatening to throw you overboard. The situation is now intolerable.'

'Why shouldn't they be able to make their own decisions?' said Grettir. 'But I would hope that one or two would join me before I went overboard.'

'This cannot go on,' said Haflidi. 'We will never survive if you and the men continue like this. I would like to offer you my advice.'

'What is it?' said Grettir.

'They hold it against you that you lampoon them. Now I would like', said Haflidi, 'that you compose a scornful verse about me. Perhaps then they might tolerate you better.'

Map 4. Grettir's First Trip to Norway. Blown off course and shipwrecked, Grettir finds shelter on the island of Haramarsey in western Norway. He sails north to Vaagan and then to Saltfjord before being summoned to Jarl Svein at Stenkjer in Trondheim Fjord. Grettir sails to Tonsberg in southern Norway and stays with his half-brother Thorstein the Galleon. Then he returns to Haramarsey for the winter before leaving for Iceland.

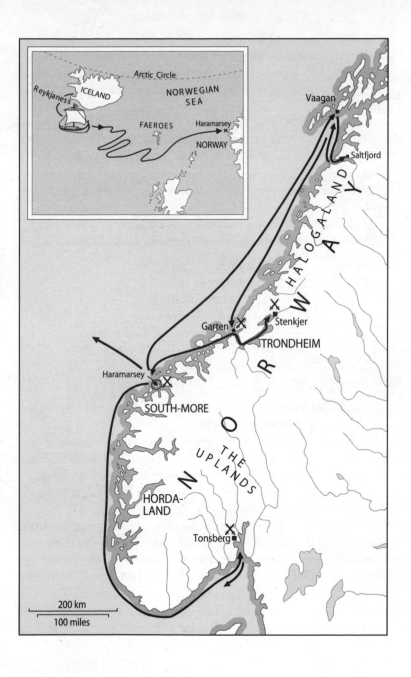

'I will never compose about you,' said Grettir, 'except to say something good. I would never compare you with these louts.'

Haflidi said: 'Nevertheless, you could make a verse which at first seems demeaning but later, upon consideration, appears differently.'

'I could do that,' said Grettir.

Haflidi went back to the crewmen and said: 'We are facing many difficulties, and it's only to be expected that you dislike Grettir.'

'We find his mocking ditties worse than anything else,' they said.

Haflidi then said aloud: 'He will surely pay for this in the end.'

When Grettir heard Haflidi rebuke him, he said this verse:

> 14.   Back then, when Haflidi
>   loudly slurped his curds,
>   snug at Reydarfell,
>   that was a different story:
>   on-board now, as our ship's owner,
>   he ensures two rations a day
>   serving to satisfy people
>   who eat like carrion-birds.

The merchants took this badly, saying there was no reason whatsoever to dishonour Haflidi.

Haflidi then said: 'Grettir surely deserves some punishment, but I, for one, refuse to stake my honour against his malice and selfishness. We are not going to seek revenge for this while we are in such great danger. But keep these slights in mind, if you like, when you are back on land.'

The men replied: 'We ought to be able to follow your example. Why should we, more than you, let his mockery get to us?'

Haflidi agreed with them, and from then on the men were much less bothered by the ditties. The trip had already been long and hard, when the ship began to leak in several places. The men were reaching exhaustion, while the captain's young wife was always on hand to sew up the sleeves* of Grettir's tunic. The crew had much to say about that.

Haflidi went to where Grettir was lying and spoke this verse:

15. Grettir! Out of your hole,
    our ship is dug deep down in its furrow,
    and don't forget your lively
    chat with your cheerful friend.
    She's stitched your sleeves up tight
    at the wrist to keep you cosy;
    some kindness from you in return
    she'd welcome, while land's out of sight.*

Grettir stood up quickly and said:

16. All right, I'm up, despite
    the sea and its constant pitching.
    I know she won't be pleased
    if Grettir lies down on the job.
    She's a fine woman, fair of
    complexion*—yes, she'll take
    a dim view of things if others
    must slave on my behalf.

Following this, he went quickly to the stern of the ship. There the men were bailing, and he asked what they wanted him to do. They replied there was little good that he might do.

Grettir said: 'Every little bit counts.'

Haflidi asked them not to reject his offer of help: 'It may be that he thinks he can get himself out of trouble if he offers to help.'

At that time there were no run-off sluices* in ocean-going ships. Instead, men used buckets or tubs, and it was wet and difficult work. The practice was to have two buckets; one was lowered and filled with water while the other was hoisted up and emptied overboard. The men said that Grettir should fill the bailing buckets, so they could test what he was capable of. He answered that would show best. He climbed down, while two men set themselves to emptying the buckets. This went on for only a short time, before the two men were overcome with fatigue. They were replaced by four men, and the same thing happened. Some men said that as many as eight men were emptying the buckets before it was all over. And so the ship was bailed. After this the merchants began to speak differently to Grettir, because they saw the kind of strength that he had. From here on he was also fully willing to carry out whatever job needed to be done.

The ship now drifted eastwards on the sea and became lost in a thick fog. One night, before they knew it, they had run aground on some rocks and the ship's bottom under the prow was ripped open. Launching the rowboat, they loaded off the women and many of the loose goods. A short distance away lay a small island, to where they ferried all the merchandise that they were able to save from the ship during the night.

When it began to grow light, they discussed where they might be. Those among them who had previously travelled between the different lands recognized that they were in Norway, in Sunnmoer (South-More). Not far from them, towards the mainland, was an island called Haramarsey. It was thickly settled, and there was also a landed-man's estate.

18. The Mound-Dweller

THORFINN was the name of the landed-man who lived on the island. He was the son of Kar the Old, who had lived there for many years. Thorfinn was an important chieftain.

When the day reached full light, the people on the island saw where the merchants were stranded. Word was sent to Thorfinn, who acted quickly, commanding his large boat to be launched. It was a *karfi*,* with sixteen oars on each side, and there were nearly thirty men on-board. They rowed as fast as they could and rescued the merchants' valuables, but the trading ship had sunk, taking with it much of its cargo. Thorfinn brought all the men from the ship to his house, where they stayed for a week, drying out their merchandise. Then the merchants left for the southern part of the country, and they are out of the saga.

Grettir stayed behind with Thorfinn. For the most part Grettir hung back and said little. Thorfinn let Grettir have his food, but otherwise paid him little attention. Grettir showed no interest in becoming Thorfinn's follower, and showed no interest in going out with him during the day. This displeased Thorfinn, but he could not be bothered to deny Grettir food. Thorfinn kept a fine household. He was a cheerful man, the kind of person who wanted others to be happy.

Grettir often left the house and walked around to the other farms on the island. Audun was the name of the man who lived at a place called Vindheim (Wind-Home). Grettir went there every day, and became very friendly with the man. Grettir often stayed long into the day, and late one evening, as he was preparing to walk home, he saw a flame shoot up from the headland below Audun's farm. This was new to Grettir, so he asked Audun what this was. Audun said that he should not concern himself with that.

'If this were seen in my country,' said Grettir, 'it would be said to be the kind of flame that comes from treasure.' The farmer replied: 'The one who is in charge of that fire is the sort about whom there is no profit in being curious.'

'Still, I would like to know,' said Grettir.

'Out on the headland stands a grave-mound,' said Audun. 'In it was laid Kar the Old, Thorfinn's father. At first, father and son owned a single farm on the island, but after Kar died he returned from the dead and started walking, so much so that in the end he drove away all those farmers who owned lands here. Now Thorfinn alone owns the whole island, and no harm from these happenings comes to those under Thorfinn's protection.'

Grettir said that he had done well in telling him. 'I will return here in the morning, so have some digging tools ready.'

'I suggest', said Audun, 'that you not concern yourself with this, because you will gain nothing but Thorfinn's hatred.'

Grettir said he was prepared to risk that.

The night passed, and Grettir arrived early next morning. The digging tools were there, ready. The farmer accompanied him to the grave-mound, and Grettir started breaking in. He worked hard at it, without stopping until he reached a row of timbers. The day was almost over as he tore his way through the wooden rafters. Audun kept trying to discourage him from entering the mound.

Grettir asked him to hold the rope, 'because I want to find out what lives down here'.

Grettir then descended into the mound. It was dark inside, and not altogether sweet-smelling. He had to feel around to get an idea of what was inside. He found some horse bones, and next bumped into the back-posts of a seat. He realized that a man was sitting there in the chair. There was a great pile of gold and silver all mixed together. There was also a chest full of silver under the man's feet. Grettir took all the treasure and carried it to the rope, but as he was making his way up out of the mound something strong grabbed hold of him. He let go of the treasure and turned to resist. A fierce fight began, and everything in their path was broken as the mound-dweller attacked with fury. For a long time Grettir tried to give way. Finally he realized there would be no chance of winning if he continued just to shield himself. Now neither spared himself, and they shoved each other until they came to where the horse bones were. There they struggled for a long time, with each at times falling to his knee. But in the end the mound-dweller fell backwards with a great crash, and with that noise Audun dropped the ropes and ran away, assuming that Grettir had been killed. Grettir now drew the sword Jokul's-Gift and struck at the mound-dweller's neck. He cut off the head and placed the head against Kar's buttocks.* Then he carried the treasure to the rope. Audun was long gone, so Grettir had to climb up the rope, leaving the treasure below. He had tied a rope around the treasure and then pulled it up.

Worn out and stiff after his fight with Kar, Grettir returned to Thorfinn's farm, carrying the treasure. All the household was sitting at the table, and Thorfinn narrowed his eyes at Grettir when he came into the drinking-hall. He asked what kind of work Grettir had found so necessary that he chose not to observe people's normal customs.

Grettir replied: 'Many small matters occur late in the evening.'

He then placed on the table all the hoard taken from the mound. There was one treasure which most caught Grettir's eye. It was a sax,* a weapon so fine that he had never seen a better one, and he put it on the table last. Thorfinn raised his eyebrows when he saw the treasure and the sax. These were heirlooms that had never left the family.

'Where did you get this treasure?' said Thorfinn.

Grettir spoke this verse:

> 17. Man with gold for the asking,
> my hopes of buried treasure
> were dashed for good. It's best
> that folk get the message promptly.
> It's clear to me that few men,
> seasoned in sword-storms, will find
> reward in that dragon's den
> if they hazard a quest for gold.*

Thorfinn answered: 'Even for one who is not a coward, this was an undertaking, and no one before you has shown any eagerness to break into that mound. Because I know that treasure hidden in the ground or buried in mounds is wasted, I will not hold your action against you, especially since you brought the gold to me. But where did you find the good sax?'

Grettir replied:

> 18. In the grave-mound's gloomy chamber,
> I snatched a short-sword, my friend—
> nothing short about the gashes
> it cuts. The ghost succumbed.
> That gleaming blade spells death
> by a sharp chop through the helmet.
> If I were this short-sword's owner,
> never would it slip from my hands.*

Thorfinn answered: 'That might be, but before I give you the sax you will have to prove yourself by accomplishing something worthy of fame, because I was never able to get it from my father while he was still alive.'

Grettir replied: 'It is not clear who will reap the most gain before it's all over.'

Thorfinn took the treasure and kept the sword beside his bed. The winter now continued to Yuletide, and nothing else worth repeating occurred.

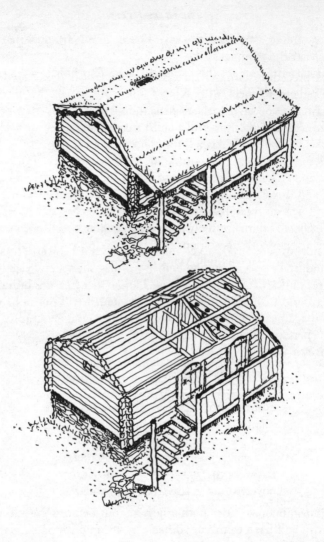

Illustration 1. The Wooden Storehouse in Norway Where Grettir Kills Twelve Berserkers. The storehouse at Haramarsey Island was separate from the main dwelling and constructed of stout timbers. It had an outside stairway and heavy doors which could be bolted. Inside, a wooden wall partitioned the building into two rooms. One room was used for locked storage for food and valuables. The other was a latrine. In medieval Scandinavia people often visited the latrine in groups.

19. Berserkers

THE preceding summer, Jarl Eirik Hakonarson* had sailed west to England to meet with King Canute the Great, his brother-in-law. In Norway Eirik had placed his son Jarl Hakon in power, but because Hakon was still a child, he was under the authority of Eirik's brother Jarl Svein.

Before leaving the country, Jarl Eirik summoned the landed-men and rich farmers to come to him. They spoke in detail about law and government, because Jarl Eirik was a wise ruler. Men found it a disgrace that in their country robbers and berserkers were allowed to roam freely and could challenge well-born men to duels over wealth or women. In such duels no compensation was required for men who fell. Many good men were dishonoured and lost their wealth; some were even killed. For this reason, Jarl Eirik commanded that duelling end throughout Norway. He also out-lawed the robbers and berserkers who had caused trouble. Thorfinn Karsson, from the island of Haramarsey, took an active part in these arrangements. The jarl listened to his counsel because Thorfinn was a wise man and a close friend.

Two brothers called Thorir Paunch and Ogmund the Ill-Willed were the worst of the troublemakers. By kinship they were Halogalanders, and they were bigger and stronger than other men. When they went berserk they spared no one. They took men's wives and daughters, keeping them for a week or half a month before sending them back home. They robbed wherever they went and caused distress. Jarl Eirik declared them outlaws throughout the whole of Norway. Thorfinn pushed hardest for the berserkers' outlawry, and because of this he seemed to them the one most worthy of their vengeance. Then the jarl left the country, as is told in his saga,* and Jarl Svein now took power and authority in Norway.

Thorfinn returned to his farm and stayed mostly at home until Yule, as was already told. With Yule approaching, Thorfinn pre-pared to travel to his estate on the mainland in Slysfjord.* He had invited many of his friends there. Thorfinn's wife was unable to accompany her husband because their daughter, who had just turned marriageable, lay sick. So both the women remained behind at home. Grettir also remained behind, along with eight of the housemen. Thorfinn set off for the Yule feast with thirty free-men.* It was a lively feast with much laughter.

As Yule evening approached the weather was clear and calm on Haramarsey. Grettir was outside for much of the day. He watched as ships went north or south along the coast, with people on their way to feasts according to different arrangements. By then the farmer's daughter had recovered and was able to walk about with her mother. So the day passed.

Then Grettir saw a ship being rowed towards the island. It was not large, but its side was crowded with shields from stem to stern. It was painted from the waterline up. The crew was rowing hard as they headed straight for Thorfinn's boathouse. When the ship touched bottom the men jumped onto land. Grettir counted twelve of them, and their intentions did not seem to him peaceful. They lifted their ship and carried it out of the water. Next they charged up to the boathouse. Inside lay Thorfinn's big rowing ship, the *karfi*. It was so large a ship that thirty men were always needed to launch it. But these twelve men quickly carried it out and set it on the gravel shore. Then they picked up their own ship and moved it into the boathouse.

Grettir realized that the newcomers intended to offer them-selves hospitality. So he went down to meet them, greeting them well. He asked them who they were and what was the name of their leader.

The man he spoke to answered quickly. His name, he said, was Thorir, and he was called Paunch. His brother Ogmund and their companions were with him. 'I would expect', said Thorir, 'that your master Thorfinn will have heard of us. But is he at home?'

Grettir replied: 'You must be very lucky men, because you've come at just the right time if you are the men I think you are. The farmer is away from home with all the freemen among his housemen, and he is not expected back until after Yule. His wife is at home, and so is their daughter. And if I had some score to settle with Thorfinn, matters are just the way I would have wished them to be. Everything needed is here, both ale and other enjoyments.'

Thorir was quiet while Grettir spoke. Afterward he said to Ogmund: 'Haven't things turned out as I said? My intention is to avenge myself on Thorfinn for having us outlawed, and this man brings good news, without our having to pull the words out of him.'

'Everyone has control of his speech,' said Grettir, 'and I would like to be of as much service as I can. So follow me home.'

Thanking him, they said they would accept his offer. When they reached the farm, Grettir took Thorir's hand and led him into the main hall. Grettir was chattering away. The mistress of the house was in the hall, hanging tapestries and decorating the room. When she heard Grettir talking, she stood in the middle of the floor and asked whom Grettir was so intent on welcoming.

He replied: 'It is a good plan, mistress, to receive guests well. Master Thorir Paunch has arrived, together with his eleven companions, and they intend to stay here over Yule. This is a fine idea, because before their arrival we were rather few.'

She replied: 'I do not count them among farmers or other good men, because they are the worst of robbers and criminals. I would have gladly given much of what I own to have prevented their coming here at this time. And you repay Thorfinn badly. He rescued you from shipwreck when you were without a penny to your name, and he has supported you throughout the winter like a freeman.'

Grettir answered: 'It would be better to take the wet clothes from our guests than to rebuke me. You will have many opportunities for that later.'

Thorir then spoke up: 'Do not be put out, lady. You will suffer no lack, even though your husband is away. You will receive a man in his place, as will your daughter and all the other women in this household.'

'Said like a man,' said Grettir. 'There's no need for the women to worry.'

Now the women fled to the back part of the house. Overwhelmed with fear, they wept.

Grettir said to the berserkers: 'Give me whatever weapons and wet clothes you want to take off. Keep some of your arms, because people need to stay scared.'

Thorir replied, saying that he paid no attention to whining women. 'But', he said, 'there's a big difference between the way we will treat you and the way we will treat the other housemen. It seems to me that we have found in you a trusted friend.'

'You will have to judge for yourself,' said Grettir, 'but I myself don't treat all men the same.'

Then they removed most of their weapons.

Next Grettir said: 'It seems right to me that you ought to take your places at the table and drink something. You must be thirsty after rowing.'

They said that they were altogether ready for some drinking, but they did not know their way around the food cellar. Grettir asked whether they would let him take care of these matters, and the berserkers said they would gladly do so. Grettir then went and found some ale and gave it to them to drink. They were very tired and they drank deeply. Grettir did not spare the ale, and gave them the strongest kind there was. The drinking continued for a while, and in the meantime Grettir told his guests amusing stories. They listened, and it was a boisterous gathering. No one else in the household had any desire to come near them.

Then Thorir said: 'I have never met a stranger as helpful as this man. What sort of repayment do you expect to receive from us for such good service?'

Grettir replied: 'I am not looking for payment right now. If, however, we are still such good friends when you leave, as I think most likely, then I would like to join your group. Even though I can do less than any of you, I will not get in your way when you are performing great deeds.'

Very pleased with this response, they wanted to take oaths of friendship immediately.

Grettir replied that they should wait, 'because it is true, as the saying goes, that ale changes a man. It would be best not to make such a decision more hastily than I have suggested. Neither of us seems to be cool-headed.'

They said they had no intention of changing their minds. So the evening passed, and it became very dark. Then Grettir saw that they were beginning to grow tired from their drinking.

He asked then: 'Do you think it's time to go to bed?'

Thorir agreed, saying that 'now I will fulfil my promise to the mistress of the house'.

Grettir went out and announced in a loud voice: 'To your beds, women. Master Thorir is now in charge.'

The women swore at him in response, and their sobs and the fury of their curses could easily be heard. The berserkers got themselves ready.

Grettir said: 'Let's go out, so that I can show you the storehouse where Thorfinn keeps his clothes.'

They let him lead the way, and came to a very large storehouse with an outer door with a strong lock. It was a solidly constructed building, and attached to one side was a big, sturdy outhouse separated from the larger storehouse by a timber wall. The buildings were tall, with some stairs in front. The berserkers, anxious to get inside, shoved their way past Grettir, who let them crowd past him. When no one was looking, Grettir slipped out through the door. He grabbed hold of the hasp, fastened it across the door, and closed the lock. Thorir and his companions thought the door was just swinging loose, and paid no attention. They had a light with them, because Grettir had been showing them Thorfinn's valuables. For a while the berserkers continued to look about, and in the meantime Grettir dashed back to the farmhouse. As soon as he reached the doorway he called out loudly, asking where the mistress was. She kept quiet, because she dared not answer.

Grettir said: 'There is a huntsman's catch outside. Are there any good weapons here?'

She answered: 'There are some weapons, but I do not know what use they would be to you.'

'We will talk about that later,' he said. 'Each of us will now do what he can. An opportunity like this will not come again.'

The housewife said: 'Now God is surely looking after the household, if our situation improves. A large barbed spear is hanging above Thorfinn's bed. It belonged to Kar the Old. There is also a helmet, a coat of mail, and the good sax. These weapons will not fail, if you have the courage to use them.'

Grettir grabbed the helmet and the spear, and before going outside he belted on the sax. The wife called the housemen, and told them to follow this brave man. Four of them ran to get weapons, while the other four scarcely dared to move.

Returning to the berserkers, there is this to tell. It seemed to them that Grettir had been gone for an overly long time, and they began to suspect that there might be some treachery. They ran to the door, but found it locked. They started throwing themselves against the wall, so that every timber in the house groaned. They finally succeeded in breaking a hole through the wooden wall. From there they made their way through the entrance-way and out onto the steps. Then the berserker fury came upon them, and they started howling like dogs.

At that instant Grettir arrived. Using both hands, he thrust the spear up through Thorir's belly just as he was coming down the stairs. The spear blade was wide and long, and it went right through him. Next Ogmund the Ill-Willed ran down the stairs. He crashed into Thorir and pushed against him with such force that the spear blade now went all the way through Thorir up to the barbs. The point came out through the back of Thorir's shoulders and sank straight into Ogmund's chest. They both fell dead from the spear-thrust.

Then, one after another, the berserkers came out of the house and down the steps. Grettir attacked each of them in turn, cutting with the sax or thrusting with the spear. The berserkers defended themselves with logs, which were lying there on the ground, and used anything else they could get their hands on. Even without weapons they were, because of their unusual strength, extremely dangerous fighters. Grettir killed two of these Halogalanders, and they lay in the field between the farm buildings. Now the four farmhands arrived; they had not been able to agree on who was to have which weapon. They started attacking when it looked as if the berserkers were about to run, but the farmhands ran back to the house as soon as the berserkers began to fight them.

Six of the vikings fell there, and Grettir killed them all. Now the other six fled. They made their way down to the boathouse. There, inside, they defended themselves with oars, landing a number of powerful blows on Grettir which nearly disabled him.

The housemen now went home and boasted about their accomplishments. The housewife wanted to know what had happened to Grettir, but she got no answer from them.

Grettir killed two more berserkers in the boathouse, but the four remaining got away. They split into two pairs, each going in a different direction. He hunted the ones who were nearest to him. The night was pitch dark. The berserkers ran into a corn barn on the farm Vindheim, mentioned earlier, and there they fought for a long time. In the end Grettir killed them both. By then he was completely exhausted and stiff. The night was almost over, and outside it was cold, with blowing snow. Deciding not to search for the two vikings who were still alive, he went home to the farmstead.

The housewife had ordered that lights be placed in the windows of the upper loft, so that Grettir could find his way home. Because of this decision, he made it back by following the lights. When he came through the door the wife approached and greeted him. 'You have now', she said, 'won great fame. You have freed me and my household from a shame. We would never have recovered from this disgrace had you not saved us.'

Grettir said: 'I think I am now the same man whom, earlier in the evening, you cursed.'

The wife then said: 'We had no idea that you had so much courage as you have now shown. Within this house you have only to ask for anything you want. All is yours which is proper for me to give and honourable for you to receive. And I can guess that Thorfinn will repay you even more when he returns home.'

Grettir replied: 'There is little need just now for us to speak of rewards, and I accept your offer until your husband comes home. I believe you can now sleep in peace without worrying about the berserkers.'

Grettir drank little that evening, and kept his weapons on when he lay down. In the morning, at first light, men were collected from throughout the island. They searched for the berserkers who had escaped the night before, and found them both late in the day. They lay against a boulder, dead from the cold and their wounds. They were taken down to the shore and buried under a pile of stones at the high-tide line.* After that everybody went home, and the islanders were glad to be left in peace.

Grettir spoke this verse to the housewife when he came home:

> 19.   At low-tide mark I've supplied
>   a dozen brutes with their graves.
>   I had no support—or remorse—
>   in undertaking their demise.
>   Tell me, gilded lady,
>   daughter of noble kindred,
>   what solo feats win esteem
>   if such as this seems trifling?

The wife said: 'Surely there are few others like you, at least among men alive today.' She placed him in the seat of honour, and showed him every respect. Time now passed until Thorfinn was expected home.

20. The Sax

AFTER Yule, Thorfinn prepared to return home. He gave valuable gifts to the many people whom he had invited to his feast, and then set sail with his companions. When he got close enough to see his boathouse, they could see that a ship was lying outside on the sand. They realized immediately that it was Thorfinn's large *karfi*.

Thorfinn had heard nothing about the vikings. He ordered his men to make land as quickly as they could, 'because I suspect', he said, 'that this turn of events is not the work of friends'.

Thorfinn was the first of his men to go on land, and went immediately to the boathouse. He saw the ship inside, and recognized that it belonged to the berserkers.

Now he spoke to his men. 'I fear', he said, 'that events have taken place here for which I would have given the island and all that I own if only they could have been prevented.'

They asked him what might have happened.

He said then: 'I see that Thorir Paunch and Ogmund the Ill-Willed are here. They are the worst vikings in all of Norway, and they wish me no good. So, too, I do not trust the Icelander.' He continued talking to his men in this way.

Grettir was at home. He arranged it so that people waited some time before going down to the shore, saying that he did not mind if the farmer got a little scared about what he might find. But the wife asked his permission to go out. He said that she could decide her own comings and goings, but he himself made no move to go. She quickly went to find Thorfinn, greeting him affectionately.

Her greeting pleased him, and he said: 'God be praised that I find you and my daughter in health and safe. But what has happened since I left home?'

She said: 'Things turned out well in the end, but we were faced with so much dishonour that we would never have rid ourselves of the shame, if your guest had not helped us.'

Thorfinn then said: 'Now let's sit down, and you tell me what happened.' She then told him carefully about all the events that had occurred, praising Grettir's courage and conduct.

Thorfinn, who listened quietly while she told the whole story, said: 'What they say is true: it takes time to test a man. But where is Grettir now?'

The wife said: 'He is home in the living-room.'*

Then they went home to the farm. Thorfinn walked over to Grettir and embraced him. He thanked Grettir, praising him for the loyalty that he had shown. 'And this I will tell you,' said Thorfinn, 'in a way that few men speak to their friends; I wish that you will find yourself in need of help. In that moment you will learn whether or not I am a man who will stand by you. But I will never be able to repay you for this deed of generosity if you do not find need of me. You will have lodging here with me whenever you want it, and you will be held foremost among my men.'

Grettir gave him great thanks in return: 'And I would have accepted such generosity even if you had offered it earlier.'

Grettir remained there during the winter, and was held in the closest affection by Thorfinn. He became famous for his courage throughout all Norway, and especially in those areas where the berserkers had caused the most trouble.

In the spring Thorfinn asked Grettir what he had in mind to do next. Grettir replied that he wanted to travel north to Vaagan,* at the time of the annual market gathering. Thorfinn said that he would provide him with whatever resources he wished. Grettir said that he had no need for funds aside from some pocket silver. Thorfinn, saying that was understood, accompanied him down to the ship, where he gave Grettir the good sax. Grettir carried it as long as he lived, and it was a splendid treasure. Thorfinn invited him to return whenever he needed assistance.

Grettir travelled north to Vaagan, where there was a large crowd. Many men extended their greetings to Grettir, though they had never seen him before. He was known because of his great accomplishment in having killed the vikings. Numbers of well-born men invited him to stay with them, but he wanted instead to return home to his friend Thorfinn. He took passage on a merchant ship owned by a man named Thorkel, who lived at Saltfjord in Halogaland and was a man of high standing. When they reached Thorkel's, Thorkel heartily welcomed him to his home and requested that Grettir remain there over the winter. Thorkel was so pressing with his offer that Grettir accepted, and he stayed with Thorkel that winter and was well treated.

21. The Bear

A MAN named Bjorn was staying at Thorkel's. He was by nature an aggressive, pushy sort, but he came from a good family and was distantly related to Thorkel. He was not popular with most people on the farm, because he would make false accusations about some of those in Thorkel's service; many of them left because of his troublemaking. He and Grettir began to dislike each other.

Bjorn found Grettir of little worth compared to himself, but Grettir stood his ground. Animosity developed between them. Bjorn was a loud man, who liked to act as if he was important. Because of this, many young men followed him, and they often got together in the evening outside the farmhouse.

Now something happened. Early in the winter a wild cave-bear suddenly came out of its den. It was so savage that neither man nor livestock was spared. Men believed that it had been awakened by all the noise made by Bjorn and his companions. The bear destroyed people's livestock and became a serious problem. Thorkel felt the damage most of all, because he was the richest man in this settlement.

One day Thorkel asked his followers to search for the location of the bear's cave. They found it in some bluffs by the sea. In a cliff there was a cave with a narrow path leading to it. Beneath the cave was a sheer drop ending below in a heap of stones, thus making death a certainty for whoever fell down from above. The bear lay in its den during the day, but would come out after nightfall. No stockade was strong enough to keep it from the livestock, and dogs were of no use. The bear became a very serious problem.

Thorkel's kinsman Bjorn said the major work was done now that the den had been found. 'Now we'll see', he said, 'how the game goes between me and my namesake.'* Grettir acted as though he had no idea why Bjorn was making so much noise.

It often happened, just as men were going to sleep, that Bjorn disappeared outside. One night Bjorn went to the den, knowing that the animal was there because it was roaring savagely. Bjorn lay down on the narrow path. He had his shield with him, and intended to wait there until the bear came out as usual. But the bear picked up the man's scent and did not come out right away. Meanwhile Bjorn was getting very tired, and lying there he could not keep awake. The bear now chose to leave its den and saw where the man was lying. It clawed the shield with its paw and, drawing it off him, threw it down the cliff. Startled, Bjorn awoke and jumped to his feet. Then he set off running back home, fearing the bear would grab him at any moment. His companions knew all about this incident, because they always kept watch on his trips. They found the shield in the morning and had great fun at Bjorn's expense.

At Yuletide Thorkel himself went to the cave. There were eight men altogether, Bjorn and Grettir along with five of Thorkel's followers. Grettir was wearing a fur cloak, but he took it off when they went to attack the bear. The attack wasn't very successful because, given the situation, all they could do was thrust at the bear with spears, which it was able to push away. Bjorn urged the men to attack, but he himself kept his distance and stayed out of danger. When no one was paying attention, Bjorn threw Grettir's cloak to the bear, still in its den. The men accomplished little, and towards the end of the day they decided to quit. Grettir prepared to leave, but could not find his cloak until he saw that the bear was lying on it.

He said: 'Who played a trick on me and threw my fur into the den?'

Bjorn replied: 'He alone did it who dares to admit it.'

Grettir answered: 'I will not make much of this.'

They set off for home, and after going some way the strap holding up Grettir's leggings broke. Thorkel told the men to wait for him, but Grettir said there was no need.

Then Bjorn spoke up: 'You need not worry that Grettir will run away from his cloak. He alone wants the honour of killing the bear, especially after eight of us gave up. He would prove what people say about him, even if he didn't do much today.'

'I do not know', said Thorkel, 'how this situation will turn out for you. But as to courage, the two of you are not equals. Leave Grettir alone.'

Bjorn said that neither Thorkel nor Grettir would choose words for him.

Then they separated, a ridge coming between them. Grettir returned to the narrow path on the cliff. Now that there was no need to have his courage compared with that of others, he drew his sword, Jokul's-Gift. He also tied a thong to the hilt of the sax, looping the other end around his forearm. He did so, thinking it better to have his hand free to grab the sax if he needed it.

Grettir went straight down the path to the cave. When the animal saw the man, it rose up on its hind legs, roaring savagely. The bear attacked Grettir, striking at him with the paw that was farthest from the cliff. Grettir defended himself with his sword, landing a blow on the paw just above the claws, slicing them off. Then the bear tried to strike at him with the other front paw, which was still whole. To do so, it shifted its weight onto the stump, but because the stump was shorter the animal lost its balance and fell into Grettir's arms. Grettir grabbed the bear and held it away from him by its ears, so that it could not bite him. Later Grettir said that holding the bear off was the greatest test of his strength. With the bear struggling so desperately, and the path being so narrow, they both fell over the cliff. The bear was heavier, so it was on the bottom when the two struck the rocks. Grettir lay on top, but the bear beneath him was badly wounded from the fall. Grettir reached for his sax and drove the blade into the bear's heart. This was the bear's death.

Grettir went home and took his fur cloak with him; it was all torn into pieces. He had with him the part of the bear's paw that he had sliced off. Thorkel sat drinking with his men when Grettir entered the hall, and the men laughed at the ripped cloak he was wearing. Grettir put on the table the part of the bear's paw which he had cut off.

Thorkel said: 'Where, now, is my kinsman Bjorn? I never saw iron bite so well for you, and I want you to offer Grettir compensation for the dishonour that you have shown him.'

Bjorn said that could wait: 'And it doesn't matter to me what he likes or what he does not like.'

Grettir then spoke this verse:

20.   My friend, godlike in war,
          paid calls on the bear last autumn.
      Come dusk, though, he'd slink back home,
          preferring to fight shy of bloodshed.
      But no one spied me as I sat
          far on at night by the cave.
      I escaped at last unscathed
          from the furry wrestler's hideout.

Bjorn said: 'You have done two things: shown your prowess and shown that you believe we are unequal. I see that you want to make little of me.'

Thorkel said: 'It is my wish, Grettir, that you do not avenge yourself on Bjorn. To make sure of that, I offer to pay as compensation the full worth of a man, if you will be reconciled with him.'

Bjorn said that Thorkel might do better things with his money than offer Grettir compensation. 'And so it will be like snow blowing from one tree onto another, if Grettir and I deal with each other.'* Grettir said that he was in full agreement.

'Then I ask you, Grettir,' said Thorkel, 'for my sake do not settle your difference with Bjorn while you are staying with me.'

'And so it shall be,' said Grettir.

Bjorn said that he would not be afraid of Grettir, no matter where they met. Grettir just grinned. He would not accept any payment for Bjorn, and the two stayed there over the winter.

22. Grettir's Vengeance

IN the spring Grettir sailed back north to Vaagan with some merchants. Grettir and Thorkel parted in friendship. Bjorn sailed west to England, in command of a ship that Thorkel was sending there. Bjorn remained in England during the summer, buying for Thorkel the goods he had been told to purchase. In the autumn he sailed back from the West.

Grettir stayed in Vaagan until the ships went their different ways. Then he sailed north with some merchants, who held their course until they came into the port called Garten at the mouth of Trondheim Fjord. They pitched their tents. After they had been there for a while, a ship came from the south, sailing along the coast. They realized right away that it was a ship returning from England. The newcomers landed a little farther out along the coast and went ashore.

Grettir and his companions walked to meet them. When they drew close, Grettir saw that Bjorn was among the crew, and he said: 'All's well now that we have met, because we have an old score to settle. Now I would like to see which of us is more capable.'

Bjorn said that, as far as he was concerned, this matter was an old one, 'and if there is still something to it, then I would like to compensate you so that your honour will be satisfied'.

Grettir spoke this verse:

> 21. I put paid to the gnasher of greedy
> teeth; grimly he ripped
> my long fur cloak to shreds.
> The news spread far and wide.
> Whose fault if not this menace
> of a man? And now he shall pay!
> Empty boasts in a quarrel
> are not my accustomed style.

Bjorn said that more important matters than this one had been reconciled with money. Grettir replied that there were few men still alive who had treated him so shabbily. Up to now he had not accepted money for insult, and nothing, this time, was going to be different. 'One of us will not be leaving here unscathed, if I am to decide, and I lay upon you the name of coward if you dare not fight me.'

Bjorn now realized that he would not be able to talk his way out of this situation. Picking up his weapons, he went up onto dry land. The two men ran at each other and began to fight. Bjorn was quickly wounded, and not long afterwards fell to the ground, dead. Bjorn's followers saw all that had happened and then they returned to their ship. They sailed north up the coast, bringing the news to Thorkel. When he had been told what had happened, he said it was no more than was to be expected.

A little later Thorkel travelled south to Trondheim to meet with Jarl Svein.

After the killing of Bjorn, Grettir went south to More. He went to his friend Thorfinn and told him what had happened. Thorfinn received him well. 'And it is good', he said, 'that you are in need of a friend. You will stay here with me until this case is settled.'

Grettir thanked him for his offer and said he would accept it.

Jarl Svein was in residence at Stenkjer in Trondheim when he learned of Bjorn's killing. At the time Hjarrandi, Bjorn's brother, was with him. Hjarrandi was one of the jarl's retainers and was enraged when he learned about Bjorn's killing. He asked the jarl for his support in the case. The jarl promised to stand by him, and sent a messenger to Thorfinn, summoning both Thorfinn and Grettir to come before him. They set off immediately, Thorfinn and Grettir, after receiving the jarl's command, and travelled to Trondheim to meet with him. The jarl called a meeting to talk about the case, and requested that Hjarrandi be present.

Hjarrandi declared that he would never carry his brother in his money pouch.* 'Either I will go the same way as he did, or I will take vengeance for him,' he said.

When the case was examined the jarl found that Bjorn had given Grettir many provocations. Also, Thorfinn was willing to compensate the heirs in a way the jarl thought was suitable to satisfy their honour. Thorfinn spoke at length about how Grettir had freed people in the northern part of the land by killing the berserkers, as has been told earlier.

The jarl said: 'What you say, Thorfinn, is quite true. It was a great land-cleansing.* It is honourable for us to accept compensation in accordance with your proposal. So, also, Grettir is a famous man because of his strength and courage.'

When Hjarrandi refused to make a settlement, the meeting ended. Thorfinn arranged that his kinsman Arnbjorn should accompany Grettir in the coming days, because he knew that Hjarrandi was planning to attack Grettir.

23. Jarl Svein and Grettir

ONE day Grettir and Arnbjorn went to amuse themselves on the town's streets.* As they passed by a gate, a man with a raised axe jumped out and, using both hands, struck at Grettir, who had let down his guard and was walking slowly. Arnbjorn, however, saw the man and shoved Grettir forward with such force that he fell onto his knees. The axe cut into Grettir's shoulder, slashing down to his armpit; it was a serious wound. Grettir turned quickly and drew his sax. He recognized the attacker as Hjarrandi. The axe had sunk into the roadway, and Hjarrandi was not quick enough in pulling it back. In that instant Grettir struck at him. The blow landed just below Hjarrandi's shoulder, taking off his arm. Now five of Hjarrandi's followers attacked. In the brief fight that followed Grettir and Arnbjorn killed the five who were with Hjarrandi. One man, however, escaped and went immediately to the jarl to tell him what had happened.

The jarl was infuriated when he learned of the outcome and summoned an assembly for the next day. Thorfinn went to the Thing.

The jarl blamed Grettir for the killing, and Grettir admitted it, saying that his hands had been full in defending himself. 'Further, I carry the mark of it,' said Grettir. 'I would have been killed if Arnbjorn hadn't saved me.' The jarl said it was a pity that he had not been killed: 'You will be the death of many men if you continue to live.'

At that time Bersi Skald-Torfuson was with the jarl. He was a companion and friend of Grettir's. He and Thorfinn approached the jarl, asking that Grettir's life be spared. They proposed that once Grettir had been granted his life and the right to stay in the country, the jarl alone should decide the case. The jarl was reluctant to take part in the settlement, but in the end he let himself be persuaded by their appeals. The outcome was that Grettir was allowed to remain free until the spring. The jarl did not want to enter into a final settlement before Gunnar, the brother of Bjorn and Hjarrandi, was present. Gunnar was a householder* in Tonsberg.

In the spring the jarl summoned Grettir and Thorfinn to come east to Tonsberg. The jarl was intending to stay there while the shipping season was at its height in eastern Norway. They sailed eastwards, and when they arrived the jarl was already in the town.

Grettir sought out his brother Thorstein the Galleon, a householder in the town. Thorstein greeted Grettir affectionately, inviting him to his home. While Thorstein listened carefully, Grettir told him about the case. Thorstein advised Grettir to be on his guard against Gunnar. Time now passed, until well into the spring.

24. Thorstein the Galleon

GUNNAR was in the town and kept a close watch on Grettir, hoping to find an opportunity to get at him. It happened one day that Grettir sat drinking, having stayed inside a tavern so he could remain out of Gunnar's way. When he was least expecting it, there was a sudden crash. The door broke apart, and in ran four men, all fully armed; they were Gunnar and his followers. They attacked Grettir, who reached for his weapons, which were hanging on the wall over his head. He withdrew to a corner where he defended himself, holding his shield in front of him and slashing with his sax. The attack quickly slowed down. He landed a blow on one of Gunnar's followers, and that was all that was required. Grettir now forced them back across the floor, and as they retreated out of the room another of Gunnar's men fell. Then Gunnar wanted to get away, as did his remaining companion, who reached the door but then tripped on the threshold. The man fell down, but was rather slow at getting up. Gunnar withdrew, holding his shield in front of him, while Grettir attacked furiously. As Gunnar stepped out the door, Grettir jumped up onto a bench against the wall next to the door. At that instant Gunnar backed out of the doorway, but his arms and his shield were still inside. Grettir now cut downward, striking between Gunnar and his shield. He sliced off both of Gunnar's hands at the wrists, and Gunnar fell backwards out the doorway. There Grettir gave him his death wound. At that moment Gunnar's follower managed to get to his feet and escape. He went immediately to the jarl and told him what had happened.

Jarl Svein was enraged when he heard this story, and he immediately called an assembly in the town. When Thorfinn and Thorstein the Galleon learned about the call, they got together a group of kinsmen and friends and went to the Thing with a large following. The jarl was so furious that it was scarcely possible to speak with him.

First Thorfinn went before the jarl, saying: 'I have come here because I want to offer you an honourable settlement for the manslaughter that Grettir has caused. You alone will have the right to decide in all matters if the man is granted a pardon.'

The jarl responded angrily: 'You do not seem to grow tired of offering truces for Grettir, but I suspect your case is not good. He has now killed three brothers, one after the other. Each was so courageous that not one of them was willing to carry the other in his money-sack. Now, Thorfinn, do not beg for Grettir. I will not allow so serious a wrong to be committed in this land by taking payment for such a crime.'

Then Bersi Skald-Torfuson came forward and requested the jarl to accept this settlement. 'I am prepared', he said, 'to add to the offer by giving all my possessions, because Grettir is a man of excellent family and my good friend. Certainly you can see, my lord, that it is better to spare one man and in return have the thanks of many. At the same time, you alone will receive the honour of deciding the compensation payment, rather than risking your honour by testing your ability to seize the man.'

The jarl answered: 'Well spoken, Bersi, and as always you show that you are a man of worth. I cannot, however, bring myself to break the laws of the land by pardoning men who have forfeited their rights.'

Then Thorstein the Galleon came forward. After greeting the jarl, he offered to make a settlement for Grettir. He addressed the issues in the case in an eloquent speech, but the jarl asked what business it was of his to be offering money compensation for this man. Thorstein replied that they were brothers.

The jarl said he had not known about the relationship. 'And your desire to help him shows the manliness in you. Because I have already decided not to accept money compensation in this case, I respond to all the pleas in the same way. Whatever the cost, we will have Grettir's life as soon as we can.'

The jarl stood up and refused to consider any more offers of settlement from Thorfinn or the others. These men, returning to Thorstein's house, began to prepare their defence. When the jarl became aware of their plans, he commanded all his followers to arm themselves. Then they marched in ordered ranks to

Thorstein's house, but before they arrived the defenders had deployed themselves and stood waiting in front of the house gate. Thorfinn, Thorstein, and Grettir in the forefront were backed up by Bersi. Each had a large following of men.

The jarl ordered them to hand over Grettir, so as not to bring disaster upon themselves. They responded by repeating all the offers made earlier, but the jarl refused to listen. Thorfinn and Thorstein also pointed out that the jarl would find it was more than a small matter to take the life of Grettir: 'Because we will all share in the same end, and it will be said, if we are all laid in the dirt, that you put much work into taking the life of one man.'

The jarl said that none of them would be spared. They were on the verge of fighting when many men of goodwill came forward. Approaching the jarl, they implored him to change his mind and avoid so much trouble. They pointed out that the defenders would cause serious damage before they were killed. The jarl, realizing that this was wise counsel, let himself be convinced. Then it looked as if an agreement could be reached. Both Thorfinn and Thorstein made it clear that they were willing to reach a settlement, if Grettir were granted a truce.

Then the jarl said: 'You should know that, although I am granting a generous compromise concerning this killing, I do not call it a reconciliation. I choose not to fight with my own men, even if you place little value on my concerns in this case.' Thorfinn replied: 'This agreement offers you great honour, my lord, because you alone will determine the payments.'

The jarl said that as far as he was concerned Grettir could go in peace. He could leave for Iceland as soon as it was time for ships to sail there, if that was agreeable to them. They said that they would accept this offer. They paid the jarl as much money as he required, but they parted without affection. Grettir went home with Thorfinn, parting from his brother Thorstein in great friendship. Thorstein became famous for his support of Grettir, having faced overwhelming odds. None of the men who supported Grettir ever again came into favour with the jarl, except for Bersi.

Grettir said this verse:

> 22. Thorfinn, a comrade
> fit for Odin's
> warband, was destined
> to bring me help,
> when Hel, that goddess
> who lives sealed up
> with the dead in their dwellings,
> laid claim to my life.*

> 23. Look at his name!
> It means a ship,
> a giant-killer,
> and a hefty rock:
> it stood for protection
> (who gave more help?)
> against Hel, true whelp
> of Loki the trickster.*

And then followed with this verse:

> 24. The king's men thought us
> no easy matter
> to deal with, when Bersi,*
> a real bear in a fight,
> set his fiery sword
> to hacking their skulls,
> thick bony redoubts
> for an arsenal of tricks.

Grettir went northwards, returning to Thorfinn's home. He stayed there until Thorfinn found passage for him with merchants who were going to Iceland. Thorfinn gave Grettir many fine clothes and a painted saddle with matching bridle. They parted in great friendship, and Thorfinn asked Grettir to stay with him if he ever returned to Norway.

25. Back in Iceland, Another Whale

ASMUND GREY-STREAK continued to live at Bjarg while Grettir was abroad, and was thought a prominent, respected farmer in Midfjord. Thorkel the Scratcher died during the time when Grettir was not in Iceland. Thorvald Asgeirsson, living at As in Vatnsdal, became an important chieftain. He was the father of Dalla, who married Isleif,* who afterwards became bishop of Skalholt. Asmund received much support from Thorvald in legal cases as well as in many other matters.

Asmund had raised in his household a man named Thorgils. He was called Thorgils Maksson, and was closely related to Asmund. Thorgils was a powerfully built man, and with Asmund's assistance he amassed much wealth. Asmund bought the land at Laekjamot for Thorgils, who settled there. Thorgils worked hard at acquiring provisions, and every year he went out to the Strands. There he collected wild foods and found whales as well as other driftage.* Thorgils was a brave man. He travelled all through the eastern common lands.

At this time the foster-brothers* Thorgeir Havarsson and Thormod Kolbrun's-Skald were making their reputations. In their coastal trading ship they sailed over a wide area, landing in many places. They were thought to be unjust men.*

One summer Thorgils Maksson found a beached whale on the common land, and he and his companions immediately started to cut it up. When the foster-brothers learned about it they went there as well, and at first the discussion seemed reasonable enough. Thorgils offered them half of the whale-meat from the part that was still uncut. But the newcomers claimed for themselves all of the part that was still uncut, or wanted to divide in two the parts already cut as well as those that were uncut. Thorgils flatly refused to give back the part that was already cut. Tempers flared. Both sides armed themselves, and they began to fight. Thorgeir and Thorgils fought each other for a long time, with no one interfering. Neither gave way, and each fought furiously. Their long and hard exchange ended when Thorgils fell dead, killed by Thorgeir.

Meanwhile Thormod fought in another place with Thorgils' followers. Thormod won the victory in this exchange, killing three of Thorgils's companions.

After Thorgils's killing, his men returned to Midfjord, taking Thorgils's body with them. People thought his death a great loss. The foster-brothers took the whole whale for themselves. Thormod tells of this encounter in the memorial *drapa*,* which he composed in honour of Thorgeir.

Asmund Grey-Streak learned about the killing of his kinsman Thorgils. Asmund was the person principally responsible for prosecuting the legal case for Thorgils' death, so he set out to name witnesses and to verify the type of wounds. He and his supporters interpreted the law in such a way that they referred the case straight to the Althing, because the event had taken place outside their quarter.* Some time passed.

26. Asmund Rallies Support at the Althing

THERE was a man named Thorstein Kuggason. He was the son of Thorkel, called Kuggi, who was the son of Thord Gellir, the son of Olaf Feilan, the son of Thorstein the Red, the son of Aud the Deep-Minded. His mother was Thurid, the daughter of Asgeir the Rash, the uncle of Asmund Grey-Streak. Thorstein Kuggason shared responsibility with Asmund Grey-Streak for prosecuting the case of Thorgils Maksson's killing. Asmund now sent a message to Thorstein to come to meet with him. Thorstein, an accomplished fighter and an aggressive man, came immediately to speak with his kinsman Asmund. They discussed the manslaughter suit, and Thorstein was adamant, declaring that no blood-money* should be accepted. He argued that they had sufficient strength in kinsmen to ensure that they could either get a judgement of outlawry* or take blood-vengeance. Asmund told Thorstein that he would stand behind him and would support whatever course he chose to take. They rode north to Thorvald,* their kinsman, and asked for his support. Thorvald quickly agreed, and they planned their lawsuit against Thorgeir Havarsson and Thormod.

Thorstein rode home to his farm. At the time he was living at Ljar Woods in the Hvammssveit region. Skeggi, who lived at Hvamm in Hvammssveit, was the son of Thorarin Foal-Brows, the son of Thord Gellir. Skeggi's mother was Fridgerd, the daughter of Thord from Hofdi. Skeggi agreed to share responsibility with Thorstein in the lawsuit. Together they took a large following to the Althing and pursued their cases vigorously. Asmund and Thorvald rode from home with sixty men and waited many nights in Ljar Woods.

27. The Foster-Brothers Sentenced

THORGILS ARASON lived at Reykjaholar. He was the son of Ari, who was the son of Mar, the son of Atli the Red. His father was Ulf the Squint-Eyed, who was the first settler to claim Reykjaness. The mother of Thorgils Arason was Thorgerd, the daughter of Alf of the Dales. A second daughter of Alf was Thorelf, the mother of Thorgeir Havarsson. Because of shared kinship, Thorgeir could count on support from there, and Thorgils at Reykjaholar was the most important leader in the Western Quarter. He was a man of such open-handed hospitality that he gave food to every freeman who asked for it, and for as long as it was needed. Because of Thorgils's hospitality, there was always a large crowd at Reykjaholar. Thorgils acquired great renown for his establishment. He was a generous man, and a wise one. Thorgeir stayed with Thorgils during the winters, but he went out to the Strands during the summers.

After the killing of Thorgils Maksson, Thorgeir went to Reykjaholar and told Thorgils Arason what had happened. Thorgils told Thorgeir that he could stay there with him. 'But I would imagine', he said, 'that they will be unbending in the lawsuit for the killing, and I am not eager to expand the troubles. I will now send a man to Thorstein, offering to pay compensation for Thorgils's killing. But if he chooses not to make an agreement, then I am not going to defend this case forcefully.'

Thorgeir said that he would follow Thorgils's advice.

In the autumn Thorgils sent a man to Thorstein Kuggason to see if an agreement could be reached. Thorstein was reluctant to accept compensation for the manslaughter of Thorgils Maksson, but as to the other killings, he indicated that he would follow the counsel of men wiser than himself. When Thorgils learned of this response, he spoke with Thorgeir, asking him what he could most usefully do for him. Thorgeir said that he would prefer to travel abroad if he was to be outlawed. Thorgils replied that he would try to arrange matters in this way.

A ship had been drawn up on land alongside Nordur (North) River in Borgarfjord. Thorgils secretly purchased passage on the ship for the foster-brothers. So the winter passed.

Thorgils learned that Thorstein and those joining him in the suit had gathered a large following to take to the Althing, and that they were waiting at Ljar Woods. Knowing about Thorstein's group, Thorgils put off leaving home. He wanted to wait until Thorstein and his group had already set out on the ride south before he would pass Ljar Woods, riding from the west. And it worked out that way. When Thorgils finally rode from the west on his way south to the Althing, the foster-brothers rode with him. On this trip Thorgeir killed Bundle-Torfi from Maskelda, then later two more men, Skuf and Bjarni, at Hundadal. Thormod says in Thorgeir's *drapa*:

> 25. Success was squarely Thorgeir's
> when he settled accounts with Thorgils,
> Mak's son, for his aggression.
> Sword-blade grated on sword-blade;
> ravens butchered bodies.
> And what a great send-off Skuf
> and Bjarni received! He gladly
> gave them the hands-on treatment.*

Thorgils immediately arranged a settlement for the killing of Skuf and Bjarni. The matter was handled right there in the valley, but that meant that Thorgils was forced to spend more time there than he had intended. Thorgeir now rode to the ship, while Thorgils continued on to the Althing, but arrived only after the court was already in session. Asmund Grey-Streak was just then calling for the defence in the manslaughter of Thorgils Maksson. Now Thorgils Arason entered the court and offered compensation for the killing, but only if Thorgeir were acquitted. As defence in the case, he raised the question of whether or not it was true that everybody had the right to the free usage of common lands.

The law-speaker was then asked whether or not this defence was legal. At the time Skapti was the law-speaker,* and he was supporting Asmund because of their kinship. He said that free usage would have been the law if the contenders had been equals, but that landowning farmers had precedence over landless wanderers. Asmund pointed out that Thorgils had offered the foster-brothers an equal division of the uncut part of the whale when they had first arrived, and that his defence was therefore invalid. Thorstein and his kinsmen pursued the case boldly, maintaining that they would accept nothing less than Thorgeir's being made an outlaw. Thorgils now could see only two choices open to him. He could either attack with all his men, even though the outcome was unclear, or he could stand back and let his opponents conclude the case as they wished. As Thorgeir was already on-board the ship, Thorgils withdrew and let the case run its course. Thorgeir was outlawed, but compensation was accepted for Thormod, who was acquitted.

Asmund and Thorstein felt they had gained considerable stature from this lawsuit. As people were riding home from the Althing some men said that Thorgils had not pushed his case very hard. Thorgils paid little attention to their opinion, letting each man say what he wished.

When Thorgeir learned of his outlawry, he said: 'My choice would be that those who are responsible for having me outlawed will receive full payment before all is ended; that is, if I am able to decide things.'

There was a man named Gautur; his father was named Sleita. He was a kinsman of Thorgils Maksson. Gautur had reserved passage on-board the same ship as Thorgeir. He snarled at Thorgeir and acted in a menacing way. When the merchants realized what was going on, they said it was obvious that the two men could not travel on the same ship. Thorgeir said that he did not care whether Gautur glared at him or not. Nevertheless, the decision was made to put Gautur off the ship, and he went to the countryside up north. Nothing more happened between Thorgeir and Gautur at this time, but, as is commonly known, this encounter led to the later quarrel between them.

28. A Boyhood Grudge

GRETTIR ASMUNDARSON arrived back in Iceland that summer. He landed in Skagafjord, and was by then so famous a man because of his strength and courage that none of the young men were thought his equal. He rode straight home to Bjarg, where Asmund greeted him honourably. By then Atli was in charge of the farm, and the two brothers got along very well together. Grettir's arrogance had increased so much that he thought nothing was beyond him.

By that time many of the young men who had earlier participated with Grettir in the games at Midfjord Lake had become full-grown men. One of them was Audun,* who lived at Audunarstead in Vididal. He was the son of Asgeir, who was the son of Audun, the son of Asgeir the Rash. Audun was a good farmer, respected and even-tempered. He was the strongest man there in the north, and was regarded as the most peaceful man in the district.

It now began to play on Grettir's mind that he had been publicly humiliated by Audun at the ball game, as has been told earlier. This bothered Grettir, and he wanted to find out which of them had grown stronger since then. With this thought in mind, Grettir left home and went to Audunarstead. It was at the beginning of the hay harvest. Grettir wore fine clothes and used the splendid painted saddle that Thorfinn had given him. He had a good horse and all his weapons were the best.

Grettir arrived at Audunarstead early in the day and knocked on the door. Only a few people were at home. Grettir asked if

Audun was there, and the people said that he had gone up to the shieling* to collect dairy goods. Grettir unbridled his horse. The home field was as yet uncut, and the horse went there to graze on the best grass. Grettir entered the hall, sat down on one of the side benches, and fell asleep.

A little later Audun came home. He saw the horse with its painted saddle loose in the home field. Audun was bringing back dairy products loaded on two horses. One of the horses carried *skyr*,* which had been placed in skin bags that were tied shut at the top and were called *skyr* bags. Audun unloaded the horse and carried the *skyr* into the house. As he went inside, his eyes had not adjusted to the dim light. Grettir stuck his foot out from the bench so that Audun fell on his face. He landed on the *skyr* bag and the top came open. Audun jumped up and asked what idiot was there. Grettir named himself.

Audun said: 'That was foolishly done. What do you want here?'

'I want to fight you,' said Grettir.

'Let me take care of the food first,' said Audun.

'As it should be,' said Grettir, 'if there's no one else to do it for you.'

Audun bent down and picked up the *skyr* bag. He flung it straight into Grettir's arms, telling him first to deal with what had been given to him. Grettir was covered with *skyr*, and this he thought more of an insult than if Audun had given him a serious wound. Now they flew at each other and wrestled fiercely, but remained standing. As Grettir pushed furiously, Audun gave ground, realizing that Grettir now surpassed him in strength. They overturned everything in their path as they staggered up and down the hall. Neither spared himself, but in the end Grettir had more stamina than Audun, who lost his balance and fell over backwards. By then he had ripped all the weapons from Grettir. The two men wrestled without stopping, and they were crashing about in the hall when a loud noise came from outside. Grettir became aware that someone had ridden up to the house, dismounted, and was now quickly entering the building. He saw the man, handsomely dressed in a red tunic and wearing a helmet, come inside the house. The man entered the hall, because he had heard the brawl going on inside. He asked what was happening.

Grettir, naming himself, asked: 'And who wants to know?'

'Bardi is my name,' said the newcomer.

'Are you Bardi Gudmundarson from Asbjarnarness?'

'The one and the same,' said Bardi. 'But what are you doing?'

Grettir replied: 'Audun and I are just playing around.'

'I have my doubts about the fun in this activity,' said Bardi. 'Besides, there's a big difference between the two of you. You are an overbearing man, arrogant and aggressive, whereas Audun is peaceful and good-natured. Let him stand up.'

Grettir replied: 'Many search in the distance while the truth is staring them in the eyes. It seems to me that you might more easily concern yourself with taking vengeance for Hall,* your brother, than concerning yourself with Audun's and my problems.'

'I hear that everywhere,' said Bardi,* 'and still I don't know whether vengeance will be taken. Be that as it may, I want you to leave Audun in peace. He is a quiet man.' Grettir did as Bardi suggested, even though it was not to his liking. Bardi asked what was the problem between them.

Grettir spoke this verse:

26.   Rest assured that Audun*
      will get his paws on your throat
      for these brave deeds. A swollen
      neck will rack you with pain.
      In just that way, long since,
      when this boy was at a loose end,
      Audun choked me in anger
      and checked my voice-production.

Bardi said that he had at least some reason for seeking to avenge himself. 'I would now like to make a settlement between the two of you,' said Bardi. 'I want you both to end this matter as it now stands. With what has now taken place, all is concluded between you.'

The two agreed to accept this advice because they, Audun and Grettir, were related. Grettir started to dislike Bardi and his brothers, but he rode off with them.

When they had not gone very far, Grettir said: 'I have heard that you plan to go south to Borgarfjord in the summer. Now I will offer to go with you, Bardi, and perhaps this offer is better than you deserve.' Bardi, pleased with the offer, accepted it quickly and gave his thanks. Then they parted.

Then Bardi turned around and said: 'I want this understood, that you will come with us only if Thorarin gives his permission, because he is in charge of the trip.'

'I liked it better when I thought that you alone were competent to make your own decisions. I do not', said Grettir, 'make my movements according to the decision of others, and I will take it very badly if I am driven from this group.'

Each then went his own way. Bardi said that he would let Grettir know 'if Thorarin wants you along'. Otherwise, Grettir should quietly stay home.

Grettir rode home to Bjarg, and Bardi returned to his farm.

29. A Horse-Fight Leads to Violence

DURING the summer a large horse-fight* was held at Langafit (Long Fertile Meadow), a little way below Reykir. Many people attended. Atli of Bjarg owned a fine grey stallion. It was of the same stock as Kengala,* with a black stripe down its back. Atli and his father, Asmund, were proud of this horse. The brothers Kormak and Thorgils* at Mel owned a brown stallion, a tough and trusted fighter. It was agreed that they would pit their horse against Atli's from Bjarg. Many excellent stallions were to be there.

Odd the Orphan-Skald, Kormak's kinsman, was chosen to goad the horse of the two brothers that day. Odd had developed into a very strong man who thought highly of himself, and could be rash and difficult. Grettir asked his brother Atli who should goad their horse.

'It's hard to decide,' said Atli.

'Do you want me to stand in?' asked Grettir.

'If so, you must keep your composure, kinsman,' said Atli, 'because here we are competing with ambitious men.'

'Each pays for his own arrogance,' said Grettir, 'if he cannot restrain himself.'

The stallions were then led forward, while the other horses were kept farther out on the riverbank. They were tied together as a group, standing on the bank just above a deep pool. The stallions fought well, providing fine sport. Odd goaded his horse aggressively, but Grettir tended to back off. He took hold of his stallion's tail with one hand, while in the other he held a stick he used to prod the horse. Odd stood near the front of his horse, and it was not clear whether he was also striking Atli's horse when he had the opportunity. Grettir acted as if he saw nothing. The horses were fighting their way towards the river when Odd struck at Grettir, landing his goading-stick on his shoulder-blade just as Grettir turned. It was no small matter; the skin ripped back over the muscle, although Grettir bled little. At that instant the horses reared up. Grettir got under the haunches of his horse and drove his goad into Odd's side so hard that three of his ribs were broken. Odd was flung out into the pool along with his horse and all the other horses that were tied together. People managed to get a hold of Odd, and they pulled him out of the river.

This action caused an uproar. Kormak and his men went for their weapons, while the men of Bjarg armed themselves where they stood. But when the men of Hrutafjord and those of Vatnsness saw the fighting, they forced them to separate. Then they all went home, but not before exchanging threats. For a time, at least, everybody stayed quietly at home. Atli said little about what had happened, but Grettir showed no such restraint, and said that if the decision were up to him they would find another time to meet.

30. The Brothers, Thorbjorn Oxen-Might and Thorodd Poem-Stump

A MAN named Thorbjorn lived at Thoroddsstead in Hrutafjord. He was the son of Arnor Hairy-Nose, whose father, the settler Thorodd, claimed land in Hrutafjord on one side of the fjord all the way north to Bakki (Bank). Thorbjorn was an unusually strong man and was called Oxen-Might. He had a brother named Thorodd, who was called Poem-Stump.* Their mother was Gerd, the daughter of Bodvar from Bodvarsholar (Bodvar's Hills).

Thorbjorn was a good fighter and kept many men around him. He had more trouble getting workmen than other farmers, and he rarely paid wages to anyone. He was not thought of as an easy man. He had a kinsman, also named Thorbjorn, who was called the Traveller. He was a seafaring merchant, and the two namesakes were partners. Thorbjorn Traveller was usually at Thoroddsstead, and it was thought that he barely improved Thorbjorn Oxen-Might's disposition. He was a clever man, who enjoyed deriding other people.

There was a man named Thorir. He was the son of Thorkel at Bordeyri. Thorir lived first at Melar in Hrutafjord. His daughter was the Helga whom Sleitu-Helgi married. After the killings at Fagrabrekka (Fair Slope), Thorir moved south to Haukadal (Hawk Valley) and lived at Skard (Pass). He sold his land at Melar to Thorhall, the son of Gamli the Vinlander. This Thorhall was the father of the Gamli who married Asmund Grey-Streak's daughter Rannveig, Grettir's sister. At that time Gamli and Rannveig were living prosperously at Melar.

Thorir from Skard had two sons. One was called Gunnar and the other was named Thorgeir. They were promising men, who had taken over the farm from their father. But they spent most of their time with Thorbjorn Oxen-Might, and became arrogant. During the summer in question, Kormak and Thorgils, as well as Narfi, their kinsman, rode south to Nordur River Valley to take care of some business. Odd the Orphan-Skald went along with them on this trip. He had by then recovered from the wounds he had received at the horse-fight.

At the same time as these men were riding south of the heath, Grettir left home, riding from Bjarg together with two of Atli's housemen. They rode to Burfell Mountain, and from there over the ridge until they reached Hrutafjord, where they arrived at Melar during the evening. They stayed three nights with Rannveig and Gamli, who were very pleased to have Grettir with them.

They wanted him to stay longer, but he decided to ride back home. Just then Grettir learned that Kormak and his companions had arrived from the south, and had spent the night at Tunga.

Grettir got ready to set out early from Melar. Gamli advised him to travel carefully, and offered to provide men to accompany him. Gamli had a brother named Grim, who was a vigorous man. Along with a second man, he rode with Grettir. They were now five altogether, and they rode until they reached Hrutafjord Ridge, west of Burfell Mountain. A boulder that lies there is called Grettir's-Lift.* Grettir spent a good part of the day trying to lift it, and in this way they awaited Kormak and his companions. As Grettir turned to meet these men, they all jumped off their horses. Grettir said that it would now be more honourable to strike with weapons rather than hitting each other with sticks like vagrants. Kormak told his men to be manly and do their best. Then they ran towards each other and started to fight. Grettir placed himself in front of his men, telling them to make sure that nobody attacked from the rear. They fought for a time, and men on both sides were wounded.

That same day Thorbjorn Oxen-Might had ridden over the ridge to Burfell Mountain, and as he and his group were riding back they saw the fight. With Thorbjorn were Thorbjorn Traveller and the sons of Thorir: Gunnar, Thorgeir, and Thorodd Poem-Stump. When they reached the fighting, Thorbjorn ordered his men to ride between the fighters in order to separate them. But the men were fighting so furiously that the newcomers could do nothing to stop them. Grettir was moving back and forth, and when the sons of Thorir got in front of him he shoved them both off their feet at the same time. This action so infuriated them that Gunnar cut at one of Atli's housemen, giving him a death-wound. When Thorbjorn saw what was happening he ordered the fighters to separate, offering to support the side that followed his command. By that time two of Kormak's men had been killed. Grettir now realized that things would go badly if Thorbjorn joined forces with his enemies, and so he abandoned the battle. Everyone who had taken part in the fighting was wounded. Grettir was thoroughly displeased at being forced to separate. When both sides rode home, no settlement had been made.

Thorbjorn Traveller made insulting remarks about this fight. The relationship between the people at Bjarg and Thorbjorn Oxen-Might began to worsen, until the two sides became full-blown enemies, as later became clear. Atli was offered no compensation for his housemen, but he acted as if he knew nothing about the issue. Grettir stayed at Bjarg until the end of the summer. No further dealings between Grettir and Kormak are reported.

31. Bardi and Grettir

MEANWHILE, after leaving Grettir, Bardi Gudmundarson and his brothers rode home to Asbjarnarness. They were the sons of Gudmund Solmundarson. The mother of Solmund was Thorlaug, the daughter of Saemund the Hebridean. He was the foster-brother of Ingimund the Old. Bardi, a noble-minded man, soon rode off to meet Thorarin the Wise, his foster-father. Thorarin, after greeting Bardi well, asked him how he was doing in gathering support, because they had earlier agreed to take part in Bardi's coming raid. Bardi said he had arranged for the man who seemed to him to offer better support than any two other men to take part in the group.

Thorarin, after listening quietly, said: 'That would be Grettir Asmundarson.'

'The wise are able to see far,' said Bardi. 'It is, foster-father, one and the same man.'

Thorarin answered: 'It is true that Grettir is far in advance of other men, at least among those now living in our land. He will hardly be brought down by weapons if he is in good health. But now there is so much violence in his nature that I doubt whether he will have any success. For you it is crucial that not all those participating in your venture are men of ill luck. You already have enough problems on your hands without taking him along. He will not go with us, if I am to decide.'

'I had not considered, foster-father,' said Bardi, 'that you would deny me the support of one of the bravest of men, whatever may happen. One cannot look out for everything when in such need as I find myself.'

'You will succeed,' said Thorarin, 'even when I make the decisions.'

In the end it was decided as Thorarin wished, and no word was sent to Grettir. Bardi rode south to Borgarfjord,* where the killings on the heath occurred.

Grettir was at Bjarg when he learned that Bardi had ridden south. He became infuriated when he realized that no word had been sent to him, and said that matters would not be left as they were. He learned when they were expected to return home from the south, then he rode down to Thoreyjargnup (Thoreyjar Peak), intending to wait for Bardi and his men as they returned north. Grettir rode up the slope near the farm, and there he waited.

That same day Bardi and his men rode northwards from Tvidaegra Heath after the heath killings. Six men, all badly wounded, were in the group.

As they were riding past the farm, Bardi said: 'There's a man up there on the slope, large and fully armed. Do you recognize him?'

They replied that they did not know who he was.

Bardi then said: 'I think that it is Grettir Asmundarson, and if so, he is waiting for us. I would guess that he disliked being left out of our journey. Right now, I don't think we are in any condition to deal with him if he wants to make trouble. I will send home to Thoreyjargnup and request some men, in order that we do not have to face his bullying.'

They all thought that was a wise plan. Bardi sent for the men, but meanwhile he and his group continued on their way. Grettir saw them riding past, and immediately turned to head them off. When they met, they greeted each other. Grettir asked for the news, and Bardi, without hesitation, told him what had happened. Grettir asked who was riding with him. Bardi said that he was with his brothers, as well as Eyjolf, his brother-in-law.

'You have now overcome your past disgrace,' said Grettir. 'What remains before you is to see which of us is the more accomplished.'

Bardi said: 'I have more urgent business than fighting with you for no reason at all. I think I am now past worrying about the problem between us.'

Grettir replied: 'To me, Bardi, you are a coward if you dare not fight me.'

'Say whatever you wish,' said Bardi, 'but find someone else to push around. And I imagine you will do just that, because your arrogance has now grown to where it knows no bounds.'

Grettir disliked Bardi's prediction, and began to wonder whether he should attack one of Bardi's men. But such action seemed unwise, because they were six to his one. At that moment the men from Thoreyjargnup arrived and joined Bardi's party. Grettir now backed off. He mounted his horse, while Bardi and his companions continued on their way. They separated with no words passing between them, and, as far as is known, Grettir and Bardi had no further dealings.

Grettir once said that he thought he was secure in a fight against most men, even if three came against him at once. Nor would he give way without trying, even if he had to face four men. But he would fight with more than that only if he was forced to defend himself, as is said in this verse:

> 27. I tell you, since you consort
>   with Odin's warrior maidens,*
>   that I trust myself to take on
>   three men, if effort is needed
>   in a noble cause of vengeance.
>   But I'm not game, if I can help it,
>   to wager my life in warfare
>   with more than four dealers of death.

After he and Bardi had separated, Grettir returned home to Bjarg. It greatly bothered Grettir that he could find no way to test his strength. He began to wonder if there was some action he might undertake.

32. Christmas Hauntings

A MAN named Thorhall lived in Forsaeludal* (Shady Valley) at Thorhallsstead. Forsaeludal runs inland from Vatnsdal. Thorhall was the son of Grim, who was the son of Thorhall. His father was named Fridmund, the settler who claimed Forsaeludal. Thorhall was married to Gudrun. Their son was named Grim, and their daughter, who was fairly well grown, was called Thurid. Thorhall was very well off. Most of his possessions were livestock, and no one else had as much grazing stock as he did. Although not a chieftain, Thorhall was a prominent farmer.

There was much haunting at Thorhall's farm, and he had trouble finding a herdsman whose work pleased him. He sought the advice of many knowledgeable men, asking what steps he should take, but no one could tell him what to do.

Thorhall rode to the Althing every summer; he owned fine horses. One summer at the Althing Thorhall went to the booth* of the lawman, Skapti Thoroddsson. Skapti was the wisest of men, who, if asked, would give sound advice. That was the difference between Skapti and his father, because Thorodd, although he could see into the future, was thought by some to be deceitful. Skapti, however, gave everyone the advice he thought would work if followed precisely. For this reason Skapti was called Father-Betterer.

Thorhall entered Skapti's booth, and Skapti greeted him well, knowing that Thorhall was a wealthy man. Skapti asked for the news.

Thorhall said: 'I have come here hoping to receive some good advice.'

'I'm of little use in that area,' said Skapti, 'but what is troubling you?'

Thorhall said: 'I have trouble keeping herdsmen. Some are injured and others leave before their contracts expire. Now no one, at least among those who know the situation, will take a job with me.'

Skapti answered: 'There must be some evil spirit at work, if men are more reluctant to look after your livestock than that belonging to others. Because you have sought my advice I will arrange for you to have the herdsman called Glam. He is from Sweden; his family comes from Sylgsdalir. He came to Iceland last summer and, although not much for keeping company with other men, he is big and strong.'

Thorhall replied that Glam's failure to mix with others would not bother him, as long as the man was competent to look after his sheep.

Skapti said that other men's chances to protect his sheep would be slim if Glam failed, given his strength and disposition. Thorhall then left. Their talk had just preceded the end of the Althing.

Two of Thorhall's pale-dun horses were missing, and he himself went to look for them. Because Thorhall went by himself, people surmised that he was not an important man. He went up to Sledge Ridge, and from there he continued south, passing under the mountain called Armannsfell (Spirit Mountain).

Then he saw where a man was coming down from Godaskog (Chieftains' Woods), leading a horse loaded with brushwood. The two men soon crossed each other's paths. Thorhall asked the man his name, and the other replied that he was called Glam. The man was extremely large and had a strange appearance, with wide-open blue eyes and wolf-grey hair. Thorhall, taken aback when he realized that this was the man who had been recommended to him, began with questions.

'What kind of work do you do best?'

Glam said that he was good at looking after sheep during the winter.

'Would you like to look after my sheep?' said Thorhall. 'Skapti has placed you in my service.'*

'My work will be of use to you only if I can make my own decisions. I become difficult when things do not go my way,' said Glam.

'I have no problem with that,' said Thorhall, 'and I would like you to come to my farm.'

'I will do so,' said Glam, 'but are there any difficulties?'

'My place is thought to be haunted,' said Thorhall.

'I am not afraid of ghosts,' said Glam. 'I find they break the boredom.'

'You will need to be thinking like that,' said Thorhall. 'It is all the better that you are not a coward.'

After that they entered into a contract, with Glam agreeing to arrive at Thorhallsstead by the time of the Winter Nights.* Then they parted, and Thorhall found his horses in a place he had just searched. Thorhall rode home, after thanking Skapti for his assistance.

As the summer passed, Thorhall had no news of the herdsman. No one knew anything about him before Glam arrived at the appointed time at Thorhallsstead. The farmer welcomed him, but nobody else liked him, least of all Thorhall's wife. Glam now took the sheep under his care, and it was an easy job for him. He had a deep, booming voice, and the sheep would come running when he called. There was a church at Thorhallsstead, but Glam would not enter it. He sang no prayers, had no beliefs, was unbending, and he always had something foul to say. He was unpleasant in almost every way.

The day before Yule, Glam got up early and demanded his food. Thorhall's wife answered: 'It is not the custom among Christians to eat on this day, because tomorrow is the first day of Christmas, and today one's first duty is to fast.'

He answered, 'You have many superstitions for which I see no use. It seems to me that people are no better off now than before they concerned themselves with such matters. I liked the customs better when men were called heathen, and I want my food without any tricks.'

The wife said: 'I know for sure that you will pay for it today if you act in so evil a way.'

Glam told her to bring his food immediately or it would be the worse for her, and she did not dare refuse him. When he had eaten his fill he went out. He was in a foul mood. Outside it was dark and overcast, with snow flurries and a howling wind. The weather worsened as the day wore on. People heard the herdsman in the morning, but less so as the day passed. Then the snow began to drift, and a powerful storm arrived in the evening.

People went to mass, and at last the day came to an end. Glam did not come home. The householders wondered whether they should go out to look for him, but because of the snowstorm and the darkness no search was undertaken. He did not come home on Christmas Eve, and people decided to do nothing until after mass.

With daylight, men went out to search. They found the sheep scattered around the mountains, buried in snowdrifts. The animals were exhausted from exposure to the weather or from being driven up into the mountains. Then the men came to a place at the head of the valley where the snow had been trodden. They believed it likely that there had been rather a fierce struggle here, because stones were ripped loose over a wide area and the ground was disturbed. Searching carefully, they saw Glam lying a short distance away from them. He was black as Hel and swollen as fat as a bull. They felt disgust, at the sight and almost lost their courage. Still, they set about trying to take him to the church, but they were not able to move him beyond a small ravine a short distance away. Then they went home and told the farmer what had happened.

He wanted to know how Glam could have been killed. The men said they had followed tracks so big that it was as if barrel bottoms had been thrown down. The tracks were in the area with trampled snow, and the men continued going up under the cliffs at the head of the valley. Alongside them was a blood-soaked trail, leading them to conclude that a monster had killed Glam, but Glam had wounded the monster so badly that it must have died, because the creature was never seen again.

On the second day of Christmas, men tried once again to bring Glam to the church. They used oxen, but once they had come down the slope they were unable to move him across the flat stretch. The men then gave up, but on the third day a priest went with them. They searched all day long, but Glam was nowhere to be found. The priest refused to go with them again, but the herdsman was found as soon as the priest was no longer in the party. They gave up trying to move Glam to the church, and buried him under a mound of stones at the place where he was lying.

A little later people became aware that Glam was not lying there quietly. He became a scourge to the local people. Many lost their senses when they saw him, some of them never recovering. Immediately after Christmas, some people thought they saw Glam inside the farmhouse. They were terribly frightened, and many of them fled the farm. Then Glam took to riding the house* in the evenings, so that the roof was nearly broken. Then he started walking about, both day and night. Men scarcely dared to go up the valley, even when they had reason to do so. For the people in the district it seemed as if a terrible misfortune had descended upon them.

33. Glam Rides the Roof

In the spring Thorhall hired new servants and began to farm again. At that time, when the days were at their longest, the hauntings decreased. This situation continued until midsummer. That summer a ship arrived in Hunavatn. On it was a foreigner named Thorgaut, a big, powerful man with the strength of two. Thorgaut, who was travelling alone, was his own master. He wanted to find work, because he had no funds.

Thorhall rode to the ship. He met Thorgaut and asked if he wanted to work for him. Thorgaut said that might well do, adding that he was not particular.

'You will need to know', said Thorhall, 'that because of the hauntings this place is not for weaklings. The hauntings have continued for some time, and I do not want to mislead you.'

Thorgaut replied: 'I don't think I am the kind to give up, even if I should see some ghosts. Few others will stay calm in a situation if I become frightened. And I won't break the bargain because of that.'

They soon came to an agreement whereby Thorgaut was to look after the sheep during the winter. After the summer had passed, Thorgaut began to herd the sheep during the Winter Nights, and everyone liked him. Glam kept coming home to ride the house.

Thorgaut found the situation amusing, and he said the slave*
would have to come closer 'if I am to be scared'.

Thorhall told him not to be concerned, saying: 'It would be
best if you were to avoid defying him.'

Thorgaut replied: 'You seem to have had your courage knocked
out of you, but I am not going to die overnight because of such
talk.'

So the winter passed until Christmas. On Christmas Eve, when
the herdsman was going out to the sheep, Thorhall's wife said:
'I need to know that the old story is not going to repeat itself.'

Thorgaut answered: 'Have no fear, lady. There will be something worth telling if I do not return.'

Then he went back to his sheep. The weather was cold and
snow was drifting. It was Thorgaut's habit to come home at twilight, but this time he did not return. People came back from
church as usual, and they soon began to think that matters were
taking a familiar turn. Thorhall wanted to go out looking for the
shepherd, but the churchgoers refused to go along, explaining
that they had no intention of placing themselves in the hands of
trolls during the night. As the farmer did not trust himself to go
alone, no search was made.

On Christmas Day, after people had eaten, a quickly assembled
group searched for the herdsman. Believing that the shepherd's
disappearance was Glam's work, they went first to his mound.
They approached the grave and saw something unusual: the shepherd with his neck and every other bone in his body broken. They
carried the corpse to the church, and after that Thorgaut caused no
harm to anyone. Glam then returned in full force, becoming so
dangerous that everyone except the farmer and his wife abandoned
Thorhallsstead.

The same cowherd had been on the farm for a long time. Thorhall
did not want to lose him, because he was a kind man who performed
his tasks well. The cowherd, although getting on in years, did not
want to leave. He realized that everything the farmer owned
would be ruined if no one remained to look after the property.

One morning, towards the middle of winter, Thorhall's wife
went to the cowshed at the usual time to do the milking. It was

full daylight. No one wanted to go out early in the morning except for the cowherd, and he had done so at first light. She heard crashing noises in the cowshed and dreadful bellowing. Screaming, she ran back inside the house, saying that something horrible was happening in the cowshed. The farmer went out, and when he reached the cattle he found them goring one another. Upset by the sight, he passed by the hay barn and saw the cowherd lying with his head in one stall and his feet in another. The man was lying face-up. The farmer approached and touched him, but quickly realized that he was dead, his back splintered. It had been broken across the stone slab separating the two stalls.

Now realizing that the farm was not safe, Thorhall left, taking with him all that he was able to carry. Glam killed all the livestock that remained behind. Then he went up and down the valley, emptying all the farms above Tunga of livestock.

Thorhall stayed with friends for the rest of the winter. No one was able to travel up the valley with a horse or a dog without fear of being killed. In the spring, however, when the days grew longer, the hauntings diminished to some extent. Thorhall decided to return to his own property. Although it was not easy to find farmhands, in the end he was able to start farming again at Thorhallsstead. All went the same way as before. As the autumn went on, the hauntings increased. This time the farmer's daughter was the one most often assaulted, and she died because of the attacks on her. All kinds of remedies were tried, but nothing worked. It seemed that all Vatnsdal would be laid waste unless a plan to save it could be found.

34. Predictions

GRETTIR ASMUNDARSON, after leaving Killer-Bardi at Thoreyjargnup, remained at home at Bjarg all through the autumn. Then, shortly before the Winter Nights, he rode from home, heading north over the ridges to Vididal, where he stayed the night at Audunarstead. He and Audun reached a complete reconciliation. Grettir gave Audun a fine axe, and the two pledged friendship to each other. Audun lived for a long time at Audunarstead, and was a popular man. His son was Egil, the one who married Ulfheid, the daughter of Eyjolf Gudmundarson. Their son was Eyjolf, who was killed at the Althing. He was the father of Orm, the chaplain of Bishop Thorlak.*

Grettir rode north to Vatnsdal and paid a visit at Tunga. At the time, Jokul Bardarson, Grettir's uncle, was living there. Jokul was a big, strong man with a violent temper. A seafarer, he was very difficult to deal with and yet extremely capable. Jokul received Grettir well, and Grettir stayed there for three nights.

At that time there was so much talk about Glam's hauntings that little else was discussed. Grettir enquired carefully about the events that had taken place.

Jokul said that, in view of what had happened, the stories were not exaggerations, 'or are you interested, kinsman, in going there?'

Grettir said it was true.

Jokul asked him not to go, saying: 'Even though it would be a great test of luck, your kinsmen are in considerable danger where you are involved. It seems to us that among our young men no one is your equal. Evil will only beget evil where Glam is concerned, and it is far better to grapple with humans than with monsters like this.'

Grettir said he intended to go to Thorhallsstead so he could see just what the situation was.

Jokul said: 'I can see now that it is of no use trying to talk you out of going. But it is true, as the saying goes, that luck and ability are not the same.'

'Danger is at your own door when it has entered your neighbour's. You might concern yourself more with how things will turn out in the end for you,' said Grettir.

Jokul replied: 'It may be that both of us are seeing into the future, even if neither of us can do much about it.'

Then they parted, and neither of them liked what the other foretold.

35. Glam's Curse

GRETTIR rode to Thorhallsstead, and was well greeted by the farmer. He asked where Grettir was heading, and Grettir replied that he was hoping to spend the night there—which pleased the farmer.

Thorhall said he was grateful that Grettir wanted to stay there with him. Then he added: 'But at present few think it wise to stay here any length of time. You probably have heard about what has been going on here, and I would not want you to have any trouble on my behalf. Even if you go away without being harmed, I know for a fact that you will lose your horse, because no one who has come here has been able to hold on to his mount unscathed.'

Grettir replied that he had enough horses, regardless of what might happen to this one.

Thorhall, pleased that Grettir wanted to stay there, welcomed him with open arms. Grettir's horse was securely locked in the stable. The two men went to sleep, and the night passed without Glam's coming home.

Thorhall then said: 'Matters have taken a good turn with your arrival, because Glam is used to rising every night. He rides astride the house or he breaks up the door, as you can clearly see.'

Grettir replied: 'Then it will be either one or the other: he will not sit long by himself, or he will have to change his usual habits for more than one night. I will stay a second night and see how it goes.'

Next they went to look at Grettir's horse, and found it had not been bothered. The farmer thought everything was going well.

Grettir stayed with the farmer for a second night, and again the slave Glam did not come home. Then it seemed to the farmer that things were looking up, and he went to see to Grettir's horse. When the farmer got to the stable he saw that someone had broken into it. The horse had been dragged out through the door, and every bone in its body broken. Thorhall told Grettir what had happened, and said that he should save himself, 'because your death is assured if you wait for Glam'.

Grettir answered: 'For my horse, I will take no less a price than seeing the slave.'

The farmer said there was no advantage in seeing him, 'because he is unlike any human being. Nevertheless, each hour that you choose to stay here pleases me.'

After the day had passed and people were making ready to go to sleep, Grettir did not take off his clothes. Instead, he lay down on the bench across from the farmer's locked bed closet. He placed a rough sheepskin cloak over himself, tucking one end of it down under his feet. The other end he pulled up over his head so that he could see out through the neck-hole. The raised board running along the outer end of the bench was very strong, and he braced his feet against it. The door-frame at the main entrance had been broken loose, and there was now only a makeshift door of branches and planks. The wooden wall separating the entrance room from the main hall was broken loose, both above and below the crossbeam. All the beds had been pushed from their places, and the room looked scarcely liveable. A light burned in the hall throughout the night.

After a third of the night had passed, Grettir heard a loud noise outside. Something had climbed up onto the house. It was riding the hall and beating down on the roof with its heels, so that every timber in the house creaked. The noise went on for a long time, until whoever or whatever caused it had climbed down off the house and gone to the door. When the door opened, Grettir saw the creature stick its head in. It seemed to Grettir to be large and horribly deformed, with strangely oversized features. Glam entered slowly, and once he had passed through the door and was inside he stood still. At his full height he reached the level of the rafters. Then he turned towards the hall, placing his arms up on the crossbeam. Bending forward, he peered into the hall. The farmer did not make a sound. It was enough for him when he heard what was going on outside.

Grettir lay still, not moving at all. Glam saw what looked like a lump on the bench and moved farther into the hall, giving the cloak a sharp tug. Grettir braced his feet against the wooden cross-frame and did not budge. Glam pulled for a second time, now much harder. The cloak did not move. The third time, Glam pulled with both hands, yanking it so hard that Grettir was pulled from the bench, with the cloak ripping in two between them. Glam looked down at the ripped piece he now held, wondering who might be pulling so hard against him.

At that moment Grettir dashed under Glam's arms. He grabbed Glam around the middle and squeezed his spine as hard as he could, thinking that Glam would topple over. But the slave grabbed Grettir's arms with so much strength that Grettir was forced to use all his power to break loose. Grettir now retreated along the bench, seat by seat. The two struggled, breaking the bench-posts and everything else in their way. Glam now wanted to get out of the house, but Grettir held onto him. Grettir braced his feet wherever he could find a footing, but still Glam was able to drag him across the hall. They struggled violently, because the slave intended to drag Grettir from the hall. As difficult as it was to fight Glam inside, Grettir saw that it would be worse dealing with him outside the house. For this reason he put all his strength into preventing Glam from getting out.

When they reached the entry-way, Glam, throwing all his strength into the fight, pulled Grettir right up to him. When Grettir saw that he could no longer resist, he did several things at once. He threw himself as hard as he could against Glam, then grabbed the slave under the arms while bracing both his feet against a stone that had been set in the entrance. The slave was unprepared for this manoeuvre. He had been trying to pull Grettir towards himself, but now he fell backwards, tumbling out through the door. As he fell, his shoulders ripped off the top of the doorframe, so that the roof rafters broke apart, dislodging both the wooden frame and the frozen turfs around it. Glam, now off balance, came crashing out of the house with Grettir on top of him. Outside it was bright in the moonlight, with gaps here and there in the cloud cover. On and off, the moon shone through.

Just as Glam fell the clouds moved, revealing the moon. Glam stared up at the light, and Grettir later said that this sight was the only one that had ever scared him. Exhaustion and the sight of

Glam's threatening eyes now took their toll, and Grettir's strength left him. Unable to draw his sax, he lay between life and death.

Because Glam had more evil power in himself than most of the other walking dead, he said: 'You have shown much determination, Grettir, in finding me. And it would be expected that you would receive only ill fortune from me. This much I can tell you: your strength and the stature which you would have reached, had you not sought me out, are now reduced by half. I will not take from you the strength you have already acquired. But it is in my power to decide that you will never become stronger than you are now—yet you are strong enough, as many will find out. You have become famous because of your accomplishments, but from now on you will fall into outlawry and killings. Most of what you do will now turn against you, bringing bad luck and no joy. You will be made an outlaw, forced always to live in the wilds and to live alone. And further, I lay this curse upon you: these eyes will always be within your sight, and you will find it difficult to be alone. This will drag you to your death.'

When the slave had finished talking, the powerlessness that had gripped Grettir slid away. He drew the sax and cut off Glam's head, placing it against his buttocks. Now the farmer emerged. He had put on his clothes while Glam was speaking, but he had not dared to come closer before Glam was killed. Thorhall praised God and thanked Grettir warmly for having overcome that unclean spirit. They set to work and burned Glam, until only his cold ashes remained. Then they carried the ashes in a skin bag, burying them at a place farthest from where people would go or livestock might graze. When they returned home it was almost daybreak, but Grettir lay down because he felt very stiff.

Thorhall sent to the neighbouring farms for people to come. He showed and told them what had happened. All who heard what he said agreed that a great feat had been accomplished. It was commonly acknowledged that there was no one else with Grettir Asmundarson's strength, courage, and abilities in all the country.

When Grettir left, Thorhall treated him honourably. He gave Grettir a good horse and fine clothes, because all his own had been ripped to pieces. The two men parted in friendship. From there Grettir rode to As in Vatnsdal, where Thorvald greeted him well, enquiring carefully about his encounter with Glam. Grettir told him about their confrontation, saying that he had never before experienced such a test of strength or faced such a long struggle as theirs was.

Thorvald advised Grettir to show restraint, 'and then things will go well. Otherwise you will face problems.'

Grettir replied that his temperament had not improved. He had much less control now over his anger than previously, and reacted even more poorly than before to affronts. One thing he found had greatly changed. He had become a man so scared of the dark that he dared not travel alone after darkness fell, since he saw in his imagination all kinds of apparitions. From this come the expressions to have Glam's eyes or Glam's sight,* said of people who see things other than they are.

Having concluded his task, Grettir rode home to Bjarg and stayed there through the winter.

36. Thorbjorn Oxen-Might's Feast

THORBJORN OXEN-MIGHT held a large, well-attended feast in the autumn when Grettir went north to Vatnsdal.

Thorbjorn Traveller was present at the feast, where there was much talk and gossip. People from Hrutafjord enquired about the encounter between Grettir and Kormak on the ridge during the preceding summer. Thorbjorn Oxen-Might, in telling what happened, spoke well of Grettir. He said that things would have gone much worse for Kormak if no one had arrived to separate the two.

Then Thorbjorn Traveller said: 'The fact is that I saw Grettir accomplish nothing that would work to enhance his fame, and what's more, he was scared when we arrived but then was thoroughly pleased to be separated from Kormak. Furthermore, I did not see him try to take any vengeance when Atli's houseman was killed. For these reasons I find no courage in him unless he is backed up by a large following.'

Thorbjorn continued to make many similarly disparaging remarks.

Many people found this kind of talk foolish, and they doubted that Grettir would stand for it if he should hear about it. Nothing else worth telling happened at the feast, and people went home. There was a lot of animosity between the two farms during the winter, but neither one attacked the other. Nothing more worth repeating happened during the winter.

37. A Father Insulted and Again to Norway

EARLY the following spring a ship arrived from Norway. It landed before the Althing had met, and the men on-board the vessel had news to tell. First, there had been a change of rulers in Norway. King Olaf Haraldsson* had come to power, and Jarl Svein had fled the country in the spring after the battle of Nesjar. Many noteworthy comments were made about King Olaf, including one claiming that he was interested in making the best men retainers in his service. The news pleased many young men who were eager to travel abroad.

When Grettir heard the news about retainers, he made up his mind to sail. Like many others, he hoped to receive honours from the king. A ship was beached at Gasir in Eyjafjord.* Grettir, arranging passage on it, began preparations to go abroad, although he still had very little in the way of trade goods.

By now Asmund was becoming infirm with old age, and seldom got out of bed. He and Asdis had a young son named Illugi, an extremely promising youth. Atli now took charge of all the farm-work and looked after the family holdings. This was thought to be a great improvement, because he was a quiet, thoughtful man.

Grettir went to the ship on which Thorbjorn Traveller had also arranged passage. Thorbjorn arrived before the merchants were aware that Grettir would also be coming aboard. Many people tried to dissuade Thorbjorn from travelling on the same ship as Grettir, but Thorbjorn said he would sail anyway. He set about preparing for his trip abroad, but he was rather late, arriving at Gasir in the north only when the ship was ready to sail.

Before Thorbjorn set out for the west, Asmund Grey-Streak became ill and was no longer able to get out of bed.

Thorbjorn Traveller arrived at the beach late in the day. The crew, preparing to have a meal, stood outside at the washing-bowls they had placed in front of their booths. As Thorbjorn rode up the path between the booths, the crew members greeted him and asked for the news.

He replied that he knew nothing worth telling, 'except that I would guess that by now the champion Asmund from Bjarg must be dead'.

Most of the men agreed that an exceptional person had left this world, and they asked: 'How did it happen?'

Thorbjorn replied: 'It was not much of an end for the warrior. He suffocated like a dog from the smoke in his own fireplace. But his death was no loss, because he was already senile.'

The others answered: 'You speak oddly of such a man, and Grettir would not like it if he were to hear such talk.'

'I can tolerate that,' said Thorbjorn, 'and if Grettir is to scare me he will have to raise his sax higher than he did last summer at Hrutafjord Ridge.'

Grettir heard everything, but remained quiet while Thorbjorn was telling the story. When Thorbjorn had finished, Grettir said: 'I foresee this for you, traveller: you will not die by suffocating in a smoke-filled room, and it may be that you will not reach old age. It is odd that you speak so scornfully about men who've done you no harm.'

Thorbjorn said: 'I have nothing to retract from what I said. You did not seem to act so bravely when we rescued you from the men of Mel, who beat you like a bull's head.'

Grettir said this verse:

> 28. How long you've got in the tongue,
> it endlessly waggles on!
> Some bowmen get strung up
> to nip that fault in the bud.

> Many who yearned for a scrap
> committed lesser offences
> than you, Traveller, and still
> they paid the price with their lives.*

Thorbjorn said: 'I do not see that I am any closer to death, whatever you mumble.'

Grettir answered: 'Until now, it has not taken long for my predictions to be fulfilled. The same will hold true here. Defend yourself now if you wish, for you will have no chance later.'

Grettir then struck at Thorbjorn, who raised his arm to ward off the blow. The sax landed on his arm, just above the wrist, and then sliced down onto Thorbjorn's neck, cutting off his head. The merchants said Grettir was a heavy striker, worthy of being a king's man. They thought that Thorbjorn's death was no loss; he had been both quarrelsome and sneering.

Shortly thereafter the merchants put out to sea. Toward the end of summer they landed at Hordaland in the south of Norway, and learned that King Olaf was holding court in Trondheim to the north. Grettir took passage with merchants who were heading north, because he wanted to meet the king.

38. Swimming for Fire

A MAN named Thorir* lived at Gard in Adaldal. He was the son of Skeggi, who was the son of Botolf. Skeggi had settled the Kelduhverf (Stagnant Pit Area) up as far as Kelduness. He married Helga, the daughter of Thorgeir at Fiskilaek (Fish Brook).

Skeggi's son Thorir was an important chieftain and a seafarer. He had two sons, one called Thorgeir and the other Skeggi.

Map 5. **Grettir's Second Trip to Norway.** Grettir arrives in Hordaland, then sails with merchants north up the coast. They land near Stad, where Grettir swims across a channel in search of fire. At Nidaros he meets King Olaf. Grettir next travels south to Jaederen, and later goes to Tonsberg to stay with Thorstein the Galleon. In the spring Grettir returns to Iceland.

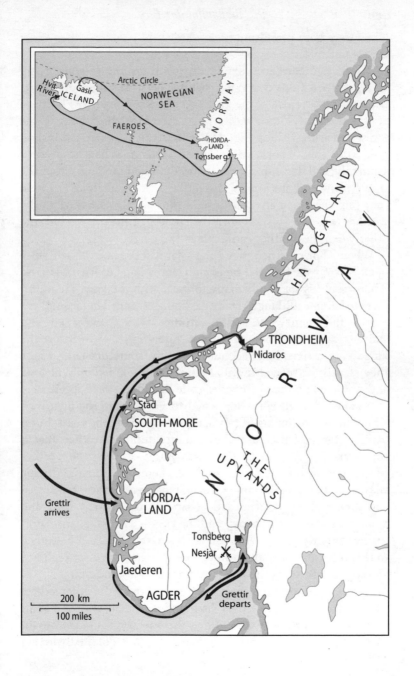

They were both promising men, almost fully grown, when these events took place.

Thorir had been in Norway during the summer when King Olaf returned from the West, having been in England. Thorir became a close friend of the king and of Bishop Sigurd. The mark of this was that Thorir had a large merchant ship* built in the forest and asked Bishop Sigurd to consecrate it, which the bishop did. After this, Thorir sailed out to Iceland. When he tired of sailing, he had the ship cut apart and mounted the beaks from the ship's prow and stern over the outer door of his house. There they remained long afterwards, and they were so sensitive to the weather that one whistled with the coming of the south wind, the other when the weather came out of the north.

When Thorir learned that King Olaf had become the sole ruler of all Norway, he believed he could claim a bond of friendship. So Thorir sent his sons to Norway to meet with the king. He meant them to become the king's retainers. The sons landed in the southern part of the country late in the autumn. They found a skiff and started rowing north along the coast, intending to come before the king. They arrived in a harbour just to the south of Stad,* where they stayed for several nights. They had a good supply of food and drink, and remained inside while outside a storm raged.

Now we can tell what happened to Grettir and the men with whom he was travelling. They set off north along the coast, but it was the start of winter, and they ran into difficult weather. Just as they were trying to make their way north of Stad, the weather turned unusually rough. One evening there was freezing, driving snow, and they were forced to take shelter along the coast. Exhausted and drenched, they succeeded in landing on a grassy bank and managed to save their money and the cargo. The merchants complained bitterly. They were unable to make a fire, and it seemed to them that their health and even their lives were at stake. They stayed there through the evening in miserable condition.

As the night wore on, they saw a large fire on the other side of the channel from where they had landed. When Grettir's shipmates saw the fire, they agreed that the one who could get fire for them would become a fortunate man. But they doubted whether they ought to launch the ship, because all agreed that could be dangerous. Next a lively discussion began over whether anyone might be fit enough to reach the fire. Grettir took little part in the discussion, yet said that once there had been men who would not have thought it much bother.

The merchants said that as far as they were concerned it was no help hearing about the past, if there were nothing to do now. 'Or do you not trust yourself to do it, Grettir? Aren't you', they queried, 'now said to be the most accomplished of the Icelanders? Clearly, you can see what we are facing.'

Grettir answered: 'To me it does not seem much of a feat to fetch the fire, but I am not at all sure how well you will repay the one who undertakes this task.'

They said: 'Why do you believe us men of such dishonour that we would not repay such a feat well?'

'I will attempt it,' said Grettir, 'provided that you believe much hangs on the outcome, even though my instincts tell me that this will turn badly for me.'

They assured him that it would not, and promised they would speak of him as the best of men.

With this, Grettir prepared for the swim. He threw off his clothes, exchanging them for a tunic and some woollen pants. He tucked in the tunic and tied a bast rope around his middle. Then he took hold of a wooden tub and jumped overboard. He swam straight across the channel and climbed up on to the land. He saw a house and heard the sounds of people enjoying themselves inside. Grettir turned and went there.

Now we can tell about those who were inside. Here were the sons of Thorir, the ones mentioned earlier. They had remained ashore many nights at Stad, awaiting a change in the weather before continuing north. They sat drinking, twelve all together, and were staying in the main harbour in a house built as a way-station for sailors travelling up the coast. Much straw had been carried into the building, and there was a large fire burning on the floor.

Grettir now burst into the house, having no idea who was inside. His tunic had frozen solid when he climbed up on to the land, and he looked horribly huge, as though he were a troll. Those inside were completely startled, thinking it was some monster. They hit him with everything they could lay their hands on. In the noise and confusion, Grettir ducked behind the protection of his arms. Some hit him with burning sticks from the fire, and the fire now spread all through the house. In the middle of this Grettir managed to get out of the house, and, taking some fire, he returned to his companions. They praised him highly for the trip and for his courage, saying no one was his equal.

The night now passed, and the merchants thought themselves fortunate that they'd been able to get a fire. The following morning the weather was good. The merchants woke early and made ready to travel. They agreed that they ought to meet the people who had given them the fire and find out who they were. So they unmoored the ship and went across the channel. They could not locate the hall, but they saw a huge pile of ashes, and in the ashes were many human bones. They now realized that the building had burned down, along with the people inside.

They asked Grettir whether he had caused this misfortune, and called it a horrible crime. Grettir said that it was just as he had suspected: they would repay him badly for getting them fire. It had been unwise, offering support to a bunch of cowards. Now Grettir found his troubles increasing. Wherever the merchants went, they spread the report that Grettir had burned to death the men inside the house.

People soon learned that it was the sons of Thorir of Gard—the ones mentioned previously—who had died in the house, together with their followers. Now the merchants forced Grettir off the ship, and no one wanted anything to do with him. He became so despised that almost no one would do anything to help him. Things began to look bleak, and Grettir wanted above all else to appear before the king. He now sought ways to go north to Trondheim, where the king was in residence. The king had already heard all about the matter before Grettir arrived, and Grettir had been badly slandered before the king. He had to wait several days in the town before he succeeded in gaining an audience.

39. Grettir Meets King Olaf

ONE day, when the king sat in open council, Grettir came before the king and greeted him well.

The king looked him over and said: 'Are you Grettir the Strong?'

He replied: 'I have been so called. I have come here because I look for your help in freeing me from the slander which has been attached to me, and for which I am not responsible.'

King Olaf said: 'You are an impressive man, but I have my doubts about whether your good luck will suffice to throw off the charges against you. But it is most likely that you have not willingly burned men to their deaths.'

Grettir said that he was determined to remove this charge from himself, if the king thought this was possible. The king asked him to tell the whole true story of what had gone on between them.

Grettir then recounted all that has been told earlier. He added that all the men were alive when he left with the fire: 'And I offer to submit to any ordeal which you think would be lawful.'

King Olaf then said: 'We will arrange for you to carry the glowing iron in response to this charge, if you are able to do it.'

This pleased Grettir, and he began to fast in preparation for carrying the iron. Time passed until the day of the ordeal. The king went to the church, together with the bishop. There was a large gathering of people, because many wanted to see Grettir since so much had been said about him. After a while Grettir was led to the church, and when he came to the church many stood looking at him. It was agreed that he was unlike most men, on account of his strength and his size. As Grettir was going up the aisle, a boy suddenly jumped out of the crowd. He was rather ugly, and spoke to Grettir: 'Strange customs are now here in this land, where men call themselves Christians, and yet criminals, robbers, and thieves go in peace, and ordeals are held for them. What wouldn't an evil man do to save his life when given the chance? Here is an evil man who is known to have carried out terrible deeds. He burned innocent men to death inside a house, and now he will undergo the ordeal. This is a terrible injustice.'

He went up to Grettir and pointed his finger at him and, making faces, he called him the son of a sea-witch and many other evil names. Grettir lost his temper at this, and could not control himself. He raised his fist and hit the boy under the ear, so that he immediately fell unconscious, and some say he died instantly. But nobody could say where this boy had come from, or what became of him, and people believe that this was an unclean spirit sent to disqualify Grettir.

Now there was an uproar in the church, and the king was told that the man who was to bear the iron was fighting.

King Olaf now went up to the front of the church, and when he saw the situation he said: 'You are a man of great misfortune, Grettir. Now the ordeal will not continue, even though everything has been prepared. It is not possible to struggle against your ill luck.'

Grettir answered: 'It had been my wish that I, on account of my family, would have received more honour from you, Lord, than now it appears will happen.' Then he told King Olaf how they were related,* as previously was recounted.

'What I so very much want,' said Grettir, 'is for you to take me on. You have many men with you who will not be thought more warrior-like than I.'

'I can see', said the king, 'that there are few men like you, on account of your strength and courage. But you are a man of such great ill luck that you cannot be with us. Go now in peace and stay wherever you wish throughout the winter. But when the summer comes, go back to Iceland, because it is there that your bones are fated to lie.'

Grettir replied: 'I wanted first to clear myself of the accusation of the burning, if I were able, because this was something which I did not willingly do.'

'That is altogether likely,' said the king, 'but on account of your having invalidated the ordeal because of your lack of patience, you will now, as matters stand, not be able to throw off from yourself the accusation in this case. Trouble always comes from thoughtlessness, and if ever there was a man who was cursed, then it must be you.'

After that Grettir stayed for a time in the town, but received no more from King Olaf than has already been told. A while later he travelled south in the country, intending to go east to Tonsberg to find Thorstein the Galleon, his brother. And there is nothing told of his journey until he arrived east in Jaederen.

40. A Berserker

AT Christmas Grettir arrived at the home of a rich farmer named Einar. He was married and had a daughter of marriageable age. Her name was Gyrid. She was a beautiful woman and was thought a very fine match. Einar asked Grettir to stay with him over Christmas and he accepted.

At that time it happened in many places in Norway that outlaws and criminals would suddenly come down from the forest. They challenged men for their women or took men's wealth with violence in those places where there were few other men for protection.

One day at Christmas a band of outlaws arrived at Einar's. A man named Snaekoll was their leader. He was a large berserker and he challenged Einar, saying that Einar should either hand over his daughter or defend her if he thought himself enough of a man. The farmer was then long past his youth and no warrior.

Einar realized that he was being drawn into a dangerous situation. In a low voice, he asked Grettir if he had a suggestion, 'because you are called a famous man'.

Grettir counselled him only to agree to whatever would not bring him dishonour. The berserker sat on a horse. He wore a helmet, but the faceguard was not fastened. In front of him he held a shield with an iron rim, and acted menacingly.

The berserker said to the farmer: 'Choose quickly, one or the other. But what is he saying to you, that big lummox standing beside you? Perhaps he would like to come play with me?'

Grettir said: 'We are in agreement, the farmer and I. Neither of us is looking for trouble.'

Snaekoll replied: 'You'd find yourself quite scared of me, if I was to get angry.'

'Only what is tested is known,' said Grettir.

The berserker now found that he was getting nowhere with this talk. He began to bellow loudly and to bite the edge of his shield, putting the shield in his mouth and grinning over the rim and getting enraged. Grettir dashed out into the field, and when he came right up to the berserker's horse he kicked the bottom of the shield so hard that the shield went right up into the man's mouth so that the jaw fell down on his chest. Then, all in one long movement, he grabbed the helmet with his left hand and pushed the viking off the back of his horse, while his right hand drew his sax and brought it down on Snaekoll's neck, taking off his head. And when Snaekoll's followers saw that, they fled in all directions. Grettir did not bother hunting them down, because he saw there was no courage in them. The farmer thanked him warmly for this work, and so did many others. This accomplishment was thought to have been brought about by both skill and courage.

Grettir was well looked after during Christmas, and the farmer gave him fine gifts when he left. After this Grettir travelled east to Tonsberg, where he met Thorstein, his brother. Thorstein received Grettir with affection, and asked about his travels and how he had defeated the berserker.

Grettir spoke this verse:

> 29.   Snaekoll's shield of iron
>   took a sharp kick from my foot
>   and rammed right into his mouth.
>   That metal intruder reshaped
>   the capacious depot for dinners
>   and collapsed its dental foundations:
>   in a case of major subsidence
>   his jawbone fetched up on his chest.*

Thorstein said: 'You would have success in many ways, kinsman, if you were not dogged by misfortune.'

Grettir replied: 'Nevertheless, people will speak of what has been done.'

41. Brothers Talk

GRETTIR now stayed with Thorstein for the remainder of the winter and into the spring.

One morning, when the brothers Thorstein and Grettir were lying in the sleeping-loft, Grettir had moved his hand out from under the covers. Thorstein awoke and noticed that. Grettir awoke a little later.

Then Thorstein said: 'I was looking at your arm, kinsman,' he said, 'and I don't think it's strange that many should find your blows hard, because I have never seen a man's arm like this.'

'You can be sure of this,' said Grettir, 'had I not been rather capable, I never would have accomplished what I have.'

'I would find it better,' said Thorstein, 'if your arms were thinner, yet had somewhat more luck.'

Grettir said: 'It is true what is said, that no man creates himself. Let me now see your arm,' he said.

Thorstein did so. He was extremely tall and thin.

Grettir smiled and said: 'No need to look at that longer. All your ribs run together, and I don't think I've ever seen arms more like tongs. I would scarcely imagine you have the strength of a woman.'

'That may well be,' said Thorstein, 'but you should know that these slender arms will be the ones to avenge you, or you will never be avenged.'

'Who can know how things will turn out in the end?' said Grettir. 'And I think that to be altogether unlikely.'

Nothing more is said about their talk. The spring now passed, and in the summer Grettir got himself passage on a ship and went out to Iceland. The brothers separated with deep friendship, and they never saw each other afterwards.

42. Asmund Grey-Streak Dies

Now we can take up the story where earlier it was left off.
Thorbjorn Oxen-Might learned about the killing of Thorbjorn
Traveller, which earlier was told. He was enraged, and said if he
had his way blows would be felt by others.

Asmund Grey-Streak lay sick for much of the summer. When
it seemed that his end was drawing near, he called for his kinsmen
and told them that his wish was for Atli to take over the management of all his wealth when his days were done. 'Yet I fear', said
Asmund, 'that you, Atli, will scarcely be left in peace, because of
unprovoked aggression. And it is my wish that all my kinsmen
support Atli as best they can. But about Grettir I have nothing
to say, because to me his life seems like a wheel spinning. Though
he is a strong man, it concerns me that he will be so deep in
troubles that he will be unable to support his kinsmen. Although
Illugi is young, he will become a full-grown man if only he can
keep himself alive.'

And when Asmund had arranged matters between his sons
according to his wishes, the sickness took hold of him. He died a
little later, and was buried at Bjarg because Asmund had had
a church built there. The men of the district thought his death a
great loss.

Atli now became a successful farmer, and he had many men.
He was a good provider. Toward the end of the summer he
travelled out to Snaefellsness to purchase dried fish. He took
with him many pack-horses and rode to Melar in Hrutafjord to
Gamli, his brother-in-law. Grim Thorhallsson, Gamli's brother,
together with another man, joined Atli. They rode west through
Haukadalsskard, following the route which leads out onto
Snaefellsness. There they bought a lot of dried fish and loaded it
onto seven horses. When they were all done, they set off on the
route home.

43. Death-Wounds

THORBJORN OXEN-MIGHT learned that Atli and Grim had set off from home. Staying with him were Gunnar and Thorgeir, the sons of Thorir from Skard. Thorbjorn was envious of Atli's popularity, and he urged the brothers to ambush him as they returned from Snaefellsness. The brothers rode home to Skard and waited there until Atli rode by with the pack-horses. When he and his men rode past the farm at Skard, the brothers saw them. Acting quickly, they rode out with their housemen to meet Atli.

When Atli's group saw the others coming, he told them to take the packs off the horses: 'They will be wanting to offer me compensation for my houseman whom Gunnar killed last summer. Let's not be the first to start anything, but we will defend ourselves if they attack us.'

Now the others came up and immediately jumped off their horses. Atli greeted them and asked the news: 'Or do you, Gunnar, want to compensate me somewhat, for my houseman?'

Gunnar answered: 'You men of Bjarg deserve something else, rather than my paying for that. It would be more worthwhile to think about paying compensation for Thorbjorn Traveller, whom Grettir killed.'

'It's not my responsibility to answer for that,' said Atli; 'besides, you're not the plaintiff in the lawsuit.'

Gunnar said that was not an issue: 'Let's attack them, using to our advantage that Grettir is not present.'

They charged at Atli, and were eight all together, while in Atli's group there were six. Atli advanced at the front of his men. He used the sword Jokul's-Gift, which Grettir had given to him.

Then Thorgeir said: 'There's much similarity between those who are thought superior. Grettir bore his sax high last summer at Hrutafjord Ridge.'

Atli answered: 'Grettir is more accustomed to performing great deeds than I am.'

Now they fought. Gunnar was in a fury, and attacked Atli fiercely.

When they had been fighting for a while, Atli said: 'There's no reputation to be had in our killing each other's workmen. Wouldn't it be better if we continued the game just among ourselves, even though I have never before killed with weapons?'

Gunnar refused.

Atli told his housemen to look after the train of pack-horses, 'while I see what these men are capable of'. Then he advanced with such force that Gunnar and his group were thrown back. Atli killed two of the brothers' followers. After that, he turned against Gunnar and struck a blow that sliced right across his shield, taking it apart below the handle. The blade landed on Gunnar's leg below the knee. Immediately Atli struck again, and this was a death-blow.

Now concerning Grim Thorhallsson, he attacked Thorgeir, and they fought for a long time because both of them were brave men. Thorgeir saw the death of his brother Gunnar and then wanted to get away. Grim ran behind him, chasing him until Thorgeir tripped and fell on his face. Then Grim chopped with his axe between his shoulders, so that the axe sank in deeply. Then they gave mercy to the three followers of the brothers. Next they bound up their wounds, replaced the packs on the horses, and returned home. They announced these killings.*

Atli stayed home with many men that autumn. Thorbjorn Oxen-Might was very displeased, but there was nothing he could do because Atli was so popular. Grim stayed with him during the winter, and so also Gamli, his brother-in-law. With them by then was Glum Ospaksson, another of his brothers-in-law, who lived at Eyrr (Gravel Bank) in Bitra* (Bitter). They had a large group keeping watch at Bjarg, and there was much cheer during the winter.

44. The Case at the Hunavatn Thing

THORBJORN OXEN-MIGHT took over the prosecution for the killings of the sons of Thorir. He built a case against Grim and Atli, and they built their defence that the brothers had forfeited their immunity by their assault. The case was brought before the Hunavatn Thing, and both sides gathered large groups of supporters. Atli had no trouble getting support, because he could count on a large kin-group. Now friends went back and forth between both sides and spoke about arranging a settlement. All said that Atli had conducted himself well, peaceful but courageous when put to the test. Thorbjorn realized there would be no other honourable course than to accept the settlement. Atli stipulated that he would accept neither being exiled from the district nor being forced to leave the country.

Then arbitrators were agreed upon. Thorvald Asgeirsson spoke for Atli, while Solvi the Proud looked after Thorbjorn's interests. Solvi was the son of Asbrand, the son of Thorbrand, who was the son of Harald Ring, the one who claimed Vatnsness all the way out to Ambattar (Female Slave) River in the West and to the east all the way up to Thver River and from there across to the Bjorg Estuary and all that side of Bjorg out to the sea. Solvi was a vain man, but he was also shrewd and, for this reason, Thorbjorn chose him to look after his interests in the arbitration.

Later, the arbitrators announced their decision. For the killing of the sons of Thorir, a half-compensation was awarded. The other half was dropped on account of the assault on Atli and the attempt to take his life. The killing of Atli's houseman, the one killed on Hrutafjord Ridge, was balanced out against the killing of Thorbjorn's two housemen who were killed along with Thorir. Grim Thorhallsson lost the right to stay in his district, while Atli chose to pay all the fines himself.

This settlement pleased Atli well, but Thorbjorn was disappointed. Nevertheless they parted with what was called a reconciliation, even though Thorbjorn blurted out that things were not ended between them, if he had his way. Atli rode home from the Thing, and he thanked Thorvald for his support. After this, Grim Thorhallsson moved south to Borgarfjord. He lived at Gilsbakki and was a prosperous farmer.

45. Broad Spears Now in Fashion

A MAN named Ali was in service with Thorbjorn Oxen-Might. He was a difficult and lazy farmhand. Thorbjorn told him to improve his work, or he would beat him. Ali said that he had no intention of doing that, and was surly in return. Thorbjorn warned him that he would not tolerate this, but the other kept up his abuse. Finally Thorbjorn could not stand it any longer. He threw him down and beat him badly.

Following that, Ali ran away. He broke his service and went north over the ridge to Midfjord, continuing without stopping until he came to Bjarg. Atli was at home and asked where he was going. Ali said he was looking for work.

'Aren't you Thorbjorn's workman?' said Atli.

'Things did not go so well with us,' said Ali. 'I was not there very long, but I found it unpleasant as long as I stayed. We parted because I felt he did not treat me well, and I will never again return to work there, whatever else becomes of me. The truth is that there is a great difference between the two of you as to who treats his servants better. I would gladly now work for you, if this were possible.'

Atli answered: 'I have enough workmen of my own, that I don't have to try to take those men whom Thorbjorn has taken into his service. And you don't strike me as being able to put up with much, so return to him.'

Ali said: 'I will never return there without being forced.'

Now Ali stayed there for a while. One morning he went out to work with Atli's housemen, and worked like a man with many hands. While Ali kept this up throughout the summer, Atli paid no attention to him, but let him have his food because he liked the man's work.

Thorbjorn now learned that Ali was at Bjarg. He rode over to Bjarg with two other men and called Atli to come out and speak with him. Atli went outside and greeted them.

Thorbjorn said: 'Once again you are starting up with me, going against my wishes and showing me disrespect. And isn't it so that you have taken one of my workmen? And isn't this improper?'

Atli answered: 'It has not been proven to me that he is your workman. And I have no wish to hold him if you can show proof that he is your servant. But I don't feel like dragging him out of my house.'

'You may decide this time,' said Thorbjorn, 'but I claim the man and forbid you his work. I will come a second time, and it is not clear that we will then separate better friends than now.'

Atli answered: 'I will wait at home and accept whatever comes to me.'

After this Thorbjorn rode home. When the workman came home that evening, Atli spoke to Ali about his talk with Thorbjorn. He told Ali to be on his way, saying that he did not want him to stay there any longer.

Ali replied: 'The old saying is true, people seldom live up to their reputations. I had not imagined that you would drive me away, now that I have worked myself nearly to death here during the summer, hoping that you would offer me some protection. All the while you have acted as though you are thoroughly good, but now I will be beaten before your eyes if you do not offer me protection or help.'

Atli was touched by his words, and could not bring himself to drive the man away. Time now passed until the haymaking began.

One day, a little before midsummer, Thorbjorn Oxen-Might rode to Bjarg equipped in the following way: he had a helmet on his head, a sword was belted at his side, and he carried a spear in his hand. It was a broad spear and the blade was very wide.* It was raining hard, and it continued all through the day. Atli had sent his housemen to cut the hay, and others of his men were north at Horn, fishing. Atli was at home with just a few other people.

Thorbjorn arrived just before noon. He was alone on this trip, and he rode up to the outer door. The door was shut and no one was outside. Thorbjorn banged on the door. Then he went around to the back of the house, so that no one inside the house could see him when they looked out of the door. People inside heard the knock, and a woman went out. Thorbjorn caught sight of the woman, but he did not let her see him, because he had something else in mind. She went back into the main room, and Atli asked her who had come. She said that she had not seen anybody outside. Just as they said this, Thorbjorn gave a loud thump on the door.

Then Atli said: 'He seems to be looking for me, whether the errand is important or not.'

He walked through the house and out into the doorway, but saw no one outside. It was sleeting rain, and because of this he did not go out. He braced himself, putting his hands on either side of the door-frame and leaned forward, looking out.

At that instant, Thorbjorn sprang forward in front of the door and, using two hands, he thrust his spear into Atli's waist so that it went right through him.

Atli took the thrust and said: 'Broad spears are now in fashion.'

With this he fell forward onto the threshold. The women, who had been in the hall, came out. They saw that Atli was dead. By then Thorbjorn was up on his horse. He announced that the killing was his, and with that he rode home.

Asdis, the mistress of the house, sent for Atli's men. Atli's body was prepared, and he was buried alongside his father.

His loss was mourned as a tragedy, because he had been both a wise and a popular man. No offer of payment was made for Atli's killing, and no settlement was sought because the prosecution fell to Grettir, whenever he came back out to Iceland. The matter was left to rest during the summer. Thorbjorn was not well regarded because of this act, but he stayed quietly on his farm.

46. Full Outlawry

THAT same summer when the events just told occurred, a ship arrived at Gasir before the Thing. Grettir's travels were then recounted, including the house-burning. Thorir of Gard was enraged when he heard the story, and felt he had a claim of vengeance against Grettir on account of the deaths of his sons. Thorir rode with a large following to the Althing, and when he arrived he began making a case for prosecuting the burning.

But men found they were unable to start the proceedings while there was no one to answer the charges. Thorir demanded nothing less than Grettir's outlawry throughout the land on account of such a crime.

Then Skapti the lawman gave this answer: 'Certainly this is foul work, if it is true as reported. But a story is always half told if only one side speaks, because many people willingly choose the worst if there are two interpretations of what happened. At the moment I will not announce a decision that Grettir should be made an outlaw in this matter, as things now stand.'

Thorir was an important chieftain, powerful in his own district and popular elsewhere with many of the country's leaders. He pushed the case with such force that there was no chance for Grettir's acquittal. Thorir had Grettir made an outlaw in every part of the country, and he was from that time on the fiercest of all Grettir's opponents, as later events will show. He placed a price on Grettir's head, as was done with other outlaws. The matter completed, he rode home. Many said that this was done more out of spite than according to the law. Nevertheless, the decision stood. There is nothing new to report until past midsummer.

47. The Saddle-Head Verses

TOWARD the end of the summer Grettir Asmundarson sailed out to Iceland, landing at the Hvit River in Borgarfjord. People from throughout the district came to the ship. Grettir received the following news all at once: first, his father had died; second, his brother had been killed; and third, he had been made an outlaw throughout the country.

Then Grettir said this verse:

> 30. That threefold onslaught stunned
> a smart verse-smith to dumbness:
> my father's death; my brother's
> slaying; myself an outlaw.

> Yet, come tomorrow morning,
> fellow swordsman, those
> who seek out strife will feel
> these griefs far more than I.

It is said that Grettir took this news without showing any change in his manner, and continued to be cheerful as before. Grettir remained at the ship for a time, because he could not find a horse which pleased him.

There was a man named Svein, who lived at Bakki, north of Thingness. A good farmer, he was a cheerful man who often composed humorous verses. He owned a black mare which was very fast. Svein called it Saddle-Head.

Grettir left Vellir in the night, not wanting the merchants to know he was leaving. He got hold of a black hooded cloak and, throwing it over his clothes, disguised himself. He went first to Thingness and then to Bakki. By then it had become light. He saw a black horse near the home meadow. He went straight for it and bridled it, and then got on and rode beside the Hvit River all the way until he passed below the farm Baer. He continued on to Flokadal River and up onto the path above Kalfaness. By then the farmhands at Bakki were awake, and they told the farmer that a man had ridden off on his horse.

Svein stood up smiling and said this:

> 31. His thieving hands he laid
>   on my fine mare Saddle-Head
>   right in my own home field
>   and off he rode to provoke me!
>   That flaunter of sword and shield
>   will show the same adroitness
>   at other foolhardy tricks—
>   Here it seems is a prankster.*

Next Svein took his horse and rode out in pursuit. Grettir continued riding until he came up to the farm at Kropp. There he met a man who called himself Halli, who said he was travelling down to the ship at Vellir.

Grettir spoke a verse:

32. Dash down to the farmlands,
    hot-tempered fighter, and say
    you've located Saddle-Head
    on higher ground at Kropp.
    On the mare was sitting a young
    darkly hooded fellow,
    who has long been trying his luck.
    Hurry off now, Halli!

Now they parted, and Halli continued down the path. He had not gone all the way down to Kalfaness before he met Svein coming the other way. They greeted each other hurriedly.

Then Svein said:

33. Did you chance to see where that sly,
    idle, scheming snake in the grass
    rode the mare from the neighbour's?
    Such a trial, this business.
    The local folk will find
    the thief a fitting reward:
    if he sails into my clutches
    he will sport a black-and-blue torso.

'You should be able to do that,' said Halli. 'I met the man who said he was riding Saddle-Head. He asked me to alert people to this, down below in the settled part of the district. He was a large man in a black hooded cloak.'

'He appears to think rather highly of himself', said the farmer. 'I intend to find out who he is,' and he rode after him.

Grettir reached Deildartunga. A woman was outside. Grettir stopped to speak with her and said a verse:

34. Well-born lady, pass on
    my jesting verse to the farmer:
    eel-like, I slipped away,
    having rustled his precious mare.
    An outspoken poem-spouter,

I'll put fury into my riding
so the mare and I will make
Gilsbakki our lodging tonight.

The woman memorized the verse, and Grettir rode off on his way.

Svein came up a little later, and the woman was still outside. As soon as he reached her, Svein said:

35.   What trouble-seeker scampered
       off on a black-maned mare
       just now in this foul weather?
       No doubt at all, he'll scurry
       a good long way today,
       like the shameful dog he is.
       Where are his feats of courage
       now his tail is between his legs?

She then said the verse which had been taught to her.

He thought over the verse, and said: 'It seems likely that this man is more than my match, yet I still want to find him.'

He continued riding past the farms, and each could see the other in the distance. The weather was both stormy and wet. Grettir arrived at Gilsbakki during the day, and when Grim Thorhallsson learned this, he welcomed him very warmly and invited him to stay there. Grettir accepted this. He turned Saddle-Head free and told Grim how he had acquired the mare.

Just then Svein arrived and dismounted. He saw his horse there and said:

36.   What man rode off on our mare?
       How will I get repayment?
       Who yet saw a bigger thief?
       And what is that hooded man playing at?

Grettir, who had taken off his wet clothes, heard the verse:

37.   I rode the mare home to Grim.
       He is a real man, no measly crofter.
       Don't look to me for repayments.
       Let's call it quits instead.

'Consider the settlement made,' said farmer Svein, 'and the horse ride fully paid.'

After that each spoke his verses, and Grettir said he could find nothing at fault with Svein's looking after what was his. Farmer Svein stayed there during the night, as did Grettir, and they had great fun together. They called these the Saddle-Head Verses. In the morning the farmer rode home. He and Grettir parted on the best of terms.

Grim told Grettir many things that had happened up north in Midfjord while Grettir was abroad. He noted that no compensation had been received for Atli, and that Thorbjorn Oxen-Might's power was now becoming so great that it was unclear whether mistress Asdis would be able to remain at Bjarg if matters continued as they were.

Grettir stayed only a few nights with Grim, because he didn't want any news about him to travel north across the heath.

Grim invited Grettir to return if he needed help: 'But I would like to avoid breaking the law and being outlawed for giving you shelter.'

Grettir replied that he had been very generous with him. 'And most likely my need will be greater later.'

Grettir now rode north across Tvidaegra Heath and then to Bjarg, arriving in the middle of the night. Everyone was asleep except for his mother. He went around to the back of the house and found a door, because he knew there was a passageway. Entering the hall, he felt his way in the dark and came to his mother's bed. She asked who was there, and Grettir spoke to her.

She sat up and embraced him. Then, sighing deeply, she said: 'I welcome you, kinsman, even though my sons are for me a fleeting joy. That son on whom I most depended is now killed, while you have been made an outlaw, a criminal for whom there will be no compensation. The third is so young that there is nothing he can do.'

'It is an old saying,' said Grettir, 'that one loss is cured by suffering an even greater one. People can be consoled by more than compensation alone, and it is likely that vengeance will be taken for Atli. It is my view that there are some who will be pleased when Thorbjorn and I fight it out.'

She said it was not unlikely. Grettir was there for a time, but only a very few knew it. He gathered information about the movements of people in the district. People were not aware that Grettir was back in Midfjord. He learned that Thorbjorn Oxen-Might was home and had only a few men with him. This was towards the end of the haymaking season.

48. Grettir Meets Thorbjorn Oxen-Might

ONE day, when the weather was good, Grettir rode west along the ridge to Thoroddsstead. Arriving just before noon, he knocked on the door. Some women came out and greeted him, but they did not recognize him. He asked after Thorbjorn. They said that he had gone to the meadows to bind up the cut hay, and had with him his sixteen-year-old son, Arnor. Thorbjorn was a hard-working man, who was hardly ever idle. Having gathered this information, Grettir left. He wished the women farewell, and rode out on the road to Reykir.

Below the ridge was a marsh with thick, good grass. Thorbjorn had already cut much hay, and this was now drying. He intended to tie up the hay and bring it home. The boy was with him, as well as a woman to rake the grass. Grettir now rode down onto the meadow. The father and son were further up the field, where they had tied up one bundle and were working on a second. Thorbjorn had left his shield and sword beside the bundle, but the boy had a hand-axe with him.

Thorbjorn saw the man coming, and said to the boy: 'Over there, a man is riding towards us. We will stop binding the hay and find out what he wants.' This they did.

Grettir dismounted. He was wearing a helmet and the sax was belted at his side. In his hand he held a large spear with no barbs. Its socket was inlaid with silver. He sat down on the ground and pulled out the nail which held the spear-blade in place. He did this so that Thorbjorn would not be able to throw the spear back at him.

Then Thorbjorn said: 'That is a large man, and I am not able to recognize anyone if this is not Grettir Asmundarson. He has a score to settle with us, so let's act bravely and show no sign of fear. We need a plan, so I will attack him from the front, and we will see how it goes between us, because I trust myself against any man if I have only one against me. But you are to go behind him and, using two hands, strike with your axe between his shoulders. You will not need to worry that he will harm you, because he will have his back turned to you.'

Neither Thorbjorn nor his son had a helmet. Grettir walked to the marsh, and when he came within range he threw the spear at Thorbjorn. The blade was looser on the shaft than Grettir had intended, and it wobbled in flight before falling off and plunging to the ground. Thorbjorn took up his shield and held it in front of him. Then he drew his sword and went to meet Grettir — now that there was no doubt who it was. Grettir drew his sword, but in doing so he turned somewhat, and realized that the boy was behind him. He positioned himself, and when he saw that the boy had come within striking distance, he raised the sax and, with its blunt back edge, struck Arnor so hard on the head that his skull broke. And this was the boy's death.

Then Thorbjorn ran straight at Grettir and struck at him, but Grettir parried with the small shield he held in his left hand, warding off the blow. Grettir then struck directly in front of him with the sax and cleaved Thorbjorn's shield in half. The blow continued and landed on Thorbjorn's head with such force that the sax stood in his brains, and Thorbjorn fell down dead. Grettir gave them no more wounds. He went looking for his spear but could not find it. Then he walked back to his horse and rode out to Reykir, where he announced the killings.

The woman who was working at the meadow saw the killings. Frightened, she ran home and announced that Thorbjorn, along with his son, had been killed. That came as a complete surprise to those who were at home, because no one knew anything about Grettir's travels. Men from the surrounding farms were summoned. Soon a large gathering had assembled, and they carried the bodies to the church. Thorodd Poem-Stump took on the

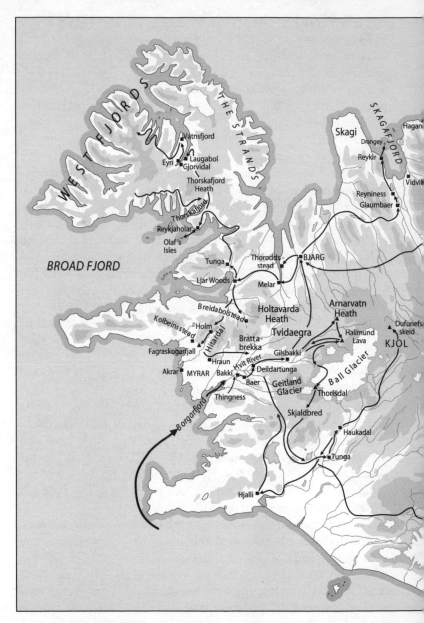

Map 6. Grettir's Travels Through Iceland as an Outlaw, Chapters 47–82.

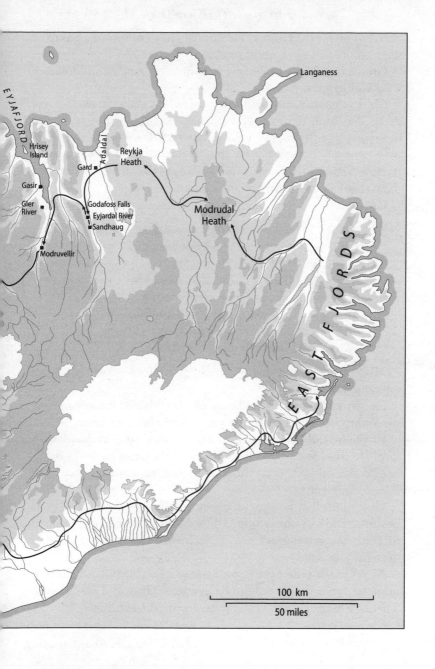

prosecution for the killings. He immediately assembled a group of men, whom he kept around himself.

Grettir rode home to Bjarg. He went to his mother and told her what had happened.

She was pleased. She said that he was now showing that he was descended from the men of Vatnsdal: 'Yet this will now be the beginning and the root of your outlawry. I know for certain that from now on you will not be able to stay here for any length of time on account of Thorbjorn's kinsmen. You have now shown them that you can be stirred into action.'

Grettir spoke this verse:

> 38.   Thor the troll-killer's namesake
> got caught by squalls of weapons
> in Hrutafjord. He fought
> in a frenzy, strong like a bullock.
> Now recompense comes to me
> for the theft of my brother's life,
> a deed unrevenged since Atli
> sank in death on his fair lands.

Mistress Asdis said that was true: 'But I am not sure what you intend to do now.'

Grettir said that he would seek out friends and his kinsmen in the West: 'But I will not cause you any trouble,' he said.

He made ready to leave, and they parted, mother and son, with love. He went first to Melar in Hrutafjord. There he told Gamli, his brother-in-law, everything that had happened concerning Thorbjorn's killing.

Gamli said that he should get out of Hrutafjord as quickly as possible, 'and stay out as long as Thorbjorn's kinsmen are grouped together. We will support you as much as we can in the legal action over Atli's killing.'

Next Grettir rode west across Laxardal Heath, and did not stop until he came to Thorstein Kuggason's farm at Ljar Woods. There he remained for a long time during the autumn.

49. Thorodd Poem-Stump Pursues Grettir

THORODD POEM-STUMP set out to learn who had killed Thorbjorn and his son. When he and his men came to Reykir, he was told that Grettir had been there and had announced his responsibility for the killings. Thorodd surmised what had happened. He now rode over to Bjarg and found many men waiting. He asked whether Grettir was there.

The house-mistress said that he had ridden away, adding that she would not have kept him in hiding: 'Were he here, you would do well to leave matters alone. What has taken place was not too much vengeance for Atli's killing. You never asked or showed interest in what I have suffered from all this. It is now best that things stand as they are.'

Thorodd and the men now rode home, as it seemed there was nothing else to do.

The spear which Grettir lost was not found until a time within the memory of people who are now alive. It was found in the last days of the lawman Sturla Thordarson,* right in the wet swampy ground where Thorbjorn fell. The place is now called Spjotsmyrr* (Spear-Mire). People hold this find as evidence that Thorbjorn was killed there, even if in some places they say he was killed at Midfitjar.

Thorbjorn's kinsmen learned that Grettir was at Ljar Woods, and gathered men to ride there. But when Gamli from Melar heard about the plans of the men of Hrutafjord, he warned Thorstein and Grettir about their movements.

Now aware of these plans, Thorstein sent Grettir over to Tunga to Snorri Godi since, at that time, there was a truce between them. Thorstein advised Grettir that he should ask Snorri for help, but if Snorri should be unwilling, then he advised Grettir to ride west to Reykjaholar to Thorgils Arason: 'And he will take you in for the winter. Stay in the West Fjords until this case is settled.'

Grettir said that he would follow this advice. He rode over to Tunga and met with Snorri Godi. The two talked, and he asked Snorri to take him in.

Snorri replied: 'I am now becoming an old man and do not feel like harbouring outlaws in my house if I am under no obligation to do so. But why has the old boy sent you away?'

Grettir said that Thorstein had often been good to him: 'But now more assistance will be needed than his alone if matters are to turn out successfully.'

Snorri said: 'I will speak in your favour if that might help you, but you must look elsewhere for a place to stay.'

With that they ended their talk. Grettir then went west to Reykjaness. The men of Hrutafjord got as far as Samsstead. There they learned that Grettir had already left Ljar Woods, so they turned back.

50. Grettir and the Foster-Brothers

GRETTIR arrived at Reykjaholar just before the Winter Nights, and asked Thorgils to take him in.

Thorgils said that he was welcome to food, like any other free man. 'But don't expect fine provisions here.' Grettir said that was no difficulty.

'There is one other problem,' said Thorgils. 'There are men staying here who are thought to be very difficult. These are the foster-brothers Thorgeir and Thormod. I don't know how well you will get along together, but they will always have the right to stay here whenever they want. You can remain here if you wish, but work it out so that none of you causes the other any harm.'

Grettir said that he would not be the first to start any trouble, especially since the head of the house wanted it that way. A little later, the foster-brothers arrived home. It was soon clear that there was no love lost between Thorgeir and Grettir, but Thormod was agreeable enough. Farmer Thorgils told the foster-brothers the same that he had said to Grettir, and since Grettir and the other two respected Thorgils so much, they exchanged no taunts, but they were not friendly. In this way, the early part of the winter passed.

It is said that Thorgils owned some islands called Olaf's Isles, which lie out in the fjord about six miles off Reykjaness. Farmer

Thorgils had left there a fine ox which ought to have been brought back home earlier that autumn. Thorgils often mentioned that he wanted to get the ox back before Christmas.

One day the foster-brothers were ready to set out to fetch the ox, provided they could find a third man to help them. Grettir offered to go with them, and they gladly accepted. A little later, the three set out in a ten-oared boat. The weather was cold and the wind was blowing from the north. The ship was beached at Hvalshausholm (Whale's Skull Island). They sailed out, and along the way the wind began to pick up. They reached the islands and got hold of the ox.

Grettir asked them which they would prefer: to put the ox on-board or to hold the ship, since there was a strong surf against the island. They asked him to hold the ship. He placed himself alongside the ship, on the side which faced the sea. The water reached up to his shoulders, but he held the boat perfectly steady. Thorgeir lifted the rear of the ox and Thormod its head, and in this way they got it into the ship. Then they set to rowing. Thormod rowed in the bow, while Thorgeir was in the middle and Grettir at the stern. They held their course back in through the bay, and when they had made it in past Hafraklett (Billy-Goat Cliff), a gale began to blow against them.

Then Thorgeir said: 'The stern is lagging.'

Grettir said: 'The stern would not be left behind, if the rowing up front were all that it should be.'

Thorgeir now worked so hard at his oars that he ripped out both oar-pins. Then he said: 'Throw yourself into it, Grettir, while I repair the pins.'

Grettir now threw himself into rowing while Thorgeir fixed the pins. And when Thorgeir set to rowing again, the oars were so worn out that Grettir shattered them to pieces on the gunwales. Thormod said that it was better to row less than to break things. Grettir grabbed two planks, which were there in the ship, and, punching holes through the ship's side, he rowed so strongly that every timber in the boat groaned. Because it was a good ship and the men somewhat fit, they finally reached Hvalshausholm.

Grettir asked whether they wanted to take the ox home or haul the ship up on land. The foster-brothers chose to pull the ship up. They did so with all the seawater and frozen ice still in it, and by now it was freezing outside. Grettir set off leading the ox, but the animal was so fat and stiff from being tied up that it could scarcely walk. The animal was so out of breath that, going past Tittlingsstead, it could walk no further.

The foster-brothers returned to the house, because neither they nor Grettir were willing to help the other. Thorgils asked about Grettir, and they told where they had left him. Thorgils sent men to go and find Grettir, and when the men were going down the path below Hellishola (Cave-Hills), they saw a man coming towards them with an ox on his back. It was Grettir carrying the ox. Everyone was amazed by Grettir's ability, and Thorgeir began to be jealous of Grettir's strength.

One day, a little after Christmas, Grettir went alone to the hot pools.

Thorgeir learned about this, and said to Thormod: 'Let's head over there and see how Grettir reacts if I attack him as he returns from the hot pool.'

'I don't like this idea,' said Thormod, 'and you will get nowhere with him.'

'Still, I want to go,' said Thorgeir.

He turned, and started down the slope with his axe raised.

Grettir was walking back from the hot pool, and when they met Thorgeir said: 'Is it true, Grettir, that you have said you would never run from just one man?'

'I don't know if that's quite so,' said Grettir, 'but I have never run far from you.'

Thorgeir raised his axe, but just then Grettir ran in under Thorgeir's arms and threw him hard onto the ground.

Thorgeir said to Thormod: 'Are you just going to stand there while this devil crushes me under him?'

Thormod grabbed Grettir's feet and tried to drag him off Thorgeir, but he was unable to do so. Thormod had a sax attached to his belt and started to draw it. Just then Thorgils arrived and told them to show some intelligence and leave Grettir alone.

They did so, and tried to make a joke of it. After this the foster-brothers and Grettir had nothing more to do with each other, as far as we know. People judged that Thorgils's great luck was shown in his being able to keep such dangerous men under control. When spring came, all of them left.

Grettir went north to Thorskafjord (Cod Fjord). He was asked how he had found the food and lodgings at Reykjaholar.

He replied: 'It was this way, that I always enjoyed my food when I was able to get it.'

Next he went west over the heath.

51. Grettir's Outlawry Discussed

THORGILS ARASON rode to the Althing with a large following. All the major leaders of the country came. Skapti the lawman and Thorgils soon met, and the two began talking.

Then Skapti said: 'Is it true, Thorgils, that during the winter you had with you the three men considered the most uncontrollable of all outlaws, and that you were able to keep them in their place so that none caused harm to the other?'

Thorgils said that this was true.

Skapti said: 'That shows great leadership. But what can you say about their different natures? What kind of courage does each of them have?'

Thorgils said: 'All of them, I believe, are thoroughly brave men. Yet two among them know what it is to be fearful. In this, however, they are different: Thormod is a God-fearing man with a deep belief, while Grettir is so scared of the dark that, if able to follow his own wishes, he dares not travel after darkness has fallen. But my kinsman Thorgeir, I think, does not know what it is to be scared.'

'Their natures must be as you say,' said Skapti, and with this they ended their talk.

At this Althing, Thorodd Poem-Stump prosecuted the case for the killing of Thorbjorn Oxen-Might, because he had not been able to bring the suit at the Hunavatn Thing on account of opposition from Atli's kinsmen. Thorodd believed that here at the

Althing his case would have a better chance. Atli's kinsmen sought the advice of Skapti concerning the case, and he said that he could see a legal defence which would bring them payments of full compensation.

Next the cases were put to arbitration, and most people believed that the killings of Atli and Thorbjorn would balance each other out. But when Skapti became aware of this, he went to the arbitrators and questioned their reasoning. They said they counted the men killed as being farmers of equal standing.

Skapti asked: 'Which came first, Grettir's being made an outlaw or Atli's being killed?'

When the answer was worked out, it became clear that there was a week's difference between the time that Grettir was made an outlaw at the Althing and when the killing took place after the Thing.

Skapti said: 'I suspected as much. In preparing your case, you have overlooked a point. You hold one of these men to be a full party to the action, when he was already an outlaw and thus ineligible to defend or prosecute his case. I tell you now that Grettir may not have anything to do with this case of manslaughter. Further he cannot, according to the law, be designated the person responsible to take on the prosecution.'

Then Thorodd Poem-Stump said: 'Who then shall be responsible for the killing of my brother Thorbjorn?'

'You will have to find that out yourself,' said Skapti, 'but Grettir's kinsmen will not rain down money for either Grettir or his actions if it buys him no peace.'

When Thorvald Asgeirsson became aware that Grettir was disqualified from the litigation for Atli's killing, he set about enquiring who was next in line. As Atli's nearest relations, Skeggi, the son of Gamli from Melar, and Ospak, the son of Glum at Eyri from Bitra, were responsible. Both were brave and aggressive men. Thorodd now had to hand over the payment for the killing of Atli valued at two hundreds of silver.

Then Snorri Godi interjected: 'Would you, men of Hrutafjord, now be willing to drop your claim to this payment, if Grettir were to be acquitted? Because in my view, he will be a dangerous man as an outlaw.'

Grettir's kinsmen took this suggestion well, and said that the money was not a concern if Grettir could get back his freedom and rights. Thorodd said that he could see that his position was becoming difficult, and for his part he would accept the agreement.

Snorri said they should first find out whether Thorir of Gard would allow Grettir to be acquitted. But when Thorir heard of the proposal he became enraged, and said that Grettir should never be freed from his outlawry: 'And rather than his being acquitted, more money should be placed on his head so that it is more than for any other outlaw.'

Nothing came of the acquittal, because Thorir was so opposed to it. Gamli and his party took the money for safekeeping, and Thorodd Poem-Stump received no compensation for his brother Thorbjorn. Both Thorir and Thorodd now placed a price on Grettir's head, each offering three marks of silver.* People thought this most unusual, because previously three marks had been the highest price offered. Snorri said that it was unwise to push so hard to keep the man an outlaw when he could cause so much damage. And he added that many would pay for this. Then the men dispersed and started the ride home from the Althing.

52. Thorbjorg the Stout

GRETTIR now travelled across Thorskafjord Heath, before heading down into Langadal (Long Valley). There he seized possessions from the small farmers and took from each whatever he wanted. From some he got weapons and from others clothes. The dealings were often different, but after he was gone all said that they had given up their possessions unwillingly.

At that time Vermund the Slender lived in Vatnsfjord (Lake Fjord). He was the brother of Killer-Styr, and was married to Thorbjorg, the daughter of Olaf the Peacock Hoskuldsson. She was called Thorbjorg the Stout.

Vermund had already ridden to the Althing when Grettir entered Langadal. He travelled down over the ridge to Laugabol (Hot Springs), where a man named Helgi lived. He was the leading man there among the farmers. Grettir took there a good horse owned by the farmer. From there he went further up the fjord to Gervidal (Almost Valley), where a man called Thorkel lived. He had ample riches but was small-minded. Grettir took whatever he wanted, while Thorkel did not dare to resist or try to keep what was his. From there Grettir went to Eyrar and then continued down that side of the fjord, taking food and clothes from everyone. He treated many people roughly, and most found this hard to endure.

Now Grettir moved about boldly and kept no watch. He continued travelling until he came into Vatnsfjardardal (Lake Fjord Valley), where he found a shieling and stayed for many nights. He lazed about in the forest, sleeping and suspecting nothing.

When the herdsmen became aware of his presence, they went down to the farms and announced that a criminal had come into the district, and he appeared to be no easy catch. The farmers now assembled, and there were thirty men. They hid themselves in the forest so that Grettir was unsuspecting. Meanwhile the shepherds kept watch to let the men know when an opportunity arose to get at Grettir. All the time, however, they had no idea who this man was.

It happened one day, while Grettir was lying sleeping, that the farmers decided to attack. When they got close enough to see him, they discussed how they should overcome him while suffering the least loss. They agreed that ten of them would hold him down while the others would tie his feet. But when they piled onto him, Grettir reacted so violently that they were thrown off. Grettir now managed to get onto his knees, but they tossed ropes around him and tied his feet. Next Grettir kicked two of them so hard on their ears that they lay there unconscious. Then, one after the other, they jumped on top of him, and for a long time he struggled violently. In the end they were able to hold him down and finally tied him up.

After that they began to argue about what they should do with him. They asked Helgi from Laugabol to take custody of Grettir until Vermund came home from the Althing.

He answered, saying: 'I have more important things to do than to let my farmhands sit around idly watching him. My lands are difficult to work, and he will never be my responsibility.'

Then they asked Thorkel from Gervidal to take care of him, saying that he was a wealthy man.

Thorkel spoke against the idea, saying there was no chance he would do that: 'Because I am alone in the house, together with my old wife. We live far from other people, and you are not going to put this burden on me.'

'You, Thorolf from Eyri,' they said, 'take Grettir and guard him carefully during the time of the Althing or place him on one of the other farms. But make sure he does not escape, and keep him tied up in the same way that you now receive him.'

He replied: 'I will not take Grettir, because I have neither the supplies nor the wealth to hold him. Besides, he was not seized on my property. It seems to me there is more trouble than honour in looking after him or in having anything to do with him, and I will never take him into my house.'

After that they asked each farmer, and all refused. Later, people who liked to poke fun composed the poem called 'Grettir's Move' about this discussion. They added humorous lines to amuse themselves. After discussing the matter for a long time, they finally came to an agreement. They were determined not to turn their good fortune into bad. So they set about building a gallows to hang Grettir right there in the forest, and thrashed about there, making a lot of noise.

Then they saw three people across the valley. They were riding up towards them. One of the riders wore coloured clothing. They guessed that this would be Mistress Thorbjorg from Vatnsfjord, and so it was. She was on her way to the mountain shieling. A commanding and clever woman, she took charge when Vermund was out of the district and made all decisions when he was not at home.

She changed direction and rode over to the group of men. She was helped down from her horse, and the farmers greeted her well.

She asked them: 'What kind of meeting are you having, or who is this thick-necked man sitting here tied up?'

Grettir named himself and greeted her.

'What drove you to this, Grettir,' she said, 'that you trouble my thingmen?'

'Some things just happen. And I have to be somewhere.'

'What a great misfortune,' she said, 'that these pathetic men should capture you without your being able to do anything about it. But what do you men now intend to do with him?'

The farmers said that they intended to hang him from the gallows because of his crimes.

She replied: 'It may well be that Grettir has given cause for this, but it would be a mistake for you men of Isafjord (Ice Fjord) to take Grettir's life. He is a famous man and from a prominent family, even if he is not a man of good luck. What will you do to save your life, Grettir, if I choose to spare it?'

Grettir answered: 'What would you suggest?'

'You will take an oath,' she said, 'to cause no more trouble here in Isafjord. And you will take no vengeance on those who attacked you.'

Grettir said that she should decide in this, and then he was untied. Later he said that it had been the greatest test of his self-control not to strike those men who had been so boastful about capturing him. Thorbjorg asked him to come home with her, and got him a horse to ride. He now travelled to her home in Vatnsfjord, and waited there until Vermund came home. As mistress of the house, she treated him well, and because of these events her fame spread widely.

Vermund grumbled when he returned home, asking why Grettir was there. Thorbjorg recounted all that had happened between Grettir and the men of Isafjord.

'What good was it,' said Vermund, 'that you saved his life?'

'There were many reasons for my doing so,' said Thorbjorg. 'The first', she said, 'is this: you will be thought a greater chieftain than previously, when it becomes known that you have a wife with the courage to act in this way. Secondly, Grettir's kinswoman Hrefna* would wish that I should keep him from being killed.

The third reason is that Grettir is, in many respects, a man who can do things others cannot.'

'You are in most matters a wise woman,' said Vermund, 'and you have my thanks.'

Then he said to Grettir: 'A rather humiliating outcome for a warrior such as yourself, when insignificant men like these take you into their power. But so it always ends for troublemakers.'

Grettir then said this verse:

> 39. In the middle reaches
>   of that fjord*
>   where the sea carries
>   a roof of ice
>   my luck ran out
>   as the swinish old men
>   tried to get
>   my head in their clutches.

'What did they intend to do with you,' said Vermund, 'after they had captured you?'

Grettir said:

> 40. They were well agreed
>   that I'd earned the reward
>   doled out by Sigar*
>   to a hopeful suitor;
>   so they said until they stumbled
>   on a rowan bush,*
>   which, so to speak, flourished
>   in a leafage of honour.

Vermund said: 'Do you think they would have hanged you, if the decision had been left to them alone?'

Grettir said:

> 41. Too rash, as ever,
>   I'd have stuck my head
>   in their dangled noose
>   but Thorbjorg, whose name
>   means 'protection of Thor',

came to the rescue
of my poetic neck:
she's wise in all matters.

Vermund said: 'Did she invite you to her home?'
Grettir replied:

42.   This willing support
of Thor's two hands
said to follow her home.
She equipped me there
with a good horse
and found safe refuge
for one whose namesake is
a snake* in the grass.

'Yours will be a great but difficult life,' said Vermund, 'and you have been taught to be on guard from your enemies. But I have no wish to harbour you here and in return receive the anger of many powerful men. Your best hope is to seek the assistance of your kinsmen, but few will be prepared to take you in if there is some way they can avoid it. Also, you are not easily disposed to becoming a follower of other men.'

Grettir stayed in Vatnsfjord for some time. From there he went to the West Fjords and sought the support of many men of standing, but always something got in the way so that no one took him in.

53. Grettir's Kinsmen

As the autumn advanced, Grettir again turned south and rode without stopping until he arrived at the farm of his kinsman Thorstein Kuggason at Ljar Wood, where he was greeted well. Thorstein invited him to stay for the winter, and Grettir accepted.

Thorstein was a very industrious man. He was a smith and kept his men hard at work. Grettir was little disposed to working, and, because of this, the two found little in common. Thorstein had a church built on his farm. He also had a bridge built some distance from the farm. It was constructed with great skill. Underneath, on the supporting beams, rings and bells were attached along the outside. If someone went across the bridge, the bells rang and were heard all the way over to Skarfsstead two miles away. Thorstein put much work into this bridge, since he was a skilful blacksmith. Grettir was very good at hammering iron, but most of the time he could not be bothered to do it. Still, he kept himself out of trouble during the winter and, given that, nothing happened worth describing. When the men of Hrutafjord learned that Grettir was with Thorstein, they assembled together in the early spring.

But Thorstein heard about this. He told Grettir that he should find another refuge, 'because I can see that you do not want to work, and I can not abide men who do not earn their keep'.

'Where do you suggest I go?' said Grettir.

Thorstein told him to head south to meet his kinsmen there: 'But come back to me if they are unable to help you.'

Grettir followed this advice. He went south to Borgarfjord to see Grim Thorhallsson and stayed with him until after the Althing. Grim directed him to go see Skapti the Law-speaker at Hjalli. Grettir headed south, travelling the lower path across the heaths and skirting round the settled areas. He continued without stopping until he came to Tunga, the farm of Thorhall Asgrimsson, Ellida-Grim's grandson. Thorhall knew Grettir from his ancestry,* but also Grettir's name was well known throughout the country on account of his feats. Thorhall was a wise man and treated Grettir well. Nevertheless, he did not want Grettir to stay there too long.

54. Lopt

GRETTIR left Tunga and travelled up to Haukadal. From there he went north to Kjol (Keel Mountain), where he stayed for a long time during the summer. By now it was certain that Grettir would relieve men of their goods when they travelled north or south across Kjol, because he had few supplies.

It happened one day, when Grettir was as usual in the northern part of Dufunefsskeid (Dove-Bill Plain), that he saw a man riding from the north across Kjol. He was a big man. He had an excellent horse with a finely worked bridle, studded with nails. He was leading a pack-horse loaded with goods. He wore a broad-brimmed hat which hid his face.

Grettir, admiring the man's horse and possessions, rode out to meet him. Grettir greeted the man and asked his name. The man said he was called Lopt. 'I know what you are called,' he said: 'you would be Grettir the Strong, the son of Asmund, and where are you going?'

'I haven't quite decided on that yet,' said Grettir, 'but I am on an errand to learn if you might lighten your baggage somewhat.'

Lopt answered: 'Why should I give to you what is mine, or is there something you want to give to me in return?'

Grettir replied: 'Haven't you heard that I offer no payment in return for what I take, yet it seems to most that I get what I want?'

Lopt said: 'You can offer those terms to whomever you please, but I will not give up what I own, and let's each go our own way.' With this, he whipped the horse and started riding right past Grettir.

'We will not part so quickly,' said Grettir. Then he seized the reins and pulled them from Lopt's hands and held them with both hands.

Lopt said: 'Go on your way. You will not take what is mine if I am able to hold onto it.'

'That will now be put to the test,' said Grettir.

Lopt reached down past the leather chin-pieces of the bridle and, grabbing the reins between the bit and Grettir's hands, he pulled with such force that the reins slipped through his hands and Lopt had them all to himself.

Grettir looked down at his palms, realizing that this was a man with big hands and not a little strength in them. Watching him leave, Grettir said: 'Where are you going?'

Lopt replied:

> 43.　To the storm's rumbling
> cauldron I venture:
> the glacier drops
> its caves of ice.
> There (solve my riddle!)
> the snake may find
> the little stone
> and the land of the fist.*

Grettir said: 'It's not clear that I will find where you live, if you don't give better directions.'

He spoke then, saying this verse:

> 44.　No easy task
> to hold back the truth,
> if you propose
> paying a visit.
> Beyond the dwellings
> of human folk
> in Borgarfjord,
> it's called Balljokul.

After this, each went his own way. Grettir saw that he did not have the strength to fight with this man. Then Grettir said this verse:

> 45.　Illugi and Atli, brave fellows
> but lukewarm about spear-showers,
> were too far off to help me—
> I'd rather not be so placed—
> when Lopt (a curse on him!) ripped
> the bridle from my hand:
> he showed no fear; if I do,
> that kind woman* wipes her eyes.

Afterwards Grettir went south from Kjol. He rode to Hjalli, where he found Skapti and asked for his protection.

Skapti replied: 'I have been told that you have been acting rather unwisely and robbing men of their possessions. This is unworthy of you, a man of such noble lineage. Your situation could be better spoken of if you were not robbing. But further, because I carry the title of lawman of the land, it is not proper that I take in outlaws and so break the law. My advice to you is to find shelter for yourself in a place where you do not find it necessary to steal others' property.'

Grettir replied that he would gladly do this, but said he had found that he could scarcely tolerate being alone because of his fear of the dark.

Skapti replied that Grettir should not expect to get what he thought best in all matters, 'and trust no one as much as you did in the West Fjords. Many a man's death has come through overconfidence.'

Grettir thanked him for his good advice and returned in the autumn to Borgarfjord. There he found his friend Grim Thorhallsson and told him what Skapti had suggested. Grim advised Grettir to go north to Fiskivotn (Fish Lakes) on Arnarvatn (Eagle Lake) Heath, and so he did.

55. The Outlaw Grim

GRETTIR went up onto Arnarvatn Heath. He built himself a hut, and its remains can still be seen. There he settled in, and since he was now determined to do anything to avoid robbing, he got himself nets and a boat and fished for his food. Life seemed to him dreadful in the mountains, because he was so scared of the dark. When other outlaws learned that Grettir had settled there many were keen to join him, thinking he would protect them.

Grim was the name of a man from the north of Iceland. He was an outlaw. The men of Hrutafjord paid him to kill Grettir, promising freedom and wealth if he succeeded. He travelled to Grettir and asked to be taken in.

Grettir answered: 'I don't think you will be safer with me, and you outlaws are untrustworthy. Still, I don't like being alone, if there were some other choice. Also, I would not mind having someone with me who was ready to do whatever needs doing.'

Grim said that this, and nothing else, was what he wanted to do, and he pressed Grettir to offer him lodgings. In the end, Grettir let himself be persuaded and took him in. Grim stayed there into the winter. He watched Grettir carefully, but found it would not be easy to get at him. Grettir suspected Grim, and kept his weapons handy night and day. Grim did not dare attack while Grettir was awake.

One morning, when Grim returned home from fishing, he went into the hut and stamped his feet. He wanted to know if Grettir was asleep, but Grettir did not stir. He just lay there quietly, with the sax hanging up above him. Grim decided that there would never be a better chance, so he made a lot of noise, wanting to see if Grettir would say something. But there was no response. Judging that Grettir was asleep, he crept quietly to the bed, reached for the sax, and took it down. But just as Grim started to raised it to strike, Grettir jumped onto the floor and grabbed the sax. Then, with his free hand, Grettir gripped Grim's shoulder and threw the man down with such force that Grim lay there almost unconscious.

'In the end you did this,' said Grettir, 'despite all your friendliness.' Then he got the truth out of Grim before killing him. Grettir now seemed to realize what it meant to take in outlaws.

And so the winter passed. Nothing distressed Grettir more than his fear of the dark.

56. Red-Beard

THORIR OF GARD learned where Grettir was hiding and set about devising a plan to kill him. A man was named Thorir Red-Beard. He was exceptionally strong and a great killer, and had been made an outlaw throughout the country. Thorir of Gard sent word to him and, when they met, he asked Red-Beard to act on his behalf and kill Grettir the Strong. Red-Beard replied that this would be no easy matter, saying that Grettir was an intelligent man and on his guard.

Thorir asked him, nevertheless, to try: 'Such an undertaking is fitting for a brave man like you, and in return I will have you released from your outlawry. What's more, I'll give you a good sum of money.'

With this offer, Red-Beard took on the task. Thorir told him what he needed to do in order to overcome Grettir. Red-Beard first travelled towards the eastern part of the country, so that Grettir wouldn't suspect he'd come from Thorir of Gard. He arrived at Arnarvatn Heath after Grettir had been there one winter. And when Red-Beard and Grettir met, Red-Beard asked Grettir to take him in.

Grettir answered: 'I cannot allow others to play with me like the man who came here last autumn. He was cunning in his flattery, but after he had been here a short while he tried to take my life. I will no longer put myself at risk by taking in outlaws.'

Thorir replied: 'I sympathize completely with your distrust of outlaws. You will probably have heard about me, my killings and violent nature, but never anything as base as betraying my master. It is no pleasure being an outlaw, with many thinking one worse than one is. I would not have come here if I had a better choice, but I think we could hold our own against most others if we help each other. You might first risk seeing how you like me, but send me away if you find me deceitful.'

Grettir answered: 'I will risk it with you, but know this for certain, if I suspect treachery in you it will be your death.'

Thorir said that was the way it should be. With this, Grettir took him in and quickly found that Thorir had the strength of two men in whatever he undertook. He was prepared to do whatever Grettir assigned him. There was nothing that Grettir himself had to do, and not since he became an outlaw had life been so good. Even so, he remained so much on his guard that Thorir never found an opportunity to get at him.

After Thorir Red-Beard had spent two winters with Grettir on the heath, he began to tire of being there. His thoughts now turned to how he might catch Grettir unawares.

One night, in the spring, a fierce storm began blowing as they slept. Grettir awoke and asked where their boat was. Thorir sprang up and ran out to the boat. He broke it apart, and threw the pieces in all directions as though the wind had tossed them about.

After that he went back to the hut and said loudly: 'Things have not gone well, my friend. Our boat is all broken to pieces and the nets lie far out in the water.'

'Then go out and get them,' said Grettir. 'My guess is that it's your fault the boat is ruined.'

Thorir answered: 'It is this way. I am not much of a swimmer, but in most other things I can hold my own against any man. Surely you are aware that I have not caused you any extra work since I came to you. I would not be asking this if I were capable of doing it myself.'

Grettir stood up, took his weapons, and went out to the lake. There was, at that spot, a narrow point of land jutting out into the water. On one side was a large cove. The water, which was deep right up to the land, had undermined the bank so that there was an overhang jutting out above it.

Grettir said: 'Swim out after the net, and let me see how able a man you are.'

'I told you before,' said Thorir, 'I can't swim, but where is your own strength and courage?'

'I will get the net,' said Grettir, 'but do not betray my trust in you.'

Thorir replied: 'Stop accusing me of treachery and cowardice.'

Grettir said: 'You alone will prove who you are.'

Then Grettir threw off his clothes and weapons and plunged in after the nets. When he had gathered the nets together, he returned to land and threw them up onto the bank. As he was climbing out of the water, Thorir grabbed hold of the sax and, raising it to strike, he ran towards Grettir, who was on the bank getting onto his feet. But just as Thorir struck, Grettir threw himself back into the water and sank like a stone. Thorir watched the lake carefully, intending to stop Grettir from getting back onto land if he surfaced. But Grettir now swam underwater skirting the bank, something which had not occurred to Thorir.

Grettir continued until he rounded the point and entered the cove behind Thorir. There he climbed onto the land, and Thorir knew nothing before Grettir was lifting him up over his head. Then Grettir threw Thorir down so hard that the sax flew from his hand. Grettir picked it up and, without saying a word, cut off Thorir's head. And so his life ended.

After this, Grettir never had anything more to do with outlaws. Still, he could not tolerate being alone.

57. Thorir Ambushes Grettir

AT the Althing, Thorir of Gard learned that Thorir Red-Beard had been killed. Now he realized that dealing with Grettir would not be easy, and decided that, after the Althing, he himself would ride west over the lower heath with nearly eighty men. His plan was to take Grettir's life. But when Grim Thorhallsson learned of these plans, he sent word to Grettir, warning him to be on his guard. Grettir now kept a sharp eye on people's movements.

One day he saw many men riding towards his hut. He quickly climbed up into a cleft, between the cliffs, but decided not to run just yet since he still had not seen the whole group. But Thorir was soon upon him with all his followers, and he commanded his men to separate Grettir's head from his body. He added that there was little the outlaw could do now.

Grettir replied: 'Arriving at the well is one thing; drinking is another. You have long sought this moment, and some of you will acquire marks of the game before we part.'

Thorir now urged his men to the attack. The cleft between the cliffs was narrow, so that Grettir could defend the opening in front of him. Yet it seemed to him strange that he was not attacked from behind, and no trouble came from there. Now some of Thorir's men fell and some were wounded, but still they made no headway.

Then Thorir said: 'I had heard it said that Grettir was a champion because of his strength and courage. Still, I had not understood that he was as filled with sorcery* as now I see, because behind him twice as many men are killed as from the group that he faces. Now I realize we are dealing with a troll and not with a man.'

With that he ordered his men to pull back, and they did so. Grettir was exhausted and himself surprised by what had happened. Thorir now turned away, and he and his men rode north through the districts. People thought his trip had ended shamefully. Thorir lost eighteen men, and many others were wounded. Grettir now climbed up the cleft, where he found a huge man sitting upright with his back to the cliff. The man was badly wounded. Grettir asked him his name.

The man replied that he was called Hallmund. 'And I can give you this clue to aid in remembering me: you found I held the reins tightly when we met at Kjol during the summer. Now I think that I have repaid you.'

'It is certain', said Grettir, 'that you have acted nobly towards me, though I do not know when I will find a way to repay you.'

Hallmund said: 'It is my wish that you come home with me, because you must find it lonely here on the heath.'

Grettir said he would gladly do that, and they set off together, travelling south to Balljokul (Ball Glacier). There Hallmund had a large cave and a large, impressive daughter. They treated Grettir well, and she healed their wounds. Grettir stayed there for a long time during the summer.

He composed a poem about Hallmund in which this verse is found:

> 46. Hallmund ascends with sloping
>   steps to the mountain hall.*
>
>   And this verse was also in it.

> 47. Swords with an adder's bite
>   glided on wounding paths
>   through flesh and bone, as fighting
>   raged at Hrutafjord.
>   Now those thugs are hosting wakes
>   for the dead killed at Kelduhverfi.
>   Hallmund climbed from his cave
>   to aid me in my escape.*

It is said that Grettir killed six men in the fight, and Hallmund twelve. Toward the end of the summer Grettir longed to return to the inhabited districts to see his friends and kinsmen. Hallmund asked him to visit him when he travelled again in the south of the country, and Grettir promised to do so.

First Grettir went west to Borgarfjord and from there to the Breidafjord (Broad Fjord) Dales. There he asked Thorstein Kuggason's advice as to where he might now turn for support.

To Thorstein, it seemed that Grettir's enemies were now increasing, and he said that few would be willing to take him in: 'You might, however, go south to the Myrar region and see how things turn out.'

In the autumn Grettir went south to Myrar.

58. Grettir's Cave

AT that time Bjorn the Champion of Hitardal (Hot River Valley) was living at Holm. He was the son of Arngeir and the grandson of Bersi the Godless, the son of Bjalki, the first settler to claim land in Hrutafjord, as previously told. Bjorn was a prominent chieftain and a hard man. He often took in outlaws. Grettir arrived at Holm, and Bjorn greeted him well because there had been friendship between their kinsmen in earlier generations. Grettir asked Bjorn if he was willing to give him some help, and Bjorn replied that Grettir now had so many enemies throughout the country that men would avoid assisting him, lest they too became outlaws: 'Nevertheless, I will help you if you leave those men in peace who are under my protection, however you treat other men here in the district.'

Grettir agreed to this.

Bjorn said: 'It has occurred to me that up in the mountain that runs along the west bank of the Hit (Hot) River there is a good defensive spot, which also could be hidden from below if you put your mind to it. It is a cave formed by lava, which at that spot bored a tunnel through the mountain. You can see it from the road just below. Between the road and the cave there is a gravelly slope, so steep that few men would make it to the top if a capable man were up there defending the lair. Now I believe that the best plan, considering your options, is for you to stay there, because from there you can get provisions below in the Myrar district and all the way out to the sea.

Grettir said that he would follow Bjorn's advice, since he was willing to offer it. Grettir then went to Fagraskogar (Fair Forest) Mountain and settled in. He covered the cave's mouth with a piece of grey homespun cloth, and from the path below this gave the impression that one could still see unobstructed into the cave. He acquired provisions down in the settlements, and the Myra-men found Grettir an unwelcome guest.

At that time Thord Kolbeinsson* was living at Hitarness. He was a good poet. Bjorn and he were enemies, so Bjorn was not displeased to see Grettir troubling Thord's men or taking their livestock.

Grettir often visited Bjorn, and they pitted themselves against each other in many contests. *Bjorn's Saga* notes that people thought the two equal in skills, but most people are of the opinion that Grettir was the strongest man to have lived in the country following the time when Orm Storolfsson and Thoralf Skolmsson* ended their contests of strength. The two of them, Grettir and Bjorn, swam the length of the Hit River all the way from the inland lake down to the sea. They also placed stepping stones across the river, and these were so large that neither the river's rise nor ice from the spring thaws under the glacier have dislodged them.

Grettir remained an entire year in Fagraskogar Mountain, and no attack was made against him even though many people lost their property. There was really nothing they could do, since he had such an easily defensible spot and was in such close friendship with those who lived nearby.

59. Gisli Sheds His Clothes

THERE was a man called Gisli. He was the son of Thorstein Kuggason whose death Snorri Godi had arranged.* Gisli was a big, strong man who liked showy weapons and clothing. He thought highly of himself and was given to boasting. He was a seafaring trader and, arriving from abroad, he put in at the Hvit River the summer after Grettir had already been one winter up in the mountain. Thord Kolbeinsson rode to the ship. Gisli greeted him well and offered him whatever he wished from the trade goods. Thord accepted the offer and the two fell to talking.

Gisli asked: 'Is it true, as I have heard, that you are having trouble finding a way to rid yourself of the outlaw who is causing you so much damage?'

Thord said: 'We have not yet tried. Many think that he is not easy to attack, as a good number of men have experienced.'

'No wonder, then, if you find the going tough with Bjorn, since you cannot get this outlaw off your back. The worst of it is that I will be too far away this winter to change matters for you.'

'You will find it is easier to listen to talk about Grettir than to deal with him,' said Thord.

'You don't need to warn me about Grettir,' replied Gisli. 'I faced greater dangers when I was out raiding with King Knut the Great in the British Isles. I was thought capable of defending my bench there on the ship. If by chance I should meet Grettir, I would put trust in myself and my weapons.'

Thord replied that if Gisli should kill Grettir, the work would not go unrewarded. 'More money has now been put on Grettir's head than on any other outlaw's. Earlier it was six marks of silver,* but now, this past summer, Thorir of Gard added another three marks. People are of the opinion that this should be enough to get the work done.'

'People will do just about anything for money,' said Gisli, 'not least we merchants. But now we should be careful about such talk. It may be that Grettir will be more on his guard if he learns that I am making plans with you and your friends. I have already planned to spend the winter out at Olduhrygg (Wave Ridge). But isn't his hideout on the way there, just off the road? He will not see anything suspicious, as I will not be dragging a crowd of men with me.'

Thord was well pleased with this plan. He rode home and kept the matter quiet.

But as the saying goes, the bushes have ears. Friends of Bjorn from Hitardal were nearby while Gisli and Thord spoke, and they told Bjorn everything. When Bjorn and Grettir met, Bjorn warned Grettir, saying that now they might see just how well this man handled himself.

'There might be some fun in it if you were to rough him up, but don't kill him if you can avoid it.'

Grettir grinned, but otherwise made little of it.

Just before the autumn sheep round-up, Grettir went down to the Flysja District to find some sheep, and was able to get hold of four gelded* rams. The farmers became aware of his movements and started tracking him. Just as he got back to the foot of the slope, the farmers caught up with him and tried to separate him from the sheep without attacking him with weapons. Altogether there were six farmers, and they placed themselves on the path, attempting to bar his way. Grettir intended to keep the sheep, and started to lose his temper. He grabbed hold of two farmers, and threw them down the slope with such force that they lay there unconscious. When the others saw that, their courage failed them. Grettir now took the sheep and, locking their horns together, he threw two over each shoulder. Then he climbed up to his lair. The farmers, aware that things had gone badly for them, turned back, and they thought themselves worse off than before.

Gisli stayed at the ship during the autumn until it was time to lay down the rollers* and haul the ship onto land. He had much to do in preparing for the winter stay, and because of this he was late in riding out and left just before the Winter Nights. He went north and spent the night at Hraun (Lava), south of the Hit River.

That morning, before setting out, Gisli said to his followers: 'Today we ride in coloured clothing to let the outlaw see that we are not the usual, everyday travellers who pass this way.'

They were three together, and they did as Gisli said. When they had ridden across the river, he spoke again: 'Here is where I have been told the outlaw lives, up in these mountains, and it is not easy to move about in this area. Don't you think he will want to come to see our belongings?' They agreed that this was his usual custom.

That morning Grettir got up early in his lair. The weather was cold and icy. Snow had fallen, though only a little. He saw three men riding from the south across the Hit River. The sun shone on their fine clothes and glanced off their enamelled shields.

Grettir realized who these men were, and began to feel the need to get hold of some expensive clothing. He was also curious to meet these men after all their talk, so he took his weapons and ran down the rocky slope. When Gisli heard the noise in the stones above, he said: 'A man, and a rather big one at that, is coming down the mountainside to meet us. Let's act bravely, because the prey is falling into our hands.'

His followers commented that this man would not be running into their hands if he were unsure of himself: 'But it is best that the one who asks for trouble gets it.' Then they leapt off their horses just as Grettir arrived. He grabbed hold of the clothes-bag attached to the saddle behind Gisli, and said: 'This I want. I often stoop for trifles.'

Gisli answered: 'Not so fast, don't you know with whom you are dealing with?'

'That is not altogether clear to me,' replied Grettir, 'but this time I will not put so much emphasis on the difference between us, since I ask for so little.'

'It may be that you think it little,' said Gisli, 'but I would rather lose thirty hundred ells of woollen cloth.* Obviously you are not a man of moderation. Attack him, boys, and let's see what he is made of.'

So they attacked him. Grettir let himself be pushed back to a boulder, which stood beside the road. It is now called Grettir's-Lift, and from there he defended himself. Gisli continually urged his men on, and Grettir now saw that Gisli was not as brave as he had made himself out to be, since he always positioned himself behind his men. Growing tired of the exchange, Grettir made a sweeping cut with the sax and it dealt one of Gisli's followers a death-blow. Then, leaping from the stone, he attacked so fiercely that Gisli was pushed right to the edge of the mountain. Next Gisli's other companion fell.

Grettir now said: 'There is little evidence from this encounter that you were brave elsewhere, and you have parted badly with your friends.'

Gisli replied: 'The fire is hottest for the one it burns, and only bad comes from fighting with a man of such extraordinary strength.'

They had not exchanged more than a few blows before Gisli threw down his weapons and started running away alongside the mountain. Grettir followed, giving him time to throw away whatever he liked, and each time Gisli saw some distance between them, he threw off a piece of clothing. Grettir never pushed so hard that there wasn't some space between them. Gisli now ran west all the way over the mountain, then right through Kaldardal (Cold River Valley), across Aslaugarhlid (Aslaug's Slope), and continued above Kolbeinsstead, after which he ran out onto Borgarhraun (Cliff Lava).

By then Gisli was down to his linen underclothes, and exhausted. Grettir followed behind, but always left an arm's length between them. He ripped off a big branch from a bush. Gisli continued without stopping and kept going all the way west to Haffjardar (Sea Fjord) River, which was swollen and difficult to cross. Gisli was about to go right into the river when Grettir rushed up and grabbed him. Immediately Grettir felt the difference in strength between them. He pushed Gisli down under him and said: 'Are you the Gisli who wanted to find Grettir Asmundarson?'

Gisli answered: 'I have now found him, but I am unclear how we will part. Keep now what you have taken, but let me go free.'

Grettir said: 'You will have trouble grasping what I am going to say to you, so I need to give you a reminder.' Then he pulled Gisli's shirt over his head and used the branch on his back and both sides. Gisli kept trying to get away, but Grettir whipped him thoroughly before letting him go. Gisli realized how little he liked taking lessons from Grettir, and was determined to avoid another whipping. From that time on he made sure that he would never again deserve a lashing.

When Gisli got back onto his feet, he jumped into a big pool in the river and from there swam across. He arrived exhausted in the night at the farm called Hrossholt (Horse Wood). There he lay for a week in bed, his body swollen. After this, he went to his winter lodgings.

Grettir went back and picked up the things Gisli had discarded. He took them home with him, and Gisli never saw them again. Many thought that Gisli had been treated reasonably, given his arrogance and bragging. Grettir made this verse about their meeting:

> 48.   When it comes to a contest at biting,
> timid horses that don't care
> to chomp outrun their toothy
> foes and don't tire first.
> Such a stranger to glory
> I saw myself today,
> when Gisli raced off with a will
> and crossed Myrar farting.*

The following spring, Gisli prepared to go to his ship and took full precautions that none of his goods were sent south by the route that lay under the mountain, saying that the devil himself was there. Gisli rode south along the coast all the way to the ship and he and Grettir never met again. He was thought of no account from then on, and he is now out of the saga.

The situation between Thord Kolbeinsson and Grettir now worsened, and Thord tried numerous ways to drive Grettir away or to kill him.

60. The Fight at Grettir's Spit

WHEN Grettir had been two winters in Fagraskogar Mountain and the third was beginning, he went south into the Myrar region to the farm called Laekjarbug (Stream Bend). There, against the owner's will, he took six gelded rams. Then he went down to Akrar (Planted Fields), where he took two cattle for slaughter as well as many sheep. Next he set about driving the livestock northwards, following the bank of the Hvit River.

When the farmers became aware of his movements, they sent word to Thord at Hitarness, requesting that he commit himself to killing Grettir. Thord refused, but the farmers insisted. In response, Thord had his son Arnor,* the one later called Jarlaskald (Jarl's-Poet), go with them, and he urged the men not to let Grettir escape. Now messengers were sent throughout the district.

Bjarni was the name of a man who lived at Jorvi in the Flysja District. He assembled men on the western side of the Hvit River, and the plan was for each group to arrive from its side of the river. Grettir was accompanied by two men. One was named Eyjolf, the son of a farmer from Fagraskogar and a capable man. Another man rode with them. Thorarin from Akrar and Thorfinn from Laekjarbug arrived first. They had with them altogether nearly twenty men.

Grettir now decided to wade across the river, but just then Thorgeir, Arnor, and Bjarni arrived with their men on that bank. A narrow spit of land jutted out into the river on Grettir's side, and when he saw the men arriving he drove the livestock out onto the tip of the spit. Grettir never wanted to give anything back once it had fallen into his hands.

The Myra-men immediately launched a spirited attack. Grettir told his followers to make sure that no one got around to attack him from behind. In front of him there was only enough room for a few men to attack simultaneously. The fighting was fierce. Grettir struck on both sides with his sax, and it was not easy for the men to get at him.

Now some of the Myra-men fell and others were wounded. The men on the west bank of the river were slow in crossing, because the ford was a good distance away. The fighting had not gone on for long before the farmers drew back. Thorarin from Akrar was old and did not take part in the attack.

By the time Thrand Thorarinsson and Thorgils Ingjaldsson arrived, the battle had stopped. With them were Thorgeir Thorhallsson from Hitardal and Steinolf Thorleifsson from Hraundal (Lava Valley). These men now urged another attack, and once more the fight was fierce.

Grettir saw that he had only two choices: either to flee or to chance everything on the fight. Now he threw himself forward with such fury that no one was able to stand against him. Because of the numbers, Grettir assumed that escape was impossible, and he set his mind to accomplishing the most he could before falling. Grettir, determined to face a worthy opponent, advanced towards Steinolf from Hraundal. He struck at Steinolf's head, cleaving it apart right down to the shoulders. Then he suddenly hewed at Thorgils Ingjaldsson, slicing into the waist so that he cut the man almost in half. Now Thrand came forward to avenge his kinsmen. Grettir struck at his thigh and cut away all the muscles, so that Thrand was immediately out of the fight. Following this, Grettir gave Finnbogi a serious wound.

Then Thorarin called out and commanded the men to retreat. 'The longer you fight with him the worse you get, because he is choosing his targets.' The men did as Thorarin said and fell back. Five of them were killed. Another five were maimed for life and on the verge of death. Almost all the others who took part in the fight had wounds.

Grettir was exhausted, though only a little wounded. Now the Myra-men retreated. They had suffered great losses, including many capable man. Because those men on the west bank of the river had found the going difficult, they did not arrive until the fight was over. When they saw how badly things had gone, Arnor decided not to put himself in danger. Later his father and many others severely reproached them, and it was people's opinion that he was no hero. The place where they fought is now called Grettisodd (Grettir's Spit).

Grettir and his men now took horses for themselves and rode up to the mountain. All of them had wounds. When they came to Fagraskogar, Eyjolf stayed behind. The farmer's daughter was outside and asked the news. Grettir gave her an account of what had happened, and said this verse:

49. I tell you, attentive lady,
    those grievous wounds to the head
    that Steinolf took won't heal
    in a hurry. Some died outright.
    And Thorgils's life's beyond hope,
    he's a bag of shattered bones.
    They say that eight other landed
    men have bitten the dust.

After this, Grettir returned to his cave and stayed there throughout the winter.

61. Grettir's Travels

WHEN Grettir and Bjorn next met, Bjorn said that it seemed to him that matters had taken a serious turn. 'And it will not be safe for you to remain here much longer. You have now killed from among my kinsmen and friends, but I will not break my promises to you as long as you remain here.'

Grettir replied that he had been forced to defend life and limb. 'But I regret that you are offended.' Bjorn replied that what was done was done.

A little later, men who had lost their kinsmen because of Grettir came to Bjorn, demanding that he should not let this outlaw stay there any longer to remind them of their shame. Bjorn answered that it would be taken care of as soon as the winter ended.

Thrand, the son of Thorarin at Akrar, was cured of his wounds. Later he became a notable man and married Steinun, the daughter of Hrut from Kambsness.* Thorleif from Hraundal, the father of Steinolf, was an important man, and from him are descended the men of Hraundal.

There are no reports of further encounters between Grettir and the Myra-men during this period of his stay in the mountain. Bjorn maintained his friendship with Grettir, although Bjorn's friends thinned somewhat on account of his allowing Grettir to stay there. People took it badly that no compensation was paid for their kinsmen.

Around the time of the Althing, Grettir left Myrar. He went once more to Borgarfjord, seeking Grim Thorhallsson's advice as to which way he should now turn. Grim said that he was not able to lodge him, so Grettir now went to his friend Hallmund, and stayed there until the end of the summer.

In the autumn, Grettir went to Geitland, and waited there until clear weather came. Then he went up onto Geitland Glacier and headed south-eastwards across the ice. He took with him a kettle and some fire flint. It is people's belief that he was following Hallmund's directions, because Hallmund was familiar with many places.

Grettir pushed on until he found a valley in the glacier. It was long and narrow, and enclosed on all sides by the overhanging ice. He found a spot where he could climb down into the valley, and once there, he saw fair slopes grown with grass and small bushes. There were hot springs, and Grettir guessed that it must be heat from under the earth that kept the ice from closing in over this dale. A stream flowed through the valley, with flat banks on both sides. The sun only reached in for a short time each day, and he was surprised by how many sheep were there. They were much healthier and fatter than any he had ever seen.

Grettir now began building a hut from the wood he found there. For food he caught the sheep, and one of them gave more meat than two sheep in other places. There was one reddish-coloured, hornless ewe with her lamb, and this one seemed to Grettir best of all on account of her size. He was curious about the lamb,

---

Map 7. Grettir Spends Three Years in the Myrar Region. He lives by robbing and stays in a cave in Fagraskogar Mountain not far from the home of his friend, Bjorn the Hitardal Champion. The local farmers attack Grettir at Grettir's Spit. Bjorn asks Grettir to leave the area.

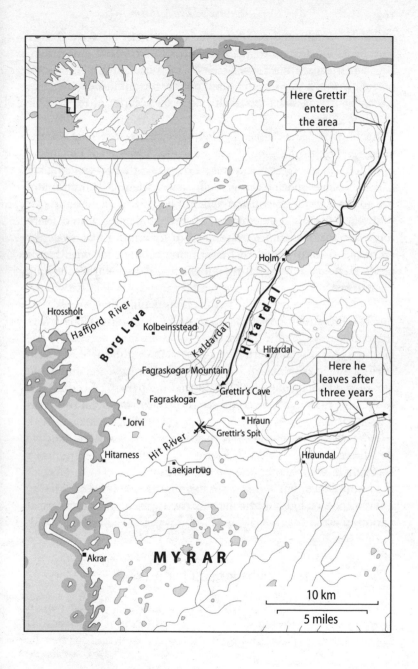

Here Grettir
enters
the area

Holm

Hrossholt

Haffjord River

Borg Lava

Kolbeinsstead

Kaldardal

Hitardal

Hitardal

Fagraskogar Mountain

Here he
leaves after
three years

Grettir's Cave

Fagraskogar

Hraun

Jorvi

Hit River

Grettir's Spit

Hitarness

Hraundal

Laekjarbug

Akrar

MYRAR

10 km

5 miles

which he caught and slaughtered. There was half a weight* of suet in it, but the meat was even better. When the ewe missed her lamb, she climbed every night up onto Grettir's hut and bleated so much that Grettir could not get a night's sleep. He came to repent having slaughtered the lamb on account of the trouble she caused him.

Each evening, as dusk settled, he heard someone up the valley calling to the sheep, and then the whole flock ran to the same fold. It was Grettir himself who said that a half-troll, a giant named Thorir, controlled the valley and that he had been under his power. Grettir named the valley Thorisdal after him. Grettir said that Thorir had daughters, and that he enjoyed himself with them and that they too were pleased to have him there, since the place was seldom visited. When it came time for fasting, Grettir observed the custom by eating only suet and liver during the long Lenten fast.

There are no reports of anything happening that winter, and finally Grettir found the place so dull that he could no longer stay there. Then he left the valley and, walking south across the glacier, arrived at the southern edge towards the middle of Skjaldbreid (Broad Shield Mountain). There he raised a large flat stone and chiselled a hole through it. He said that if a person placed his eye to the hole in the slab, he could see the ravine running down from Thorisdal.

After this, Grettir travelled throughout the southern districts and then went to the East Fjords. He continued this journey throughout the summer and into the winter. He went to meet all the leading men, but was received so poorly that nowhere was he offered food or lodging. So he returned to the north, staying at various places.

62. Hallmund's Death Poem

A LITTLE before Grettir left Arnarvatn Heath, a man named Grim came up onto the heath. He was the son of the widow at Kropp. He had killed the son of Eid Skeggjason, and for that he was made an outlaw. Now he settled in where Grettir had previously stayed, and he found the fishing in the lake good. Hallmund grew resentful that Grim had taken Grettir's spot and decided that the newcomer should not benefit from being there, even if he fished well.

It happened one day that Grim caught one hundred fish. He brought them home to his hut and hung them outside. But the following morning, when he went out, all the fish were gone. He found this strange, but went down to the lake and now caught two hundred fish. These he brought home and prepared them outside. But everything went the same way as before, and in the morning all the fish were gone. Now he knew that things were not as they should be.

The third day he caught three hundred fish and took them home. But this time he kept watch, peering out through a hole in the outer door to see if anyone approached the hut. Evening fell, and before a third of the night had passed Grim heard someone walking outside, and these were not light steps. When he was certain something was going on, he picked up his axe. It was a very sharp weapon. He wanted to know this person's intentions. The stranger had a large basket on his back. He set it down and looked around, but saw no one outside. He examined the fish and, liking what he saw, stuffed all the fish into his basket. He filled it completely, and there was so much fish that Grim guessed a horse could not have carried more. The stranger now strained to lift his burden, and just as he was getting to his feet Grim ran out of the hut and struck at the man's neck, using two hands.

The axe sank up to the hammer end. But the stranger sprang up, and set off at a run with the basket on his back. He headed southwards towards the mountain, with Grim following behind, wanting to know the outcome. They went all the way south to Ball Glacier, where the man entered a cave. A fire burned brightly inside the cave, and a woman sat beside it. She was large but good-looking. Grim heard her greet the man as father. She called him Hallmund, and when he threw off his burden it landed hard and he sighed loudly. She asked why he was bloody.

He answered, saying this verse:

> 50.   No man can trust
>   in his own unaided
>   strength, that's clear
>   to me — because
>   the courage of heroes
>   ebbs away
>   on the death day
>   as their luck runs out.

She enquired closely about the events, and he told her everything.

'Listen now,' he said, 'I will recount my deeds in a poem which you shall carve in runes* on a staff.

She prepared to do this. Then Hallmund spoke his poem, and this is part of it:

> 51.   My strength was esteemed
>   when with force enough
>   I buffeted Grettir
>   away from my reins.
>   With a glance I saw
>   how he stood gazing
>   a good long while
>   down at his palms.*

> 52.   Next was the time
>   that Thorir ventured
>   onto the heath
>   by Arnarvatn,
>   and just the two
>   of us enjoyed
>   a game of spear-points
>   against their eighty.

> 53.   Grettir's hands
>   showed the form of a master,
>   with glancing blows
>   against their shields;

I heard, though, that our
opponents rated
the marks left by me
more severe by far.

54.   As for those fellows
who sneaked from behind,
I sent their hands and
their heads flying,
with the end result
that eighteen bodies
from Kelduhverfi
littered the heath.

55.   Trolls and their kindred,
who dwell in the crags,
I have dealt with harshly.
I have taken on many
evil creatures.
Half-breeds and half-trolls
met death through me.
Likewise, I've shown
hatred to almost
all children of elves
and evil spirits.

Hallmund recounted many exploits in the poem, since he had travelled widely throughout the country.

Then his daughter said: 'This was not the kind of man to let things pass, nor is it surprising, considering how you treated him. But who will now avenge you?'

Hallmund replied: 'It is not certain that vengeance will be taken. I believe Grettir would seek to avenge me, if he were able to come. Still, it will not be easy to go against this man's good luck, because his future is bright.'

Hallmund's strength ebbed as the poem progressed, and as soon as it was completed, he died. His daughter, overcome with emotion, broke down and wept.

Then Grim came forward and told her to take heart: 'Everyone must die when his time is up, and this end was largely caused by his own actions. I could scarcely sit by and watch him rob me.'

She agreed that there was much in what he said, 'and bullying ends badly'.

Her spirits picked up with this talk. Grim remained in the cave many nights. He learned the poem and theirs was a gentle exchange.

Grim stayed up on Arnarvatn Heath the winter following Hallmund's death. After that, Thorkel located Grim on the heath and they fought. Their encounter ended with Grim's holding Thorkel's life in his hands but choosing not to kill him. Thorkel then brought Grim back home with him and arranged his passage abroad. He gave him a good sum of money, and it was thought that the two had acted well towards each other. Grim later became a trader, and many stories are told about him.

63. A Fine Joke

Now it is time to tell that Grettir set out from the East Fjords. He travelled secretly, taking care not to be noticed, because he wanted to avoid Thorir. During the summer he camped out on Modrudal Heath. He also stayed at other places, and sometimes was on Reykja Heath. Thorir learned that Grettir was on Reykja Heath, and gathered men to ride up onto the heath. This time he was determined not to let Grettir get away. Grettir had scarcely any warning before the men were upon him. At the time he was staying in one of the summer dairy huts close by the path. There was a second man with him. When they saw the others approaching, they knew they had to act quickly. Grettir told the other man that they should force the horses onto the ground and then drag them into the hut. And this they did. Thorir now rode past, heading north over the heath, and missed the friends in their hiding-place. Finally, he turned back.

When the men had ridden past, heading west, Grettir said: 'They will not think much of their journey if we do not meet.

You look after the horses, while I will go to meet them. Wouldn't it be a fine joke if they don't recognize me?'

His companion tried to dissuade him, but Grettir decided to go anyway. He changed clothing and put on a cloak with a broad-brimmed hat that hung down over his face. With a staff in his hand, he walked onto the path to meet them. They greeted him and asked if he had seen men riding across the heath.

'I think I have just seen the men you are looking for. You have almost found them, because they were just to the south of the marshy ground over there on the left.'

When they heard this, they galloped out into the swamp. The bogs were so deep that they made little progress, and they had to pull their own horses out. They spent much of the day doing this, and cursed the vagrant for making fools of them.

Meanwhile Grettir returned quickly to his companion. When they were reunited, Grettir spoke this verse:

> 56.　I will not ride into a clash
> 　　　with loud-mouthed, shield-toting men;
> 　　　for now I leave on my own,
> 　　　though some day I must fight to the end.
> 　　　I have no wish to confront
> 　　　shield-bashers keyed up for a skirmish.
> 　　　Don't fret that I've lost my mind —
> 　　　I am just awaiting my chance.
> 　　　Thorir's got strength of numbers,
> 　　　so best I draw back for now.

The two now rode west as fast as they could. Grettir rode right past Thorir's farm at Gard, and this was before Thorir and his men had returned home from the mountains. Just as the two riders approached the farm, they crossed paths with a man. He joined them without recognizing who they were. They saw a woman standing outside. She was young and finely dressed. Grettir asked who she was, and the man said she was Thorir's daughter. Then Grettir said this verse:

> 57.　Mention this to your father,
> 　　　wise woman with gold trinkets,

> even though what I say
> seldom has much impact:
> The ride I did took me round
> these broad acres, past your home field.
> Only two companions I had.
> My war-band has shrunk of late.

From this verse the newcomer guessed who they were. He rode to the farm and announced that Grettir had ridden past. Even before Thorir returned home, many were of the opinion that Grettir had pulled the wool over his and his men's eyes. Thorir now set spies to keep watch for Grettir, wherever he might appear. Grettir decided to send his follower into the west with the horses. Then he walked up into the mountains, disguised in a hooded cloak. The plan worked, and at the beginning of winter Grettir went north without being recognized.

Everyone now thought that Thorir had come off equally badly or even worse than in his previous dealings with Grettir.

64. More Christmas Hauntings

STEIN was the name of a priest who lived at the farm of Eyjardal River in Bardardal. He was a good farmer and a wealthy man. His son was named Kjartan. He was a strong young man, almost full grown.

Thorstein the White was the name of the man living at Sandhaugar (Sand Hills) south of Eyjardal River. His wife was named Steinvor, a young woman full of life. The couple had small children at this time. People thought the farm at Sandhaugar was much haunted by trolls.

It happened, two years before Grettir came north, that Steinvor, the housewife at Sandhaugar, went according to custom to Christmas mass at Eyjardal River. Her husband stayed at home that evening. In the night, after people had gone to bed, they heard a loud noise in the hall, and moving towards the farmer's bed. No one dared to get up and see what was causing the noise, because so few people were inside. In the morning the housewife returned home, but her husband was missing, and no one knew what had become of him. The year now passed with no change.

The following winter, the housewife again wanted to attend Christmas mass. She asked her farmhand to stay at home. He was reluctant, but said she should decide. Everything went the same way as before, and now the farmhand disappeared. The people thought this very strange, but when they saw traces of blood in the outer entrance-way, they surmised that a monster had taken both men. News of these happenings spread widely through the countryside.

Grettir learned of these events and, because he was so good at putting a stop to hauntings and the walking dead, he went to Bardardal. He arrived at Sandhaugar the day before Christmas, and hid his identity, saying his name was Gest (Guest). The housewife could see that he was an exceptionally large man, but the people of the household were scared of him. Gest asked for lodgings.

The housewife said that she would offer him food: 'But you must look after your own safety.'

He replied: 'That is how it should be. I will stay here at your home, but you should go to mass if you want.'

She answered: 'I think you are a brave man if you dare to stay in this house.'

'I do not allow myself to be bothered by just anything,' he replied.

'I dislike the thought of staying at home,' she said, 'but I can't get across the river.'

'I will get you across,' said Gest. Then she made ready and took her little daughter with her. Outside there was a big thaw. The ice on the river was breaking up under the flood, and big pieces of ice flowed in the current.

The housewife said: 'The river is impassable both for men and horses.'

'It can be forded,' said Gest, 'don't be scared.'

'Take the little maid first,' said the housewife, 'she is lighter.'

Illustration 2. An Icelandic Turf Longhouse. Icelanders constructed their homes with turf. Around frames of timber, they built longhouses with thick, heat-retaining turf walls and roofs. The timbers of the frame and the inside panelling and benches were mostly fashioned from driftwood which collected on the coasts. The longhouse portrayed in this reconstruction is based on written and archaeological sources. A building of this size was worthy of a chieftain or a prominent family such as Grettir's.

Illustration 3. Inside the Longhouse, seen from the rear. The main room (to the left in the drawing) of the Icelandic longhouse or hall was called a 'fire hall' or *eldskáli*. It had a 'long fire' down the centre and wooden sitting- and sleeping-benches along the walls. Icelandic halls of chieftains and prosperous landowners tended to have several rooms, and the drawing shows a small pantry or food-storage room at the rear of the building. To the right of the long hall is a second large room called a *stofa*, so named because the room was warmed by a 'stove' made of large flat stones which radiated heat. The *stofa* is often mentioned in *Grettir's Saga* as the living-room where women worked the looms during the day, families sat in the evenings, and feasts were held.

'I don't feel like making two trips,' said Gest, 'and I will carry you on my arm.'

She crossed herself and said: 'That is impossible, and what will you do with the little girl?'

'I will find a way,' he said. Then he picked them both up. He set the young girl on her mother's knee and carried them both in his left arm. He kept his right arm free. In this way, he waded out into the ford in the river. The women did not even dare scream, they were so scared. The water quickly rose to his chest. Next a big chunk of ice came straight at him, but his free hand shot out and warded it off. Now the river became so deep that the current flowed over his shoulders. Putting all his strength into it, he continued wading forward until he reached the opposite bank. There he threw the women up onto dry land.

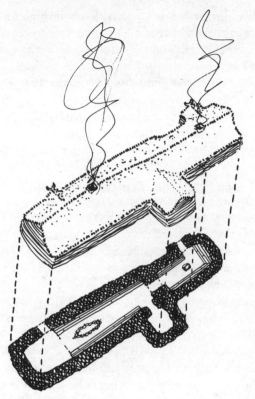

Then he turned back, and it was almost dark by the time he reached home at Sandhaugar. He called for his food, and when he had taken his fill, he told the people of the household to go to the furthest end of the living-room. Taking the table and some loose boards, he placed them sideways across the room. He constructed a barrier wall so high that none of the household people could climb out over it. No one dared argue with him or even grumble. The entrance to the house was through a small passageway that jutted out from the long side wall of the living-room. This entrance lay towards the room's far end, near the corner with the gable wall. The room had a raised wooden floor. Gest lay down, but kept his clothes on. A light burned in the room across from the doorway. Gest lay there into the night.

The housewife arrived at Eyjardal River in time for mass, and people were surprised that she had been able to cross the river. She said that she did not know whether it was a man or a troll who had helped her across.

The priest said it was undoubtedly a man. 'But there are few his equal, and let's keep this quiet,' adding: 'It may be that he is intended to bring about an end to your troubles.'

The housewife remained there that night.

65. The She-Troll from the Falls

RETURNING now to Grettir, there is this to be told. Toward the middle of the night he heard crashing noises outside. Next, a large troll woman came into the room. She held a trough in one hand, and in the other a cleaver which was not little. As she entered she looked around, and when she saw where Gest lay, she leapt at him. He jumped up to meet her, and the fight there in the room was grim and long. She was the stronger, but he gave ground skilfully. They broke everything that got in their way, even pulling down the dividing wall between the entry-way and the main room. She managed to pull him out through the inner door and into the outer entrance hallway, yet he still stood his ground. She wanted to drag him out of the house, but she was unable to do this until the two had ripped loose the whole outer door-frame, carrying it outside on their shoulders. Now she dragged him down towards the river and all the way out to the edge of the gorge. By then Gest was out of breath, but he knew that either he must fight on or she would throw him down into the chasm. They fought all night long, and it seemed to him that he had never before fought such a monster, as far as strength was concerned. She held him so tightly against her that he could free neither hand for anything more than holding on around her belly.

When they came to the edge of the cliff, he tried to lift her up and throw her down, and in that instant his right hand came free. He grabbed for the short-sword in his belt and, drawing the sax, he struck at the troll's shoulder, cutting off her right arm. In this way he broke free, while she fell into the gorge and then was sucked down under the waterfall. Gest was by then stiff and exhausted, and lay for a long time on the edge of the cliff. Then, with the first light, he returned to the house and got into his bed. He was swollen and black-and-blue all over.

When the housewife returned from mass, it seemed to her that her house was a shambles. She located Grettir and asked what happened, since all was broken and ruined. He told her everything that had taken place. She was awed, and asked who he was. He told her the truth and asked her to send for the priest, saying that he wanted to meet with him. This was done.

When Stein, the priest, arrived at Sandhaugar, he soon learned that the man calling himself Gest was Grettir Asmundarson. The priest asked Grettir what he thought had become of the men who had disappeared. Grettir replied that they must have vanished into the gorge. The priest said that he could not trust Grettir's story without evidence. Grettir answered that this would come later. The priest now returned home, and Grettir lay in bed for many days. The housewife looked after him with special care, and in this way time passed after Christmas.

As Grettir told it, the troll woman, after being wounded, threw herself down into the gorge. The men of Bardardal, however, say that she was still above ground wrestling with Grettir when the first light of dawn touched her, and that she died from this just as he cut off her arm, and there she still stands on the cliff—a woman turned to stone. The people of the valley hid Grettir that winter.

One day, after Christmas, Grettir went to Eyjardal River, and when he and the priest met, he said: 'I can see, priest, that you put little trust in my account. Now I want you to come with me to the river and see for yourself what you think is the truth. The priest went with him, and when they came to the top of the falls they saw that the cliff-top jutted out and overhung the gorge. The face of the cliff rose ten fathoms* above the water, and it was so sheer that there was no way to climb up. They had a rope with them.

Then the priest said: 'It seems to me impossible for you to climb down there.'

Grettir replied: 'Certainly it is possible, but such work is best left to men of quality. I am curious to learn what is in the falls. You stay here and guard the rope.'

The priest said that Grettir should decide, and he drove a peg into the ground on the top of the cliff and then piled stones over it.

66. Behind the Falls

Now there is this to be told about Grettir. He attached a stone to a loop at the end of the rope and then lowered the rope into the water.

'What are you intending to do?' asked the priest.

'I do not want to have a rope binding me,' said Grettir, 'when I surface behind the waterfall. That idea worries me.'

After that he got himself ready. He wore only a few clothes and belted on the sax; otherwise he had no other weapons. Then he plunged off the cliff and down into the falls. The priest watched as the soles of Grettir's feet disappeared. After that, the priest had no idea what became of him. Grettir meanwhile dived down under the falling water; the going was difficult. The current was so strong that he had to dive all the way down to the bottom before he was able to begin rising to the surface behind the falls. A big rock jutted out into the pool, and there he managed to climb up. A large cave lay hidden behind the falls.

Grettir went into the cave. A large log fire was burning. He saw a giant lying there, horribly huge and terrifying to look at. As Grettir approached, the giant leapt to his feet and grabbed hold of a pike. He hewed at the newcomer, because with such a pike one can both hew and thrust. The pike had a wooden shaft, and men call this kind of weapon a heftisax.* Grettir countered with his sax, and his blow landed on the shaft of the giant's weapon, cutting it in two. Now the giant tried to reach behind him for a sword hanging on the cave wall, but in that instant Grettir thrust straight into the giant's chest, cutting away almost all of the rib-cage and belly so the guts poured out of him and fell into the river, and the current carried them downstream.

As the priest sat beside the rope he saw bloody pieces of flesh carried on the stream, and now he lost his nerve. He assumed that Grettir was dead, so he abandoned the rope and ran for home. By then it was night, and the priest announced that Grettir was certainly dead. He said that such a man was a great loss.

Now there is this to be told about Grettir. He kept raining blows on the giant until it was dead. Then he went into the back of the cave and, striking a light, he searched. It is not told how much wealth he found in the cave, but people believe it was considerable. He stayed there through the night and found the bones of two men. These he placed in a bag, but when he tried to leave the cave he found the rope and shook it, expecting the priest to be there. When he realized that the priest had gone home, he was forced to pull himself up the rope. In this way, he climbed back up the cliff.

Once he returned to the house at Eyjardal River, he placed the bag containing the bones in the entrance-way to the church. He added a wooden rune-stick, on which these verses were carved with exceptional skill:

58. Into the dark gorge I ventured;
the waterfall, tumbling rocks,
gaped with its chill spouting
mouth at me and my sword.
Against my chest the air-borne
torrent surged in the chasm,
a haunt for trolls; the giant
came down hard on my shoulders.*

And this one also:

59. The ugly mate of some she-troll
emerged from his cave to greet me.
For a long stretch—I tell no lies—
I was grabbed by that hulking wrestler.
I wrenched the hard-edged short-
sword from its shaft. The bright
blade sliced right through the black
monster—both breast and chest.

The runes also told that Grettir had taken these bones from the cave. In the morning, when the priest went to church, he found the rune-stick and the other things and read the runes, but Grettir had gone home to Sandhaugar.

67. Gudmund the Powerful's Advice

WHEN the priest next met Grettir, he enquired carefully about the events. Grettir told him the whole story of what had happened, and said that the priest had not been trustworthy in guarding the rope. The priest agreed that this was true. People were certain that these monsters must have been the ones who caused the men's disappearance in the valley. Never afterwards in that valley was there any harm from hauntings or the walking dead, and Grettir was thought to have carried out a great land-cleansing. The priest buried the bones in the churchyard.

Grettir remained at Sandhaugar during the winter, and tried to stay out of sight. But when Thorir of Gard heard a rumour that Grettir was in Bardardal, he sent men to take his head. People then advised Grettir that he should look for another place to stay, and so he travelled west. When he came to Modruvellir, where Gudmund the Powerful lived, he asked Gudmund for his help. Gudmund replied that he was not inclined to take him in, 'but the most important thing for you', said Gudmund, 'is to find yourself a place where you will not be afraid for your life'.

Grettir answered that he did not know where that might be.

Gudmund said: 'There is an island in Skagafjord called Drangey (Cliff Island). It is such a good defensive place that there is no way to get up onto the island except by ladders. If you were to get there, I know of no one who might hope to attack you either with weapons or by other means, as long as you keep a close watch on the ladder.'

'I will try this,' said Grettir, 'but I have become so scared of the dark that I cannot for the life of me stand being alone.'

'Be that as it may,' said Gudmund, 'trust no one so well that you do not rely best on yourself. Still, many men are difficult to judge.'

Grettir thanked him for his good advice, and left Modruvellir. Now he travelled without stopping until he arrived at Bjarg. Both his mother and his brother Illugi greeted him warmly. He stayed there several nights, and learned of the killing of Thorstein Kuggason in the spring before he set out for Bardardal. Now it seemed to Grettir that many of his friends were being cut down.

Grettir then rode south across Holtuvordu Heath. He intended to avenge Hallmund, if he could locate Grim. Coming to Nordurardal (North River Dale), he learned that Grim had already departed two or three years earlier, as previously told. Grettir was so late in hearing the news of Hallmund's killing because, first he had been in hiding for two years, and then during the third year he was up in Thorisdal. During all this time he had met no one who wanted to tell him any news.

Now he went to Breidafjord Dales, where he robbed people travelling through Brattabrekka (Steep Slopes Pass) and gathered valuables from the local small farmers. This was during midsummer.

Toward the end of that summer, Steinvor from Sandhaugar gave birth to a boy named Skeggi. At first he was thought to be the son of Kjartan, the son of Stein the priest at Eyjardal River. Skeggi was unlike his brothers and sisters on account of his strength and build. When he was fifteen winters old he was the strongest man in northern Iceland, and then people realized he was Grettir's son. It was assumed that Skeggi would become an exceptional man, but he died when he was sixteen winters old, and there is no saga about him.

68. Snorri Godi's Son

AFTER the killing of Thorstein Kuggason, Snorri Godi treated with great coldness his son Thorodd, and Sam, the son of Bork the Stout. It is not known what their major offence was, except that they had opposed Snorri in carrying out some important undertaking that he had requested of them. For this Snorri drove

Thorodd from his presence and told him not to return until he had killed some outlaw. And that was the way it was. Thorodd next set out for the dales.

At that time there lived at Breidabolstad in Sokkolfsdal a widow named Geirlaug. She kept a shepherd who had | been outlawed for causing a wound. He was a young lad, though grown beyond his years. Thorodd Snorrason learned about this, and rode to Breidabolstad where he asked where the shepherd was.

The housewife said he was with the sheep: 'But what do you want with him?'

'I intend to have his life,' said Thorodd, 'because he is a convicted outlaw.'

She replied: 'There is no gain for you, such a great hero as you think you are, in killing him, a poor creature. I would direct you to much more of a challenge, if you are so determined to put yourself to the test.'

'What is that?' he asked.

She answered: 'Grettir Asmundarson is here up in the mountains. Go try yourself against him. That is more on your level.'

Thorodd took this proposal well, saying: 'So it will be.'

He now set his spurs to his horse and rode up through the valley. When he reached the hills below the East River, he saw a pale, dun-red-coloured horse with a saddle on its back. Then he saw a big man armed with weapons, and immediately he rode over to him. Grettir asked who he was.

Thorodd named himself, and said: 'Why not ask my errand rather than my name?'

'Because', said Grettir, 'your errands will come to little. But aren't you the son of Snorri Godi?'

'That I certainly am,' said Thorodd, 'but now we will see which of us is the more capable.'

'Of course,' said Grettir, 'but haven't you heard that few who try me find much profit in it?'

'I know that,' said Thorodd, 'nevertheless it will be tried.'

Then, drawing his sword, he attacked Grettir fiercely. Grettir protected himself with his shield but did not use his weapons to strike back at him. This went on for a while without Grettir's being wounded.

Then Grettir said: 'Let's stop this game, because our encounter will bring you no victory.'

Then Thorodd struck as hard as he could. Grettir now grew tired of dealing with him and, reaching out, he took hold of Thorodd and forced him to sit down beside him, and said: 'I could do whatever I want with you, and I have no fear that you will be my death, but I do fear your grey-haired father Snorri Godi and his schemes. They have brought many men to their knees. Better you concern yourself with what you can accomplish, and it is not child's play to fight with me.'

When Thorodd saw there was no way that he was going to win, he calmed down somewhat, and with this they parted. Thorodd rode home to Tunga, and told his father about his meeting with Grettir.

Snorri Godi smiled and said: 'Many a man deceives himself, and between the two of you there was a considerable difference. You attacked him, but while Grettir could have done whatever he wanted with you, he nevertheless acted wisely in not killing you, because I would not have tolerated leaving you unavenged. I will try to help him if his case comes within my reach.'

It was obvious that Snorri was touched by Grettir's having treated Thorodd so well, and from then on he was always a friend to Grettir in his proposals.

69. A Mother's Prophecy

SHORTLY after he and Thorodd parted, Grettir rode north to Bjarg, where he stayed secretly for a while. By then his fear of the dark had grown so much that he dared not travel after twilight turned to dusk. His mother invited him to stay, but said she could see that her help would not be enough; his enemies were now everywhere in the country.

Grettir replied that he would not bring trouble to her on his account: 'But I cannot stand being alone, not even to save my life.'

Illugi, his brother, was then fifteen years old and a very capable man. He was present while Grettir and his mother talked. Grettir told his mother about Gudmund the Powerful's advice, and said he would try, if possible, to get to Drangey Island. He added, however, that he would not be able to stay there unless he found some trustworthy man to accompany him.

Then Illugi said: 'I will go with you, brother. Still, I do not know if you will find any value in my assistance, beyond that I am trustworthy and will not desert you as long as you remain standing. There is also this: I will know more of what happens to you if I accompany you.'

Then Asdis said: 'Now I can see that I am caught between two approaching tragedies. I do not think I can bear to lose Illugi, but I know that Grettir is struggling with so many problems that he must find some solution. Even though I will be deeply disturbed in seeing both my sons depart, I choose that, if it will help Grettir.'

Illugi was pleased when he heard this, because his choice was to go with Grettir. Then she gave them a considerable sum of money, and they began preparing for the trip.

When the time came, Asdis led them out from the farm, and before they parted she said: 'Now, my two sons, you are leaving. You will share the same death, and this will be my greatest sorrow. Still, no one can escape the fate that has been shaped for them. I will never see either of you again, but let yourselves share one end. I do not know what luck you will find on Drangey, but there you will leave your bones, and many will begrudge you your stay. Keep your eyes open for treachery; nevertheless, you will be cut down by weapons. I have had strange dreams, and so I say to

---

Map 8. Drangey Island. The hardened core of an old volcano, Drangey rises like a fortress from the waters of Skagafjord. Eroded since Grettir's years, the island still reaches a height of 135 metres. In the medieval period a rope ladder, probably at Uppgonguvik (Ascent Inlet), was the only way up Drangey's sheer cliffs. According to tradition, Grettir's hut was located at the spot marked on the inset map. The arrows show Grettir's land route to Drangey and Thorbjorn Hook's route when he sails from his farm at Haganess to attack Grettir on Drangey.

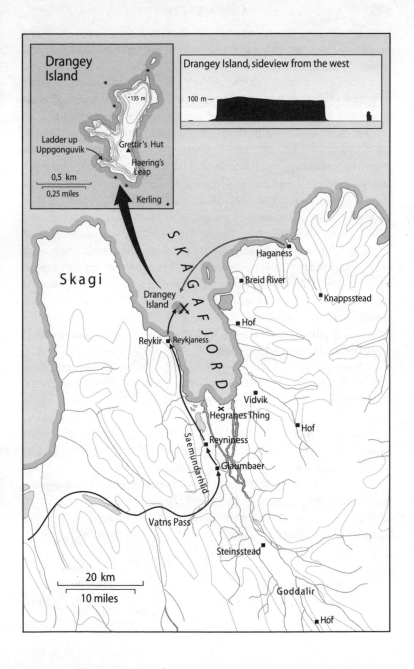

Drangey Island

135 m

Ladder up
Uppgonguvik

Grettir's Hut

Haering's
Leap

0,5 km

0,25 miles

Kerling

Drangey Island, sideview from the west

100 m —

S K A G A F J O R D

Haganess

Breid River

Knappsstead

Skagi

Drangey
Island

Hof

Reykir   Reykjaness

Vidvik

Hegranes Thing

Hof

Saemundarhlid

Reyniness

Glaumbaer

Vatns Pass

Steinsstead

20 km

10 miles

Goddalir

Hof

you, be on your guard against witchcraft. Few things are more powerful than the old ways of sorcery.' When she finished, she broke down and wept bitterly.

Then Grettir said: 'Mother, don't cry. Later it will be said that you had sons and not daughters, that is, if we are attacked with weapons. And now farewell, and may you keep your health.'

Following this, they parted. The brothers now travelled northwards through the districts, visiting their kinsmen and staying with them during the autumn and into the winter. When they turned towards Skagafjord, they made their way north through Vatns Pass, then over Reykja Pass before descending across Saemundarhlid (Saemund's Slope) and then to Langholt (Long Stone Hill). They reached the farm of Glaumbaer at the end of the day. Grettir meanwhile had thrown back the hood of his cloak onto his shoulders, just as he always did in good or bad weather.

They passed Glaumbaer, but after going just a short distance a man came out to meet them. He had a big head, was tall, thin, and poorly clothed. He greeted them, and they asked each other's names. The brothers told who they were, while he named himself Thorbjorn. He was a lone vagrant, who did not much like working and was given to boasting. Some people found him amusing and he was the butt of jokes. He was extremely friendly to them, and told them many stories about people in the district. Grettir found him very amusing.

Thorbjorn asked whether they did not feel they needed a man to work for them. 'I would gladly travel with you,' he said. In the end he convinced them, and they let him follow along. There was heavy drifting snow, and it was cold. Because this man was loud and a prankster, he was nicknamed Glaum.*

'They were very impressed at Glaumbaer,' he said, 'when you rode past the farm in this weather without wearing a hood, and they wondered whether you were tougher for not being bothered by the cold. The two sons of the farmer were at home, and both are extremely capable men. The shepherd was asking them to help him round up the sheep, but they could scarcely find enough clothes to put on against the cold.'

Grettir said: 'I saw one young man in the doorway putting on his mittens, and there was another walking between the cowshed and the dung-heap. Neither of them would scare me.'

After that they travelled down towards Reyniness, where they stayed the night. From there they went out to the coast, heading to the farm called Reykir. A man called Thorvald lived there. He was a good farmer. Grettir asked Thorvald for his help and told him the plan to go out to Drangey. The farmer said that the people of Skagafjord would not take that as a sign of good-will, and he refused. Grettir then took out the pouch of money, the one which his mother had given him, and he gave it to the farmer. The farmer cheered up with the money. He ordered his housemen to use the moonlight and to take them out to the island that same night. Reykir is the closest place to the island—the distance of a league.*

When they were ashore on the island, Grettir assessed the situation and it looked good. The top of the island was covered with grass, but the sides were sheer stone cliffs, so steep that getting up was impossible except where the ladders were placed. If the upper ladder were withdrawn, there was no other way to climb up. Then, too, there was this: the cliffs teemed with seabirds during the summer. Just at that time there were eighty sheep on the island.* These were owned by the farmers on the mainland, and most were rams and ewes that had been selected for slaughter. Grettir now settled in, intending to stay. By then, he had been an outlaw for fifteen or sixteen winters, according to Sturla Thordarson.

70. Ownership in Drangey

WHEN Grettir arrived on Drangey, these were the chief men in Skagafjord. Hjalti lived at Hof in Hjaltadal. He was the son of Thord Hjaltason, the son of Thord Skalp. Hjalti was a chieftain, a man of noble bearing, and he was popular. His brother was named Thorbjorn Hook. He was big and strong, ruthless and difficult to deal with. Their father, Thord, had in his old age married a woman who was not the mother of these brothers. She treated her stepchildren badly, and to Thorbjorn she was worst, because he was difficult and unbending.

Once Thorbjorn was playing a board-game. His stepmother walked by and noticed he was playing *hneftafl*.* The board pieces were large and had pegs at one end. She thought Thorbjorn was careless and spoke harshly to him. When he replied sharply, she grabbed one of the pieces and shoved it, peg side out, against his cheek. But the piece glanced up into his eye, which then popped out of its socket and lay hanging on his cheek. Thorbjorn jumped up and grabbed hold of her, and shook her with such force that she took to her bed and later died. People said that she had been pregnant at the time. After this, Thorbjorn became a serious troublemaker. He took his share of the property and lived first at Vidvik (Wood Bay).

Halldor was the son of Thorgeir, the son of Thord from Hofdi (Headland). He lived at Hof on Hofdastrand (Headland Beach), and was married to Thordis, Thord's daughter, the sister of the brothers Hjalti and Thorbjorn Hook. Halldor was a prominent and wealthy farmer. Bjorn was the name of a man who lived at Haganess (Grazing Point) in Fljot (River District). He and Halldor from Hofdi were friends, and they always supported each other in disputes.

There was a man called Tungu-Stein, who lived at Steinsstead. His father was Bjorn, the son of Ofeig Thin-Beard, the son of Crow-Hreidar, the man to whom Eirik of Goddalir (Valleys of the Gods) gave the tongue lands down below the marsh at Skalamyri (Swampy Hollow). Stein was a famous man.

Eirik was the name of a man, the son of Starri the Dueller (Holmganga-Starri), whose father was Eirik of Goddalir, the son of Hroald, the son of Geirmund Bushy-Beard. Eirik lived at Goddalir. These were all men of standing. There were two brothers living at the place called Breid (Broad) River in Slettahlid (Flat Slope), and both were named Thord. They were exceptionally strong yet peaceful men.

All of those mentioned owned a share in Drangey. It is said that there were no less than twenty who owned parts in the island, and no one was willing to sell his share to another. The sons of Thord, Hjalti and Thorbjorn, owned the largest shares, because they were the wealthiest.

71. Farmers Claim Their Sheep

TIME now passed until the winter solstice. The farmers made ready to go out to the island to round up their sheep for slaughter. They manned a large boat, and each owner had with him a man, and some brought two. But when they came close to the island, they saw people moving about. This they thought strange. They guessed that a ship must have been wrecked and its men come ashore. They rowed to where the ladders were, but the men on the island had pulled them up. The farmers were surprised, and they called out, asking these men who they were. Grettir named himself and his companions. The farmers asked who had taken them out to the island.

Grettir answered: 'He brought me, who owns the boat and had the strength in his arms, and he is more a friend of mine than of yours.'

The farmers replied: 'Allow us to collect our sheep, then you can sail back to the mainland with us. You can have for free the sheep that you already slaughtered.'

Grettir answered: 'A nice offer, but each will keep what he has. I can tell you right now that I will not leave here except if I am dragged away dead. I do not give back what I have my hands on.'

The farmers grew silent, realizing that an unwanted guest had arrived on Drangey. Next they proposed several choices, offering both money and handsome promises. But Grettir refused everything. So in the end the farmers left, unhappy with their lot. They told the men of the district that a wolf was now on the island. People were very surprised, and didn't think there was much they could do about it. They talked the matter over throughout the winter, but could not find a plan for getting Grettir off the island.

72. Grettir in Disguise

TIME passed until the spring, when men travelled to the Hegraness (Heron Point) Thing.* A great crowd of people came from all the districts that fell within the boundary of the assembly, and they stayed there long into the spring, involved with cases and just enjoying themselves. This was because at that time there were many in the districts who knew how to have fun. When Grettir learned that most people would be going to the Thing, he made arrangements with his friends. He always had good relations with those who lived nearest to him, and never held back from them whatever he acquired. He said to his companions that he wanted to go to the mainland in order to get provisions, but Illugi and Glaum should remain behind. Illugi thought the plan unwise, but he did not stand in Grettir's way. Grettir asked him to guard the ladder, adding that much depended on it.

Then Grettir went to the mainland and collected what he thought was needed. Wherever he went he hid his identity, and no one knew he was ashore. Then he learned about the Thing meeting and how much people were enjoying themselves. Grettir became curious, and he too wanted to go to the Thing. He got hold of some old clothes, really poor rags, and in this way he arrived at the Thing just as men were returning to their booths from the legislative council.*

At that moment, some of the young men were suggesting that, the weather being so fine, it would be a good idea for the younger men to set up wrestling matches and other amusements. People liked the idea, and a crowd started to gather down below the booths, where they sat and talked. The sons of Thord had most say in arranging the games.

Thorbjorn Hook was especially loud, and he threw himself into arranging the sport. Everyone had to follow his orders. One by one, he grabbed men by the shoulders and pushed them onto the field. Those who were weakest wrestled first, followed by the others. It was great fun.

When most of them, except for those who were strongest, had wrestled, the farmers began discussing who still remained to take on the two Thords, the brothers mentioned previously. But no one volunteered. They approached various men and asked them to come forward, but the more the men were urged, the less they were willing.

Thorbjorn Hook now looked around and saw where a big man was sitting. He was unable to see the man's face clearly, as it was partly covered. Thorbjorn went and grabbed hold of the man, yanking him hard, but the man sat quietly and did not budge.

Then Thorbjorn said: 'No one but you has withstood me equally well today. But who is this fellow?'

The man answered: 'I am called Gest (Guest).'

Thorbjorn said: 'You will want to join us in the fun, and you are a welcome guest.'

Gest replied: 'Things, I believe, have a way of changing quickly, and I will not jump into a contest with you. I am completely unfamiliar with this place.'

Many now spoke up, saying that he, an unknown man, would be treated well, if he wanted to provide some entertainment. The man enquired what it was that they wanted him to do, and they asked him to wrestle with someone.

He said that he had given up bothering about such things, 'even though I found it fun for a while'. But as he did not completely refuse, they urged him even more.

He answered: 'If you think it so important that I be drawn in, then arrange it so that, here at the Thing, I am granted a truce of safe-conduct, and this truce should last until I get back home.'

Next everyone jumped to their feet, saying that this they would gladly do. Hafur was the name of the one who argued most that the unknown man should be given safe-conduct. Hafur was the son of Thorarin, the son of that Hafur who was the son of Thord Knapp, the settler who first claimed the land from above Stifla (Blockage) in Fljot up to the Tungu (Tongue) River. Hafur lived at Hnappsstead, and was an orator. He pronounced the truce with great authority, and began in this way:

'Here I establish a truce,' he said, 'between all men, but especially with the man called Gest, the same one who is sitting here. The truce encompasses all the chieftains and worthy farmers as well as all the fighting-men of the people, those capable of bearing weapons and all the other district men in the Hegraness Thing or from wherever each has come, men who are named and those unnamed. Let us bind a truce by publicly shaking hands, thereby granting full peace to that newly arrived man, the unknown person who calls himself Gest. We do so for enjoyment, wrestling, and for other sports, while he is here and during his journey home, whether he needs to travel by sea or by land or by other means of conveyance. He shall have truce in all places, named and unnamed, for as long as he requires in order to return home safely protected by these pledges.

'I establish this safe passage on our part and for our kinsmen, bondswomen, slaves, servants, and freemen. Be he a cursed truce-breaker who breaks this truce or destroys this trust, expelled from God and good men, driven out from the Kingdom of Heaven and away from all holy men. Let him find nowhere suitable to live among men and so be driven out from the company of all, as wolves are driven furthest, wherever Christians seek their churches, heathens sacrifice in temples, fire burns, the earth grows, a speaking child calls to its mother, a mother bears a son, people kindle fires, ships advance, shields glimmer, the sun shines, snow lies, the Lapp moves on skis, pines grow, and falcons fly throughout the long spring day with a good wind under both wings, where heaven turns, where the world is settled, where the wind provides water for the sea, and slaves sow grain. He shall be barred from churches and the company of Christians, from heathen farmers, and from house, cave, and every world except from Hell.

'Now we shall be at peace and in agreement, each with the other, in good-will, whether we find ourselves in the mountains or on the shore, on ship or on skis, on firm earth or on a glacier, on the sea, or on horseback, just as one finds his friends on the water or one's brother on the road; as much in peace, each with the other, as a son with the father or a father with a son in all dealings. Now let us take each other's hands in agreement, all of us, and let us hold to this truce and to all the words said in this pledge as witnessed by God and good men and by all those who hear my words or are nearby.'

Many said that a great oath had been spoken.

Gest then replied: 'Well pronounced and all has been said, provided that you do not break your word later. Now, I will not delay what is mine to reveal', and with that he threw off his hooded cloak and then his shirt. Everyone was amazed, and they looked at each other with concern. They realized now that this was Grettir Asmundarson, because Grettir, with his size and powerful body, was unlike other men. All became quiet, and Hafur felt that he had been made a fool of. The men of the district now turned to one another, each blaming the other, but most of all they blamed the one who had proclaimed the truce.

Finally Grettir said: 'Tell me exactly what is on your minds, because I do not intend to sit here long without my clothes. You have much more at stake than I, in whether or not you respect the truce.'

The men said little in response, but sat down. Hjalti, Thorbjorn Hook, and Halldor, their brother-in-law, now spoke among themselves. Some of the farmers wanted to honour the truce and others did not. As the men were nodding their heads and speaking among themselves, Grettir spoke this verse:

> 60. Many a meritorious farmer
>   missed my incognito.
>   Fleeting indecision
>   fogged their pugnacious minds.
>   They found the tables turned,
>   these harshly spoken heroes:
>   their deeds didn't match their speeches.
>   All Hafur's drivel dried up.

Then Tungu-Stein said: 'Is that what you think, Grettir? But what will these chieftains decide? It is clear that you are quite a man as far as courage is concerned. Can't you see the way they collude, their noses in each other's faces?'

Grettir then said this verse:

> 61. These martial artists decided
>   to put their heads together;

the nose and beard of one man
nudged another's in the huddle.
They rued their noble pledge
to hold to their pact with me with me.
As soon as they knew their guest
they split up into factions.

Next Hjalti, the son of Thord, spoke: 'It will not be so. We will hold to our truce, even though we have not been equally clever. I do not want people to use this as a precedent that we reneged on a truce which we ourselves arranged and to which we pledged. Grettir shall go freely wherever he wishes, and he will be under truce until he reaches his home at the end of this journey. At that point the truce is over, whatever we arrange at this time between us.' All thanked him, and they thought that, with matters as they were, he had acted like a chieftain. Thorbjorn Hook said nothing.

The suggestion was made that one of the Thord brothers should fight Grettir, who for his part told them to decide. Grettir was standing there waiting, when one of the brothers came forward and suddenly threw himself with all his might at him. But Grettir's feet never budged. Then he reached down over the man's back until he got hold of his pants and yanked him up off his feet. Grettir threw the man backwards over his head so that he landed on his shoulder. It was a very hard fall.

Next, men said that both brothers should fight Grettir at the same time. Now the real contest began, with each side at times getting the better of the other. Although Grettir usually had one of the brothers down, both of them were in turn brought to their knees, and each was thrown. They fought so fiercely that they were black-and-blue and covered with blood. Everyone thought this great entertainment.

When they finally stopped, everyone thanked them for the wrestling. It was the judgement of those present that the two brothers together were not stronger than Grettir alone, even though each of them had the strength of two full-bodied men. The sides were so equally matched that neither had an advantage over the other, no matter how they tried.

Grettir did not stay long at the Thing. The farmers asked him to give up the island, but he refused and there was nothing they could do about it. Grettir returned to Drangey, and Illugi greeted him joyfully. Now, they stayed there quietly. Grettir recounted the events of his trip, and time passed into the summer.

Everyone thought the men of Skagafjord had acted with particular honour, especially in how well they held to their truce. From such action one can take the mark of the men of this time and judge how ethical they were, considering the wrongs Grettir had done them.

The least wealthy among the farmers now spoke among themselves and decided there was little profit in owning small parts in Drangey, so they offered to sell their shares to the sons of Thord. Hjalti said that he was not interested in buying. The farmers had made it a condition of the sale that whoever bought their shares should either kill Grettir or get him to leave. Thorbjorn Hook said that he would not refrain from committing himself to attacking Grettir, if they wanted to make it worth his while. Now his brother Hjalti turned over his part of the island to Thorbjorn, since Thorbjorn was the harder of the two and unpopular. Then many of the farmers did the same. In this way, Thorbjorn Hook acquired a large part of the island at small cost, but he took upon himself the task of removing Grettir.

73. Grettir Asked to Leave Drangey

TOWARD the end of the summer Thorbjorn Hook sailed a large, fully manned boat out to Drangey. Grettir and his men came out to the edge of the cliff. They spoke, and Thorbjorn asked Grettir to do him the favour of leaving the island. Grettir replied that there was no hope of this.

Thorbjorn then said: 'It may be that I will be able to help you in return, if you do so. Most of the farmers have now transferred to me their shares in the island.'

Grettir replied: 'Now that you tell me this, I am even more determined than before never to leave. You say that you own most

of the island, and I find it suitable that the two of us will now split
the cabbage. It is true that previously I found it difficult having all
the people of Skagafjord against me. Now, however, there is no
longer a reason for moderation, since neither of us will ever drown
in popularity. You might as well give up your trips here, because,
as far as I am concerned, everything has now been decided.'

'Each awaits his appointed hour,' said Thorbjorn, 'and you can
expect trouble.'

'I will take that chance,' replied Grettir. With this they parted,
and Thorbjorn returned home.

74. The Fire Goes Out

IT is said that by the time Grettir had been two winters in Drangey,
he and his companions had slaughtered almost all of the sheep on
the island. But one ram, according to the story, they let live. The
ram was grey-bellied and had large horns. It provided them with
many humorous moments, and became so tame that it waited outside their hut and ran after them wherever they went. In the evening
it came home to the hut, and banged its horns against the door.

They found life was good on the island, because with the birds
and the eggs, there was plenty of food. But firewood was scarce,
and Grettir kept the slave continually on the lookout for driftage.
Wood often washed ashore, and this he brought home for the fire.
The brothers did not have to work except for climbing the cliffs
after birds and eggs when they felt like it.

The slave began to grow lazy. He started to complain and grew
more careless than before. He was supposed to look after the fire
every night, and Grettir had given him a sharp warning about
being careful, since they had no boat.

It happened one night that their fire went out. Grettir was furious and said that Glaum deserved to be whipped. But the slave
said that his life was bad enough staying here as an outlaw, being
abused and beaten if something went wrong. Grettir asked Illugi
what he thought they should do. Illugi answered that all he could
think of was that they should wait until a boat came by.

Grettir thought there was little hope in that, 'and I would rather take my chances in seeing if I can make it to the mainland'.

'That is taking a big risk,' answered Illugi, 'because we are lost if something happens to you.'

'I will not drown while swimming,' said Grettir. 'More to the point, I would put less trust in the slave from now on, especially when, as in this matter, much depends on it.'

From the island to the mainland it was a league's distance, at the shortest point across the open water.

75. Grettir Swims to Get Fire

GRETTIR now prepared for the swim. He put on a woollen cloak, which he tucked into his pants, and, in order to swim better, he let his companions web his fingers together. The weather was good, and he was ready to set off from the island towards the end of the day. Illugi thought the prospects bad.

Grettir now swam out into the fjord towards the mainland. The current was with him and the sea calm. He swam hard and made land at Reykjaness after sunset. From there he walked to the farm at Reykir. Chilled, he got into the outdoor hot pool and baked himself in the hot water for a long time. It was well into the night before he entered the hall. Inside it was very warm. There had been a fire lit that evening, and the room had not cooled off. Grettir was exhausted and fell fast asleep. He lay asleep long after daybreak.

As the morning passed, the people of the household got up. The first into the room were two women, a maidservant and the farmer's daughter. Grettir was still asleep. His covers had fallen off onto the floor. The women saw a man lying there and recognized him.

The maidservant said: 'Bless me, sister, Grettir Asmundarson is here. He seems quite powerfully built in the chest and is lying there naked, but it amazes me how small he is between his legs. This does not otherwise match his excellence.'

The farmer's daughter replied: 'What makes you talk so much? You're no more than half a fool, be quiet.'

'I can't remain quiet about this, sweet sister,' said the maid, 'because I would never have believed it if somebody had told me.' She kept running over to take a closer look and then back to the farmer's daughter, where she burst out laughing. Grettir heard what she said, and when she crossed the floor again he grabbed hold of her and said this verse:

> 62.   Giddy woman, you tease me.
> Few who yearn for combat
> succeed in glimpsing the sword
> that's sheathed in another's hair.
> As to the spear-bearers here,
> I'd lay bets that their balls
> are not a bit bigger than mine,
> however long their pricks.

Next he threw her up onto the bench, while the farmer's daughter ran out. Now Grettir said a verse:

> 63.   Lonely seamstress, you gossip
> that a small sword is all I'm hung with.
> You've touched on the truth, you taunting
> lass with fondling fingers:
> yet a small curled creature, nestling
> in the bush of a youthful owner,
> may grow many sizes in stature.
> Woman, prepare for action!

The maidservant screamed at the top of her lungs, but by the time they parted she no longer taunted Grettir. A little while later Grettir got up and went to find the farmer, Thorvald. He explained his problem, and asked Thorvald to ferry him back to the island. The farmer agreed and launched his boat. On reaching the island, Grettir thanked him for his kindness. When it became known that Grettir had swum a whole sea league, everyone marvelled at his strength both on land and in the water.

The people of Skagafjord criticized Thorbjorn Hook heavily for not removing Grettir from Drangey. They said that they would take back their shares. Thorbjorn now found himself in a difficult situation, and asked people to be patient.

76. Haering's Leap

THAT summer a ship came out to Iceland and put in at Gonguskards-Estuary. On-board was a young Norwegian named Haering. He was so agile that he could climb any cliff. Haering took lodgings with Thorbjorn Hook, and stayed there well into the autumn. Haering kept pressing Thorbjorn to go to Drangey, saying that he wanted to see whether the cliffs there were so formidable that there was no way up. Thorbjorn told him that the work would not go unrewarded if he managed to get up onto the island and wound or kill Grettir. Thorbjorn made it tempting for Haering.

Next they sailed to Drangey, and found a place to set the Norwegian ashore. They left him to see if he could sneak up and attack those on the island. Meanwhile, the others sailed round to where the ladder was kept and started bantering with Grettir and his companions. Thorbjorn asked Grettir whether or not he intended to leave the island. Grettir replied that without doubt he was determined to stay.

'You have surely toyed with us,' said Thorbjorn, 'and however close we are to seeing this avenged, you don't seem much worried.' They continued like this for a long time, without reaching any agreement.

About Haering there is this to be told: he scaled the face of the cliff, moving back and forth until he finally succeeded at a place where no one else had climbed before or after. When he got up onto the top of the cliff, he saw where the brothers were standing with their backs towards him. Now he thought to win, in an instant, wealth and fame. The brothers were unaware of his presence, thinking the cliffs impassable except where the ladders were. Grettir was busy trading insults with Thorbjorn and his men, and neither side lacked for words.

Just then Illugi happened to glance around and saw where a man was almost upon them. He said: 'A man with a raised axe is just behind us, and to me his intentions seem unfriendly.'

'Turn and face him,' said Grettir, 'while I secure the ladder.'

Illugi now rushed at Haering, and when the Norwegian saw this he fled back across the island. Illugi chased him all the way, and when Haering reached the edge of the cliff he jumped off and broke every bone in his body. In this way Haering's life ended, and the place where he was lost became known as Haering's Leap. When Illugi returned, Grettir asked how he had parted with his man.

'He didn't want', said Illugi, 'to depend on me to sort things out for him, so he broke his back down below the cliff. The farmers may want to say prayers for him, since by now he should be dead.'

When Hook heard this, he ordered his men to row away. 'I have now made two trips out to see Grettir, and I will not travel here a third time, unless I learn something new. As things stand, I think we can expect that these men will remain on Drangey whatever I do. Still, it is my guess, that Grettir's remaining time on the island will be shorter than it has been up to now.'

They returned home, and this trip was judged worse than the previous one. That winter Grettir remained on Drangey, and during this time he and Thorbjorn did not meet again. That same winter the law-speaker Skapti Thoroddsson died. For Grettir this was a great loss. Skapti had promised to seek acquittal for Grettir after he had been an outlaw for twenty years. The events just recounted took place in the nineteenth winter* of his outlawry. In the spring Snorri Godi died, and at this time many other events occurred which are not discussed in this saga.

77. The Outlawry Debate

THAT summer, at the Althing, Grettir's kinsmen repeatedly brought up the question of his outlawry. To some it seemed that Grettir had served out his sentence, since he had been an outlaw for more than nineteen years. But those who had charges against him were opposed. They claimed that during these years he had committed many offences punishable by outlawry, and for this reason they believed his outlawry should be extended.

The Althing now elected Stein, the son of Thorgest, as the new law-speaker; he was the son of Stein the Great-Traveller, the son of Thorir Autumn-Darkness. Law-speaker Stein's mother was Arnora, the daughter of Thord the Bull-Roarer. Stein, a wise man, was asked to decide about Grettir. First he requested that the matter be investigated in order to determine if this was the twentieth summer since Grettir became an outlaw. And so it proved to be.

Thorir of Gard now came forward and raised all the objections against Grettir that he could. According to his reckoning, Grettir had been one winter out here in Iceland, during which he was not an outlaw, and because of this he had been an outlaw for only eighteen winters. Then the law-speaker ruled that no one should remain an outlaw for longer than twenty winters,* even if there were some overlapping winters between outlawries. 'But before this number of years is reached, I cannot release anyone from outlawry.' As a result, the appeal was quashed for the time being, but it was now thought certain that Grettir would be pardoned the following summer.

The men of Skagafjord did not like the prospect that Grettir would be released from his outlawry, and they gave Thorbjorn Hook the choice either to give them back Drangey or to kill Grettir. Thorbjorn realized that he had a problem on his hands. He wanted to hold onto the island, but could not devise a plan to overcome Grettir. Now he explored all possibilities for getting the better of Grettir, whether by force, trickery, or any other means that might work.

78. The Curse

THORBJORN had an old nurse named Thurid. She was his foster-mother. People dismissed her as feeble, but when she was young and people were still pagan, she had been skilled in magic and sorcery. Now it seemed as if she had forgotten everything, but even though the country had become Christian, many sparks of heathenism remained. The law here in the land was that sacrificing or performing pagan rites was not banned if done in private, but if such acts were carried out in public, the punishment was lesser outlawry. For many, youthful habits remained, and there were many people who were set in their ways. Since Thorbjorn Hook had exhausted all other stratagems, he sought help where most others would have thought it least likely, and that was to ask his foster-mother what advice she had to offer.

She spoke, saying: 'Matters are now as in the old adage: "Many go to the goat-shed looking for wool." But should I now think myself cleverer than other people in the district, having been considered a person of no value in important matters? Still, I do not see that I could do worse than you have done, even though I can scarcely rise out of my bed. But if you seek my advice, then it is I who will decide what to do.' He agreed to this, saying that she had long before proven the value of her counsel.

Time now passed until late summer.* Then one day, when the weather was good, the old woman said to Hook: 'The weather is now calm and bright, and it is my wish that you go to Drangey and trade insults with Grettir. I will accompany you in order to hear how carefully he guards his words. This way, I will learn for certain if I can determine how long their luck will last. After that I will be able to find the right words to say over them.'

Hook answered: 'I am tired of these trips to Drangey, since I always leave there in a worse mood than when I arrived.'

The old crone replied: 'I will not advise you, if you don't let me decide.'

'We don't want that, foster-mother,' he said, 'but I have sworn that if I return there for the third time, then something must happen in our favour.'

'It is a chance that you will have to take,' said the old crone, 'and you will face many difficulties before Grettir is forced to the ground. Often it will be unclear to you where your advantage lies, and you will suffer from the way it ends. Nevertheless, you are so committed that some solution must be found.'

Following this, Thorbjorn commanded that a ten-oared boat be launched, and he climbed aboard with eleven other men. The old woman went with them, and they sailed out to Drangey. When the brothers saw them coming they went to the ladder, and once again they all started discussing the issue. Thorbjorn said that he had come once more to enquire whether Grettir was willing to leave. Thorbjorn added that he was still willing to consider his losses as a small matter, and would agree to ignore their stay on the island if they would leave without trouble.

Grettir replied that he had no intention of discussing any compromise about leaving. 'I've repeated this often before,' he noted, 'and there is no point in speaking to me about it. You can do whatever you want, but here I will wait for whatever comes.'

Now Thorbjorn thought he could see how things were turning out this time, and said: 'I thought I was aware of what kind of hellish men I was dealing with, even before I came, but now it is more than likely that time will pass before I come again.'

'I would not count that a great loss,' said Grettir, 'if you never return.'

The old woman lay in the stern of the boat, hidden under some blankets. Now she stirred and said: 'These men are brave but not lucky, and there is a great difference between you. You make them good offers and they refuse everything. Few things lead more certainly to misfortune than not being able to accept what is good. Now I pronounce the following on you, Grettir: your good fortune has now left you along with your luck, your defences, and your good sense. Things will become worse for you the longer you live. I expect that, from now on, you will have fewer carefree days than you have had up to now.'

When Grettir heard this, he was startled and said: 'What sort of devil is with them in the boat?'

Illugi replied: 'I think it is the old woman, Thorbjorn's nurse.'

'Curse that old witch,' said Grettir. 'This is just about the worst we could expect, and words have never disturbed me more than those she just spoke. Of this I am sure: she and her sorcery will lead to harm. But she ought to have something from me in return, since she came to visit us.'

Then he picked up a big rock, and he threw it down into the boat, where it landed on the pile of clothes. The stone's throw, which was longer than Thorbjorn had imagined a man could make, was followed by a loud shriek. The stone had landed on the old woman's thigh, breaking the bone.

Then Illugi said: 'I would have preferred that you hadn't done that.'

'Do not regret it,' said Grettir. 'What bothers me is that too little came of it. The value of one old woman is hardly overcompensation for us both.'

'How could she equal us?' said Illugi. 'If so, our value would be judged little.'

Now Thorbjorn turned for home, and no words of farewell were exchanged at their parting. Thorbjorn said to the old woman: 'It went as I expected, you found little honour in your trip to the island. Despite your being crippled, we are in no way closer than before to an honourable settlement. We endure without compensation one disgraceful insult on top of another.'

She replied: 'This will be the beginning of their ill luck, and I would guess that from now on matters will go badly for them. I have no worry that, if I live, I will be able to avenge the harm that has been done to me.'

'It seems to me that you are high-spirited, foster-mother.'

Now they reached home, and the old woman went to her bed, where she lay for almost a month. During this time her leg healed. Finally she was able to get up and move about. People made great fun of Thorbjorn's and the old woman's trip, and it was thought that Thorbjorn endured frequent setbacks in his dealings with Grettir. The first setback was at the springtime assembly with the grant of a truce. The second was when Haering was lost. The third was now, with the breaking of the old woman's thigh-bone. Thorbjorn's counter-moves in this game brought little success, and he was deeply disturbed by this talk.

79. Driftwood

Now time passed into the autumn, until three weeks before the start of winter. Then the old woman requested that she be driven down to the sea in a cart. Thorbjorn asked what she intended to do.

'It is a small errand,' she said. 'Still, it might be that it will cause more important events.'

Things were done as she requested, and when she reached the shore she hobbled along the water's edge as though she were being guided. Lying there before her was a tree-trunk with the roots attached.* It was as big as a man could carry on his shoulders. She looked at the log and asked them to turn it over for her. It appeared burned and scraped on the other side. She had them shave a small smooth surface at the spot where it had been scraped. Next she took out her knife and carved runes on the root, reddening the letters with her own blood as she chanted spells. Then she walked backwards around the trunk, moving counter to the sun's course while pronouncing powerful charms over it. Following this, she had them push the trunk back into the sea, and she spoke a spell that it should drift out to Drangey, 'and bring full harm to Grettir'.

From there, she returned home to Vidvik. Thorbjorn said that he had no idea what would come of this, but the old woman replied that he would learn in time. The wind was blowing off the sea inwards towards the shoreline of the fjord, but the old woman's root moved against the wind away from the shore, and it did not seem to go slowly.

For now Grettir remained on Drangey, as previously told. With him were his companions, and they were pleased with their lot. The day after the old woman put the spell on the tree, Grettir and Illugi went down to the shore under the cliff to look for firewood. When they came to the western part of the island, they found a tree-trunk washed ashore with the roots attached.

Illugi said: 'That is a big piece of firewood, kinsman, let's carry it home.'

Grettir kicked it with his foot, and replied: 'An evil tree and sent with ill intent. We should look for other firewood.' Then he threw it back into the sea, and told Illugi to take care not to bring it home, 'because it has been sent to harm us'.

After that they went back to the hut, but said nothing about this to Glaum. The next day they again found the tree, but now it was closer to the ladder than on the previous day. Grettir pushed it back out to sea, and said this was never to be brought home. The night passed, and the next day a gale started blowing with driving rain. The brothers didn't feel like going outside, so they told Glaum to go and look for driftwood. Glaum became surly. He said he was badly treated and forced to go out in every storm. He climbed down the ladder and found right there the old woman's root. To him, it seemed things had gone well. He lifted it up and, struggling, he carried it back to the hut. There he threw it down with a loud crash.

On hearing this, Grettir said: 'Glaum must have unloaded something. I'll go and see what it is.' He picked up an axe used for wood-chopping, and went outside.

Glaum said: 'Do as good a job cutting it apart as I did in bringing it home.'

Grettir lost his patience with the slave, and raising the axe with two hands, he swung it at the root without noticing which tree it was. The instant the axe struck the wood, it turned flatside and, glancing off, slashed into Grettir's right leg above the knee. It cut to the bone, and was a serious wound.

Now he looked at the tree-trunk, and said: 'The one who wishes me harm has turned out to be the more powerful, and this will not be the last of it. Here is the same tree which I twice threw back out to sea.

'Glaum, you have now caused two accidents. The first was when you let our fire die out, and now you bring home this cursed tree. If you make a third blunder, it will be your death and that of all of us.'

Illugi bound Grettir's wound; it bled little. Grettir slept well that night, and this continued for three nights with no pain from the wound. When they opened the bandages, the wound had closed as though almost healed.

Illugi said: 'I would say that you will not be bothered long by this wound.'

'That would be good,' said Grettir, 'but this has come about so strangely, whatever the outcome. My thoughts, however, tell me that matters will go differently.'

80. The Spell Takes Its Toll

THEY went to sleep that evening, but in the middle of the night Grettir began to toss violently. Illugi asked why he was so restless. Grettir replied that his leg pained him, 'and most likely there is some change in its colour'.

They fetched some light, and when the bandage was opened the leg was swollen and dark blue. The gash had split apart and looked far worse than it had at first. The wound caused him so much pain that he was unable to lie still or close his eyes in sleep.

Grettir said: 'We ought to prepare ourselves. This sickness, which I have now, has not come by chance. It is the result of sorcery, and the old woman intends to avenge the blow from the stone.'

Then Illugi said: 'I told you that nothing good would come from that old hag.'

'Still, it is all the same in the end,' said Grettir and spoke five verses:

> 64. The sword-blade carved men's fates
> time after time when, hacking
> at thugs run amok, I staunchly
> defended that birchwood house.
> And that cost Hjarrandi, your
> man, an arm. As for Bjorn
> and Gunnar, they forsook
> both their lair and their life in short order.

> 65. To Iceland and Dyrholmar
> I sailed once more on a cutter.
> I kept my ship for a time,
> as a young spear-bearing fellow.
> Then Torfi, an excellent man,
> Vebrand's son, brought heavy

forces to challenge my serene
self to a spear-throwing contest.

66.   Though most men held up well
      as we sported with cutting points,
      my rashly fierce assailant
      took a fond farewell from this poet
      when the one-time oarsman slumped
      to the ground, unfit to move,
      courtesy of Grettir's hands.
      He left me his horse as a keepsake.

67.   Word reached me from far and wide
      that Thorfinn, son of Arnor,
      had a reputation for reckless deeds.
      He uttered death-threats against me.
      Though he found me on my own,
      the steadfast chieftain proved
      no keeper of firm resolve.
      I gave him a cool reception.

68.   Time after time I saved
      my neck from their probing spears
      by trusting my strength
      to spoil each ambush.
      But, mumbling her spells, that haggard
      crone with her stone-set necklace
      stumbled me: a godlike power
      resides in her cruel decrees.

'Now we must be on our guard,' said Grettir, 'because
Thorbjorn Hook and his people have no intention of leaving
matters where they stand. Glaum, I ask that every day from now
on you keep careful watch over the ladder and pull it up in the
evening. Make sure that you do this faithfully; much depends on
it. But if you betray our trust, things will soon go badly for you.'
Glaum swore to do this. Then the weather began to worsen, and
a cold wind from the north-east started to blow. Each evening
Grettir asked if the ladder had been drawn up.

Glaum answered: 'Surely this would be the best time to expect visitors! Do you think people are so set on taking your life that they are prepared to kill themselves? This storm has long since made travel impossible. I think your great courage is at an end, when you assume that everything will cause your death.'

'You will find it harder to bear than either of us will,' said Grettir, 'wherever this leads. But for now, guard the ladder even if you do so unwillingly.' Each morning they forced Glaum to go outside, and he could barely contain his anger.

The pain now grew in the wound so that the whole leg swelled up, while the thigh, both above and below the cut, began to fester. The infection spread to the point where Grettir could expect to die. Illugi sat with him day and night and paid attention to nothing else. By then, a second week had passed since Grettir had cut himself.

81. Hook Sails Again to Drangey

THORBJORN HOOK remained home in Vidvik, displeased that he could do nothing against Grettir. When a full week had passed since the old woman had cast the spell on the root, she came to speak with Thorbjorn. She enquired whether he was not intending to pay Grettir a visit. He replied that without doubt he wanted to do so: 'But you, foster-mother, do you want to meet with him?'

'I will not go to meet him,' said the old woman, 'but I have sent him my greetings. And I expect that they have reached him. It seems to me that it would be a good plan if you acted quickly. Set out immediately and go find him. Otherwise, you will never succeed in overcoming him.'

Thorbjorn Hook replied: 'I have made so many failed trips that I am reluctant to go there again. Besides, the gale that is blowing makes the journey impossible, whatever the urgency.'

'You have no plan,' she answered, 'and you do not see a way to accomplish this. Now I will once again advise you. First go and collect your men. Then ride out to Hof and meet with your brother-in-law, Halldor, and seek his advice. If I should have a certain power over Grettir's health, can it not be expected that I control the wind which has now been blowing for a time?'

It now seemed to Thorbjorn that the old woman might have more foresight than he had surmised, and he immediately sent word up through the district calling for men. Replies came back quickly from those who had already given Thorbjorn their share in the island. They said they would take no action, but that Thorbjorn was welcome to both their shares in the island and the attack on Grettir. Tungu-Stein, however, sent two of his followers, while Hjalti, his brother, sent three men. Eirik of Goddalir sent him one man, and from his own household Thorbjorn chose six men. Altogether twelve men* rode out from Vidvik to Hof, where Halldor offered them lodgings and enquired about their journey. Thorbjorn answered in detail, and Halldor wanted to know whose plan this was. Thorbjorn replied that his foster-mother was urging him on.

'This will lead to no good,' said Halldor, 'because she uses sorcery and that is now forbidden.'

'A man can't worry about everything,' replied Thorbjorn. 'One way or another this matter is now going to end, if I am to decide. But what else can I do to get myself onto the island?'

'I can see', said Halldor, 'that you are putting your trust in something, yet I am not convinced of its wisdom. But if you insist on continuing, then go out to Haganess in the Fljot area to my friend Bjorn. He has a good boat. Say that I ask him to lend you the boat. From there one can sail to Drangey, but to me your trip looks rather uncertain, especially if Grettir is not ill but in good health. You should recognize the certainty that, if you and your men do not overcome Grettir by honourable means, many will seek redress for him. Do not kill Illugi if there is any way to avoid it. To my mind, there is something not quite Christian in these plans.'

Halldor gave Thorbjorn six men for the trip. One was named Kar, another Thorleif, and a third Brand. The others are not named. Altogether there were eighteen men, and they now set out for Fljot. When they came to Bjorn's at Haganess, they gave him Halldor's message. Bjorn said that he was obligated as far as

Halldor was concerned, but owed Thorbjorn no favours. To Bjorn this trip seemed a mad undertaking, and he let them know how much he opposed it. Nevertheless, they would not let themselves be dissuaded and went down to the shore and launched the ship. The gear was close at hand in the boathouse, and soon they had the ship ready to sail. Those back up on land thought the crossing impossible.

The men hoisted the sail and the ship shot forward, moving quickly out into the fjord. When they had gone a good distance and reached the fjord's deep water, the weather shifted. It now seemed as though they were no longer dealing with a strong opposing wind. They arrived at Drangey in the evening, just as darkness fell.

82. Thorbjorn Attacks

Now there is this to tell. Grettir became so ill that he was unable to stand. Illugi sat with him while Glaum was supposed to keep a look out. He kept refusing to go outside, saying that they worried about losing their lives when there was nothing happening. Finally he left the hut, but unwillingly. When he reached the ladder he started talking to himself, and said that this time he would not pull the ladder up. He grew tired and lay down and slept the whole day. In the meantime Thorbjorn arrived at the island, and he and his men saw that the ladder was down. Then Thorbjorn said: 'Matters have now taken a change from the usual. There is no sign of movement and even the ladder is down. It may be that more will come from our trip than we thought at the outset. Let's go quickly to the hut, and this is no time for indecision. We know for certain that if they are in good health, then each of us will need to do his best.'

They climbed up onto the island, and when they looked around they saw where a man was lying a short distance from the top of the ladder. He was snoring loudly. Thorbjorn recognized Glaum. He went up to him and slapped him on the ear with his sword-hilt, telling the stinking man to wake up.

Thorbjorn said: 'Truly he is in bad straits, who lets his life depend on you.'

Glaum sat up and said: 'Now you are acting as usual. Or do you find I have too much freedom, even as I lie here, out in the cold?'

Hook said: 'Are you crazy, or don't you realize that you are in the hands of your enemies, and they are going to kill all of you?'

Glaum said nothing, but when he recognized who these men were, he began to scream as loudly as he could.

'Do one or the other,' said Hook, 'either be quiet and describe your living-quarters, or I will kill you.'

Then Glaum became as silent as though he were being held under water.

Thorbjorn said: 'Are the brothers in the hut, and why are they not up and about?'

'Things are not at their best,' said Glaum. 'Grettir lies sick and near to death, and Illugi sits with him.'

Hook enquired about Grettir's health, wanting to know what had happened, and Glaum described how Grettir had got his wound.

Then Hook laughed and said: 'The old adage is true. Close friends are the last to part, and true also is the saying that no good comes from having a slave as your friend. And so it turned out with you, Glaum. You shamelessly betrayed your master, even though he was not a good one.'

The men now struck Glaum because of his faithlessness. They beat him almost senseless, and then left him lying there. Next they went to the hut, where they started knocking on the door, and not lightly.

Illugi said: 'The grey-bellied ram is knocking at the door, brother.'

'This time he knocks rather hard,' said Grettir, who added, 'and not in a kindly manner either.'

Just then the door burst apart. Illugi grabbed his weapons and defended the doorway, denying the men entry. For a long time the men attacked. They got no further than thrusting in with their spears, but Illugi cut the spear-blades from their shafts.

When the men saw that they were getting nowhere, they climbed up onto the roof of the hut and started ripping it open. Grettir now got to his feet and, seizing a spear, he thrust it up between the rafters. The spear struck Kar, one of Halldor's men from Hof, and it passed right through him. Hook then called to his men, warning them to take care and look after themselves: 'Because we can overcome them, if we keep our wits about us.'

Now they ripped the covering from the ends of the roof-beam and pulled on it until it broke. Grettir could not get up from his knees; still, he took hold of his sax, Kar's-Gift, just as the men jumped down into the hut. A hard fight followed, and Grettir struck with the sax at Vikar, one of Hjalti Thordarson's followers, just at the instant that the man jumped into the hut. The blow landed on Vikar's left shoulder-joint and then, cutting across the upper part of his back, the sword came out on the man's right side, slicing him apart. The body fell in two pieces on top of Grettir, so that he was unable to raise his sax back up as quickly as he needed. Just then, Thorbjorn Hook thrust at Grettir between the shoulders. It was a serious wound.

Now Grettir said: 'Bare is the back of each man, except those who have a brother.' Illugi then threw a shield over Grettir, and protected him so fiercely that everyone praised his defence.

Grettir now said to Hook: 'Who guided you to the island?'

Hook replied: 'Christ showed us the way.'

'I would guess,' said Grettir, 'that evil old woman, your foster-mother, showed you the way, because you would be one to trust her counsel.'

Hook replied: 'It is now all the same for you, whomever I trusted.'

The men now attacked fiercely, but Illugi fought bravely and defended them both. Then Hook ordered his men to trap Illugi between their shields, 'because I have never seen his like, though he is such a young man'. The men did so. They used against Illugi both wood from the hut and their weapons, until he was unable to defend himself. Finally they captured and held him. Illugi had wounded most of the attacking men, and had killed three of Hook's followers.

Now they turned back to Grettir, who had fallen forward. No fight was left in him; he was already at the point of death from the wound in his leg. The thigh had festered all the way up into his intestines. They gave him many wounds, but there was little or no bleeding. When they thought he must be dead, Hook reached for the sax, saying that Grettir had carried it long enough. But Grettir had locked his fingers tightly around the handle and held the sword fast. Many of the men attempted to loosen it, but none could. Eight of them tried before it was over, and all without success.

Then Hook said: 'Why should we spare this outlaw? Lay his hand over that beam.' And when this was done, they chopped the hand off at the wrist. Then the fingers unfolded, releasing the handle. Hook took the sax, and then, using two hands, he struck Grettir's head with it. The heavy blow was too much for the short-sword, and a piece broke off from the middle of the sax's cutting-edge. When the men saw that, they asked why he was ruining so fine a treasure.

Hook answered: 'This way people will easily recognize it, if they ask.' They answered that there was no need for this. The man was already dead.

'Nevertheless, there is even more to be done,' said Hook, who then struck two or three blows at Grettir's neck before cutting the head off.

'Now I know for sure that Grettir is dead,' said Hook.

In this way Grettir, the boldest man ever in Iceland, lost his life. At the time he was killed he was one winter short of forty-five years of age. When Grettir killed his first man, Skeggi, he was fourteen winters old. All then went well for him for a time, and everything turned to his advantage until he was twenty winters old and fought with the wretch Glam. When Grettir fell into outlawry he was twenty-five, and remained under that sentence for more than nineteen winters. His manhood was often put to difficult tests, but he held onto his faith as much as possible. He was a person who could foresee what was going to happen, even though he could do little about it.

'We have felled a great champion,' said Thorbjorn. 'We will take his head with us to the mainland, because I do not want to miss the price placed on it. This way they will not be able to doubt that I have killed him.'

The men said that he should decide, but they showed little enthusiasm because it seemed to all of them that this was unseemly.

Then Hook said to Illugi: 'It is a great shame that a man of your courage has acted so unwisely as to join this outlaw in his crimes, and for that you can be killed with impunity.'

Illugi replied: 'Only after the Athing is over this coming summer will you know who is the outlaw. Neither you nor your old foster-mother will judge in this case, because it was your magic and sorcery that killed Grettir. Even though you struck him with iron weapons, he was already a dying man, and so you have added disgraceful acts to your sorcery.'

Then Hook said: 'You speak courageously, but it will not turn out as you say. I want to show that I recognize that killing you would be a great loss, and so I will grant your life if you are prepared to swear an oath not to take vengeance on any of those who have joined in this.'

Illugi replied: 'That might have been for me a matter of discussion, if Grettir had been able to defend himself and you had overcome him honourably and with courage. Now, however, there is no chance that I would seek to spare my life by becoming a coward like you. Right now I can tell you that no one will be more an enemy than I, if I should live, because it would be a very long time before I forget how you killed Grettir. I would rather choose to die.'

Then Thorbjorn spoke with his companions about whether or not they should let Illugi live. They said that Thorbjorn ought to decide, since he was in charge. Hook then said that this man could not be allowed to stay alive and threaten him, since he had refused to swear an oath.

When Illugi realized that they intended to kill him, he laughed and said: 'Now you have decided what was closest to my wishes.' As the first light from the east shone on the island, they led him out and executed him. Everyone praised his courage, and they all agreed that, among his age-group, no one was his equal. They buried both brothers on the island under a pile of stones.

They took Grettir's head* with them, carrying it off along with everything else of value, whether weapons or clothes. Hook did not allow the fine sax to be included among the shared goods, and he wore it long afterwards.

They kept Glaum with them, but he continued whining and complaining. During the night the wind eased, and in the morning they rowed to the mainland. Hook landed near his home and sent the ship back to Bjorn. When they approached Osland, Glaum began whimpering so shamelessly that they wished to have nothing more to do with him. He screamed as they cut him down.

Hook went home to Vidvik, and thought things had gone well on this trip. They put Grettir's head in salt and kept it there at Vidvik in a storehouse, called Grettir's Shed. There it lay through the winter. Hook became very unpopular because of his actions, as soon as people learned that Grettir had been overcome by witchcraft.

Hook stayed quietly at home until Yule had passed, then rode to see Thorir of Gard. He reported the killings to Thorir, and added that he believed he had a right to the money placed on Grettir's head.

Thorir said he would not deny that he had been behind Grettir's outlawry. 'And I often suffered injury at his hands, but I never intended to take his life by making myself a criminal or a conjurer as you have done. Rather than seeing you paid, it seems to me that you deserve death for magic and sorcery.'

Hook replied: 'I think this is more from your stinginess and pathetic nature than your caring how Grettir was killed.'

Thorir said that the surest way was for them to wait for the Althing and accept what the law-speaker found proper. Thorir and Thorbjorn Hook now parted with only ill-will between them.

83. Kinsmen Call for Blood-Vengeance

GRETTIR and Illugi's kinsmen were incensed when they learned of the killings. They believed that Hook had acted deceitfully. Not only had he killed a man already dying, but he had also used witchcraft. They consulted the wisest men, and everyone spoke against Hook's case.

After four weeks of summer had passed, Hook rode west to Midfjord. When his movements became known, Asdis sent out a call for men to come to her aid. Many friends heeded the call, and among them were her sons-in-law, Gamli and Glum, as well as their sons, Skeggi, called the Short-Hand, and Ospak, the one who previously was mentioned. Asdis was so well liked that all the people of Midfjord supported her, even those who had earlier been Grettir's enemies. Prominent among these was Thorodd Poem-Stump, and with him were most of the men of Hrutafjord.

Hook arrived at Bjarg with twenty men, and they carried Grettir's head with them. But at that moment not all who had promised Asdis support had arrived. Hook and some of his men went into the hall. He carried the head with him and set it down on the floor. The mistress of the house was there in the living-room, and with her were many others. No greetings were exchanged, but Hook spoke this verse:

> 69.   I've brought back from his island
> Grettir's insatiable head.
> As you sew, well may you shed
> tears for your red-haired son.
> See, on the floor, this trophy,
> from a lawless man, yours to view.
> It will rot on you quickly, woman,
> so take care to cake it with salt.

The lady of the house sat quietly while Hook said his verse. Then Asdis spoke this verse:

> 70.   The north salutes with scorn
> you chieftains who drip with gold.
> Think how sheep leap down
> to the sea when a fox gives chase:
> for that's how you'd have fared
> on Grettir's turf had you faced him
> before his sickness struck.
> I don't mock when praise is earned.

Many now said that it was no wonder that her sons were so courageous, when she herself was so brave in the face of such an ordeal as this.

Ospak was outside and spoke with Hook's followers, those who had not gone inside. He asked about the killings, and all praised Illugi's defence. Then they told how Grettir had held fast to the sax even in death. They marvelled at this.

Suddenly large bands of men were seen riding in from the west. Now the many friends of the lady were coming, and among them were Gamli and Skeggi from Melar in the West. Hook's intention had been to hold a court of confiscation* at Bjarg to take Illugi's property, because Hook and his men claimed for themselves all his possessions. But with so many men coming, Hook saw that this was not possible.

Ospak and Gamli were enraged and ready to fight. They wanted to attack Hook, but those who were wiser advised them instead to follow the counsel of their kinsman Thorvald and the other chieftains. They pointed out that the more men of wisdom who involved themselves in the case, the worse it would be for Hook.

Men separated the opposing sides and Hook rode away. He took with him Grettir's head, intending to bring it to the Althing. Hook now rode home. It seemed to him that matters were looking bleak, since most chieftains of the country were related by either blood or marriage to Grettir and Illugi. That summer Skeggi Short-Hand married Valgerd, the daughter of Thorodd Poem-Stump. Now Thorodd allied himself with Grettir's kinsmen.

84. Hook Rides to the Althing

Now men rode to the Althing, and fewer supporters joined Hook on the ride than he had expected, because people spoke so badly about his actions. Then Halldor asked whether they ought to be taking Grettir's head with them to the Althing. Hook replied this was his intention.

'That would be unwise,' said Halldor. 'You already have enough enemies without further reminding people of their sorrows by offering such an affront.'

By then they were well on their way, and were about to ride south over the Sands. Hook now had the head buried in a small sand-hill, which today is called Grettir's Sand-Bump.

The Althing was well attended, and Hook presented his case. He praised his own deeds highly, pointing out that he had killed the land's greatest outlaw. He claimed that he had a right to the price on Grettir's head. But Thorir of Gard gave the same answer as before. Then the law-speaker was asked to give a ruling. He said that he was ready to listen if any counter-charges were brought against Hook that would disqualify him from claiming the reward. Otherwise, Hook would be entitled to whatever price had been placed upon Grettir's head

Then Thorvald Asgeirsson called upon Skeggi Short-Hand to bring forward their charges. Short-Hand formally charged Thorbjorn Hook with causing Grettir's death by means of sorcery and witchcraft, then advanced a second charge that Thorbjorn and his men had assaulted a man already half dead. Short-Hand demanded the penalty of full outlawry.

Men gathered into groups, taking sides, and those who supported Thorbjorn Hook were few. Matters now were developing differently than Hook had expected, because Thorvald and his son-in-law Isleif argued that slaying a man through the use of witchcraft was an act punishable by death. Finally, at the suggestion of wise men, the case was concluded in this way: Thorbjorn Hook was to sail abroad that same summer, and he was not to return to Iceland while there were any men still alive who held claims against him for killing Illugi and Grettir. Then a law was passed outlawing all sorcerers.

After weighing his options, Hook chose to leave the Althing, because by then Grettir's kinsmen were preparing to attack him. He was unable to get any of the money placed on Grettir's head since Stein the Law-speaker made it clear that he would not reward such foul work. No compensation was paid for the men on Thorbjorn Hook's side killed on Drangey. Their deaths were considered to balance out Illugi's slaying, a decision that greatly displeased Illugi's kinsmen.

Men now rode home from the Althing, and all claims that people previously held against Grettir were dropped.

Grettir's nephew Skeggi Short-Hand, the son of Gamli and the son-in-law of Thorodd Poem-Stump, travelled north to Skagafjord. He had the approval of all the common people and was aided by Thorvald Asgeirsson and his son-in-law Isleif, the one who later became bishop of Skalholt. After acquiring a boat, Skeggi sailed to Drangey in order to find the bodies of the brothers Grettir and Illugi. These he transported to the farm of Reykir on Reykjastrand, and buried them there at the church. And this is the proof that Grettir lies there: in the days of the Sturlungs,* when the church at Reykir was moved, Grettir's bones were dug up,* and they were thought to be exceptionally large. Illugi's bones were reinterred north of the church, but Grettir's head was reburied back home at the church at Bjarg.

Mistress Asdis remained at Bjarg. She was so well liked that no harm was ever done to her, not even while Grettir was an outlaw.

Skeggi Short-Hand took over the farm at Bjarg after Asdis, and he became an important man. His son was Gamli, the father of Skeggi at Skardssteads and of Asdis, the mother of the monk Odd.* Many people are descended from Skeggi Short-Hand.

Map 9. Thorstein the Galleon Travels to Southern Lands. Grettir's Norwegian half-brother, Thorstein, takes two trips to Mediterranean lands. The first time he crosses the Baltic and journeys down the rivers of Russia to the Black Sea and then to Constantinople, capital of the Byzantine empire. The map shows the empire in 1027, a few years before he arrives. Thorstein serves in the imperial bodyguard before finally returning home to Norway by the same eastern route. In his second journey, Thorstein and his wife travel from Norway to Rome. The common pilgrimage route between Scandinavia and Italy is marked on the map, but many travellers also entered northern Italy through the Alpine passes. Both routes were popular in late viking times.

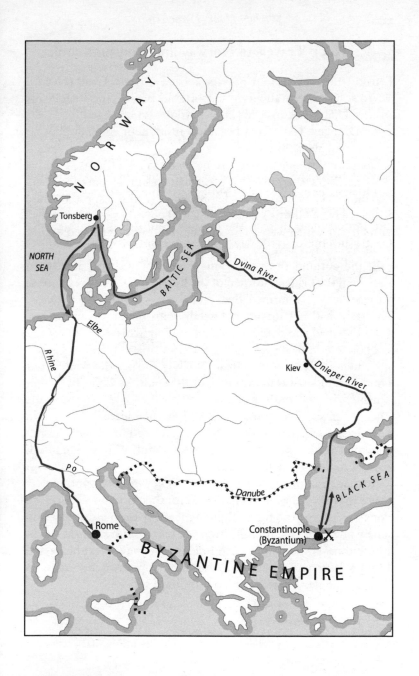

85. Hook Travels to Norway and Constantinople

THORBJORN HOOK took passage aboard a ship at Gasir (Geese). He took with him all his transportable possessions, while his brother Hjalti took over his lands. Hook also arranged for Hjalti to get Drangey. Hjalti later became a prominent chieftain, but no more is said about him in this saga.

Hook went to Norway, where he made much of himself. In his view, he had accomplished a great feat in killing Grettir. Many who did not know what really happened gave him respect, because people knew of Grettir's fame. Hook told only those of his dealings with Grettir which were to his credit, and dropped from the story whatever did not advance his renown.

In the autumn the news came east to Tonsberg, and when Thorstein the Galleon learned of the killing he became very quiet, because he was informed that Hook was capable and ruthless. Thorstein had not forgotten his talk with Grettir years before, when they had compared the shape of their arms.

Thorstein now began gathering information about Hook's movements. They were both in Norway during the winter, but Thorbjorn Hook was in the north of the country, while Thorstein remained in the south at Tonsberg. Neither had ever seen the other. Even so, Thorbjorn Hook had by then learned for certain that Grettir had a brother in Norway, something which he felt presented a risk, since he was in a foreign land. With this in mind, he tried to devise the best plan.

At that time many Norwegians travelled to Constantinople,* where they served as mercenaries. With this in mind, Thorbjorn Hook was eager to go there, thinking it a way to amass wealth and fame while removing himself from the reach of Grettir's kinsmen in Scandinavia. So he prepared to leave Norway. Next he passed through different lands, and did not stop until he came to Constantinople. There he entered military service.

86. Vengeance in Constantinople

THORSTEIN THE GALLEON was a rich man, and enjoyed great respect. When Thorstein learned that Thorbjorn Hook had left the country and was heading to Constantinople, he reacted quickly, placing his property into the hands of his kinsmen, and set out in pursuit of Thorbjorn Hook. But each time Thorstein arrived somewhere, Thorbjorn Hook had just left. Meanwhile, Thorbjorn Hook knew nothing about Thorstein's pursuit.

Thorstein the Galleon arrived in Constantinople shortly after Hook, and wanted more than anything to kill him. But neither of them knew what the other looked like. They both decided to enlist in the Varangian Guard,* and each was accepted into service when they made it known that they were northerners. At that time Michael Katalak* was king in Constantinople.

Thorstein the Galleon tried to locate Thorbjorn Hook, but because there were so many men he could not identify him. Thorstein lay awake at night discontented with the situation. He felt he had suffered a grievous loss.

Next it happened that the Varangians were commanded to set out on a military expedition to free the country from piracy. Before leaving their home quarters, it was their custom and law to assemble for an inspection of their weapons and equipment. And this they did as usual. When the weapons assembly was announced, all the Varangians and any others who intended to join them on the expedition were required to come and present their arms for inspection. Both Thorstein and Thorbjorn Hook came to the assembly, and Thorbjorn was the first to present his weapons. He had Grettir's sax, called Grettir's-Companion. When he showed the sword, many admired it. They agreed that it was an excellent weapon, but commented that it was a pity that it was badly flawed by the piece broken off from the middle of the cutting-edge. They asked Hook what caused this.

Hook said that was worth a story: 'It began out on Iceland,' he said, 'where I killed the champion called Grettir the Strong. He was the greatest, most courageous warrior there, because no one could cut him down before I arrived. But I was fated to over-come him and so I killed him, even though he had many times my strength. With the sax, I struck him a blow on the head which broke out a piece from the edge.'

Those who were standing nearest commented that the head of this Grettir must have been hard, and they passed the sword around, examining it. Thorstein now recognized Hook, and, like the others, he too asked to see the sword. Hook readily agreed, since everyone was praising his boldness and courage. Thinking that this man too would do the same, it did not cross Hook's mind that Thorstein or any of Grettir's kinsmen might be in Constantinople.

As soon as the Galleon got hold of the sax, he raised it and struck. The blow landed on Hook's head with such force that the cut ran all the way down to his jaws. There the sword came to rest, and Thorbjorn Hook died ignobly, falling to the ground.

The men were speechless, but the official in charge immedi-ately took Thorstein into custody. He asked what could be the reason for Thorstein's doing such a terrible act at an assembly hallowed by a truce.

Thorstein replied that he was the brother of Grettir the Strong, and that previously there had been no opportunity for vengeance-taking. Then many of the men marvelled at how important this strong man must have been, since Thorstein had travelled so far out into the world to avenge him. The officials in charge tended to believe Thorstein, but because there was no one there who could bear witness for him, it was their law that whoever killed a man should forfeit nothing other than his own life. Thorstein received a quick judgement and a rather hard one. He was to be placed in a dark cell, there to await his death, unless someone ransomed him by paying the fine.

When Thorstein was led into the cell, there was a man already there. He had been there for a long time and was on the verge of death from misery. It was foul-smelling and cold.

Thorstein asked the man: 'How are you doing?'

The other answered: 'Rather poorly, because no one wants to help me, and I have no kinsmen to ransom me.'

Thorstein said: 'The future is not always clear, but let's be cheerful and have some fun.'

The other replied that for him there was no joy.

'Nevertheless, we will try,' said Thorstein. Then he began to sing. He had such a fine voice that there was scarcely anyone his equal, and now he held nothing back. There was a main street not far from the prison. Thorstein sang so loudly that his voice rang throughout the walls, and the other prisoner, the one who earlier had been half dead, now found it great fun to be there. Thorstein continued his singing into the evening.

87. Spes Hears Singing

SPES was the name of a noble woman there in the town. She was rich and came from an important family. Her husband was named Sigurd. He was very wealthy but less well born than she. Spes had been married off to Sigurd for his money. There was little love between husband and wife, and she found her marriage unworthy of her. Spes was proud and strong-willed.

That same evening, as Thorstein was singing, Spes passed by in the street near the prison. She heard a voice coming from the prison so beautiful that it seemed to her she had never heard its like. She was accompanied by many servants, and she commanded them to change their route in order to determine the owner of this splendid voice. They called out, asking who was so cruelly imprisoned. Thorstein named himself.

Then Spes said: 'Are you equally as capable a man in matters other than singing?'

He replied that mostly there was little proof of this.

'What is your offence,' she asked, 'that you are being tortured to death?'

He said that he had killed a man to avenge his brother. 'I had no witnesses to attest to my story, and because of this I was sent here, where I will stay unless someone ransoms me. But I think there is no hope of that, because I have no kinsmen here.'

'It would be a great loss if you are killed. But tell me, was the brother you avenged such a famous man?'

Thorstein replied that his brother was more than twice as worthy a man as he.

> 71.   I tell you, woman, whose arm
>   bears golden rings, eight
>   keen swordsmen could not part
>   Grettir from his short-sword,
>   so firm his grasp, until
>   at last these brutes, who keep
>   their swords well whetted, hacked
>   away both sword and arm.

Those who understood the verse said: 'How excellent.'

And when Spes heard this, she said: 'Would you accept your life from me, if it were possible?'

'I would gladly,' said Thorstein, 'but only if my companion, who is here with me, is also freed. Otherwise we will remain here together.'

She responded: 'I think there is more value in you than in him.'

'However that may be,' said Thorstein, 'either we both get out of here together or neither of us leaves.'

Spes now went to where the Varangians were stationed and sought Thorstein's freedom, offering to pay the money. The Varangians were agreeable. Because of the position she enjoyed and her wealth, she had them both freed. When Thorstein was released from the prison, he went to meet Spes. The lady took him into her home and kept him there in secret. But sometimes he joined the Varangians when they set out for war, and he proved himself the bravest of men under all conditions.

88. The Husband

AT that time Harald Sigurdarson* was in Constantinople, and
Thorstein and he became friends. Thorstein was highly regarded,
because Spes did not let him want for money. Thorstein and Spes
now fell in love, and she greatly admired his abilities.

Spes spent lavishly and enjoyed popularity. Her husband
thought he noticed a change in her mood, and in other ways also,
especially the way she depleted their wealth. He began to miss the
gold and valuables, which disappeared from her keeping.

One time her husband Sigurd remarked that she seemed to be
undergoing a strange change: 'You pay no heed to our property.
Instead you squander it in various ways. You act as though you
are sleepwalking, and never want to be in the same place as I am.
I know now for certain that something is going on.'

She answered: 'When we were married I told you, as did my
kinsmen, that I intended to remain free and independent and that
I would be able to use your money in all matters that concerned
me. This is why I do not spare your wealth. Or is it that you want
to talk to me about something else that might dishonour me?'

He replied: 'I am not without my suspicions that you are keeping some man, and that you think more of him than you do of me.'

'I do not think', she said, 'that you know much about what
you are saying, and I doubt if you have any evidence to support
your talk. The two of us will never speak alone again if you accuse
me of this unverifiable foul charge.' Now he dropped the matter
for a while.

Thorstein and Spes continued in the same way as before. They
were not careful to shield themselves from the gossip of malicious
people, because she trusted in her own cleverness and popularity.
They frequently sat talking and enjoying themselves.

One evening they sat together high up in the house, in a room
where her valuables were kept. She asked Thorstein to sing a
little verse, because she thought that her husband was off drinking, as was his custom. She locked the door, but after Thorstein
had been singing for a while, someone tried to break the door

down and called out that she should open it. It was her husband, accompanied by many of his men.

The lady had previously unlocked a large chest to show Thorstein her treasures, and when she realized who had arrived, she decided not to open the door. She said to Thorstein: 'Here is a plan made in haste. Get into the trunk and make no sound.'

Thorstein did so, and she closed the lock on the chest and sat on it. Just then, the husband and his men broke down the door and entered the room.

'Why force your way in with such commotion?' she asked. 'Are your enemies after you?'

The husband responded: 'Now is a good time for you to show us just who you are, and where the man is who was singing so loudly. My guess is that you find his voice prettier than mine.'

She replied: 'No one is a complete fool if he knows how to keep quiet, and you might want to act accordingly. You think you are so clever, planning to catch me with your lies, but here the matter will be put to the test. If you speak the truth, then seize him, because there is no way he could escape through the walls or ceiling.'

The husband searched but found nothing. Then she said: 'Why haven't you taken him, since you are so sure of yourself?'

Now the husband became silent. He was unable to work out what kind of trickery he was facing, and asked his followers whether they had not heard the same as he had. But when they saw the lady's anger, they were not much help. They said only that one often hears things that are not really there. The husband now left. He was sure he knew the truth, even if he could not find the man, but for quite a while he stopped spying on his wife.

Another time, a good deal later, it happened that Thorstein and Spes went into a storeroom used for clothing. It was where the husband and wife kept their clothes and uncut cloth. Spes showed Thorstein the many fabrics and spread them out, but when they least expected it, the husband arrived with a large following and began breaking down the storeroom door. While the husband and his men were forcing their way in, Spes piled the cloths on top of Thorstein, and when the husband entered she was leaning on the pile.

'Do you still intend to deny', said the husband, 'that you have a man with you? There are now people here who saw you both.'

She told them to calm down. 'No one will hinder your search, only leave me in peace, neither touching nor pushing me in any way.'

They searched throughout the building but found nothing. Finally they gave up.

Then the wife said: 'It is always satisfying to offer better proof than people are expecting, but in this instance there was no hope that you would find what is not here. But, husband, will you not give up this foolishness and retract the slanderous accusation?'

The husband replied: 'I will in no way retract the charge, because I am certain of the truth of my accusation. You will have to clear yourself of the charge, if you can.'

She said she was not opposed to this, and so they ended their talk.

After this, Thorstein stayed mostly with the Varangians. It is said that he sought the advice of Harald Sigurdarson, and it is believed that Thorstein and Spes would never have found the right plan had they not been able to avail themselves of Harald's sage counsel.

A while later, Sigurd the husband let it be known that he would be leaving home on some business. His wife made no objection. When the husband had left, Thorstein came to Spes, and the two of them were constantly together. Her house was built in such a way that it projected out over the sea, with water flowing up under part of the house. It was in this part of the house that Spes and Thorstein frequently sat together. There was a small trap-door in the floor, which no one knew about except the two of them. It was left open in case they had to act quickly.

Now, there is this to tell about the husband: rather than leaving, he hid himself so as to spy on his wife. One evening Thorstein and Spes, amusing themselves, sat in the room overlooking the city. When they were least on their guard, the husband arrived unexpectedly with a large following. First he led some of his men up to a window, telling them to look in and see whether or not he was telling the truth. They all said he spoke the truth now, and must have done so previously. Then they burst into the room.

When they heard the noise, Spes said to Thorstein: 'You must, whatever the cost, go down the trapdoor, but send me a sign if you manage to escape from beneath the house.'

He agreed, and plunged down through the hole in the floor. Then, with her feet, the lady pushed the trapdoor shut. The lid fell back into place, and no one could see any traces that the floor had been newly altered. The husband and his men came into the room. They searched, but, as was to be expected, they found nothing. The room was empty, with nothing in it except the smooth floor and the benches. The lady sat there playing with her gold finger-rings, and seemingly unconcerned, she paid them little attention.

The husband was bewildered, and asked his followers whether they hadn't seen the man. They said that they had seen him for certain.

Then the wife said: 'It is just as in the old saying—by the third time everything is clear. And so it is with you, Sigurd,' she said. 'You have now, according to my reckoning, disturbed me three times, but are you now more knowledgeable than you were at the start?'

'This time I was not alone in making the claim,' he said, 'and in all these matters you will have to prove your innocence, because I will not in any way allow this dishonour to go unpaid.'

'As far as I am concerned,' said the wife, 'you are proposing exactly what I would have myself offered, because I'm perfectly willing to clear myself of this slander. You have, by now, made this matter so public that I would be badly disgraced if I did not clear myself of this charge.'

'In only one way can you deny the charge,' said the husband, 'and that is by proving you have never given away any of my money or my treasure.'

She replied: 'When I am put to the test, I will, in one action, free myself from all your accusations. Meanwhile you might consider the consequences. Tomorrow I will go immediately to the bishop and ask him to arrange the process by which I can clear this slander from my name.'

The husband was pleased, and left with his men.

Now there is this to be told about Thorstein. He swam under the house and, finding a suitable spot, came ashore. He got hold of a burning piece of wood and held it up so that it could be seen from the lady's house. She had remained outside long into the evening and then into the night, anxious to know if Thorstein had come ashore. When she saw the flame, she knew that he was safe on land, because they had previously decided on this signal.

The next day Spes asked her husband to go with her to the bishop to present their case, and the husband was all prepared. They came before the bishop, and the husband repeated the same charges against her as were told earlier. The bishop enquired whether she had previously faced similar accusations, but no one had heard any.

Then the bishop asked the husband what evidence he had for bringing such charges against her. The husband now produced witnesses who had seen her sitting in the locked room alone with a man. This led, the husband said, to the conclusion that the man had seduced her. The bishop declared that she was welcome to try to clear her name from this accusation, if she wished.

She replied that this was exactly what she wanted. 'For I believe', said Spes, 'that in this case I will have many women supporting me with their sworn oaths.'

Next the nature of the oath was determined, and the day was set when she was expected to come and swear to it. Following this, she went home and seemed pleased. Thorstein and Spes met and made a plan.

89. The Oath

THAT day passed and so also the time until Spes should swear her oath. She asked all her friends and kinsmen to come, and she dressed herself in her finest clothes. Many wealthy women accompanied her. It had rained that day, and the road was wet.

There was a large pool of stagnant water on the road, which had to be crossed before reaching the church. When Spes and her company came to the pool, many people were already gathered there. Among them was a large group of poor people begging alms, since this was a main street.

All the poor took it as their duty to greet her as warmly as they could, because she had often helped them. Among them was a tall beggar with a long beard.

The woman, always alert, stopped when she came to the muddy section, and the courtly people realized that, by crossing it, they would become filthy.

When the tall beggar saw the lady, he recognized her because she was better dressed than the other women. He said the following: 'Good lady, will you condescend to allow me to carry you across this muck? We beggars are required to serve as best we can.'

'How can you carry me,' she replied, 'when you can scarcely stand upright?'

'Be that as it may, it would be proof of your humility,' he said, 'and while I cannot offer more than what I have, matters will go altogether better for you if you do not treat a poor man with arrogance.'

'Know this for certain,' she said, 'if you do not carry me well, you will be flogged or receive an even worse disgrace.'

'I will gladly risk that,' he said, and waded out into the muck.

She appeared distressed about his carrying her. Nevertheless, she climbed up on his back. He stumbled along ever so slowly, supporting himself with two crutches.

When he reached the middle of the pool, he began to sway to both sides. She told him to get control of himself: 'And you will never have taken a worse trip than this, if you drop me here.'

The pathetic tramp now struggled forward and even seemed to gain strength. Using all his might, he almost reached the opposite side, only just then to lose his footing. Falling forward, he threw her onto the bank, while he himself landed in the ditch up to his armpits. Struggling there, he reached out and grabbed at the lady but was unable to grip her dress. Then his filthy hand landed on her knee and slid across her bare thigh.

She jumped up and cursed him, saying that one always received the worst from evil tramps. 'And it would be fitting for you to lie there till you die, if I did not feel that I myself would be shamed, given your sorrowful state.'

He replied: 'People's fortunes are so different. My intention was to help you, and in return, I looked forward to your reward of alms. But rather than receiving any gain, all that I have got are curses and abuse,' and he appeared overcome with emotion. Many felt pity for him, but she said he was faking. When many people pleaded for him, she took out her purse. It contained gold coins, and she shook out the money, which fell onto the ground, and said: 'This is for you, old man. It is proper that you not be denied full payment, after my treating you so harshly. We now part with your receiving a return for your labour.' He picked up the gold and thanked her for her kindness.

Spes now went to the church, where a large crowd had gathered. Sigurd opened his case vigorously, demanding that she clear herself of the charge he was bringing against her.

She answered: 'I give no credence to your accusation. But what is the name of the man that you claim to have seen with me in the house? There must always be some capable man in my service, and, because of this, I declare myself above reproach. I am prepared to swear an oath that I have given gold to no man, nor has any man touched my body in a defiling manner, except for my husband and that foul tramp who put his dirty hand on my thigh while carrying me over the ditch today.'

There was now general agreement that her oath had been satisfactory, and that she could not be reproached, even if the old man had accidentally touched her in an unseemly manner. She said that her words were a full accounting of what had happened. After this, she swore the oath according to what has been previously described. Many noted that she was holding true to the saying that little should be left unsaid in an oath. She said it was her belief that, in the eyes of sage men, she had removed all suspicion.

Now her kinsmen spoke up. They said that it was an insult for a well-born woman to have faced such slanderous accusations without compensation, because in that land, charging a woman with adulterously deceiving her husband carried the death-penalty if it were publicly proven. Spes next requested that the bishop declare her divorced from Sigurd, because she no longer wished to tolerate his accusations. Her kinsmen pleaded her case and, with their support and intervention, it came about that she and Sigurd were divorced. Sigurd received little of the property. He was forced to leave the country, and matters transpired, as is often the case, that those of lower rank have to give way. Sigurd had been unable to make any headway, even though he was the one in the right.

Spes now took all of the couple's wealth, and she was thought a woman of prominence. But later, when people considered her oath more closely, it seemed somewhat suspicious, and some were of the opinion that clever men might have dictated its wording to her. Then it became known that the beggar who had carried her was Thorstein. Even with this, Sigurd received no justice in the matter.

90. Thorstein and Spes Marry

THORSTEIN THE GALLEON remained with the Varangians while the case was the subject of public gossip. He became renowned among them, and it was thought that rarely had a man of such accomplishments joined them. Harald Sigurdarson granted him the highest honour when he openly recognized their kinship, and people came to understand that Thorstein had followed Harald's advice.

Shortly after Sigurd was driven from the country, Thorstein made a marriage proposal to Spes. She responded favourably, but deferred the decision to her kinsmen. They now held meetings, and it was decided that she should make the decision. Then the arrangements were made between the couple with the agreement of her kinsmen. Their union was a happy one, and they enjoyed ample wealth. Thorstein was thought to be a man of great luck, considering how he had overcome difficulties.

The couple had been together for two years in Constantinople when Thorstein said to his wife that he wanted to see to his property in Norway. She replied that he should decide, so he sold his possessions, which brought in a huge amount of money. Then they travelled with a fine retinue and continued the journey until arriving in Norway. Thorstein's kinsmen received both of them with exceptional warmth, and it was quickly seen that Spes was a generous and magnanimous person. She was soon extremely well liked. They had children together, and now well contented with their lives, they remained on their property.

At that time Magnus the Good was king of Norway, and Thorstein soon sought an audience. The king received him well, because Thorstein had become so famous, having avenged Grettir the Strong. People were hard put to find an example, beyond that of Grettir Asmundarson, in which an Icelander was avenged in Constantinople. It is said that Thorstein became a retainer of King Magnus.

Thorstein remained quietly at home for nine years after his return to Norway, and both man and wife were considered people of high distinction. Then King Harald Sigurdarson returned from Constantinople, and King Magnus gave him half of Norway as his share. For a time, both were kings of Norway.* When King Magnus died, his many friends became distressed, because they had all loved him. At the same time, there was an unease about King Harald's nature, because he was hard and vengeful.

Thorstein the Galleon was, by then, getting on in years, although he still remained vigorous. By now, sixteen years had passed since Grettir Asmundarson's killing.

91. Thorstein and Spes Attend to Their Souls

MANY urged Thorstein to meet with King Harald and enter his service, but Thorstein was reluctant. Then Spes said: 'It is my wish, Thorstein, that you do not seek an audience with King Harald, because we owe more of a debt to another king, and we need to think about this. We both are now getting older, and our youthful days are behind us. We have until now been more concerned with our own desires than with Christian teaching or the call of righteousness. I know now that the debt we owe can be settled neither by our kinsmen nor by our wealth, but only if we ourselves offer recompense. My wish is that we change our manner of living. We will now leave this land and travel to the pope's palace, and I believe that only there can my case be settled.'

Thorstein answered: 'The matters that you describe are as well known to me as they are to you. It is fitting that you should decide now when righteous issues are at stake, since you allowed me to decide when matters were headed in a far less seemly direction. This time, we will change things according to your wishes.'

People were much surprised by this decision. Thorstein was now two years short of sixty-five, but still active and capable in all his undertakings. He invited all of his kinsmen and relations to his house and announced his plan. The wise among them approved, but they looked upon the departure as a great loss. Thorstein said that he was not certain of returning.

'I want to thank all of you', declared Thorstein, 'for the manner in which you looked after my property the last time I was out of the country. Now I turn to you again, and ask that you take my children's property into your keeping and so also the children themselves. Raise them in accordance with your own values, because my age is such that, even if I survive the journey, the chances are good that I will not return. Look after everything that I leave behind, as though I shall not return to Norway.'

They answered that matters would be in good hands, 'if the lady of the house remained behind to look after things'.

Then she spoke up: 'The reason that I travelled from my homeland, leaving behind both kinsmen and wealth in Constantinople, was my wish that Thorstein and I should share one fate. I have greatly enjoyed being here, but I have no wish to remain longer in Norway or in the northern regions if he should leave. We have always loved each other, and nothing has yet come between us. We will now journey together, since we are the ones who know most what has happened since we first met.'

When they had arranged their affairs in this way, Thorstein asked men of integrity to divide the property into two equal shares. Thorstein's kinsmen took the half which the children were to inherit, and the children were brought up with their father's kinsmen. They became impressive people, and a great family is descended from them there in the Vik region. Thorstein and Spes then divided their share of the wealth in half. Some they gave to churches for their souls, and some they took with them. Then they set out for Rome, and many prayed for them.

92. Rome

THE couple travelled all the way until they reached the city of Rome. When they appeared before the man appointed to hear people's confessions, they gave a truthful account of everything that had occurred. They described the kinds of deception they had employed in bringing about their marriage, and they submitted meekly to whatever penance he chose to lay upon them. Because they had undertaken on their own to make amends for their misdeeds without any pressure or because of the wrath of church leaders, they received light treatment and they were relieved, as much as possible, from all fines of penance which might otherwise have been expected. They received absolution for all their concerns, and they were gently urged to arrange for their souls in a sensible matter and to live pure lives from then on. They were thought to have acted wisely and properly.

Then Spes said: 'It seems to me that matters have now gone well. We are successfully bringing our case to an end, and we can now say that we have shared more than misfortune. Because foolish people may find a model for themselves in our previous behaviour, we ought to arrange the conclusion of our life in an exemplary way. We will contract with men skilled in stonemasonry and have them build a stone hut for each of us. In this way, we may atone for our transgressions against God.

Thorstein then arranged payment for the construction of both stone huts. He also saw to whatever else they could not do without in order to live. At the conclusion of this work, when the time was suitable and all matters attended to, they ended their worldly life together. They did so of their own accord, that they might instead enjoy eternal life together in the next world. Each then entered a stone cell, and there they lived for as long a time as God chose. And so ended their lives.

Many say that Thorstein and his wife Spes were among the luckiest people, considering their troubles. There is no account that any of his children or any of his descendants have ever come to Iceland.

93. Sturla's Judgement

STURLA THE LAWMAN said that, in his opinion, no other outlaw was comparable to Grettir the Strong. He based his view on three factors. First, he found that Grettir was the cleverest, as witnessed by the fact that he lived in outlawry longest of all men and was never overcome while he had his health. Second, he was the strongest man in the land among those of the same age, and he was better than others at removing the walking dead and monsters. The third was that Grettir, unlike any other Icelander, was avenged out in Constantinople. To this can be added how much Thorstein the Galleon, the one who avenged Grettir, was a man of good luck in the latter part of his life.

Here ends *The Saga of Grettir Asmundarson*, our countryman. Let those who listened be thanked, but small thanks be given to the one who scribbled the saga. The work now concludes, and may we all be committed to God. Amen.

APPENDIX

GRETTIR'S JOURNEY THROUGH OUTLAWRY

A FEW years before Grettir's death, a controversy developed between his supporters and his opponents over the exact number of years that Grettir had been an outlaw. According to the saga, if Grettir reached a total of twenty years, first as a lesser outlaw and then as a full outlaw, he would have been freed from his outlawry. *Grágás* (the 'Grey Goose' law of the Old Icelandic Free State) does not mention this provision, and it is not certain that this was a formal law. The saga, however, makes much of this possibility, and Grettir's supporters argue that he had been an outlaw for twenty years. Grettir's opponents contend that he had been an outlaw for only nineteen years. The debate over Grettir's eligibility for freedom from his sentence has gone on for centuries.

The following charts divide Grettir's outlawry into two parts. The first lists Grettir's years as a lesser outlaw and the second, Grettir's years as a full outlaw. Both chronologies give the corresponding years, chapters, places, and events.

Outlawry: Legal Background to the Controversy and the Saga

In Iceland, people were outlawed rather than formally executed. The legal process of banishing people from the island served to keep the peace and to reinforce the integrity of the social order by removing dangerous or troublesome individuals, especially those who could not or would not abide by the rules. Outlawry served as a legalized step towards blood-taking and replaced a legal judgement of execution. Once a full outlaw, a person could be killed with impunity, that is, with no vengeance expected.

Outlawry provided Icelandic society with an efficient and cost-effective means of dispensing with troublemakers. It exempted the government from maintaining policing or coercive bodies to enforce an executive role, allowing the simplified government to focus on making laws and overseeing courts at the Althing. The responsibility for delivering executions to persons adjudged outlaws fell to private individuals, usually wronged parties or their agents.

The laws name two basic types of outlawry: *fjörbaugsgarðr*, lesser outlawry, and *skóggangr*, full outlawry (literally 'forest-going'). Both punishments included the confiscation of property. Lesser outlawry brought a sentence of a three-year exile abroad. Grettir received such a sentence for his first killing. A full outlaw (*skógarmaðr*) was not banished, nor was he permitted to travel abroad. During full outlawry, the law demanded that outlaws such as Grettir stay in Iceland, where they were denied all assistance. Although the law was sometimes broken, a full outlaw was not to be harboured by anyone, nor could he be helped to leave the country. In consequence, this punishment was a death sentence. Because of the seriousness of the penalty of full outlawry, and because it often resulted from arbitrated settlement, substantial consensus was required to sentence an individual. Sometimes, as is the case with Grettir, prices were placed on the heads of outlaws by enemies who wished to accelerate the execution of justice.

I. *Grettir's Lesser Outlawry*

In Chapter 76 the saga notes, concerning the death of the law-speaker Skapti Thoroddsson, that 'Skapti had promised to seek acquittal for Grettir after he had been an outlaw for twenty years. The events just recounted took place in the nineteenth winter of his outlawry. In the spring, Snorri Godi died, and at this time many other events occurred which are not discussed in this saga.' To reach these figures, the medieval author combined the years Grettir spent as a lesser outlaw (see Chronology 1 below) with those he spent as a full outlaw (see Chronology 2), but the author also counted some additional time.

Boys in Free State Iceland were treated as men after the age of twelve, and Grettir's lesser outlawry begins when, at the age of fourteen winters in the year 1011, he kills his first man. For this act he was made a lesser outlaw at the Althing and was banished from Iceland for three years. Grettir remains in Iceland a full year before setting out on his three-year banishment to Norway, adding an extra year to the time of his first outlawry. Grettir's lesser outlawry ends in the year 1014. He returns to Iceland, where he lives as a free man for a year until he returns to Norway in the autumn of 1015. How to count this year of freedom from outlawry in 1014 to 1015 becomes an issue. Grettir's enemies do not count this year as part of his combined time of outlawry.

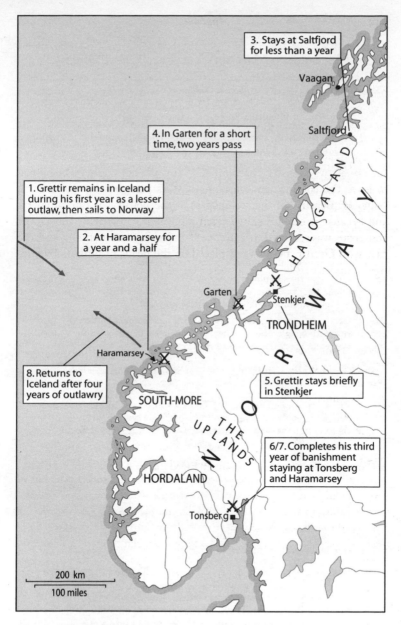

Map 10. Grettir's Lesser Outlawry (Three Years' Banishment). The numbers in the boxes correspond to the phases of Grettir's years in Norway during his lesser outlawry. See Chronology 1, below.

Chronology 1. Grettir's Years as a Lesser Outlaw

Chapter	Places and Events	Year

1. Young Grettir in Iceland (first year as a lesser outlaw)

16	Grettir kills Skeggi while travelling with Thorkel to the Althing. At the Althing Grettir is made a lesser outlaw.	1011
17	Grettir takes passage from Iceland to Norway with Haflidi and merchants. A storm drives their ship off course and they are shipwrecked off the coast of west Norway on the island of Haramarsey.	1011

2. Haramarsey Island in Norway (Grettir remains there for a year and a half)

18	Grettir stays with Thorfinn on Haramarsey. Grettir robs the burial mound of Thorfinn's father, Kar the Old.	1011–12
19	Jarl Svein rises to power in Norway. Grettir wins fame by killing the berserkers who plan, while Thorfinn is away, to rape Thorfinn's women and pillage his farm.	1012–13
20	Grettir travels to northern Norway. He receives many offers to stay with people who have heard of his deeds. He chooses to stay with Thorkel at Saltfjord in Halogaland.	1013

3. Saltfjord in Halogaland (Grettir stays at Saltfjord in northern Norway for less than a year)

21	Bjorn is a contentious guest of Thorkel's. A cave-bear kills animals and people. On the expedition to kill the bear, Bjorn throws Grettir's cloak into the bear's den. Grettir stays behind, kills the bear, and retrieves his cloak.	1013

4. Garten at the mouth of Trondheim Fjord (the specific time of Grettir's stay is not given, but it appears brief. By this time, Grettir has served two years of banishment.

21	Grettir meets Bjorn again and kills him for his past insults. No settlement is made.	1013

5. Stenkjer in Trondheim Fjord (Grettir's stay in Stenkjer is brief)

22	Bjorn's brother Hjarrandi hears of Bjorn's killing and attacks Grettir, who kills Hjarrandi. The jarl, coerced by Bersi Skald-Torfuson and Thorfinn, spares Grettir's life. He allows Grettir to remain free in Norway until the spring, when a meeting will be held in Tonsberg with Gunnar (Bjorn's other brother).	1013–14

Chapter	Places and Events	Year

6. Tonsberg and the Island of Haramarsey (the time spent first at Tonsberg and then at Haramarsey completes Grettir's three years of banishment from Iceland)

24   Gunnar attacks Grettir in a tavern, and Grettir kills Gunnar.   1013–14
Jarl Svein is enraged. He refuses any compensation for Gunnar
and tries to seize Grettir. Men come forward on Grettir's behalf.
The jarl rules that Grettir must leave Norway and return to
Iceland as soon as it is time for a ship to sail.

7. Grettir awaits passage home

24   Grettir stays with Thorfinn at Haramarsey until he finds   1014
passage.

8. Grettir's return to Iceland

28   Grettir returns to Iceland. Four years have gone by and his   1014
three-year term of lesser outlawry is served. News of his
deeds in Norway have reached Iceland before him, and
Grettir returns a hero.

II. Grettir's Full Outlawry

Freed from his lesser outlawry, Grettir returns in 1015 to Norway. Just after he arrives in Norway he accidentally burns to death Thorir of Gard's two sons. When Grettir returns to Iceland in 1016 at the age of twenty, Thorir has already had him declared an outlaw at the Althing. Chapters 46 to 82 focus on the years from 1016 to 1031, the time of Grettir's full outlawry. This was an exceptionally long period for an outlaw to survive, and during these years Grettir never leaves Iceland. At first he wanders through the different districts, living mostly with friends and kinsmen. He seeks but never finds a safe refuge. As time passes, most people, even kinsmen, are unwilling to harbour him. Despite Grettir's growing fear of the dark, he is often forced to live alone or with outlaws in the desolate inland regions.

The Chronology below begins in 1016 and continues until the year 1031, when Grettir is killed at the age of thirty-five. In Chapter 77 the law-speaker rules that anyone who remains alive as an outlaw for

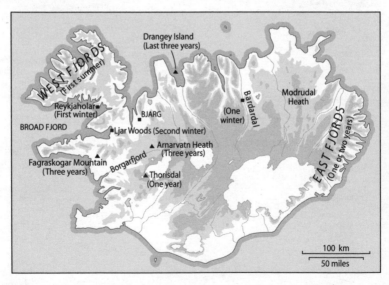

Map 11. Grettir's Full Outlawry. This map gives the places and the number of winters where Grettir stays as a full outlaw. During the summers he is mostly on the move.

twenty years has earned his freedom. If the one year, 1015, between Grettir's lesser and full outlawries is counted, then Grettir reaches the necessary twenty years. His enemies, however, argue that his one year as a free man between lesser and full outlawry should not be counted, and that Grettir has been an outlaw for only nineteen years. If this is so, then Grettir is killed in his twentieth and last year as an outlaw.

Chronology 2. Grettir's Years as a Full Outlaw

Chapter	Places and Events	Year

1. Grettir's case at the Althing and his return home

| 46–7 | At the Althing Grettir is made a full outlaw by the chieftain Thorir of Gard. Toward the end of the summer Grettir returns to Iceland. | 1016 |

2. Grettir, home at Bjarg for a short time

| 48 | Grettir takes vengeance for the death of his brother Atli by killing Thorbjorn Oxen-Might. Grettir then goes to Ljar Woods and stays with Thorstein Kuggason. Men gather to attack, and Grettir moves on. | 1016 |

3. At Reykjaholar, Grettir's first winter

| 49 | Grettir is refused shelter by Snorri the Godi. Thorodd Poem-Stump prepares to avenge the death of his brother, Thorbjorn Oxen-Might. | 1016 |
| 50 | Grettir stays one winter with the chieftain Thorgils Arason at Reykjaholar. The foster-brothers Thormod and Thorgeir are also there. Grettir spends the spring and early summer at Langadal. | 1016–17 |

4. The Althing and travels to the West Fjords

| 51–2 | At the Althing Thorodd is required to pay compensation for Atli. Thorir of Gard, Grettir's sworn enemy, prevents the ending of Grettir's outlawry. In the summer Grettir journeys to the West Fjords, where the farmers capture him. Thorbjorg the Stout, wife of the chieftain Vermund, orders the farmers to release Grettir. | 1017 |

5. Ljar Woods during Grettir's second winter of full outlawry

| 53 | At Ljar Woods during the winter, Grettir stays with Thorstein Kuggason. In Borgarfjord Grettir stays with Grim Thorhallsson. At Tunga Grettir stays with Thorhall Asgrimsson. | 1017–18 |

Chapter	Places and Events	Year

6. Kjol for most of the summer

54   At Kjol Grettir encounters Lopt (Hallmund), who bests him in   1018
       strength. At Hjalli, Grettir meets Skapti the law-speaker. In
       Borgarfjord Grettir visits Grim Thorhallsson. In the autumn he
       goes up onto Arnarvatn Heath.

7. Arnarvatn Heath for three winters

55   On Arnarvatn Heath Grettir kills the outlaw Grim.   1018–19

56–7   On Arnarvatn Heath Grettir kills the outlaw Thorir Red-Beard.   1019–21
       Thorir of Gard and his men attack Grettir, but Hallmund saves
       him. Grettir and Hallmund go to Ball Glacier, and Grettir stays
       in Hallmund's Cave. Grettir travels to Borgarfjord in the autumn
       and then to Myrar.

8. Fagraskogar Mountain for three winters

58   Grettir settles in at Fagraskogafjall above the Myrar   1021–2
       district for the first winter.

59   The merchant Gisli arrives at Fagraskogafjall in the autumn   1022–3
       before Grettir's second winter there.

60   Grettir battles local farmers at Grettisoddi. He spends his third   1023–4
       winter at Fagraskogafjall.

**9. A year in Thorisdal in the middle of a glacier. Then travels
seeking support**

61   Grettir meets with Grim Thorhallsson in Borgarfjord in late   1024–5
       spring. He stays with Hallmund near Geitland Glacier during
       the summer. Later he lives under the protection of a half-troll,
       the giant Thorir, and Grettir calls the valley Thorisdal.

61   Grettir travels south and then to the East Fjords. He stays in the   1025–7
       East during the summer and through the winter, unsuccessfully
       seeking the support of the chieftains.

10. Travels through Modrudal Heath and Reykja Heath

63   Grettir stays a summer on Modrudal Heath and Reykja Heath.   1027
       He tricks Thorir of Gard, who is hunting him.

11. Sandhaugar in Bardardal for one winter

64   Grettir hears of the hauntings in Bardardal and goes there.   1027

65   Arrives in Bardardal at the farm of Sandhaugar just before   1027
       Christmas. Grettir defeats a troll-woman by cutting off her arm.

66   After Christmas Grettir dives under a waterfall in Bardardal   1027
       and kills a male troll.

Chapter	Places and Events	Year
67	In the spring Grettir goes to Modruvellir. He seeks the advice of Gudmund the Powerful, who tells Grettir to go to the island of Drangey. Grettir travels to Bjarg.	1028

12. Broad Fjord by mid summer

68	Grettir spends the summer in Broad Fjord. Thorodd, Snorri the Godi's son, attacks him. Grettir refuses to harm the young man.	1028

13. Three winters on Drangey Island

69	In the autumn, Grettir returns for a short time to Bjarg to see his mother Asdis. He and his younger brother, Illugi, part from their mother and head north. In Skagafjord they meet a vagrant named Glaum and take him with them as their servant. Grettir denies them the farmer at Reykir to ferry them out to the island.	1028
70	Chieftains and farmers in Skagafjord, including Thorbjorn Hook of Vidvik, own shares in Drangey. They graze their sheep in common on the island, fattening the livestock for slaughter on the rich grass. Grettir denies them their rights.	1028
71	The farmers in Skagafjord try to retrieve their sheep from Drangey. Grettir refuses because he is eating the sheep. Grettir, Illugi, and Glaum spend their first winter on the island.	1028–9
72	In the spring at the Hegraness Thing Grettir, disguised as Gest, is promised immunity. He wrestles in the games. The farmers of Skagafjord sell their shares in Drangey to Thorbjorn Hook.	1029
73	At the end of the summer Grettir refuses Thorbjorn Hook's request to leave Drangey.	1029
74	At the end of the second winter on Drangey the servant Glaum allows the hearth fire to go out.	1029–30
75	Because they have no fire on Drangey, Grettir swims to Reykir, the nearest farm on the mainland.	1029–30
76	In the summer Thorbjorn Hook hires Haering to climb up onto Drangey and kill Grettir. Illugi chases Haering, who jumps off the cliff to his death at Haering's Leap. The third winter on Drangey passes.	1030–1
77	At the Althing arrangements are made to release Grettir from his outlawry after one year.	1031
78	Thorbjorn Hook sails to Drangey with his foster-mother, Thurid. Grettir hits her with a rock.	1031
79	Thurid curses a piece of driftwood and sends it to Drangey. Grettir tries to chop it up and cuts himself.	1031
80	Grettir's leg festers and he becomes deathly ill.	1031

Chapter	Places and Events	Year
81	Thorbjorn Hook sends for men and sails from Haganess to Drangey. Glaum forgets to raise the ladder. Thorbjorn and his men get on to the island.	1031
82	Grettir and Illugi defend themselves, but Thorbjorn and his men overcome them. Thorbjorn cuts off Grettir's head to use as proof of Grettir's death. Thorbjorn ends Grettir's outlawry but is himself accused of using sorcery.	1031

GENEALOGICAL TABLES

Genealogy 1. *Grettir's Saga*

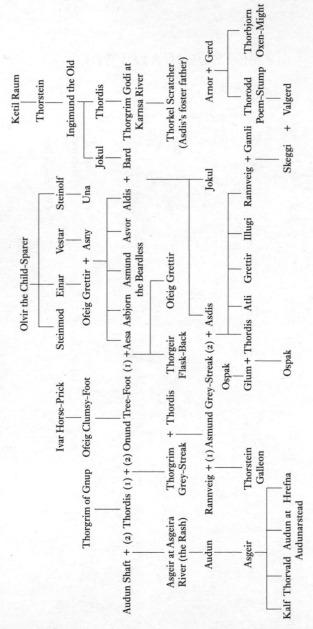

Genealogy 2. *Grettir's kinship with King Olaf the Saint of Norway*

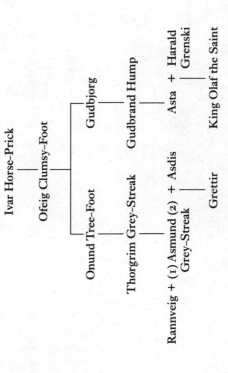

Genealogy 3. *Shared kinship between three founding families in the dispute over the second beached whale: descendants of Onund Tree-Foot, Ulf the Squint-Eyed, and Aud the Deep-Minded; despite kinship, the four individuals in the last generation are on opposing sides of the dispute*

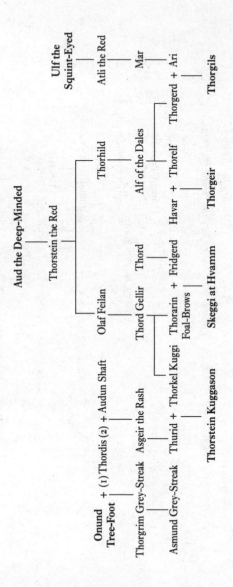

Genealogy 4. *The relationship between Grettir and Thorbjorg the Stout: kinship between the families of Onund Tree-Foot and Egil Skallagrimsson*

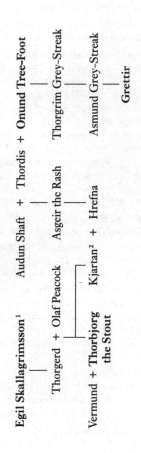

[1] The hero of *Egil's Saga*.

[2] Although married to Hrefna, Kjartan's love for Gudrun, the daughter of Osvif, is one of the central aspects of *Laxdaela Saga* and one of the most famous love-affairs in sagas.

EXPLANATORY NOTES

9 *Onund*: this important pedigree shows that Onund, who lived in the late ninth and early tenth centuries, came from a family of prominence and that his descendant Grettir is related to the Norwegian king, St Olaf, who reigned from 1015 to 1030. St Olaf and Grettir meet later in the saga.

The West: for medieval Norwegians and Icelanders, 'the West' or 'the West across the sea' meant the British Isles. See Map 1.

The Hebrides: the Hebrides, to the west of Scotland, were early occupied by Norse settlers. *Grettir's Saga* and other Old Icelandic writings note that many of Iceland's prominent first settlers, the 'land-takers' as they were called, spent some time in the Hebrides towards the end of the ninth century before setting out for Iceland. Several Icelandic sources refer to Kjarval (Irish *Cearbhall*) as king of the Irish. He was king of Ossory in southern Ireland for around forty years, and died in 887 or 888. Several early Icelandic families trace their ancestry to him. The Barra Isles at the southern tip of the Outer Hebrides were an ideal base for raiding in the 'West'. Norwegian seamen sailed past Shetland, Orkney, and Scotland, from where they had easy access to the Hebrides, whose islands play a significant role in the early part of the saga. See Map 1.

Harald Shaggy-Haired: the legend is that young Harald, initially one of many small kings, swore an oath not to trim or comb his hair until he had gained control over the whole of Norway, hence the nickname 'shaggy-haired'. After completing the conquest (*c*.870), Harald's hair was combed and cut, and he received the new name Harald 'fairhair'.

10 *Helskin*: 'helskin' (*heljarskinn*) meant skin that was either dark or pale as death. Geirmund was a royal prince from one of Norway's many regional families. After a career as a successful viking captain, he eventually settled in Iceland, where he was famous for living in the grand style of a viking prince, surrounded by retainers. Later Icelanders venerated Geirmund as a prominent ancestor.

Hafursfjord: the battle of Hafursfjord (*c*.885) took place not far from modern-day Stavanger. The battle, which gave Harald undisputed control over a good part of Norway, especially the coastal regions, is mentioned in many Old Icelandic writings, both sagas and histories. See Map 1.

the fleet: sea-battles were often fought as if they were floating land-battles. Ships of allies were tied together, allowing men to move from one ship to another.

berserker: berserkers were warriors who went into a frenzy or a 'berserker rage' in battle, and in their abandon they seemed almost invincible. According to numerous sagas and medieval writings, Scandinavian kings were expected to keep a small retinue of these fearless warriors (see *The*

Saga of King Hrolf Kraki). Berserkers probably were connected with the cult of the war-god Odin. Here in the saga such fighters are called the 'wolfskins', a select group of men who fought on King Harald's ship and went into frenzies during battle.

10 *forecastle men*: the king placed his best men on the prow, or the forecastle as the prow was called on medieval ships. It was an honour to be posted at this dangerous spot.

11 *Onund*: the line makes more sense if 'Onund' is replaced by 'Geirmund'. Perhaps it is a scribal error.

Grettir: the meaning of the name *Grettir* is unclear; it could be 'grimacer' or 'frowner', but the word also means 'serpent', 'snake', or 'penis'.

12 *Easterner*: 'Easterners', literally 'east-men' (*austmenn*), was the Icelandic term for Norwegians. Icelanders, whose island was to the west of Norway, tended to call all Norwegians east-men. Norwegians distinguished themselves by their home regions or *fylki* within Norway.

Eyvind's mother . . . Ondott Crow: this line and the following one show that Thrand and Eyvind had different mothers.

Hersir: *hersir* were regional military leaders. They are frequently mentioned in Icelandic writings as rapacious king's-men. King Harald, who abolished the small kings, kept the title of *hersir* and gave it to some of his own followers. Although not royal, a *hersir* had noble status and functioned much like a local chieftain.

13 *Helgi the Lean and Snaebjorn*: Helgi the Lean became one of Iceland's most prominent settlers. He claimed land in Eyjafjord in the north. His brother Snaebjorn claimed land in northern Iceland farther to the west in Vatnsfjord.

'The day . . . despair': verses 1, 3, 4, and 5 are all spoken by Onund and could possibly be fragments of a typical 'old warrior's lament', a poetic genre well represented in medieval Icelandic as well as in Old English and early Welsh.

15 *trolls*: 'troll' (*tröll*) had a broader meaning in Old Norse than it does in modern English, designating a variety of harmful supernatural creatures, including fiends, ghosts, witches, and giants.

'The trolls . . . boatload': short versified jibes of this kind, technically called *kviðlingar*, were a staple type of informal verse-making in Iceland.

16 *warriors*: one of the kennings (poetic circumlocutions employed by Norse poets) for 'warrior' in verse 3 illustrates how subtle and at times untranslatable kennings can be. The kenning *snerru Gjalpar brjótr* means 'warrior', but translates literally as 'breaker of the giantess of the skirmish'. We get from 'breaker of the giantess of the skirmish' to 'warrior' by solving a two-stage riddle, the first part of which is: *What is the 'giantess of the skirmish'?* Answer: *An axe.* The axe is thought of as sweeping down on its victim like a giant or troll. The feminine gender of the word *øx* ('axe') no doubt influenced the comparison with giantesses or troll-women in particular.

In verse 11 we shall see Grettir basing one of his characteristic witticisms on just this equation. The second part is: *What is the 'breaker of the axe'?* Answer: *The warrior*. To add to the complexity, puns and other word-play might be at work as well. Thus this particular giantess is named Gjalp, a word which also means 'boasting'. When Onund uses this word, it ties in with his accusation of 'mouthing off' in the previous line.

16 *Iceland*: Iceland had been newly discovered, and rumours of its large expanses of free land circulated in the Scandinavian homelands and the viking overseas encampments.

Skalavik: *vík* is the Old Norse word for bay or inlet, and there are many such place-names in the saga and throughout Scandinavia.

17 *abroad in the West*: the implication is that Thrand was an outlaw in Norway.

Thrand: Thrand was the son of Ondott's daughter, Bjorn's second wife. See Genealogy 3.

18 *Steinsholt . . . Skaftaholt*: *holt* originally meant a 'wood', but came to mean a 'rough stony hill' or 'ridge'. The meaning is often unclear and may have changed over time with deforestation and erosion. In this sentence 'Skafta' in the place-name Skaftaholt may derive from Skafti, a man's name.

Godi: 'godi' (*goði*) was the Icelandic word for chieftain. The title derives from the word for 'god', showing that Icelandic chieftains originally had a priestly function under the pre-Christian religion. Icelandic chieftains were small-scale leaders. In many ways, they functioned along the lines of what anthropologists term local 'big men'.

Thjors River: 'thjor' (*þjór*) is a bull. *The Book of Settlements* says that Thorarin Thorkelsson brought his ship into the *Þjórsárós* (Thjors River Estuary) and had a bull's head on his prow. The river was named for this.

19 *foster-father*: fosterage was the custom of having a child raised in another household in order to extend kinship bonds or to form political alliances.

Soknadal: The '-dal' at the end of many Norwegian and Icelandic place-names such as Soknadal comes from Old Norse *dalr*, meaning 'dale' or 'valley'.

Yuletide: Yule, the pre-Christian winter feast later assimilated to Christmas, was an occasion for drinking-bouts, swearing of oaths, and general merry-making. In Scandinavia the event is frequently associated with supernatural encounters.

Agder: Agder is the region just south of Rogaland.

Jarl: 'jarl' was a noble title roughly equivalent to English 'earl'.

20 *landed-man*: 'landed-men' (*lendir menn*) were nobles responsible for keeping the peace and maintaining defence. Many landed-men who received their lands directly from the king were among the king's major regional representatives.

21 *mount*: in the language of kennings, ships are often spoken of as 'horses of the sea'.

22 *tacked*: the Old Icelandic reads *beittu* (they 'beat'), meaning they tacked into the wind.

Hris Island: Hris Island (*Hrísey*) is the large island at the entrance to Eyjafjord. Eyjafjord (Island Fjord) takes its name from this prominent island.

Asgrim: Asgrim Ellida-Grimsson plays a prominent role in *Njal's Saga*. His son Thorhall appears in Ch. 53 of this saga.

houseman: see note to 'hired hand' p. 26

23 *'While . . . Cold Back'*: although several days' sailing have passed since Onund recited his previous verse, verses 4 and 5 read as if they constitute a single present-tense narrative, with verse 5 taking up the story where verse 4 left off. Connected verses, separated by prose narration, are frequently found in the sagas. In some cases, this may be because the prose embroiders upon a story originally told more economically in verse.

Kaldbak Cliffs: *Kaldbak*, where Onund settles, has several meanings. The simplest is 'a mountain with snow on the top', hence 'cold back'. The word also means 'the back of a whale', and steep sloping mountains without cliffs were sometimes named *kaldbak* and the site could be translated as 'cold slope'. Cliffs, named *kaldbakskleifar*, stand out distinctly in the Icelandic landscape. Onund's family becomes known as the 'men of Kaldbak'.

Reykjarfjord . . . side: reyk- is found in many place-names in Iceland. In Old Norse it meant smoke, but in Iceland *reyk-* sites are located in areas of thermal activity and named after smoke or steam coming from natural steam vents. Many of the *reyk-* sites, including the farms named Reykir, had surface hot pools used as thermal baths.

driftage: Iceland lies at the convergence of strong polar currents and the Gulf Stream. The waters carry drifting objects from as far away as the forests of northern Siberia and Central and South America, but only certain Icelandic coasts receive driftage. With wood and meat often in short supply, rights to driftage, especially timber and beached whales, were disputed. A significant portion of Iceland's medieval law is devoted to such issues.

24 *Onund . . . south*: Onund has much responsibility here Ofeig was both Onund's friend and his father-in-law.

Aud the Deep-Minded: she was one of the foremost settlers (*landnámsmenn*) of Iceland. A resourceful and respected leader, she is thought to have been the wife of one of the viking kings of Dublin. After his death she arranged for the escape of her family, leading them to Iceland and settling at Hvamm in the Breidafjord region. Aud, who is sometimes called Unn, is mentioned in many Icelandic writings, especially in *Laxdaela Saga* (*The Saga of the People of the Salmon River Valley*).

Kjalarness Thing: the Kjalarness Thing was a local district assembly of the type which the early settlers established to govern regionally before the

Althing was created in the year 930. After the Althing started, the local things became springtime assemblies which met annually before the June Althing.

24 *Singed Kari*: Kari Solmundarson plays an important role in *Njal's Saga*. His nickname comes from his escape from Njal's burning farmhouse.

25 *Midfjord-Skeggi*: Midfjord-Skeggi appears in a number of Icelandic sagas, including *Laxdaela Saga*, *Kormak's Saga*, and *Thord's Saga*. *The Book of Settlements* tells the story that Skeggi, before he settled in Iceland, raided as a viking in the Baltic. Once he came to Denmark he broke into the grave-mound of Hrolf Kraki and stole Hrolf's famous sword Skofnung. Hrolf, in *The Saga of King Hrolf Kraki*, uses Skofnung to cut off the buttocks of King Adils of Sweden.

26 *games*: little is known about how these ball games were played, although the sagas frequently mention them. Individuals apparently competed one-on-one and used sticks to hit the ball. Games were held mostly in the autumn, when people were free after the haying, sheep round-up, and slaughter time.

hired hand: *húskarl* or 'houseman' has several meanings. It could be 'a short-term hired worker' or 'a longtime servant'. It could be 'a trusted freeman', sometimes even 'a kinsman who lived with a landowner' or 'a chieftain accepted as an armed follower'. The plural of the word could be 'farmhands', 'servants', 'housemen', 'retainers', or simply 'men', depending on the context.

27 *'In better days . . . whey'*: verses pouring scorn upon an adversary are a staple in Old Icelandic poetry. The verse adheres passably well to the rules of the *dróttkvætt* (court-measure) stanza, with alliteration, internal rhyme, fixed metrical patterns, a division of the eight lines into two four-line units, and some use of kennings. The great majority of verses in *Grettir's Saga* belong to this stanza-form.

28 *Thorgrim*: Thorgrim Grey-Streak's brothers, Ofeig Grettir and Thorgeir Flask-Back, seem to have been present in this episode. There were four brothers in all, and it may be that all the brothers were involved.

30 *Hel*: Hel, the daughter of the trickster god Loki and a giantess, is the Norse goddess of death and the underworld. The name, as here, is sometimes used for the underworld itself.

ships: the saga generally uses the word *skip*, but many of these are small coastal boats, mostly rowing skiffs, some with rudimentary sails and perhaps some ferries. When larger ships are mentioned, the saga often refers to them as *hafskip* (ocean-going ships).

31 *'At Rifsker . . . pranks'*: here heroic vocabulary is used about a distinctly unheroic fight. Verses 60 and 61 also contain mock-heroic diction.

law-speaker: the only significant national leader of the Old Icelandic Free State was the law-speaker. He was elected at the Althing as head of the legislative council for a three-year term. At the Law Rock, the law-speaker annually recited a third of the law from memory. The law-speaker's advice in matters of law and procedure was frequently sought in legal cases.

Ingolf: Ingolf Arnason was Iceland's first settler.

32 *Saga of Bodmod, Grimolf, and Gerpi*: this saga is now lost.

Grey Locks: a characteristic of hair prematurely turning grey ran in his family. See comments on his father in Ch. 11.

33 *prime-signed*: 'prime-signed' is a Norse term meaning 'provisional baptism', adopted from Latin *primum signum* or *prima signatio*. It often consisted of making the sign of the cross over non-Christians.

34 *His children . . . are these*: Illugi is not mentioned. This much younger son, who later becomes Grettir's companion, is born when Asmund is an old man. See Ch. 37.

'The Saga of the Confederates': or *Bandamanna Saga*.

35 *long fire*: the Icelandic term for a long-house or hall is *eldaskáli*, the 'fire-hall', so named after the fire down the centre of the main room.

36 *'Your purse-proud . . . home in!'*: the vocabulary here reflects a heroic age, with gifts and hoards. The association of birds of carrion with human bloodshed is a standard heroic theme in Old Icelandic poetry, as also in the poetry of Anglo-Saxon England and many other societies.

Kengala: Kengala is named after the dark stripe down her back. Horses of this colour (*bleikálóttr*) have a natural parting of the hair at the highest point of the back, exposing the darker roots of the horsehair from the mane back to the tail.

38 *'That fine mare . . . poetic words'*: in the final line the aggrieved Asmund uses a poetic formula that normally would be at home in poems of praise, not censure as here.

44 *handshake*: a contractual, witnessed handclasp was termed *handsal*. This public gesture (perhaps a loud hand-slap) bound the parties. Thorkel is putting his honour on the line by publicly demonstrating support for Grettir. The gesture shows that Grettir has the support of people of substance, adding honour to a settlement.

three years: three years' banishment was lesser outlawry.

Grettir's-Lift: two other stones in the saga are also called Grettir's-Lift (*Grettishaf*). See Chs. 30 and 59.

45 *'As a seafaring man . . . child'*: incorporation of proverbs was a popular device among Old Icelandic poets. Successfully employing proverbs within the constraints of *dróttkvætt* stanza-form was a sign of poetic virtuosity.

48 *sleeves*: in the Middle Ages, before the introduction of buttons, sleeves on outer clothes were wide at the cuffs, which were sewed closed when the item was put on.

49 *'Grettir! . . . out of sight'*: the text and meaning of this verse is unclear. This saga and fragments of the late medieval poem *Grettisfærsla* indicate that Grettir was associated with sexual exploits as well as mischief.

49 *fair of complexion*: in keeping with the (mock) heroic tone of verses like this one, the woman is spoken of as fair-complexioned. The poem *Rígsþula* indicates that such complexion was a mark of the highest social class.

sluices: sluices were troughs that were attached between the gunwales across the width of the ship, and buckets of bilge-water were emptied into these gutters during bailing. This arrangement allowed the bailing water to run off on its own as the ship rolled.

50 *karfi*: a *karfi* was a fast coastal rowing ship often used in raiding. Long and narrow with six, twelve, or sixteen rowers on each side, such boats were also used on large lakes.

52 *mound-dweller's neck . . . buttocks*: ghosts in Icelandic tradition are not shadowy spirits but corporeal beings in the manner of the walking dead. Cutting off the head of a revenant and placing it alongside the buttocks is repeated later in the saga in the episode with Glam.

sax: hoards of buried treasure often contain valuable weapons. *The Book of Settlements* recounts that when Midfjord-Skeggi broke open the funeral mound of King Hrolf Kraki, he discovered among the other valuable items the dead king's sword, Skofnung, as well as the axe once wielded by Hjalti, one of Hrolf's legendary champions. The type of weapon mentioned here, the sax, is the same kind of broad, single-edged short-sword with which Grendel's mother attempts to kill Beowulf during the battle in her underwater lair.

53 *'Man . . . for gold'*: the content of this verse contradicts the prose. Perhaps in some versions of the story Grettir's sole discovery in the mound was the short-sword mentioned in the next verse.

slip from my hands: that Grettir lives up to this pledge is attested in verse 71.

55 *Jarl Eirik Hakonarson*: Jarl Eirik and his brother Jarl Svein were sons of Jarl Hakon, the hereditary leader of the Trondelag region of northern Norway. Eirik and Svein came to power after King Olaf Tryggvason died in the battle of Svold in the year 1000. Information from the kings' sagas indicates that Jarl Eirik died in 1013 and that half of Norway was then transferred to his young son Hakon. The other portion, and perhaps his nephew's share as well, was ruled by Jarl Svein. In 1014–15 Svein was forced to share his rule with St Olaf, who took control of young Hakon. In 1015 Olaf crushed Svein's power in the battle of Nesjar, and Hakon sailed to England, seeking the protection of Canute the Great. Hakon drowned in 1028. Canute the Great was the Danish conqueror and ruler of England from 1016/17 to 1035. Knut's father, Svein Forkbeard, the king of Denmark, was the father of Gyda, Eirik's wife.

his saga: there are no existing versions of this saga.

Slysfjord: Slysfjord in South-More was most likely a part of Storfjorden.

56 *freemen*: *frelsingi* (freeman) has two meanings, either 'one who was born free' or 'one who was set free'.

62 *buried . . . high-tide line*: the Old Norwegian Law of the Gulathing assembly specifies that 'each man shall be taken to church, when dead, to be buried in hallowed earth except for evil-doers, traitors, murderers, truce-breakers, and thieves as well as those men who themselves take their own lives. And those men, now specified, shall be buried at the tidal edge, where the sea meets the green grass'.

63 *living-room*: many larger houses had a sitting- or living-room, called in Old Norse a *stofa* (stove room). The *stofa* often had wooden benches along the panelled wooden walls and a wooden floor. Sometimes there was a raised wooden dais at the far end.

64 *Vaagan*: Vaagan (Old Icelandic *Vogar*), part of the Lofoten Islands off northern Norway, is close to excellent fishing grounds. In the Middle Ages a well-attended yearly fair was held at Vaagan. Saltfjord or Saltenfjord in Norwegian (Old Icelandic *Sálfti*) lies approximately 90 km south of Vaagan.

65 *Bjorn . . . namesake*: 'Bjorn' in Old Norse means 'bear'. It was, and remains, a common name.

68 *And . . . other*: this line makes little sense, and numerous critics have commented on it. The idea seems to be that one man's death is another's good fortune.

70 *Hjarrandi . . . pouch*: meaning that he would not accept a financial settlement in lieu of his taking vengeance.

land-cleansing: the Icelandic term is *landhreinsun* (land-cleansing).

streets: 'street' (*stræti*), though sounding modern, was an Old Norse word referring to a road within a town. Probably of Latin origin, the word was in usage by the twelfth century, and perhaps even earlier. It may have been borrowed from Old English.

71 *householder*: the term *garðsbóndi*, translated here as 'householder', was a rank denoting a property-owner within a town.

75 *'Thorfinn . . . my life'*: like many of the verses attributed to Grettir, this one is composed in *kviðuháttr*, a short-line metre.

'Look . . . the trickster': the first half of this verse is a riddle. The answer is the name 'Thorstein the Galleon'. The 'giant-killer' stands for Thor, who was famed in myth for such exploits; the 'hefty rock' stands for *steinn* ('stone'); and the 'ship' stands for a Mediterranean type galleon (*drómundr*). Hel, who presided over the world of the dead, was the daughter of Loki, the subversive god who contributed to the death of Baldur.

Bersi: Bersi's name literally means 'bear', and is punned on in this verse. Bersi's sword, in the language of kennings, is a *'fire* of the shield' which *burns* the *'arsenals* of tricks' (i.e. hacks the skulls of the enemy).

76 *Isleif*: Isleif was bishop of Skalholt from 1056 to 1080. Skalholt was one of Iceland's two bishoprics. Isleif was chosen to serve as Iceland's first bishop by the chieftains at the Althing. He went abroad for consecration.

76 *wild foods . . . driftage*: 'wild foods' refers to eggs, seals, and all that was useful along the coast. Driftage in old Icelandic had a wide meaning, including most of what could be hunted, found, or gathered along the shore including beached whales.

foster-brothers: men who swore an oath of allegiance to each other were often referred to as sworn- or foster-brothers.

unjust men: the use of the word 'unjust' is an understatement. Thorgeir and Thormod are the leading ruffians in *The Saga of the Sworn Brothers* (*Fóstbrœðra saga*).

77 *drapa*: a *drápa* was a formal poem of praise. Fifteen stanzas of Thorgeir's *drápa* are preserved in *The Saga of the Sworn Brothers*.

quarter: in about 965 Iceland was divided into quarters. When an event took place that involved people from different quarters, the prosecution had the option of taking the case directly to the Althing rather than prosecuting in a court located in the quarter where the event had occurred or the defendant was domiciled.

blood-money: financial compensation in lieu of vengeance. The suggestion here is that Thorstein finds a financial settlement dishonourable.

outlawry: a judgement of outlawry meant that the man could be killed with legal sanction, while taking blood-vengeance meant going outside the law. The latter was a viable option only when the offended party felt, as in this instance, that it had sufficient strength on its side.

Thorvald: the godi Thorvald Asgeirsson lived at As in Vatnsdal. The prosecutors and defendants are related, descending from Thorstein the Red, the son of Aud the Deep-Minded.

79 *'Success . . . hands-on treatment'*: this stanza is found in the 'Lay of Thorgeir' (*Þorgeirsdrápa*) in *The Saga of the Sworn Brothers*.

80 *law-speaker*: here the author uses the term 'lawman' (*lögmaðr*) from his own time, rather than the earlier term 'law-speaker' (*lögsögumaðr*) from the time of the events recounted in the saga. 'Lawman' means a man who has a wide knowledge of the law, but this word did not come into frequent use until introduced in the Norwegian-influenced lawbooks *Jarnsíða* (*Iron Sides*) from 1271 and the later *Jónsbók* (*Jon's Book*). The use of the term 'lawman' reflects the late date of the saga's composition, most probably in the early fourteenth century.

81 *Audun*: this is the same Audun who, at the ball game in Ch. 15, beat Grettir at wrestling. Information from *The Book of Settlements* suggests that there is a scribal error here, and that the great-grandfather of Audun at Audunarstead was Audun Shaft rather than Audun the Rash.

82 *shieling*: during the summer months Icelanders followed Norwegian practice and moved their livestock to upland pastures, where pens and sheds for the animals, dairy-making huts, and living-quarters for the herdsmen and dairymaids were located. The Icelandic word for these summer dairy stations is *sel* (singular and plural). The Scottish term

'shieling' is somewhat known in English. Icelandic *sel* were private property and for the most part on private land.

skyr: milk curds.

83 *Hall*: the sons of Harek killed Bardi's brother Hall Gudmundarson without sufficient provocation. Then they themselves were lost at sea. Bardi from the north inherited the claim of blood-vengeance and ultimately would ride south to attack the killers' kinsmen in Borgarfjord. Bardi Gudmundarson's act of vengeance is described in *Heiðarvíga saga* (*The Saga of the Heath Slayings*), in which Bardi is the main hero.

Bardi: although here described as a moderate man intervening in the face of Grettir's arrogance, Bardi is widely known in the literature as Killer Bardi (*Víga-Barði*) because of his vengeance-taking. At the time of this incident in *Grettir's Saga*, Bardi and his supporters from the northern part of the country have not yet ridden south into the Borgarfjord region where they will attack their enemies.

Audun: the Icelandic turns on untranslatable word-play on two proper names, *Auðunn* (= '*Óðinn*') and the name of the author of the verse, *Grettir* (= 'snake').

84 *horse-fight*: horse-fighting was commonly organized as a popular spectacle in medieval Iceland, rather as cock-fighting was elsewhere. The sport was highly competitive, dangerous, and frequently led to quarrels.

Kengala: the horse owned by Grettir's father, the one Grettir flayed as a boyish prank.

Kormak and Thorgils: the same brothers who were at the ball game in Ch. 15.

86 *Poem-Stump*: Thorodd's nickname, 'poem-stump' (*drápustúfur*), refers to part of a *drápa*, a poem of praise.

87 *Grettir's-Lift*: this is the second stone called *Grettishaf*. The first one is mentioned in Ch. 17. Another is found in Ch. 59.

89 *Borgarfjord*: Bardi's famous journey south to take vengeance in the Borgarfjord region is thought to have occurred about the year 1014. Grettir may not have been the only one left behind. After bitterly inciting her sons to vengeance, Bardi's mother was, according to *The Saga of the Heath Slayings*, stopped from taking part in the trip when her saddle-girth was cut and she fell into a creek.

90 *Odin's warrior-maidens*: the Valkyries, who selected the finest slain warriors to aid him in the defence of his hall *Valhöll* (Valhalla).

91 *Forsaeludal*: Shadow Valley was so named because for several weeks in the depth of winter the sun did not reach into the valley.

booth: booths were simple temporary structures used yearly at the assemblies. They were made of turf walls and roofed with cloth. Each chieftain and many important farmers had their own booths.

92 *Would . . . service*: this sentence is curious. The Icelandic phrase *undir mitt vald* gives the impression that Glam was not free to make his own

decisions and that he is being passed, much like a slave, from master to master.

93 *Winter Nights*: summer and winter were the only two seasons in medieval Iceland. Winter began each year on Saturday in the week of 11–17 October. The first three days of the new season were called Winter Nights (*veturnaetur*), a time that was originally observed as a pagan feast. The term is often used to mean the time just before the beginning of winter.

95 *riding the house*: ghosts were thought to sit astride the roof-beam, riding the house like they might ride a horse.

96 *the slave*: why Glam is referred to as a 'slave' (*þræll*) is unclear. It may be just a pejorative term. Glam's story has many folkloric elements, and the use of 'slave' may be one way to distinguish between humans, non-humans, and creatures. Earlier, when Glam and Thorhall made their bargain, Glam passed from one master to another much as a slave or a bound servant.

98 *Bishop Thorlak*: Thorlak the Holy Thorhallsson (1133–93), bishop of Skalholt, later saint. His story is told in *The Saga of Thorlak the Holy* (*Þorláks saga helga*).

103 *Glam's sight*: Glam's sight (*Glámsskyggn*) is still an expression in modern Icelandic.

104 *King Olaf Haraldsson*: Olaf the Stout, who after his death was called Olaf the Saint, returned to Norway from England in 1014. The next year he defeated Jarl Svein at the battle of Nesjar (now Brunaland, in Oslo Fjord). These events are described somewhat differently in *Heimskringla*, Snorri Sturluson's saga history of the kings of Norway.

Gasir in Eyjafjord: this was the major port in northern Iceland. Ships arrived in the spring and summer, and Gasir was a seasonal market-place, not a town. Foreign merchants beached their ships and traded with people who arrived from all over the northern part of the country. Merchants and visitors pitched tents or stayed in turf booths roofed with sailcloth.

106 *'How long . . . their lives'*: the warning about hasty speech is semi-proverbial and has counterparts in the Old Icelandic poem *Hávamál* and Old English poetry.

Thorir: Thorir of Gard becomes Grettir's determined opponent later in the saga.

108 *merchant-ship*: the *knörr* (pl. *knerrir*) was the major ocean-going merchant ship of Viking Age Scandinavia. The *knörr* was a short, stubby craft, differing from the graceful lines of the often narrower and swifter longships, which were used for war. Single-masted and square-sailed, the *knörr* was exceptionally seaworthy, sacrificing speed for cargo capacity. Capable of long voyages on the open sea, *knerrir* carried cargoes and passengers almost everywhere the Norse went.

Stad: Stad, a mountain, serves as a prominent landmark along the coast of South-More. See Map 5.

112 *how they were related*: Grettir and King Olaf were third cousins. See Genealogy 1.

114 *'Snaekoll's shield . . . his chest'*: the kennings used for Snaekoll's mouth and teeth are humorously evocative of a trading town.

118 *They announced these killings*: according to Iceland's medieval Grey Goose Laws (*Grágás*, so called perhaps because of the leather used to bind one of the medieval lawbooks), a killer had to publicly announce his slaying (*lýsa vígi*) within half a full day, i.e. a twenty-four-hour period. By publicly announcing his deed, the killer avoided a charge of murder. The latter was a secret killing, which carried a penalty of outlawry, as opposed to an announced manslaughter, which was treated as a subject for arbitration or adjudication, often involving compensation.

Bitra: someone who is *bitur* is disappointed and angry. The place Bitra (Bitru) is also called Bitrufjord, and *The Book of Settlements* tells that its settler was Thorbjorn Bitra. It is not clear which came first, the nickname (if Thorbjorn existed) or the name of the bay.

121 *It was . . . wide*: the spear-point was shaped like a leaf and was called a blade-spear (*fjaðraspjót*).

124 *'His thieving hands . . . prankster'*: the *Söðulkolluvísur* (verses 31 to 37) appear to represent an Old Icelandic version of the flyting genre, where insults are exchanged in a quasi-ritual fashion. The clearest Icelandic examples are the eddic poems *Lokasenna* and *Hárbarðsljóð*. Probably such exchanges were enacted or performed as entertainment.

133 *the lawman Sturla Thordarson*: Sturla (1214–84) was a nephew of Snorri Sturluson and a major participant in the later struggles of the Age of the Sturlungs. Sturla was the author of *The Saga of the Icelanders* (*Íslendingasaga*), the central story in the thirteenth-century compilation of sagas called *Sturlunga saga*.

Spjotsmyri: the Icelandic word *mýri*, cognate with English 'mire', is often translated 'marshland' or 'bog', but in Iceland the term means 'wet, swampy land', not quite a marshland or bog.

139 *marks of silver*: a mark was eight ounces of silver.

142 *Hrefna*: she was married to Thorbjorg the Stout's brother, Kjartan. Their father was Olaf the Peacock, who figures prominently in *Laxdaela Saga*.

143 *fjord*: the fjord referred to here is Isafjord. This verse begins another series of *kviðuháttr* compositions.

Sigar: he was a figure of early Scandinavian legend and condemned the suitor of his daughter to be hanged.

rowan bush: this line and the next stanza allude to the god Thor. The rowan bush refers to the story where Thor escapes drowning in a swollen river by clinging on to a rowan tree, which is called *Thors bjorg* (Thor's Protection), a name nearly identical to that of Thorbjorg, Grettir's protector in his current crisis.

144 *snake*: here the word-play is on the 'snakc' meaning in Grettir's name.

145 *ancestry*: Grettir and Thorhall shared a bond because Onund Tree-Foot, Grettir's great-grandfather, sailed to Iceland with Asmund, the brother of Thorhall's great-grandfather.

147 *There . . . fist*: the 'snake' is Grettir, as previously, while the 'stone' (*hall-*) and the 'fist' (*mundr*) supply the name of Hallmund (known to Grettir at this point in the prose narrative as Lopt).

kind woman: verses relating to fighting and warfare are often addressed to a woman or imply a woman's interest in or judgement of the speaker's deeds.

152 *sorcery*: the word *fiölkyngi*, here translated as 'sorcery', literally means 'very cunning' and also refers to 'the black arts' and 'witchcraft'. The word often had negative connotations, especially when contrasted with the more neutral *galdr*, even though the two terms are sometimes used interchangeably.

153 *'Hallmund . . . mountain hall'*: the poem is preserved more completely in *Bergbúa páttr*, where it is called *Hallmundarkviða*.

'Swords . . . in my escape': despite the statement in the prose, this verse does not seem to belong to the *Hallmundarkviða*. If anything, the verse has closer links with verse 38, and might originally have formed part of a series of verses in which Grettir, as speaker, reviewed some of his greatest exploits.

155 *Thord Kolbeinsson*: a fighter as well as a poet, Thord was the major opponent of Bjorn the Hitardal Champion. The bitter animosity between the two is recounted in *The Saga of Bjorn: Champion of the Hitardal People* (*Bjarnar saga hítdælakappa*).

Orm Storolfsson and Thoralf Skolmsson: *The Story of Orm Storolfsson* (*Orms páttr Stórólfssonar*) tells that Orm and Thoralf competed at the Althing. Thoralf is also spoken of in Bard's Saga (*Barðar saga snæfellsáss*) and in *Heimskringla*.

156 *Thorstein . . . arranged*: Thorstein's slaying and the involvement of Snorri Godi in the killing are spoken of in *The Saga of the Heath Slayings* (*Heiðarvíga saga*) and *Eyrbyggja Saga*. See also Ch. 68, where Snorri shows coldness to his son.

six marks of silver: forty-eight ounces. Thorir of Gard adds three more marks: twenty-four more ounces.

157 *gelded*: gelded rams were fatter and better eating.

the rollers: whalebone or wooden rollers were placed under the keel when the ship was pulled up on to land for the winter.

158 *ells of woollen cloth*: Gisli is setting value in homespun woollen cloth (*vaðmál*), which was one of the major trade goods produced by the Icelanders. *Vaðmál* was measured in ells. One ell in Old Icelandic usage was about half-a-yard long (*c*.45 cm). In this instance, it is not clear what

Gisli is putting value on. Probably it is his valuable clothes, but it could be the trade goods that Grettir is taking from Gisli's horse.

160 *'When it comes to a contest . . . farting'*: for horse-fighting, from which the poet takes a simile here, see note to p. 84.

161 *Arnor*: a master of skaldic poetry, Arnor Thordarson lived in the eleventh century along with the earls of Orkney.

163 *Hrut from Kambsness*: he appears in the early chapters of *Njal's Saga* and *Laxdaela Saga*.

166 *half a weight*: here the term is *hálf vætt* or 'half a weight'. The measurement of weight used, *vætt*, was 80 pounds (such a pound equalled 540 grams).

168 *runes*: runes were the alphabet used by the Germanic peoples for writing on bone, wood, metal, and stone. In addition to practical uses, runes had magical properties.

'My strength . . . his palms': here, and in the next four verses, Hallmund reviews his exploits in a type of poem sometimes termed a 'life poem' (*ævikviða*). For a comparable example, also supposedly inscribed in runes, see *Arrow-Odd's Saga* (*Örvar-Odds saga*).

177 *fathoms*: a fathom was three ells long, measured as the length between the fingertips of a person's outstretched arms. The cliff is approximately 15 metres high.

178 *heftisax*: a short-sword with a shaft attached. This weapon is mentioned in the Icelandic texts only once, at this point in *Grettir's Saga*. In the Old English epic *Beowulf* the hero borrows a *hæftmece*, a hilted sword named Hrunting, from Unferth to kill Grendel's mother.

179 *'Into the dark gorge . . . shoulders'*: these lines are possibly reminiscences of the poem *Thor's Drapa* (*Þórsdrápa*) by Eilif Godrunarson, a tenth-century skald. The stanzas appear to take up the poem at the point where it describes the god's struggle with a river swollen by his giant adversary. More remotely, this and the following verse also invite comparison with the episode in *Beowulf* where the hero invades the lair of Grendel's mother, but the relationship between saga episode and the Old English poem remains obscure.

186 *Glaum*: the name means 'noisy merrymaking'.

187 *league*: a sea league was approximately 4 miles (*c*.7.5 km).

sheep on the island: the sheep were being fattened on the island's rich grass, fertilized by sea-bird droppings.

188 *hneftafl*: also known as *hnettafl*, a board game mentioned several times in the sagas that seems to have been a kind of elementary chess. Light and dark playing-pieces found in graves are thought to be from this game. Little is known about the rules, but there appears to have been a king who needed to be protected from attack. The individual pieces sometimes had pegs at their bottoms which fitted into holes in the board and held the pieces in place.

190 *Hegraness . . . Thing*: the local springtime assembly in the Skagafjord region.

legislative council: aside from this passage, there is no mention of a legislative council (*lögrétta*) being held at a springtime assembly (*várþing*). The writer may have meant to say that the men were returning from a court (*dómþing* or *dóma*), as lawcourts were routinely held at such assemblies.

200 *nineteenth winter*: that is, almost to the twentieth year. The medieval laws (*Grágás*) do not mention the twenty-year arrangement. In *Grágás* full outlawry is a lifetime sentence that could be mitigated only by the outlaw killing other outlaws. Although Grettir kills outlaws, he does not seem to have benefited.

201 *twenty winters*: other manuscripts of the saga mention that the year-count would hold even if acts punishable by outlawry had been committed.

202 *late summer*: *tvímánaðr*, the next-to-last month of the summer, began on a Thursday. In the modern calendar this would have been towards the end of August.

205 *tree-trunk with the roots attached*: driftwood logs only infrequently have their roots still attached by the time they reach Iceland.

210 *twelve men*: legally it makes sense for Thorbjorn to have twelve witnesses with him.

216 *Grettir's head*: in the sagas, victors often take the heads of their opponents. For example, concerning the heads of people mentioned in *Grettir's Saga*, other sagas tell us: 'Thorarin killed there seven men and cut the head off Thorgeir [Havarsson] . . . and placed it in salt when he came home'; *The Story of Thorarin the Overbearing* (*Þórarins þáttr ofsa*). 'Thord took the head of Bjorn [the Champion of Hitardal] . . . and let it hang from his saddle'; *The Saga of Bjorn the Champion of Hitardal* (*Bjarnar saga*).

218 *court of confiscation*: a court of confiscation (*féránsdómr*) was an execution of judgement for the benefit of claimants. The *féránsdómr* was usually held two weeks after the closing of the Thing at which a judgement had been obtained. The property to be confiscated was called *sektarfé*. Men who could prove their claims had first right to the property, and then the chieftain or leader who had prosecuted the case could take his fee. In this instance, it does not seem that a binding judgement had been reached; nevertheless, Thorbjorn Hook and his men appear to have intended taking the lion's share of the property.

220 *the Sturlungs*: an important family of chieftains especially active in the decades from 1220 to 1260, a period which in modern studies is called the Age of the Sturlungs.

bones were dug up: bones are reported dug up and moved in five sagas: *The Saga of Bjorn the Champion of Hitardal*, *Egil's Saga*, *Eyrbyggja Saga*, *Floamanna Saga*, and *Laxdaela Saga*.

Odd: Odd Snorrason (d. *c.*1190) was a monk at the monastery of Thingeyrar. He wrote in Latin *The Saga of King Olaf Tryggvason*, which is preserved in an Icelandic translation.

222 *Constantinople*: the Norse name was *Miklagarðr*, meaning 'the great city'. The name is formed from the adjective *mikli* meaning 'great' or 'large' and the masculine noun *garðr* (cognate with English 'yard') meaning 'enclosure', in this instance a walled city.

223 *Varangian Guard*: Scandinavians in the Greek-speaking Byzantine empire were called Varangians. The emperor's palace guard, known as the Varangian Guard, was composed mostly of Scandinavians. The name 'Varangian' comes from the Norse *várar* 'pledges' or 'oaths', and the Varangians (*Væringjar*, sg. *Væringi*) were thus 'men of the pledge', referring to the oath taken by Scandinavian traders and raiders moving up and down the Russian rivers.

Michael Katalak: Michael IV, the Paphlagonian Catalactus, ruled from 1034 to 1041. He was called by the Norsemen *stólkonungr*, 'throne king'. Michael came to power by marrying Zoe, the widow of a previous emperor, and he reigned in conjunction with his powerful wife. See *King Harald's Saga* (chs. 3, 5, and 11) from *Heimskringla*.

227 *Harald Sigurdarson*: Harald Hardradi (*Haraldr harðráði*, Harald the Ruthless) was king of Norway from 1046 to 1066. Harald was half-brother to St Olaf, and his difficult ascent to the throne is told in *King Harald's Saga* from *Heimskringla*. As part of his long exile in the East, Harald, as a young man, entered the service of the Greek emperor in Constantinople. He rose to be commander of the Varangian Guard and amassed a fortune. Harald died in England at the battle of Stamford Bridge in 1066.

235 *kings of Norway*: the following summer King Magnus died and Harald became sole ruler of Norway.

GLOSSARY

THIS glossary is divided into two parts. Part I lists the names of important persons, groups, animals, and objects appearing in the saga. Included in Part I are cultural and folkloric terms and supernatural creatures that play significant roles in the saga. Part II lists the most important place-names. The entries in both parts are alphabetized in anglicized form, followed by the Old Icelandic within parentheses. Numbers in the entries refer to chapters.

I. Personal Names, Animals, and Objects

Ali (*Áli*), servant of Thorbjorn Oxen-Might: runs away and is taken in by Atli, 45

Althing (*Alþingi*), the national assembly of Iceland: lawsuit brought by Ofeig Grettir's kinsmen against Thorbjorn Jarl's-Champion referred to Kjalarness Thing, before Althing was instituted, 10; dispute between Flosi and Kaldbak Men referred to Althing, 12; Grettir attends Althing with Thorkel Scratcher; Grettir sentenced to three years outlawry, 16; Asmund Grey-Streak refers case of killing of Thorgils Maksson to Althing, 25; Asmund and Thorstein Kuggason ride to Althing with large following, 26; Thorgeir Havarsson outlawed at Althing, 27; Skapti Thoroddson the Law-speaker advises Thorhall at the Althing, 32; suit brought against Grettir at Althing for killing of Thorbjorn Oxen-Might, 51; Thorir of Gard rides from Althing with a large force to kill Grettir, 57; Stein Thorgestsson elected new law-speaker; he rules that no one may be an outlaw for more than twenty years, 77; Thorir of Gard tells Thorbjorn Hook to await ruling of the law-speaker at Althing, 82; Thorbjorn Hook outlawed at Althing, as is sorcery, 84. *See also* 34, 83

Asdis (*Ásdís Bárðardóttir*), mother of Grettir, brought up by Thorkel Scratcher: marries Asmund Grey-Streak, 13; has sons Atli and Grettir, daughters Thordis and Rannveig, 14; presents Grettir with her grandfather Jokul's fine sword, 17; agrees that Illugi should go to Drangey with Grettir, 69; stands up to Thorbjorn Hook's demand for Illugi's possessions, 83; stays on at Bjarg until her death, 84. *See also* 16, 37, 45, 47, 48

Asgeir of Asgeirs River (*Ásgeirr at Ásgeirsá Auðunarson skökuls*): son of Thordis and Audun Shaft, 11; father of Audun, Grettir's childhood rival, 28

Asgrim (*Ásgrímr Öndóttsson kráku*), son of Ondott Crow and brother of Asmund: takes vengeance on Grim for murder of his father; defeats Grim's ally, Jarl Audun; kills Hallstein Horse, 7; father of Ellida-Grim; settles in Iceland, 8

Asmund Grey-Streak (*Ásmundr hærulangr Þorgrímsson hærukolls*), father of Grettir, a farmer at Bjarg: travels to Norway; marries Rannveig, sister of Thorstein and mother of Thorstein the Galleon; becomes a seafarer after Rannveig's death; settles in Iceland and marries Asdis, 13; comes into conflict with Grettir after assigning him farm chores, 14; sends Grettir to the Althing with Thorkel Scratcher, 16; sends Grettir, without a weapon, to stay with Haflidi, 17; rides to the Althing with Thorstein Kuggason to bring a lawsuit over the killing of Thorgils Maksson, 26; he and Thorstein have Thorgeir Havarsson outlawed, 27; Grettir kills Thorbjorn Traveller for insulting his ailing father, 28; dies, 42. *See also* 25, 37

Atli (*Atli Ásmundarson hærulangs*), brother of Grettir, a farmer at Bjarg: Atli placed in charge of the farm at Bjarg, 28; Grettir leads Atli's stallion in a horse-fight at Langafit, 29; one of his servants is killed by Gunnar Thorisson, 30; Atli and his men fight off the attack; they kill the Thorissons of Skard, 43; Atli pays half compensation for the deaths of the Thorissons, 44; Atli takes in Thorbjorn Oxen-Might's abused servant, Ali; Thorbjorn kills Atli, 45; Grettir avenges Atli by killing Thorbjorn, 48; Thorodd is ordered to pay compensation for Atli's death, 51. *See also* 14–16, 36–7, 42, 49

Audun Asgeirsson (*Auðunn Ásgeirsson*), farmer at Audunarstead in Vididal, Grettir's childhood opponent: bests the young Grettir during a ball game, 15; is overcome in a fight with the adult Grettir, 28; he and Grettir reconcile and become friends, 34. *See also* 16

Audun Shaft (*Auðunn skökull Bjarnarson*) of Vididal: marries Thordis after Onund's death, 11

Bardi Gudmundarson (*Barði Guðmundarson*), farmer of Asbjarnarness: breaks up the fight between Grettir and Audun, 28; based on his foster-father Thorarin's advice, Bardi refuses Grettir's offer of help, 31. *See also* 34

Battle of Nesjar (*Nesja orrosta*), AD 1015: battle at which King Olaf Haraldsson comes to power in Norway and Jarl Svein is driven out of the country, 37

Bear (*björn*): Grettir slays ferocious bear that was terrorizing Thorkel's district in Halogaland, Norway, 21

Berserkers (*berserkir*), frenzied warriors thought to be unstoppable in battle: Onund and his companions battle King Harald's berserkers, called Wolfskins, 2; berserkers led by Thorir Paunch and Ogmund the

Ill-Willed invade Thorfinn's farm; Grettir uses stealth to slay them, 19; Thorfinn tells Jarl Svein how Grettir freed people from berserkers, 22; Grettir kills the berserker Snaekoll, 40; *see also* Wolfskins. *See also* 20

Bersi Skald-Torfuson (*Bersi Skáld-Torfuson*) of Torfustead, a friend of Grettir: Bersi and Thorfinn convince Jarl Svein to spare Grettir's life, 23; Bersi supports Grettir against Jarl Svein, 24. *See also* 15

Bjarg, Men of (*Bjargsmenn*), Grettir's kinsmen and supporters: 29–30; 43; *see also* place-name Bjarg.

Bjorn, the Hitardal Champion (*Björn Hítdælakappi Arngeirsson*), chieftain and farmer at Holm: gives lodging to Grettir, 58; informs Grettir of Gisli's plan to kill him, 59; tells Grettir he must leave Fagraskogafjall, 61

Bjorn (*Björn*), a kinsman of Thorkel in Norway, brother of Hjarrandi and Gunnar: insults Grettir; runs away from the bear that Grettir later kills, 21; is killed by Grettir, 22. *See also* 23

Bjorn Hrolfsson (*Björn Hrólfsson*), father of Thrand and Eyvind the Easterner: flees from Gautland after burning Sigfast alive; escapes from the chieftain Grim, who wanted to murder him for his money; stays with Ondott Crow; Ondott gives his daughter Helga to him in marriage, 3; Bjorn dies; Grim fails in an attempt to seize his property, 6. *See also* 5

Canute the Great (*Knútr inn ríki Sveinsson tjúguskeggs*), Danish king in England: visited by his brother-in-law Jarl Eirik Hakonarson, 19

Eirik Hakonarson (*Eiríkr jarl Hákonarson*), Norwegian jarl: outlaws duels in Norway; leaves rule in the hands of his son, Hakon, while he visits his brother-in-law Canute the Great in England, 19

Eyvind (*Eyvindr*), brother of Ingolf and Ofeig, father of Olaf: one of three brothers who settle in Iceland; Eyvindarfjord named after him, 11

Eyvind the Easterner (*Eyvindr austmaðr Bjarnarson*), brother of Thrand Bjornsson, head of the coastal defence forces in Ireland: visited by his brother Thrand and Onund Tree-Foot, 5

Flosi Eiriksson (*Flosi Eiríksson snöru*), farmer at Arness: incites his servant Thorfinn to attack Thorgeir Flask-Back, 11; receives serious wound from Thorgrim, 12. *See also* 3–4

Gamli Thorhallsson (*Gamli Þórhallsson Vínlendings*), farmer at Melar, Grettir's brother-in-law: marries Grettir's sister Rannveig, 14; warns Grettir of Thorbjorn's kinsmen's plan to kill him, 49; one of the kinsmen who supports Asdis against Thorbjorn Hook, 83. *See also* 30, 42, 43, 48, 51

Geirmund Helskin (*Geirmundr heljarskinn Hjörsson konungs*), chieftain in Hordaland: most famous viking in the west; declines Onund and Thrand's offer to help him regain lands taken by Harald Shaggy-Hair, 3. *See also* 2

Gest (*Gestr*: 'Guest'): alias used by Grettir when he arrives at Thorstein the White's farm to drive out trolls, 64; Grettir uses the alias again at the Hegraness Thing, 72. *See also* 65

Giant (*jötunn*), a huge giant who lived in a cave behind a waterfall: killed by Grettir, 66

Glam (*Glámr sauðamaðr*): a herdsman from Sweden who haunts Thorhallsstead after his death, 32; during fight with Grettir, prophesies misfortune for the hero; is killed by Grettir, 35. *See also* 33–4

Glaum (*Þorbjörn glaumr*), a vagrant: accompanies Grettir and Illugi to live on Drangey, 69; is threatened with flogging by Grettir after allowing fire to go out, 74; brings to camp the tree of bad luck sent by the sorceress Thurid to harm Grettir, 79; enjoined by Grettir to tend to the ladder, 80; forsakes duty by not pulling up the ladder, allowing Thorbjorn's men access to island; killed by Thorbjorn, 82. *See also* 72

Glum Ospaksson (*Glúmr Óspaksson*), farmer at Eyr in Bitra, brother-in-law of Grettir: later married to Grettir's sister Thordis, 14; stays winter at Bjarg in support of Atli, 43; joins others in supporting his kinswoman Asdis against Thorbjorn Hook, 83. *See also* 51

Grettir Asmundarson (*Grettir Ásmundarson*), the hero of the saga: his father Asmund Grey-Streak is not fond of him, but he is loved by his mother Asdis; fails to properly perform the three tasks assigned him by his father; in the third task, he mutilates father's mare, Kengala, 15; kills Skeggi, servant of As, in a dispute over a food bag; sentenced to three years outlawry at the Althing, 16; receives his great-grandfather Jokul's sword as a gift from Asdis; sails from Iceland after being outlawed; after his initial laziness brings him into conflict with the crew, he helps bail out their ship, 17; stays with the Norwegian chieftain Thorfinn; vanquishes mound-dweller Kar the Old, father of Thorfinn, 18; kills berserker brothers, 19; is insulted by Bjorn; kills marauding bear, 21; kills Bjorn at Garten, 22; kills Bjorn's brother Hjarrandi, 23; kills a third brother, Gunnar; banished from Norway by Jarl Svein, 24; returns to Iceland; is prevented by Bardi from killing his childhood opponent Audun Asgeirsson, 28; leads Atli's stallion in a horse-fight at Langafit, 29; with four other men he fights Kormak and his men, 30; Grettir and his uncle Jokul trade disastrous prophecies about each other's fate, 34; is cursed by the monster Glam before destroying him, 35; kills Thorbjorn Traveller, 37; while retrieving fire for merchants, accidentally burns to death the sons of Thorir of Gard; is blamed for their deaths, 38; is supposed to undergo ordeal of hot iron, but loses this chance to prove his innocence after striking a youth, 39; kills the berserker Snaekoll, 40; avenges Atli by killing Thorbjorn Oxen-Might and his son Arnor, 48; the spear that Grettir used to kill Thorbjorn is found in bog many years later; receives advice from Thorstein Kuggason, 49; with the help of the sworn brothers Thorgeir and Thormod, brings an ox from island to mainland, 50; disqualified as litigant in the case brought by Thorodd Poem-Stump, 51; captured by farmers of Vatnsfjord; saved from hanging by Thorbjorg the Stout, 52; stays with Thorstein Kuggason, 53; meets Lopt (an alias of Hallmund); is unable to steal from him because of Lopt's strength, 54; kills a bribed outlaw, Grim, 55; kills another bribed outlaw, Thorir Red-Beard, 56; fights off attack by Thorir of Gard with Hallmund's help; stays with Hallmund (Lopt) in a cave near Ball Glacier, 57; stays in a cave at Fagraskogafjall, 58; routs attackers and thrashes Gisli, their leader, 59; bravely fends off attack by Myrar men, 60; stays in Thorisdal, a valley surrounded by ice, under the protection of the half-troll Thorir, 61; while disguised, tricks Thorir and his men, 63; under the alias Gest, arrives at the haunted farm of Sandhaugar, 64; rids Sandhaugar of a female troll, 65; descends a gorge to destroy a giant who lives in a cave behind a waterfall, 66; is unable to avenge Hallmund; easily thwarts Thorodd's attempt to kill him, 68; visits his mother Asdis for last time; settles on Drangey with his brother Illugi and Glaum, a vagrant, 69; refuses to leave Drangey, 71; visits Hegraness Thing in disguise; is induced to fight as part of entertainment; is granted safe passage before his identity is revealed, 72; refuses Thorbjorn's offer to leave Drangey, 73; becomes angry with Glaum for letting their fire go out, 74; swims to mainland; discovered lying naked by women at Reykir; sports with a maiden, 75; speaks again with Thorbjorn, 76; is denied acquittal of outlawry until twenty years have passed, 77; wounds the sorceress Thurid with a stone, 78; wounds himself when he strikes the tree of bad luck with an axe, 79; his magically inflicted wound becomes life-threatening, 80; is killed by Thorbjorn Hook, 82; his head is taken by Thorbjorn Hook to Bjarg, 83; his head is buried by Thorbjorn Hook in a sandhill at Sand; the place is now called Grettir's Dune, 84; Thorstein avenges Grettir by killing Hook, 86; Sturla the Lawman calls him Iceland's most distinguished outlaw, 93. *See also* 14, 20, 25, 31, 36, 41–3, 45–7, 62, 67, 70, 81, 85, 87, 90

Grim (*Grímr skógarmaðr*), an outlaw bribed by men of Hrutafjord to kill Grettir: talks Grettir into letting him stay at Arnarvatn Heath; killed by Grettir, 55

Grim the Hersir (*Grímr hersir Kolbjarnarson sneypis*): chieftain in Norway who lodges Bjorn for winter; wants to murder him for his money, 3; kills Ondott Crow; burned to death by Ondott's sons Asgrim and Asmund, 7. *See also* 6

Grim Thorhallsson (*Grímr Þórhallsson*), a farmer at Gilsbakki, brother of Grettir's brother-in-law, Gamli: helps Grettir against Kormak, 30; kills

Thorgeir Thorisson, 43; legal settlement requires him to leave the district, 44; Grettir stays with Grim at Gilsbakki, 47; tells Grettir to go to Skapti the Law-speaker, 53; advises Grettir to go north, 54; warns Grettir of Thorir of Gard's forthcoming attack, 57. *See also* 42, 61

Gudmund the Powerful (*Guðmundr inn ríki Eyjólfsson*), a chieftain at Modruvellir: advises Grettir to go to Drangey, 67. *See also* 69

Haering (*Hæringr*), a good climber: hired by Thorbjorn to scale cliffs of Drangey to kill Grettir; plunges to his death, 76; *see also* Haering's Leap

Haflidi (*Hafliði*), seafaring trader from Reydarfell along the Hvita River: provides transport to Norway for Grettir after he is outlawed, 17

Hafr Thorarinsson (*Hafr Þórarinsson*) of Knappstead: foolishly proclaims safe conduct for the disguised Grettir at Hegraness Thing, 72

Hall Gudmundarson (*Hallr Guðmundarson*), unavenged brother of Bardi Gudmundarson: 28

Halldor Thorgeirsson (*Halldórr Þorgeirsson*), a farmer of Hof in Hofdastrand: supporter and brother-in-law of Thorbjorn Hook, 70; despite his misgivings about Thorbjorn's use of sorcery, Halldor gives him hospitality and advice, 81. *See also* 72, 84

Hallmund (*Hallmundr*), alias Lopt (*Loftur*), mysterious friend of Grettir who lives in wilds at Ball Glacier: Grettir makes unsuccessful attempt to steal from stranger who calls himself Lopt, 54; Hallmund, as he is now called, helps Grettir fight against Thorir of Gard, 57; gives lodging to Grettir, 61; steals fish from the outlaw Grim; killed by Grim, 62. *See also* 67

Harald Shaggy-Hair or Fine-Hair (*Haraldr lúfa* or *hárfagri*), king of Norway: wins a great battle at Hafursfjord, defeating Onund and others, 2; outlaws those who fought against him, 3; Onund and companions revenge themselves on Harald by attacking his followers, 7

Harald Sigurdarson 'Hardradi' (*Haraldr inn harðráði Sigurðarson*), leader of Varangian Guard in Constantinople: consulted by his kinsman Thorstein, 88; holds Thorstein in the greatest honour; later given half of Norwegian kingdom by King Magnus, 90. *See also* 91

Harek (*Hárekr*), steward of King Harald Shaggy-Hair: receives the possessions of Onund that are confiscated by King Harald; killed by Onund, 7

Heath-Killings (*Heiðarvíg*): battle fought at Tvidaegra Heath in Iceland between Bardi Gudmundarson and his enemies, 31

Hedin of Soknadal (*Heðinn*), foster-father of Signy, the wife of Ondott Crow: takes in the sons of Ondott Crow after his murder, 7

Hjalti Thordarson (*Hjalti Þórðarson*), a chieftain at Hof in Hjaltadal, brother of Thorbjorn Hook: he and his brother have greatest shares in

Drangey, 70; sends three of his men to join Thorbjorn's attack on Grettir, 81; takes charge of Hook's estate, 85. *See also* 72

Hook: *see* Thorbjorn Hook

Hrutafjord, The Men of (*Hrútfirðingar*), the men of Thorbjorn Oxen-Might's home territory: Thorbjorn Oxen-Might gives a good account of Grettir's prowess to Men of Hrutafjord, 36; gather a force to kill Grettir, 53; bribe the outlaw Grim to kill Grettir, 55; Thorodd Poem-Stump and most of Men of Hrutafjord help Asdis, 83; *see also* place-name Hrutafjord. *See also* 30, 49, 51

Illugi Asmundarson (*Illugi Ásmundarson hærulangs*), brother of Grettir: accompanies Grettir and Glaum to Drangey, 69; chases Haering; chastises Grettir for throwing a stone at Thurid, 76; dresses Grettir's wound, 79; defends against Thorbjorn's attack; killed, 82; buried at Reykir, 84. *See also* 37, 42, 54, 67, 72, 74–5, 80, 81, 83

Jokul Bardarson (*Jökull Bárðarson*), seafaring uncle of Grettir: warns Grettir against confronting Glam; Grettir, in turn, predicts disaster for him, 34

Jokul's-Gift (*Jökulsnautr*) also called Jokul's Companion, Grettir's fine sword: belonged to Grettir's great-grandfather Jokul and others in Vatnsdal; given to Grettir by his mother Asdis, 17; Grettir uses the sword to strike off head of Mound-dweller Kar, 18; Grettir kills a bear with the sword, 21; Atli kills Gunnar and two of his men with Jokul's-Gift after Grettir gives it to him, 43

Kar (*Kárr*), one of Halldor's men: joins Thorbjorn's attack on Grettir on Drangey; killed by Grettir, 82. *See also* 81

Kar the Old (*Kárr inn gamli*), mound-dweller at Vindheim in Norway, father of Thorfinn: Grettir cuts his head off, 18; Grettir uses his spear and short-sword to kill berserkers, 19; Grettir wields the short-sword taken from Kar's mound to defend against Thorbjorn, 82; *see also* Revenant; Sword

Kengala (*Kengála*), Asmund Grey-Streak's mare, who could predict the weather: mutilated by Grettir; in a horse-fight at Langafit, Grettir leads Atli's stallion of Kengala's stock, 29. *See also* 14

Kormak (*Kormákr*) of Mel, brother of Thorgils: his horse is pitted against Atli's in horse-fight, which leads to conflict between Kormak's men and the men of Bjarg, 29; Kormak and his men fight with Grettir and his companions, 30. *See also* 15, 36

Leif Kolbeinsson (*Leifr Kolbeinsson*), brother of Ivar: accompanies Thorgrim and his brothers to the site of a stranded whale; avenges his brother's wounding by killing one of Stein's companions with a whale rib, 12

Lopt (an alias of Hallmund): *see* Hallmund

and Thrand sail from the Hebrides to Norway to see Ondott Crow, 6; kills Harek, the steward of King Harald, who had confiscated Onund's property; aids the sons of Ondott Crow in taking vengeance on the chieftain Grim and Jarl Audun; spends the winter with Eirik Ale-Lover, 7; sails to Iceland, 8; given land by Eirik Snare; builds a farm at Kaldbak, 9; helps arrange the marriage of Olaf, grandson of Aud the Deep-Minded; rides to Kjalarness Thing with the sons of the slain Ofeig Grettir to bring a lawsuit against his killer, Thorbjorn Jarl's-Champion, 10; Onund and Aesa have two sons, Thorgeir and younger Ofeig Grettir; after Aesa's death he marries Thordis and has son Thorgrim by her; dies and is buried in Treefoot's Mound, 11. *See also* 12

Ospak Glumsson (*Óspakr Glúmsson*), Grettir's nephew: one of kinsmen who supports Asdis against Thorbjorn Hook after Grettir's death, 83. *See also* 14, 51

Rannveig (*Rannveig Ásmundardóttir hærulangs*), daughter of Asmund Grey-Streak, sister of Grettir: marries Gamli, 14; Rannveig and Gamli live prosperously at Melar; they give a warm welcome to Grettir when he visits, 30

Revenant, 'the walking dead' (*draugr*, 'ghost', 'spirit'; *haugbúi*, 'mound-dweller'; *aptrganga*, 'one who comes back'): Grettir kills the revenant Kar the Old in his grave-mound, 18; Glam is said to have more power for evil than any other revenant, 35; *see also* Kar the Old, Glam. *See also* 34

Runes (*rúnar*), an alphabet of written characters, sometimes possessing magical power: Grettir carves verses in runes on a staff describing his battle with a giant, 66; the sorceress Thurid cuts runes on a tree, by which she lays a spell to harm Grettir, 79

Saddle-Head (*Söðulkolla*): a swift horse that Grettir 'borrows' from Svein, 47

Signy (*Signý Sighvatsdóttir*), wife of Ondott Crow: gathers all her valuables after her husband's murder and sails to her father Sighvat's home with her sons Asmund and Asgrim, 7

Sigurd (*Sigurðr*), a rich landowner in Constantinople, husband of Spes: accuses his wife of infidelity, 88; forced to leave country after Spes evades the charges he brings against her, 89. *See also* 87

Skagafjord, The Men of (*Skagfirðingar*), farmers who come into conflict with Grettir during his stay on Drangey: the leading men of Skagafjord are named, 70; considered to have acted honourably toward Grettir in upholding their pledge of safe passage, 72; threaten to take back their shares in Drangey from Thorbjorn Hook, 75; tell Hook to kill Grettir or return the island to them, 77; *see also* place-name Skagafjord. *See also* 73

Skapti Thoroddson (*Skapti Þóroddson*), law-speaker of the Althing: sides with Asmund against Thorgils Arason, 27; called the wisest of men because he is not deceitful like his father Thorodd, 32; disqualifies Grettir as litigant in the case brought against him by Thorodd Poem-Stump, 51; advises Grettir to live where he won't have to steal to survive, 54; dies, 76. *See also* 46, 53

Skeggi (*Skeggi*), servant of As in Vatnsdal: killed by Grettir in a dispute over a food bag, 16.

Skeggi Gamlason, 'Short-Hand' (*Skeggi skammhöndungr Gamlason*), Grettir's nephew: one of the kinsmen who supports Asdis against Thorbjorn Hook; marries Valgerd, daughter of Thorodd Poem-Stump, 83; indicts Hook at Althing for Grettir's death; brings back the bodies of Grettir and Illugi from Drangey for burial, 84. *See also* 51

Snorri Godi (*Snorri goði Þorgrímsson*), a chieftain at Tunga: gives advice to Grettir, 49; becomes hostile towards his son Thorodd, 68; dies, 76. *See also* 51, 59

Solvi the Proud (*Sölvi inn prúði Ásbrandsson*): arbitrator for Thorbjorn Oxen-Might at Hunavatn Thing, 44

Solvi (*Sölvi*), king of Gautland: 3

Sorcery and Witchcraft (*fjölkynngi*; *galdr*; *forneskja*): Asdis warns her sons to avoid practitioners of witchcraft (*forneskja*; *gjörningar*), 69; Grettir realizes that he will suffer from the old woman Thurid's sorcery (*fjölkynngi*; *forneskja*; *galdr*), 78; Thurid chants spells over runes carved into tree (*galdr*), 79; Grettir asserts that his illness is caused by sorcery (*gjörningar*), 80; Illugi accuses Thorbjorn of killing Grettir through sorcery and witchcraft (*fjölkynngi*; *forneskja*; *galdr*; *gjörningar*), 82; kinsmen of Grettir are angered that Thorbjorn has resorted to sorcery to kill him (*fjölkynngi*; *görningar*), 83; Thorbjorn outlawed for sorcery and witchcraft in the death of Grettir (*fjölkynngi*; *forneskja*), 84; *see also* Thurid; Witch

Spes (*Spes*), rich wife of Sigurd in Constantinople: after hearing the beautiful singing of Thorstein the Galleon, has him released from prison, 87; falls in love with Thorstein, 88; carried across muddy ditch by Thorstein disguised as tramp; by a false oath she is granted a divorce from her husband Sigurd, 89; marries Thorstein; they move to Norway, 90; Spes and Thorstein journey to Rome to do penance for sins, 92. *See also* 91

Stein (*Steinn*), priest at Eyjardalsa River in Bardardal: falsely assuming Grettir is killed by trolls, he deserts his post of watching over the rope; Grettir leaves a bag containing the bones of two men killed by trolls and a rune-carved staff on the porch of Stein's church, 66. *See also* 64, 65, 67

Stein Thorgestsson (*Steinn Þorgestsson*), the law-speaker: becomes lawspeaker after Skapti's death; rules that no man should be an outlaw for more than twenty years; determines that Grettir, however, has been an outlaw for only nineteen years, 77; denies reward to Thorbjorn Hook for killing Grettir, 84

Steinvor (*Steinvör*) of Sandhaugar, wife of Thorstein the White: husband disappears from their troll-haunted farm, 64; Grettir rids Sandhaugar of trolls, 65; gives birth to Skeggi, thought to be Grettir's son, 67

Sturla Thordarson the Lawman (*Sturla lögmaðr Þórðarson*), a thirteenth-century historian and authority on Grettir cited by the sagaman: spear that Grettir used to kill Thorbjorn Oxen-Might is found in the bog where he was killed in the time of Sturla Thordarson, 49; according to Sturla the Lawman, Grettir had been outlaw for fifteen or sixteen years when he arrived on Drangey, 69; asserts that no outlaw was ever as distinguished as Grettir, 93

Sturlungs (*Sturlungar*), one of the outstanding families of thirteenth-century Iceland: 84

Svein (*Sveinn*), farmer at Bakki: owner of the horse Saddle-Head that Grettir takes; regains his horse and parts from Grettir on friendly terms, 47

Svein Hakonarson, Jarl (*Sveinn jarl Hákonarson*), ruler of Norway: 19; meets with Thorfinn and Grettir, 22; banishes Grettir from Norway, 24; driven out of Norway by King Olaf, 37

Sword (*sax*), a fine, one-edged short-sword used by Grettir: Grettir takes a short-sword as plunder from Kar's mound; Grettir gives the sword to Thorfinn, 18; Grettir uses Kar's short-sword to slay berserkers who are raiding Thorfinn's farm, 19; Thorfinn gives short-sword to Grettir in gratitude for killing the berserkers, 20; Grettir drives short-sword into the heart of a fierce bear, 21; Grettir fights off Gunnar and his men with the short-sword, 24; Grettir cuts off Glam's head with the short-sword, 35; Thorbjorn the Traveller's head cut off by Grettir with his sword, 37; Grettir uses the sword to decapitate the berserker Snaekoll, 40; Grettir crushes skull of Thorbjorn Oxen-Might's son Arnor with the flat of his sword; Grettir kills Thorbjorn with his sword, 48; Thormod Kolbrun's-Skald is armed with a short-sword in a tangle with Grettir, 50; the outlaw Grim snatches Grettir's short-sword, but fails to kill Grettir with it, 55; the outlaw Thorir attempts to kill Grettir with his short-sword; Grettir seizes sword and strikes off the outlaw's head with it, 56; Grettir wields his short-sword in fighting off Myrar Men, 60; Grettir slices off a female troll's arm with his sword, 65; a huge giant attacks Grettir with a wooden-shafted pike (*hepti-sax*); Grettir counter-attacks with his short-sword, 66; when attacked by Thorbjorn, Grettir seizes his short-sword (called Kar's-Gift: *Kársnautr*); Grettir does not release his grip on the sword after being killed by Hook; Hook cuts off Grettir's hand to free sword; a piece of sword's edge breaks off as Hook cuts off Grettir's head, 82; *see also* Jokul's-Gift. *See also* 43, 59

Thorbjorg the Stout (*Þorbjörg in digra Óláfsdóttir pá*), daughter of Olaf the Peacock, wife of Vermund the Slender: rescues Grettir from being hanged by peasants, 52

Thorbjorn Glaum: see Glaum

Thorbjorn Hook (*Þorbjörn öngull Þórðarson*), a farmer at Vidvik, brother of Hjalti Thordarson: one of leading men of Skagafjord; a troubled youth who killed his stepmother; one of the owners of Drangey, 70; induces the disguised Grettir to fight as part of entertainment at Hegraness-Thing; is unable to convince Grettir to leave Drangey, 73; distracts Grettir with another offer while Haering scales the cliffs; the men of Skagafjord tell him to give Drangey back to them or kill Grettir, 76; borrows a boat from Halldor, 81; attacks and kills Grettir and Illugi, 82; outlawed for killing Grettir, 84; leaves Iceland for Norway; travels to Constantinople to become mercenary, 85; killed by Thorstein the Galleon, Grettir's half-brother, 86. *See also* 72, 75, 78–80, 83

Thorbjorn Oxen-Might (*Þorbjörn öxnamegin Arnórsson hýnefs*), son of Arnor Hairy Nose, a farmer at Thoroddsstead in Hrutafjord: 30; holds a great autumn feast at which Thorbjorn the Traveller disparages Grettir, 36; persuades Thorissons to ambush Atli, 43; brings legal proceedings against Atli, 44; kills Atli, 45; he and his son killed by Grettir, 48; after Thorodd Poem-Stump receives no compensation for his brother's killing, he and Thorir offer a huge reward for Grettir's head, 51. *See also* 42, 47, 49

Thorbjorn the Traveller (*Þorbjörn ferðalangr*), a seafaring trader, kinsman of Thorbjorn Oxen-Might: 30; makes insulting remarks about Grettir, 36; killed by Grettir, 37; Thorbjorn Oxen-Might infuriated by his killing, 42

Thords, The (*Þórðr hvárrtveggi*), two brothers with the same first name, Thord, who farm at Brieda (Broad River) in Slettahlid: owners of a share in Drangey, 70; fight together against Grettir as part of entertainment at Hegraness Thing, 72

Thordis (*Þórdís Ásmundardóttir*), daughter of Asmund from under Asmund's Peak, Grettir's grandmother: wife of Thorgrim Grey-Streak; mother of Asmund, Grettir's father, 13

Thordis (*Þórdís Ásmundardóttir hærulangs*), daughter of Asmund Grey-Streak, sister of Grettir: later marries Glum, 14

Thordis (*Þórdís Þórðardóttir*), wife of Halldor; sister of Hjalti and Thorbjorn Hook: 70

Thordis (*Þórdís Þorgrímsdóttir*), daughter of Thorgrim of Gnup: Onund's second wife, after the death of Aesa; marries Audun Shaft after Onund's death, 11

Thorfinn Karsson (*Þorfinnr Kársson ins gamla*), a landowner in Haramarsey Island, Norway, son of the mound-dweller Kar the Old: gives Grettir hospitality; accepts a sword and other treasures that Grettir brings back from Kar's mound, 18; takes part in outlawing robbers and berserkers in Norway; is away from home when berserkers arrive to plunder his estate, 19; gives Kar's fine short-sword to Grettir for protecting his family and property, 20; offers to pay compensation for Grettir's killing of Bjorn, 22; supports Grettir against Jarl Svein; gives Grettir many fine gifts; finds him passage to Iceland, 24. *See also* 23, 28

Thorgaut (*Þorgautr*): hired by Thorhall to replace Glam as shepherd; killed by Glam, 33

Thorgeir Flask-Back (*Þorgeirr flöskubakr Önundarson tréfóts*), son of Onund Tree-Foot: in charge of farm at Reykjafjord; ambushed by Flosi's servant Thorfinn; receives his nickname from an axe-blow that lands in a flask on his back but doesn't wound him, 11; kills Thorfinn during a fight over a stranded whale, 12; divides the family property with his brother Thorgrim, 13

Thorgeir Havarsson (*Þorgeirr Hávarsson*), one of the 'Sworn-Brothers', an outlaw: kills Grettir's kinsman, Thorgils Maksson, 25; kills Bundle-Torfi at Maskelda, Skuf and Bjarni at Hundadal, 27; shares lodgings with Grettir at Thorgils Arason's farm; fights Grettir, but is restrained by Thorgils, 50

Thorgeir Thorisson[1] (*Þorgeirr Þórisson*), son of Thorir of Gard: accidentally burned to death with his brother Skeggi by Grettir, 38.

Thorgeir Thorisson[2] (*Þorgeirr Þórisson*), son of Thorir of Skard, brother of Gunnar: one of the men with Thorbjorn Oxen-Might who broke up the fight between Grettir and Kormak's men, 30; at Thorbjorn's urging, he and Gunnar ambush Atli and his men; killed by Grim Thorhallsson, 43.

Thorgils Arason (*Þorgils Arason*), a chieftain at Reykjaholar, north Iceland: kinsman of the outlaw Thorgeir Havarsson, one of the 'sworn-brothers'; Thorgils takes in Thorgeir after his killing of Thorgils Maksson, 27; gives hospitality to Grettir; the sworn-brothers Thorgeir and Thormod also spend the winter with Thorgils, 50; Thorgils rides to the Althing with a large contingent of men, 51. *See also* 49

Thorgils Maksson (*Þorgils Máksson*), a farmer at Laekjamot, Grettir's kinsman: killed by outlaw Thorgeir Havarsson in a dispute over a stranded whale, 25; Thorstein Kuggason and Asmund Grey-Streak bring legal proceedings against Thorgeir and his 'sworn-brother' Thormod, 26; Thorgeir outlawed for killing of Thorgils, 27

Thorgrim Grey-Streak (*Þorgrímr hærukollr Önundarson tréfóts*), son of Onund Tree-Foot and grandfather of Grettir: by age 25 his hair turns grey, resulting in his nickname Grey-Streak, 11; he and his brothers fight Flosi's men over rights to a stranded whale; loses part of his lands in the settlement reached at the Althing, 12; moves south to Midfjord, buys farm at Bjarg; dies in Iceland, 13

Thorhall Grimsson (*Þórhallr Grímsson*) of Thorhallsstead, a farmer at Forsaeludal: hires Glam of Sweden as a shepherd for his haunted farm; Glam later haunts farm himself after being killed by monsters, 32; Thorhall hires the foreigner Thorgaut to take Glam's place; Thorgaut killed by the revenant Glam, 33; welcomes Grettir to his farm; Grettir destroys Glam, 35

Thorir (*Þórir*), a giant half-troll: provides protection for Grettir in Thorisdal, an isolated valley named by Grettir in his honour, 61

Thorir Skeggjason of Gard (*Þórir farmaðr Skeggjason*), the father of the Thorissons, a farmer at Gard and stalwart enemy of Grettir: 38; has Grettir outlawed, 46; he and Thorodd offer unusually large reward for Grettir's head, 51; hires Thorir Red-Beard to kill Grettir, 56; attacks Grettir with almost eighty men, 57; he and his men become stuck in a bog after being tricked by the disguised Grettir, 63; sends men to kill Grettir, 67; raises objections to Grettir's acquittal at Althing, 77; refuses to pay Thorbjorn his reward for Grettir's head because of the cowardly manner in which Grettir was killed, 82. *See also* 59, 62, 84

Thorir Red-Beard (*Þórir rauðskeggr*), an outlaw: offered bribe by men of Hrutafjord to kill Grettir; convinces Grettir to allow him to stay at Arnarvatn Heath; slain by Grettir after revealing his treachery, 56. *See also* 57

Thorir of Skard (*Þórir Þorkelsson*), father of Gunnar and Thorgeir, a farmer at Melar in Hrutafjord: sells his farm to Thorhall and moves south to Skard at Haukadal after the killings at Fagrabrekka, 30; 43–4

Thorkel (*Þorkell*) of Saltfjord in Halogaland, Norway, a wealthy farmer: gives hospitality to Grettir, 20; Grettir comes into conflict with Bjorn, a kinsman and guest of Thorkel; Grettir kills a fierce bear that has been destroying the flocks of Thorkel and others, 21; Grettir goes north with Thorkel's men, 22

Thorkel Moon (*Þorkell máni Þorsteinsson*), law-speaker of the Althing: arbitrates the dispute between Kaldbak men and Flosi's followers, 12

Thorkel Scratcher (*Þorkell krafla Þorgrímsson Kárnsárgoða*), a chieftain at Karnsa River in Vatnsdal: invites Asmund Grey-Streak to stay with him; Asmund marries Thorkel's foster-daughter Asdis, 13; Grettir accompanies Thorkel and his men to the Althing, 16; Thorkel dies, 25

Thormod Kolbrun's-Skald (*Þormóðr Kolbrúnarskáld Bersason*), one of the 'Foster-Brothers': kills three of Thorgils Maksson's men during a dispute over a stranded whale, 25; Thorstein Kuggason and Asmund bring charges against Thormod and Thorgeir Havarsson, 26; receives a fine and is acquitted at the Althing, 27; shares lodgings with Grettir at Thorgils Arason's farm, 50. *See also* 51

Thormod Skapti (*Þormóðr skapti Óleifsson breiðs*), a viking and settler in Iceland: with his kinsman Ofeig Grettir, flees west across the sea from

King Harald; Thrand and Onund become close friends with Thormod and Ofeig in the Hebrides; Thrand is later betrothed to Thormod's daughter, 3; Ofeig and Thormod go to Iceland with their households; settles at Skaptaholt, 6; Thrand and Thormod both invite Onund Tree-Foot and Olaf Feilan to stay with them, 10

Thorodd Godi (*Þóroddr goði Eyvindarson*) of Hjalli, father of Skapti Thoroddson the Law-speaker: helps the Kaldbak men at the Althing in a dispute over a stranded whale, 12; his son Skapti is called the Father-Betterer because he is not deceitful like his father, 32. *See also* 6

Thorodd Poem-Stump (*Þóroddr drápustúfr Arnórsson hýnefs*), brother of Thorbjorn Oxen-Might: starts proceedings against Grettir for the death of his brother, 48; rides with his men to Bjarg seeking Grettir, 49; receives no compensation for death of his brother Thorbjorn, 51; Grettir's nephew Skeggi married to his daughter Valgerd; becomes a supporter of Grettir's kinsmen against Hook, 83. *See also* 30, 84

Thorstein the Galleon (*Þorsteinn drómundr Ásmundarson hærulangs*), Grettir's half-brother, son of Asmund and Rannveig: receives his nickname because of his slow movement, 13; supports Grettir in his conflict with Jarl Svein, 24; prophesies that he will avenge Grettir's death, 41; after hearing of Grettir's murder, keeps track of Thorbjorn Hook's movements in Norway, 85; follows Hook to Constantinople; kills Hook; imprisoned by the Varangians, 86; after hearing his beautiful singing, the rich woman Spes has him released, 87; dallies with the married woman Spes; escapes detection by her husband, 88; disguised as a beggar, he helps Spes across a muddy ditch, 89; marries Spes; the couple moves to Norway, 90; Thorstein and Spes journey to Rome to do penance for sins, 92. *See also* 40, 91, 93

Thorstein Kuggason (*Þorsteinn Kuggason*), farmer at Ljar Woods, a kinsman of Grettir: Asmund and Thorstein start proceedings against the sworn-brothers Thorgeir and Thormod for the killing of Thorgils Maksson, 26; Thorstein and a large group of his followers travel to Althing, 27; Grettir stays with Thorstein for most of the autumn, 48; Gamli warns Thorstein and Grettir of a force of Thorbjorn Oxen-Might's vengeful kinsmen, 49; Grettir again stays with Thorstein; in the spring Thorstein asks Grettir to leave Ljar Woods on account of Grettir's laziness and because another force of men have gathered to kill him, 53; Thorstein advises Grettir, 57; Grettir hears that Thorstein had been killed, 67; after Thorstein's killing Snorri Godi becomes hostile toward his own son Thorodd, 68

Thorvald Asgeirsson (*Þorvaldr Ásgeirsson*), a chieftain at As in Vatnsdal: a great supporter of Asmund Grey-Streak, 25; supports Asmund and Thorstein Kuggason's proceedings against the foster-brothers, 26; gives hospitality and advice to Grettir, 35; arbitrator for Atli at the

Hunavatn Thing; again advises Grettir, 44; supports Skeggi's journey to retrieve the bodies of Grettir and Illugi, 84. *See also* 15, 51

Thorvald Kodransson (*Þorvaldr víðförli Koðránsson*): one of first men to preach Christianity in north Iceland, 13

Thrand Bjarnarson Fast-sailing (*Þrándr mjöksiglandi Bjarnarson*), a friend of Onund Tree-Foot: helps Onund escape from battle against King Harald, 2; Onund and Thrand offer support to Geirmund Hell-Skin; Onund and Thrand travel to the Hebrides and befriend Ofeig Grettir and Thormod Skapti; helps Onund find a wife; is betrothed to the daughter of Thormod Skapti, 3; Onund and Thrand defeat the vikings Vigbjod and Vestmar, 4; Onund and Thrand sail west to Ireland to visit Thrand's brother Eyvind the Easterner; after participating in raids with Eyvind they return to Hebrides, 5; his father Bjorn dies; Onund and Thrand travel to Norway; Thrand takes charge of his father's inheritance and settles in Iceland at Thrandarholt, 6; Thrand and Thormod Skapti both invite Onund and Olaf Feilan to stay with them, 10

Thurid (*Þuríðr kerling*), sorceress foster-mother of Thorbjorn Hook: while in boat she curses Grettir and is wounded by him with a stone, 78; carves runes on uprooted tree in order to wound Grettir; Grettir wounds himself while striking the tree with an axe, 79; Grettir realizes that his wound was caused by old woman's sorcery, 80; responsible for raging storm; Thurid urges Thorbjorn to attack Grettir on Drangey, 81

Troll (*tröll*), a monstrous being: residents of Vatnsdal unwilling to go out at night to search for missing shepherd Thorgaut for fear of trolls, 33; Grettir compared in size to a troll, 38; Thorir refers to Grettir as a troll, 57; Hallmund claims to have beaten half-trolls (*blendingir*), 62; Sandhaugar haunted by trolls, 64; Grettir destroys a female troll, 65. *See also* 4, 16

Tungu-Stein (*Tungu-Steinn Bjarnarson*), a farmer at Steinsstead in Skagafjord: owner of a share of Drangey, 70; sends two of his men to join Thorbjorn's attack on Grettir, 81. *See also* 72

Varangian Guard (*Væringjar*), an elite corps of mostly Scandinavian mercenaries in the service of the Byzantine emperors: Thorbjorn and Thorstein the Galleon both attempt to join the Guard, 86; Spes pays the Varangians to release Thorstein from prison, 87; Thorstein spends most of his time with the Varangians after Spes is accused by her husband of infidelity, 88. *See also* 90

Vermund the Slender (*Vermundr inn mjóvi Þorgrímsson*), a chieftain at Vatnsfjord, husband of Thorbjorg the Stout: is away at the Althing when Grettir is in Langadal; after Vermund's return Thorbjorg convinces her husband of the wisdom of saving Grettir's life, 52

Witch (*gjörninga-vættr*): Grettir curses the witch Thurid, 78; *see also* Sorcery; Thurid

Witchcraft: *see* Sorcery

Wolfskins (*úlfheðnar*): King Harald's unstoppable berserker warriors, 2; *see also* Berserkers

II. Place-names

Adaldal (*Aðaldalr*), Norway: location of Gard, home of Thorir Skeggjason, 38

Armannsfell (*Ármannsfell*), Iceland: mountain on which Thorhall first meets the fierce shepherd Glam, 32

Arnarvatn Heath (*Arnarvatnsheiðr*), Iceland: wild place where Grettir ekes out a living by fishing, 54; Grettir agrees to take in the bribed outlaw Grim at Arnarvatn Heath; Grim killed by Grettir, 55; Thorir of Gard bribes another outlaw, Thorir Red-Beard, to kill Grettir; he is slain by Grettir, 56; a second outlaw named Grim, son of the widow at Kropp, comes to live at Arnarvatn Heath after Grettir leaves; Grim kills Grettir's friend Hallmund, 62

Ball Glacier (*Balljökull*), Iceland: home of Grettir's friend Hallmund (Lopt), 54. *See also* 57, 62

Barra Isles (*Barreyjar*), Hebrides: islands where Onund meets Kjarval, 1

Bjarg (*Bjarg*), Midfjord, north Iceland, farm of Asmund Grey-Streak, father of Grettir: bought by Grettir's grandfather Thorgrim Grey-Streak at Skeggi's suggestion, 13; Grettir stays home at Bjarg throughout the autumn after his encounter with Bardi Gudmundarson, 34; Thorbjorn Oxen-Might kills Atli at Bjarg, 45; Hook brings Grettir's head to Asdis at Bjarg, 83; Grettir's head buried at church at Bjarg, 84; *see also* Bjarg, Men of. *See also* 14, 16, 25, 28–31, 35, 37, 42–3, 47–9, 67, 69

Borgarfjord (*Borgarfjörðr*), Iceland: Grettir stays with Grim Thorhallsson in Borgarfjord, 53. *See also* 27, 47, 54

Byzantium: *see* Constantinople

Constantinople (*Miklagarðr*): Thorbjorn travels to Constantinople from Norway to become a mercenary, 85; Thorbjorn killed by Thorstein here, 86; Thorstein and Spes are married in Constantinople, 90. *See also* 88, 91

Drangar (*Drangar*), Iceland: location of Olaf's farm, 11

Drangey (*Drangey*), Skagafjord, north Iceland, Grettir's island sanctuary; Gudmund the Powerful advises Grettir to seek refuge on Drangey, 67; Grettir, Illugi, and Glaum settle on Drangey, 69; Grettir refuses to leave the island or allow access to its owners, 71; Grettir wounds the sorceress Thurid with a stone cast from the island, 78; Grettir wounds himself with axe on Drangey while striking the enchanted tree sent as a weapon by Thurid, 79; Hook and his men kill Grettir and Illugi on the island, 82; Skeggi Gamlason recovers the bodies of Grettir and Illugi from island, 84; Hook gives Drangey to his brother Hjalti, 85. *See also* 70, 72–6, 81, 83

Dufunefsskeid (*Dúfunefsskeið*), north Iceland: place where Grettir meets Lopt (an alias for Hallmund), 54

England (*England*): Jarl Svein left in charge of Norway while Jarl Eirik Hakonarson sails to England to visit his brother-in-law, King Canute the Great, 19. *See also* 22, 38

Fagraskogafell (*Fagraskógafjall*), west Iceland: mountain cave inhabited by Grettir, 58. *See also* 60

Garten (*Gartar*), Norway: harbour at the mouth of Trondheim Fjord where Grettir kills Bjorn, 22

Gasir (*Gásir*), Iceland: port from which Grettir takes ship to Norway, 37; the outlawed Thorbjorn sails from Gasir, 85

Geitland (*Geitland*), Iceland: Grettir stays here as an outlaw; Grettir climbs a glacier at Geitland, 61

Gnupverja-Hrepp (*Gnúpverjahreppr*), Iceland: settled by Ofeig Grettir and Thormod Skapti, 6

Goda Wood (*Goðaskógr*), Iceland: place from which the shepherd Glam has come when he first meets Thorhall, 32

Grettir's Dune (*Grettisþúfa*), Iceland: sandhill in which Hook buries Grettir's head, 84

Grettir's Shed (*Grettisbúr*), Iceland: shed at Vidvik in which Thorbjorn stores Grettir's head in salt for the winter, 82

Grettir's Spit (*Grettisoddi*), near the Hitar River, west Iceland: place where Grettir fights off men of Myrar, 60

Hafursfjord (*Hafrsfjörðr*), Rogaland, Norway: location of a great battle won by King Harald Shaggy-Hair, 2

Haramarsey Island (*Háramarsey*), South-More, Norway: island on which Grettir stays with the chieftain Thorfinn, 17. *See also* 19

Haering's Leap (*Hæringshlaup*), north Iceland: cliff-face on Drangey where Haering jumps to his death after being chased by Illugi, 76

Hebrides (*Suðreyjar*), islands off the west coast of Scotland: Thrand and Onund become friends with Ofeig Grettir and Thormod Skapti in the Hebrides, 3; Thrand and Onund return to the Hebrides from Ireland, 5. *See also* 1, 4, 6

Hegraness Thing (*Hegranessþing*), Skagafjord, north Iceland: Grettir visits the Thing in disguise; is induced to fight as part of entertainment; is granted safe passage before his identity is revealed, 72

Hordaland (*Hörðaland*), Norway: home territory of the family of Onund's father, 1; site of the battle fought against Harald Shaggy-Hair, 2; Grettir lands in Hordaland after leaving Iceland, 37. *See also* 3

Hrutafjord (*Hrútafjörðr*), north Iceland: area where Balki settles, 5; home region of Thorbjorn Oxen-Might, 30; *see also* Hrutafjord, Men of. *See also* 14–15, 42, 48, 58

Hvamm (*Hvammr*), west Iceland: home of Aud the Deep-Minded, 10. *See also* 26

Hris Island (*Hrísey*), Iceland: Asmund shelters in the lee of this island during the storm that separates his ship from Onund's, 8

Ireland (*Írland*): Thrand and Onund visit Thrand's brother Eyvind the Easterner, head of defence forces in Ireland, 5. *See also* 1, 3

Jaederen (*Jaðarr*), Norway: Grettir travels here after losing the opportunity to prove his innocence in the death of Thorissons, 39

Kaldbak (*Kaldbakr*), north-west Iceland: Onund's farm south of Kaldbaksvik, which is named after a nearby mountain, 9. *See also* 11–12

Kjalarness Thing (*Kjalarnessþing*): one of local assemblies held in early Iceland before advent of Althing, 10

Kjol (*Kjolr*), Iceland: Grettir spends the summer here, stealing from travellers, 54

Langaness (*Langanes*), Iceland: peninsula by which Onund and Asmund orient themselves during their voyage to Iceland, 8

Laxardal Heath (*Laxárdalsheiðr*), Iceland: Grettir rides across on his route to Thorstein Kuggason's farm at Ljar Woods, 48

Laekjamot (*Lækjamót*), Iceland: Bishop Fridrek and Thorvald Kodransson stay here, 13; location of Thorgils Maksson's farm, 24

Ljar Woods (*Ljárskógar*), Hvamm District, west Iceland: home of Thorstein Kuggason, 26; Grettir stays with Thorstein for most of the autumn, 48; Grettir spends the winter at Ljar Woods; on account of Grettir's laziness, as well as a force of Hrutafjord Men gathered to kill him, Thorstein asks him to leave, 53. *See also* 27, 49

Melar (*Melar*), Hrutafjord, north Iceland: farm sold by Thorir to Thorhall, father of Gamli, Grettir's brother-in-law, 30; Gamli and Skeggi of Melar come to the aid of Asdis, 83. *See also* 14, 42, 48–9, 51

Midfjord Lake (*Miðfjarðarvatn*), north Iceland: lake at which the young Grettir is bested by Audun during a ball-game, 15. *See also* 28

Midfjord (*Miðfjörðr*), north Iceland: place to which Thorgrim moves, 13; Asmund Grey-Streak considered the foremost man at Midfjord, 25. *See also* 11, 45, 47, 83

Modrudal Heath (*Möðrudalsheiðr*), Iceland: place where Grettir stays, 63

More (*Mærr*), Norway: Grettir travels here after killing Bjorn, 22

Myrar (*Mýrar*) Iceland: Thorstein Kuggason advises Grettir to go south to Myrar, 57; while staying in cave at Fagraskogafjall, Grettir makes himself unwelcome in Myrar by seeking out supplies, 58; Grettir steals livestock in Myrar; he is attacked by the Myrar men, 60; *see also* Myrar Men, The. *See also* 59, 61

Thorisdal (*Þórisdalr*), west Iceland: valley surrounded by ice that Grettir names in honour of the half-troll Thorir, 61. *See also* 67

Thorskafjord (*Þorskafjörðr*), Iceland: Grettir goes north to, 50

Tunga (*Tunga*), Iceland: home of Snorri Godi, 49. *See also* 34, 53–4, 68

Tonsberg (*Túnsberg*), Norway: home of Gunnar, 23; Grettir travels here to meet his brother Thorstein, 40

Trondheim (*Þrándheimr*), Norway: Grettir meets Jarl Svein at Trondheim, 22; 37; Grettir tries to reach the residence of King Olaf at Trondheim, 38. *See also* 37

Trondheim Fjord (*Þrándheimsmynni*: The Mouth to Trondheim Fjord), Norway: 22. *See* Garten

Tvidaegra Heath (*Tvídægra Heiðr*: Two-Day Heath), Iceland: location of the killings on the heath, 31. *See also* 16, 47

Uplands (*Upplönd*), district of Norway: site of Harald Shaggy-Hair's kingdom, 2

Vaagan (*Vágar*), Halogaland, Norway: Grettir is welcomed by strangers at Vaagan because he has killed vikings; he gets passage from here to Thorkel's farm, 20. *See also* 22

Vatnsdal (*Vatnsdalr*), north Iceland: home territory of Thorkel Scratcher, 13; location of Thorvald Asgeirsson's farm at As, 25; farms in Vatnsdal laid waste by the revenant Glam, 33; Grettir visits Thorvald at As in Vatnsdal, 35. *See also* 16, 32, 36

Vesturhop (*Vestrhóp*), Iceland: one of places from which people come to attend the ball-games at Midfjord Lake, 15

Vidvik (*Viðvík*), Skagafjord, north Iceland: home of Thorbjorn Hook, 70; also home of Thorbjorn's foster-mother, the sorceress Thurid, 79. *See also* 81, 82

Vik (*Vík*), Iceland: site of a shipwreck, 12

Westfjords (*Vestfirðir*), north-western Iceland: Thorstein Kuggason advises Grettir to seek out Thorgils Arason at Reykjaholar in this region, 49. *See also* 53

The Oxford World's Classics Website

www.worldsclassics.co.uk

- Browse the full range of Oxford World's Classics online

- Sign up for our monthly e-alert to receive information on new titles

- Read extracts from the Introductions

- Listen to our editors and translators talk about the world's greatest literature with our Oxford World's Classics audio guides

- Join the conversation, follow us on Twitter at OWC_Oxford

- Teachers and lecturers can order inspection copies quickly and simply via our website

www.worldsclassics.co.uk

American Literature

British and Irish Literature

Children's Literature

Classics and Ancient Literature

Colonial Literature

Eastern Literature

European Literature

Gothic Literature

History

Medieval Literature

Oxford English Drama

Poetry

Philosophy

Politics

Religion

The Oxford Shakespeare

A complete list of Oxford World's Classics, including Authors in Context, Oxford English Drama, and the Oxford Shakespeare, is available in the UK from the Marketing Services Department, Oxford University Press, Great Clarendon Street, Oxford OX2 6DP, or visit the website at www.oup.com/uk/worldsclassics.

In the USA, visit www.oup.com/us/owc for a complete title list.

Oxford World's Classics are available from all good bookshops. In case of difficulty, customers in the UK should contact Oxford University Press Bookshop, 116 High Street, Oxford OX1 4BR.

ÉMILE ZOLA

L'Assommoir
The Attack on the Mill
La Bête humaine
La Débâcle
Germinal
The Kill
The Ladies' Paradise
The Masterpiece
Nana
Pot Luck
Thérèse Raquin

Travel Writing 1700–1830

Women's Writing 1778–1838

WILLIAM BECKFORD   Vathek

JAMES BOSWELL   Life of Johnson

FRANCES BURNEY   Camilla
Cecilia
Evelina
The Wanderer

LORD CHESTERFIELD   Lord Chesterfield's Letters

JOHN CLELAND   Memoirs of a Woman of Pleasure

DANIEL DEFOE   A Journal of the Plague Year
Moll Flanders
Robinson Crusoe
Roxana

HENRY FIELDING   Jonathan Wild
Joseph Andrews and Shamela
Tom Jones

WILLIAM GODWIN   Caleb Williams

OLIVER GOLDSMITH   The Vicar of Wakefield

MARY HAYS   Memoirs of Emma Courtney

ELIZABETH INCHBALD   A Simple Story

SAMUEL JOHNSON   The History of Rasselas
The Major Works

CHARLOTTE LENNOX   The Female Quixote

MATTHEW LEWIS   Journal of a West India Proprietor
The Monk

HENRY MACKENZIE   The Man of Feeling